I CROW RIVER

JAMAN TREE

First Edition published 2012 by:

For information visit:

www.caferevolution.org

Book title: I CROW RIVER

Author: Jaman Tree

ISBN: 978-0-646-91625-5

Dedication

To all my relations: big and small - seen and unseen - here and beyond.

This book is to give a voice to the voiceless – be it the four-legged, the winged, the deep-rooted, the tall-branched, the silent, the formed and the formless.

And to my fellow humans: my brothers and sisters who live at the margins of the so-called miracle of economics. The ones dispossessed so others can have.

THE DALAI LAMA

Foreword

The book, *"I Crow River"* by Jaman Tree, is on the need for caring for our planet, our only home.

It challenges us to question whether we are doing all we can to avert the environmental catastrophe unfolding before us.

I agree with the author and feel that the increasingly frequent environmental disasters of recent years are our mother earth's warning of what awaits us if we do not take care of our environment.

July 22, 2016

Acknowledgments

I acknowledge it all. Everything and everybody that shaped me into the being that I am, right here – right now.

I thank you for being part of my life: be it, family, friends, the kookaburra laughing outside or the screeching cockatoo.

A few individuals have been intimately related to this particular journey and without their dedicated support 'I Crow River' would not have been possible.

For the hours upon hours of editing, proof reading, suggestions and coffees, and mostly for believing in the call of the river; I am in deep gratitude to Jemma Masters, Barbora Butkova, Donal O'Cofaigh and Yvette Harvey.

For the impressive crow and the book cover - Anastasia Lubitckaya and Interior design and layout - Veronika Repková.

And to my father, who from an early age made me understand that the written word is a powerful instrument to initiate change in the world.

Preface

Some years ago I was sitting on the banks of the river Ganga in a small town called Rishikesh in northern India.

It's a place that has always been a source of inspiration for me; you might call it a sacred site or a power spot.

I had this idea to write a book based on some of my past work with sustainability and organics. The title was going to be *Organic Farming for Fools.*

After a week of sitting in front of my laptop, I couldn't get past page one. It just felt stuck, even though I already had much of the material ready.

Then one night I just gave up.

I walked outside and sat by the river, enjoying the calming effect of flowing water and the light of an almost full moon.

Suddenly I heard the river talk—no joking, I heard her voice. Now anyone that knows me would vouch that I am quite a grounded person. Though that night the river did talk to me, and what she said was: "Start writing, don't worry about the book you were planning to write, write the book I am going to give you."

I went back to my room and commenced typing and it just flowed, one page after the other. I never knew what the story would be, what the next sentence would be, though I trusted it was coming—the river did say it would.

In a few weeks the whole story was there, though it took a couple more years to polish the rough edges.

So this was the birth of I CROW RIVER, and I promise to you, it wasn't me, it was the river.

*Note on pronunciation – the 'u' in the name Nulla is pronounced N(a)lla with an open sound such as 'uplift'.

The Songline

I want to touch your lips tonight and kiss you and kiss you and kiss you, until you run out of breath and only the silence of passion remains.

I want to dance and dance and dance and dance, until the dancer is no more and only the silence of passion remains.

I think of you, I die for you and eternally reborn for your touch. At first I thought that this story was about you, and then it dawned on me that you were in everyone. And that I, will forever fly amongst the stars, whispering stories to the sparks of earth's kin residing in our Mama's home.

They say that the whales, they keep the chronicles of time within their body of wisdom. They dance in the space where the spirit of air meets the movement of water to witness the story of the ages.

So am I the story or the storyteller, the witness or the one that acts? Well, I guess it's up to you to decide this, though in truth, this is not my story or your story.

This is a story of Nobi the crow. He flew in one dark night and whispered a prayer in my ear — your ear — our ears.

Stories are like spider webs, they are made of many strands that constantly overlap and meet each other.

Nobi is the spider weaving this story, for he speaks in the voice of the Mother, the Whale, the Rock, the River, and the Crow.

In a way — a way most of us have not comprehended yet — he is your and my voice as well.

Nobi appears to tell us we have strayed far from the centre of silence, away from the celebration of unity into the debilitating spiral that abides within the fear of separation. We may ignore the message, or choose to ridicule the messenger. We do this at our own peril.

Do we want to be baptised by fire in order to effect the change that within our heart of hearts, we all desire to see?

A whisper within the silence of the night tells me there is another way: some call it understanding, others compassion. A few speak about caring, while others talk of the embrace of all life as our relations in creation. Myself, I call the secret prayer — love.

In pain I love, in joy I love, in despair I love, in ecstasy I love. Within it all, I find a touch of freedom — the freedom to be.

My love for you is like a river. It moves and changes, runs dry, and floods.

My love for you is a river — forever still, at times chaotic, always there.

My love for you was born by a river and by her banks it may die, only for the promise of a rebirth she holds within her caress.

I can talk of my love for you forever and ever, though beneath my feet I can hear the sound of my earthly mother softly crying.

How can it be? What have I done to bring tears to the mother that gave birth to all mothers wherever they may be?

The night is clear and warm, while the stars shine a light of compassion over our weeping Mama. I stare at the stillness, listening to a voice born from empathy that abides in peace.

My earthly Mother she is crying, since one of her children, the one called *human being*, is slowly but surely killing the rest of her offspring. What should I do? Will I sit and watch the massacre that is taking place, or will I leap to the defence of my siblings in creation?

My earthly Mother she is hurting, while being stripped bare of her mane. Her clothes ripped apart — she is left naked to blister in the scorching sun, a sun that will soon burn all of her children.

Tears flow down the face of my Mama, for the laughter,

that once was the prevailing song of life in her abode, has turned into worries, stress, insecurity and hatred, all born of the illusion of separation.

Will I shine in my magnificence to make the children smile again, or will I keep my concern with *me* and *me* and *me* and what *I* need in order to feel secure in this world?

I listen to the hush of a falling leaf in the gentle breeze and it lets me know that I cannot be happy while the rest of creation is crying. I hear it asking me, can a joy born of *want* encompass within it the ecstasy of laughter, or would it be another moment of a fleeting illusion, soon to be overtaken by the wailing of despair?

The whale sings because it has a song. The eagle glides in the sky for the reason that it has wings. The frog calls the rain. A tree grows in and out at the same time. The deeper it sinks its roots into the ground, the taller it stands. The closer it gets to the centre of the earth, the nearer it is to touching the sky. Am I a brother to the trees? Perhaps, for I constantly touch the trees asking them to carry my song on their wings of presence and tell you of my love — the love that forever grows deeper and bigger — my love for you.

Within us all abides a divine power we have not dreamt to touch. This power is our call, our birthright and our song. The time is upon us to make choices that will reverberate within the sphere of presence of *all that is*. The time is always *now*!

My love for you and my love for my earthly mother are one and the same. It is a song born with the innocence of renewal and danced in playing fields of change.

The Story

The river feels so silent tonight. I stare at her calm dark waters as she bears witness to my heart's space increasingly mirroring the deep surrender reflected in her flow.

This time the silence has penetrated to a deeper core, a subtler place than ever before. I can feel the stealth of an eagle's gaze becalming me as I ready myself for the catastrophe she is about to unleash. Bit by bit, I plummet into the terrain of nothingness, floating as a free-ranging particle suspended in the radiance of space.

The whole whirling universe inside of me has come to a halt. There are no more questions to be asked, desires to be fulfilled, or battles to be waged. The moment is perfect and is exactly what it is meant to be. I don't wish it to be anything else to what it is.

Nothing separates any longer the river and the body sitting on its bank. We have become one and the same, as we have always been, born of the source that cycles and recycles, turns to ashes and rises with the new dawn.

My presence with life is at last total.

It's been a while now since she vanished from my life, left without a trace as she has done, time and time before. She said it was final, that there was nothing more we had to give each other. Our karma was lived. It wasn't the first time she left with the same profound certainty, always to be followed by the echoes of return.

She knows and I know and every atom in the universe knows that the same gravity that pulls us apart will always bring us together again. We knew this to be true from the time we first touched many lives ago on the island with the big rock.

It was some lives and cycles ago, still in my heart the story
has been told again and again. How can it be any different?
It is a story of the birthplace of love and the spreading of
her wings that carried me through life and space, a journey
and return.

As we all know to every story there is a twist and turn.
The life of celebration we experienced for timeless moons
had come to an abrupt end when the invader with the
white skin landed on our shores. He carried a book that he
said was written by his Gods, and he drank this water that
burned the throat and made you angry. He carried these
sticks that spat fire from them and made our people die.
Eventually he wanted us to believe in his book too, though
we could never understand how God could live in a book,
when she lives in the sky and the rocks, the rivers and the
trees.

They looked like ghosts and eventually there were so
many of them and we were just a few.

They took the land and said that now they owned it. We
never knew that the land could be owned before. How could
she? She is free and she takes care of us! They had these
coins and papers, and they said that if you had enough of
these coins, the land that you lived upon was yours. And
more so, even if you didn't live there, she could be yours,
just because you had papers and coins.

It all was so very strange to us, so that with time we
started to forget the laughter that was our song.

What I never did forget though, was that first time I met
her.

I will never forget that day. No matter how many lives I
lived or how many times I returned from the stars.

And luckily enough, it was before the ghost landed on
our shores.

✳ ✳ ✳ ✳ ✳ ✳ ✳

There was a time — a long, long time ago if we measure it by today's clock yet just a mere moment ago as far as universal dreaming is concerned — that we, one of the tribes from the big island, roamed the earth as desert nomads, celebrating the sounds of silence as a way of life.

It was a time when our entire lives and the meaning we attached to them revolved around listening to the still sounds of silence emanating from the heart of the desert. We knew that silence had different qualities to it; that it wasn't only about the absence of sound. We recognised that an ever-alive stillness encompassed the touch of the unseen world, a deeper more expansive domain of being, where silence serves as a luminous light shining on the walls of illusion. We knew beyond all doubt that this was the secret garden where spirit lived in and we learned with the experience of the passing desert summers, that there was nothing more sure to chase spirit away than our inner chatter. We had to stop the world inside us to listen to the wind, and that is exactly what we did.

I can still remember so clearly, after many lives of return, the instance when my eyes first met hers. When my heart first trembled and a quiver coiled up and down my spine, shaking the core essence of my being.

It was a cool morning at the time of the year when the sun was low on the horizon and the nights were laced with a cold, sometimes freezing desert chill. The smell of smoke filled the camp as fires were lit to fend off the morning dew. Children were running around everywhere and a buzz of excitement filled the camp. News had just come in, that a neighbouring nomadic group passing through our country would be arriving at our camp some time that day. They were the people of the Rainbow Serpent, our relatives and kin who shared with us the vast desert tracts south of the great rock. Our people were preparing to receive the guests. We knew many of them; they passed through our country in the cold season every year, some of our sons and daughters were married to them: they were our next of kin.

Upon their arrival we welcomed them with song and dance and later in the day we all shared a feast of some animal relations caught by the hunters and offered for the nourishment of the tribes. We celebrated our kinship as neighbours who shared the banks of the great dry river. We affirmed again that peace is our way; that if disputes ever arose we would resolve them in understanding and love, with our hearts guiding the way.

We shared the warmth of the fire and endless stories into the night, stories of the adventures and lessons of the year gone by. Of course, there was a fair amount of gossip and story-telling, of loves that had been sparked, others that had wilted, babies to be born, new techniques to soften animal skins and any other information relevant to life under the vast desert skies.

Our life, our culture, our walk on mother earth, was manifested through our song, dance, and silence. We sang the land and in return she offered us her dance, she shone a pathway for us, so we could discover ourselves as part of the source of all things. She never gave us clear answers and always showed us a way.

It was on the afternoon of the third day after their arrival, while we all sat down to feast on a couple of large desert lizards caught by the hunters, that my eyes first met hers. It felt like a flash, a thunderbolt, a bang that shook my entire existence. It was as though the whole beauty, magic and wonder of the desert were present in her big brown eyes. My world brought to a halt by a princess from the people of the Rainbow Serpent.

Rocked to my core, I felt breathless as I stared at her across the fire, the smoke allowing me glimpses of her light and then shielding me from exposing my own folly. I had to get away, quick, for I felt that any moment I would lose my balance and do or say something stupid. I got up quietly and left the circle, slowly walking into the desert sands to regain my lost composure.

It felt as if all my life, all my lives, I had been waiting for this particular woman; that in the beginning we came forth manifest from the same star. I had no doubt that the same spark placed us beyond the galaxies into the cycle of earth relations. Still, is this real or am I just hallucinating? Nothing has ever moved or touched my being in such a way before — the force of love felt stronger than the fiercest of desert storms.

One thing I did know for sure; my heart was on fire and one does not approach the woman they have known since the beginning of time with a raging fire consuming them. I knew that to be true. I was a warrior of heaven and earth: it was before the white ghost came with his book of knowledge in one hand and a gun in the other. Many of us were warriors. We fought our battles with our own hearts and, as a warrior, I knew that the first gift you bring love - is peace.

Quietly I strolled into the desert chaparral to call upon my sister the *wind* so I could probe her on what she knew of the story of love in order to place some clarity in my heart. Where does love owe its birthing place to, the human heart, the sky or perhaps the desert sands?

I needed to know. From that moment onwards there was nothing I sought more than to *see* the story of love, to understand where this overwhelming emotion came from. Did it have a birthplace? Did it ever die?

※ ※ ※ ※ ※ ※ ※

"Does love ever really begin or end?" I mutter to myself, as I exit my internal wonderland to be present in this present moment, by the river. "Is love a raging fire or the peaceful flow of water, or does it encompass both? Where does this mystery hail from?" Yes, the whereabouts of the birthplace of love is still a mystery to me after so many loves of return; such a simple question, yet the most puzzling riddle ever to be composed by the spider that weaves the story of creation.

While absorbed deep within an inner space transcending time, I fail to notice that three crows have come and perched on a piece of driftwood by my side. They are still and silent. I have watched many crows in my time, except I have never come across a silent one before. I sense that they know something I don't. They too want to watch this grand show by the river as the drama of what she is about to unleash unfolds.

Sure, they must have observed us for long enough now to witness how we have lost touch with anything and everything that is sacred. How with the passing of the seasons we have forgotten the true purpose of our walk on earth. How we have been hypnotised by the allure of the demi gods and have come to bow in deep worship in the temple of desire, greed, fear and separation. They certainly must have watched how we turned around from being an integral part of the great web of life to the ruler and conqueror of it; a ruler bent on subduing all life forms and exploiting them for *his* own perceived benefit.

The crows lift their heads in unison, cocking them to one side and looking at me intently; it is as though they are saying, "Yes, there is nowhere to run to anymore, it's all over." Anyway they must know I am going nowhere, even after they fly away to take refuge in the air, I will still be here, waiting for the river.

20

I may not have learned much in my journey through the many cycles of earthly return, though one thing I have learnt is how to wait. The desert taught it to me a long time ago. The desert taught me that one *must* wait. The rain will come when it's her time to come. Food will arrive when we are hungry. Love will knock at our door when we least expect her. And as they come, they will always move on one day, continue on their journey, for the cycle of life is continuously spinning and turning, evolving and dissolving.

It took me a long time and many lives to trust that she will always return. Countless trees would have grown from the rivers of tears I shed at the altar of love. That was before I really looked deep into her eyes to fathom her eternal being. Yet now there are no tears, nor fears, nor wants. There is nothing to fight for, nothing to strive for, beyond this reality of the present moment. Does it matter if a warrior finally knows love a moment before the river comes to embrace him?

No, it doesn't.

I can feel some sadness in the stillness of the night. No fear or regret, just pure sadness. The sadness that one feels when they first look into the eyes of a lover and knows that this too will pass.

❋ ❋ ❋ ❋ ❋ ❋ ❋

I was sixteen when fate grabbed me by the hand one day and set me on a journey that changed my life forever. Previous to that I was a normal teenage boy, a middle class product programmed to join the corporation.

I was going to go to university and fulfil my father's dream of my becoming a lawyer, doctor, or businessman. In reality, they weren't his dreams or aspirations either;

then again, the masters who pull the strings in the club of material achievements had long ruled his brain. In short, I was going to make it in this world - be somebody. But I chose to be nobody.

In my first journey into the land of vision I *saw* life as it is, recognising how far we have strayed away from the source. How dense and fragmented we have become. How far removed we have turned out to be from the divine nest that sparked us into life. I felt the infinitum of possibilities life's banquet has on offer. In that first moment of insight behind the veil of illusion I saw what was to come, for you, for me, for all of us.

Sitting by the river now, I finally appreciate how lucid my perception was in those early years of dreaming with the fairies, that time when the illuminating spark first penetrated the realms of my innocent heart. The narrative, the plot, did of course evolve in a different way to my original projection, yet the spirit of the journey remains the same as I felt it that first day, when it all came to be, as it is now.

Every journey in life has a different ending than what we can perceive on the first step. In fact, it has a different beginning and no ending and only when we are utterly still, can we ever touch the wind. It's been a long time since I did touch the wind, though on that trip I did.

I saw the tribes, all the colours that make up humanity, coming together as one again, in a celebration of love and unity. I felt us all shed the illusion of separation and make a conscious choice to hold each other in a deep embrace. I saw the torchbearers of the future, who through their deeds and actions shone their light and inspired the people as a whole, of the new way, the old way, the magic way. I felt the brilliance and joy—our eternal birthright—emanating from the harmony of walking in balance with mother earth and one another. I was young and the corrupt ideas of the world had not penetrated me past the point of no return.

When we are young we always have hope and we know we can do anything. We *know*, beyond a mind fed with doubts, that every dream can be made reality; every song can become our dance. The old folk teach us that dreams are dreams, still the young know better. I have chosen to stay young, although I have walked many circles around the sun since then. Yet now, here by this river, I feel old, as ancient as time itself, and the river she keeps whispering, asking me questions.

Something about the presence of crows always makes me want to talk to them, make contact, relate to them, although at this present moment I am lost for words. It feels as though the dam that broke upstream and the earth that shook disintegrated the world of words within me and only silence remains.

It is a normal quiet night by the Ganga, as if anything, ever, in this place can be described as quiet or normal. In this country, silence only exists within oneself; one does not dare look for it anywhere else. Perhaps this is the reason why the art of meditation was mastered in this land.

They worshipped the river since the beginning of time.

The river was their mother, ever nurturing and giving.

The river was their lover, capricious and moody, ever changing with what she was ready to share.

The river was their sister, a good companion to sit by in the evenings and gaze beyond their fears.

They loved the river and disrespected her at the same moment, as we all do sometimes with our lovers, mothers and sisters. Sometimes they took more than they should and the river withdrew her giving.

Haven't we all noticed how, every time in life when we take more than we are welcome to, the giving runs dry?

The river was everything to them, she gave them love and sorrow.

There is now nothing I can feel anymore. I am here, the river is here, and a story is about to unfold.

※ ※ ※ ※ ※ ※ ※

Yet before the present story is allowed to make it self known, a tale from the past keeps calling to me from within the hidden recesses of my mind, as though to hint that it embodies within something that is an allusion to what is taking place at present. Like all parables, it's a legend of love.

Back in time, the central Gondwana desert was a harsh place, especially in summer, though we knew that when the sun blazed the sky and scorched the earth, it was her way of telling us that it was time for us to take a deep breath and pause.

We listened to the majestic sun, which sustains our life, and withdrew into the bushes during the long hot days. It was at this period of the year that we had the time to stop and take an honest look into what lives in the secret chambers of our hearts. It wasn't only about self-reflection. We felt deeply all our relations in this cosmic dance, the four-legged ones, the reptiles, and the winged ones, how they all must be hiding from the sun at this time. We recognised that, in every step we took in the great desert our fate was shared by all our relations. It's the same sun that nurtures all our lives. It's the same rain that sprouts the shoots that will sustain us all.

Often we sat and contemplated the magic and awe of the great expansive desert while thanking the mother of creation for giving us such a *whole* life. Yet me, I thought of her only. Ever since that fateful day when I gazed at her eyes through the veil of smoke rising from the campfires, no other thought occupied my mind. My heart knew no desire other than her.

Slowly and steadily, like an army of ants taking siege of a tiny crumb, the original fire grew inside me stronger and brighter, transforming itself into a dazzling flame that

24

sparked my being into a new equilibrium. Like a light that shines in a spiritual unknowing, a light that floods every cell of our being and illuminates us in the presence of all that is divine. A radiance, that each and every one of us has felt sometime in our life, when love first sneaks its way in, tricks our hearts to trust and open wide to the joy and agony to come.

We worship the dance of opposites that creates her mystery and to attempt to name her seems to take something away from the magic she spins through the veins of our existence. I felt restless in the presence of these feelings and decided to go for a walkabout, endeavouring to find peace in my heart.

Walking the tracks of the country I knew so well I finally crossed paths with our ever-unpredictable sister the wind. "Hey, Sister Wind, I have been looking for you everywhere, I want to know if you are familiar with the land where love comes from?" I pleaded with her. She laughed her head off, whirled around and told me to look up in the sky and pose my question to our great grandmother, the *Sun*. I asked the wind to carry me to the Sun so she can tell me about love, yet she tricked me again and whispered to me to look at all life on earth and see the sun's love reflected in it.

I kept on querying the wind with questions on love and asked her if is it wise to bring the *water spirit* over so I can ask her about love. She told me to be patient and walk back to the camp, while she went and talked matters over with the *water spirit*.

The following day, big grey clouds gathered over our camp, with the air smelling of the coming of the *water spirit*. We knew the rain would come and with it the desert would turn into a garden in bloom. The rain came that night; it didn't stop for three days. We all got soaked, yet we were happy. Now all the water holes would be full, the butterflies dancing, and in a few weeks the desert would turn into a rainbow of colour and food.

The wind returned later with a big smile on her face, saying that love may reveal itself in many ways and often, like the rain in the desert, it may take some time before we see all the colours of love. I wanted to know more about the story of love, though the wind got a bit tired of my questions and decided it was time for her to blow on her merry way. Before she flew away on her journey, she whispered a great secret in my ear. "There is nothing, nothing that is not love . . ."

❋ ❋ ❋ ❋ ❋ ❋ ❋

The crows look at me intently as though to say, "Isn't it time for you to snap out of your dream state so we can have conversation, mate?"

I smile at them, recalling what the wind whispered to me that day a long, long time ago. It's all love, the river is about to love us and one day, many times from now, we will understand why it had to happen and thank her for loving us this way. And like time and again in life, it takes a long time and much pain to recognise — love is always present.

Sitting motionless by the river, a gentle stream of tears surfaces from my eyes, bearing testimony to the love I feel, and have always felt, in the presence of this river. Over and over again she has nurtured me, guided me and given me hope that there is a life worth living; that a sacred walk is here to be experienced on our passage through planet earth.

Over the years she kept on whispering to me that my trust and intent were required if I was to reclaim the path of the brave.

When it comes to freedom of the soul, India must be the greatest country on earth; where love was born, where the smile was conceived and where the impossible is always possible. It is a place where more than one thousand million dreamers, lovers, smilers live together in relative harmony in an almost impossible situation.

India is a country where *hope* is a sermon that shines in every face you look in to. India is an oasis where people still sense *who* you are, rather than ask you *what* you are. At the same time, it is a country where despair, cruelty, corruption and oppression have become a way of life for many, yet somehow she is a grand trickster, managing to mask the latter.

The three crows perched on the piece of driftwood by my side unexpectedly call for my attention. It is as though they are saying in unison, "How dare you sit and ignore us for so long, while we are perched by your side. Who do you think you are, another arrogant human?"

Throughout time and legend, crows have always been assigned the role of the bridge makers, the link between our world and the world of magic and myth. They are a highly evolved species, perhaps more advanced than we would be willing to acknowledge, as they operate in a well-organised social and spiritual order. The one crow that seems slightly larger than the other two, takes a couple of hops closer, while staring at me with fierce eyes emanating defiance.

"Hey you, mister human, how come you built this stupid dam if you knew all along it was in the highest seismic zone of this country? It never made any sense to any of us. Look at what's happened now! Check out this big mess you mob have created again!" he says, with blame in his voice, as though I was personally responsible for the construction of this dam.

I stare back at him, caught off guard by the fact that I suddenly have company by my side, demanding attention. Funny, it doesn't really surprise me that the crows are talking, what I don't get is why they would want to talk to me.

"Yes, it doesn't make any sense whatsoever to have built

this dam, I agree with you. Many human actions these days don't make sense to me either. For some reason, though, we still do it, since the masters that rule the earth don't seem to care anymore about anything that stands in the way of their profit." I answer him, hoping he will let me return to my silent dream state.

"Who are these masters you talk about, that keep on doing things which end up harming even their own species?" He continues his probe, obviously wanting to have an in-depth conversation on the subject, more than I am willing to offer at present. Here I am, wanting my own space at what could be the final chapter of my crusade on earth, and I have to contend with these crows, bent on annoying me with questions I don't really feel like contemplating anymore. Neither do I feel I have any time left to find answers I myself am lost for.

I sense I would have to start explaining the whole state of stupidity and ignorance in which humanity is living. Really, there is much more to clarify than the current insanity that is taking place on planet earth. I would have to reach to find a way to describe to them how a whole race was led like sheep by a consent, manufactured by the few rich and powerful. I would have to try and understand myself how the masses, although exploited by these very people, still support their own exploitation, for in their state of mindlessness they are convinced that their own good will and survival depends on the ones who rule them.

The longer I search for words to describe the present state of our human civilization, the more I recognize how insanely fucked up we have all become. However, instead of going into a long complicated answer, I decide to keep it simple in an attempt to cut the conversation short. "As you have noticed for long now, we humans often do things without thinking of the consequences of our actions and how they might affect the world around us," I answer him, while looking intently at my new companions and trying to figure out what it is they want of me.

The crow doing the talking seems really annoyed by my answer. "Yes, we can understand when you humans do things which keep eliminating more and more species from the planet because you simply don't care about others. Still, when you do things that result in eliminating your own species . . . hmm, maybe you are more brainless than what we perceived all along."

I need to return to my silence, I really don't like what's starting to take place here. I can feel where the crow is heading and I know that everything he is saying is true. Then again, I don't really feel like explaining the stupidity of the human race to them, a state of being that I myself have no rational description for. Neither do I wish to make a case in defence of humanity, which often I do not feel is a mob I can call my true family.

Staring at my new companions I can sense that there is something more profound than the destruction that is currently taking place, which seems to really sadden these three crows. I am not really sure that they care that much if the earth is going through a cleansing process and is about to clear up a river basin and wipe a few million people off the face of the earth. I feel it's not the real heart of the matter. They know there is much more to come, and still more than that, they know beyond all doubt that the human race has severed its ties of kinship with the world they are attuned to—the natural world.

The crows shatter the silence of the night. I am rattled by their talk; many questions surface within me, swelling into a torrent, like the river is about to do. Is it really right for me to sit here, seeking my own peace and salvation while all this is happening? Have I reached a state where nothing can touch me anymore—Nirvana, Enlightenment, Moksha, or whatever other dirty word I can use to describe this state of mind? Or am I just escaping from *what is* as so many of my peers have done during the years of the struggle for a *new earth.* Have I taken the easy road, where self-comfort rules supreme—a path chosen by many folk who have stopped caring for anything else other than their own happiness?

Hey, wait a minute! I stop my mind's rumblings as I notice myself sinking deep into an intense space of inner chatter. There is really nothing I can do anymore, other than find the still point in my being, nothing else matters . . . or does it? I wonder as I watch an old lady scramble up the hill with her few belongings in her hand.

I close my eyes and shift my sitting position, as though to say to the crows, "I am going back to my own space. This is too much for me to handle right now. Do not disturb!"

❋ ❋ ❋ ❋ ❋ ❋ ❋

I shut off the world around me in an attempt to ignore the crows while allowing my head space to drift back into memories of the time before time. The time before the circle was broken.

Each and every landscape on earth offers a different reflection to the human soul. The desert mirrors stillness as a guide and ally, thus continually supporting our endeavour to cultivate the silence within. However, the quest for a clear inner gaze never came at the expense of our obligations and duties to the circle we were part of. Each and every one of us had a role to play in caring for the world we lived in and only once we had rendered our service to the circle of life, did we wander into the desert to have a conversation with the *all that is* . . .

Our visitors left some time ago now, yet her image remained vivid within me. I learned from one of my friends that her name was "Nukaya." Many days I wandered into the desert chaparral, whispering her name: "Nukaya, Nukaya," with the hope that the wind would carry my song to her. I was searching for a plan, an idea, a piece of magic to win her heart over, before I made the journey to her country and asked her to be my wife.

"What can I bring her? Shall I make her something, an ornament, from desert seeds and stones, shall I bring her a fine skin?" my mind kept roaming in circles. After a while of being lost in a constant inner debate, I decided it was time to seek again the wisdom of my sister the wind and ask for her advice: I needed a piece of the insight she held. Isn't the wind the one who carries us through change when the time for transformation is upon us?

"Hey, Sister Wind, come and talk to me I need your help, we never actually concluded our conversation about love. You got a bit tired of my questions the other day." I yelled out into the open desert sky. "What did you mean when you said that 'all is love?' I don't really understand this."

At last, after making me wait for half a day, the wind came whirling, laughing her head off as she often does. "Hey, it's you fool again! Are you still lost in your quest for love? Haven't the sun, earth and rain taught you the meaning of the thing you call love?" she asked me mischievously.

"Yes, yes, Sister Wind. I do understand that love is everything that is nurtured, and I do know that love needs time to grow. Still, Sister Wind, my heart is on fire and the mosaic of life has suddenly turned into a single-minded quest." I pleaded with her as she kept on whirling all around me.

"That is no good, my friend," answered the wind with some concern in her voice. "True love does have fire in it, though the core of love is *still*, it always is — it must be. Go and search for that stillness in your heart and then take it as a gift to your beloved, she will feel your calm, even before you arrive. And remember, learn from the rock spirit, how it is always so still and ever present." That said the wind blew away, leaving me alone to comprehend the meaning behind her words.

"Be as a rock, ever present," I kept reciting to myself, hoping that the more I spoke the words the closer I might come to grasping the meaning of what the wind had just shared with me.

I conjured a plan of action and decided that the next day I would walk over to a cliff overlooking the next valley, where a rock formation with very powerful energy stood. If I sat there long enough I might *hear* what the rock spirit has to say on the subject of stillness. It was an old dreaming spot used by many of the tribe's men and women in a quest for a vision.

Early next morning I set on my way. It was a day's walk and I took my time, walking slowly, enjoying the sights, smells and feel of the country I loved so much. The place where my ancestors and their great grandfathers have all walked before me, their lasting imprints alive within every grain of sand in this great land we have care-taken since time could remember itself.

By dusk I reached the sacred rock formation. I scanned the surrounds and sat down in a corner, with a low natural rock wall offering me shelter from the ever-howling evening winds.

I marvelled at the endless miracles offered by this magnificent desert, as all around me the glitter of the rock crystals reflected the setting sun. I sat there for a while; meditating on the glory of creation while, bit-by-bit, the rock dreaming started whispering her story to me.

Tranquillity is the essence I am born of, so what is it that agitates me? What is it that sends a calm mind into a frenzy of thought and desire? I asked the shadows of the setting sun. With the fall of night, I became aware of only one sound. I was listening to my own breath, as its resonance and rhythm were instilling a deep sense of calm within me. Then I noticed that, when my mind raced again out of control, my breath would turn shallow, lose its rhythm or stop altogether.

"Breath," I heard the rocks around me speak with the deep voice of a choir of baritone singers " . . . the secret is breath. Never forget to breathe, and if the mind goes wild, breathe even deeper, and watch—watch as all dissipates into the stillness of the desert night."

Gradually, without clearing a space for my body to lie down, I found myself sinking into a deep space, in-between the worlds of wake and sleep, and the desert's voice dissolving, as echoes fading away . . .

❋ ❋ ❋ ❋ ❋ ❋ ❋

Opening my eyes to the presence of the river and the three crows, I am somehow confused by the parallel time frames juggling for my attention. The crows hop closer to remind me of my presence *here* and *now*. If they move any closer, I will become their piece of driftwood to perch on.

The river seems to have gathered some ripples in her flow, as though she can already feel the immense body of water pushing her from behind, agitating her peaceful rhythm. At the same time, cracks appear in my silence. It's not perfect anymore: there is something uneasy in this peace. Is it a tinge of doubt, or perhaps a challenge that I am refusing to acknowledge? What are the crows trying to point out and why are they here? After all, they have been assigned the role of messengers since time begun and I should at least endeavour to grasp the message in their presence with me.

I stare at the vast open space offered by the blanket of darkness—there is something special in the air. I feel the hum of the earth vibrating all around me, buzzing with a unique, distinct voice.

The river is projecting herself as a being, a life-force with its own intelligence and personality that is about to bestow its might and healing. The divine earth mother must have asked the river to do a bit of a cleanse; enact a Kali[1] dance of destruction; send a message to the human race. A race that, for some time now, has lost its ability to feel its space of unity with the earth mother, as it has become bewitched by the illusion of materialism—a race that has totally severed its connection to its own roots and is about to lose the last remaining thread that links it to the very fabric that sustains life.

How often do any of us stop for a moment to listen to the voice of the earth mother? And she has a voice, a song, a melody and a celestial sound, so distinct and so soothing; after all she is the mother of all mothers. Nonetheless, we have all turned deaf and live in different times. These days, the folk who speak the language of all things and *know* that everything in our universe is sharing a sermon in silence with us, these folk are considered crazy and labelled insane, and many times are put away to be dosed with drugs to make them *normal* again. We live in times when only one point of view is tolerated, the one *manufactured consent* we are all supposed to believe in and follow. Diversity has been sacrificed at the altar of uniformity, which is easier to control and manage. A mosaic of ideas and different worldviews is not encouraged. You are either one with the machine walking in support of the common agenda or you are an enemy, a threat to the ruling elite. We have been homogenised into a meaningless monoculture. Someone out there wants us all to dress in the same clothes, eat the same food and think the same thoughts—all, of course, produced by the same corporation in charge of our lives.

"Where did it all go wrong?" I whisper, hoping that the river or perhaps the crows can offer me an answer.

A reply I really don't need . . .

I look at the crows, long and deep, and in return they

---

1   ⁺Kali—Hindu Goddess associated with destruction, death of illusions and rebirth.

offer me their compassion. They don't press for more talk at present, for they know, and I know, and the river knows, that a part of the great web of life, the manifest mystery, is bleeding, wounded, disconnected from its source.

At the same time, I feel a sense of peace, which surpasses my understanding, a stillness untouched by any outer storm, a calm in which I am fully present, regardless of circumstance. A silence unmoved by my mind's wandering into journeys of past, present and future.

"So where does truth shine? Does it sit amidst the grace of the river's flow, the stillness of a majestic tree, or does it find a place in action and struggle for change. Do the likes of Jesus, Gandhi, and Martin Luther King offer us an ultimate path to salvation? Do we walk in sacrifice of our smaller self – our individual journey – for the greater good of all, while serving humanity at large? Or is it the sitting Buddha in his journey into silence that carries us to the highest realisation? Perhaps there is a place where these two energies overlap and serve each other.

Yet why should there be a goal at all?" My mind keeps sinking into a raging inner paw-wow, while I notice my crow mates beginning to feel impatient with me. They shift from one foot to another, looking around restlessly. I sense that at any moment they might take off.

My perfect silence beginning to crack, I seek solace in the memories of a time when living on earth was a quest to be lived rather than a question to be answered.

In the time before time, the notion of separation from creation did not exist. We lived one with the earth and the life that surrounded us. We didn't perceive ourselves as some entity ordained to be the ruler of all things. We gave thanks daily to be part of the puzzle of life, where every piece enacts a role in the great play of creation.

We lived for each other, with each other, celebrating each other, in an inter-depended reality. We needed everyone and everything and we acknowledged the unity that governs the cosmos.

While walking back to camp that day from the sacred rock formation, I noticed how, for the first time in my life, I really paid attention to my breath and was actually conscious of its presence. How could I have missed it for so long, when it's so close to me—right under my nose? Breath is the secret to a calm mind; in fact breath is the secret of life, the reference point to presence.

Nukaya was still present in my mindscape, yet her *felt-being* within me had a new quality now. I wasn't agitated or consumed by the flames of my desire for her, just happy to feel her unseen presence with me. My breath told me that all was well, that separation was not possible, and that separation is never really an option within the ever-present unity of life. She was already with me, from the moment the spark first went off in a faraway galaxy, even if her body was still roaming the hills on the other bank of the great dry river.

This is the real story of love. Our beloved is always alive within us, residing in a special room within our heart.

I had to wait for the right moment to approach her, timing is everything, I can't push this with my *will*. I had to listen, watch and be alert. After all, I was a hunter, and I knew that, if you wait long enough, everything you want always comes to you.

Approaching the camp I could hear the sound of laughter everywhere. Laughter was the main song of my people. Laughter and a smile full of gratitude to all of creation for taking such good care of us and always giving us what we need, when we need it.

And, yes, we did dance a lot. We danced for the rain

gods, which brought the water when we needed it, and we danced to the sun to thank her for her life-giving rays. We danced to the wind and thanked her for bringing us change. We danced to the animal spirit and thanked it when it nurtured our body. We sang and danced and within it all we found that even the heart of dance rests in silence. The silence reflected in the stillness of a perfect desert night.

I walked away from the camp into the sparkling desert night. The stars were smiling at me from every conceivable corner of the galaxy. Sitting on the warm sand, I started *dreaming* the courting dance I would bring Nukaya. It would act as a bridge between our two souls which were yet to touch in the realm of the body.

Little did I know, back then, that Nukaya would walk with me again and again as my shining light, time and return until the moment when we as a people almost brought life on earth to an end.

❋ ❋ ❋ ❋ ❋ ❋ ❋

I had walked twenty-four cycles around the sun on my earth journey and was living in a small village in the western Indian desert, when I first met her in this lifetime. Really, it might have been the first time we'd ever met. My whole stream of memories of where our love was born eons ago might be a fantasy conjured up by my ever-wandering mind. I myself believe in this story because—I feel it. I felt it the first moment I met her eyes as a young man in search of an answer. I knew I had seen those eyes before, though at the time my knowing petrified me.

The place where I lived at the time was a relatively small village by Indian terms. It was a holy place and a sacred pilgrimage site set amongst the vast desert sands. The houses in the village blended perfectly with the surrounding desert. Most were built within the parameters of an enclosed courtyard. The courtyards were usually a mix of vibrant garden space and flat concrete or stone, which served as a work area for all the various household chores and a sitting place in the cool of the late afternoons and evenings. The surrounding walls were thick, really thick, as to offer protection from the scorching desert heat. All of the houses wore a fresh coat of white wash every couple of years and, if you looked at it from a distance, you could easily mistake the village to be part of the flora of the desert: a testimony that the people there lived in tune with an environment that offered them an oasis to call home.

My shelter in the village was a small room inside an old temple that had a couple of rooms set aside for pilgrims. The rooms were separated from the main temple by a majestic garden of jasmine and roses.

The temple building was about two hundred years old and comprised of a courtyard surrounded by a few rooms where the priest and his family lived. At the centre of the courtyard was an open space with a small platform raised directly in the middle. This podium was draped with beautiful thick red velvet, and served as an altar which housed the resident deity.

The deity was Karni Mata—the Rat Goddess. Karni Mata was a 15th century mystic who was considered to be an incarnation of the Goddess Durga. According to legend, once a storyteller brought her a child that was dying. She failed to revive the child and thus got infuriated with the god of death, Yama, who preys on souls migrating from body to body, and who had taken hold of the child's soul. From then on, she decreed that none of her tribe would fall into Yama's hands again. She declared that all members of her tribe would first be reborn as rats before they returned to human form, thus avoiding passing through the vicious clutches of the ever-hungry Yama.

Rats in this part of the world are therefore considered

to be storytellers awaiting their rebirth into human form. They are called *Kabas* and are much revered by the semi-nomadic desert folk.

And my oath, these giant rodents were running around everywhere as if they owned the joint. They seemed to keep to a routine, though; they always knew when it was feeding time, so in reality they didn't bother me too much. Nor did they make their presence felt in my room, apart from the few times when one strayed in for a look and a sniff.

Nevertheless, it took me some time to get used to the fact that the place was swamped with rats and they were the ones ruling the roost. The rats were being served, fed and worshipped as living Gods! For some strange reason I accepted this fact with a sense of joy. The rebel within me really liked the idea of a rat Goddess and I knew it would freak out the folks back home when I shared with them this story. Surely, most of them would think I was pulling their leg.

The small field that separated the temple courtyard and the building with my room was planted with jasmine and roses. In the evenings, it filled the warm desert night with a fantastically intoxicating aroma – a divine bliss to make the senses drunk. The building where I lived had three rooms all facing the flower garden. I occupied the first room, while the other two were empty most of the months I lived there. When, on rare occasions, the priest felt right about it, the rooms originally built to house pilgrims were let out to foreigners like me who came to the village for a visit longer than only one night's stay. In festival season or on sacred pilgrimage days, the two rooms adjacent to mine would be occupied by a whole host of people from the nearby villages who had come to pay homage to the rat goddess. They were usually fascinated at how I was the only one living in my room, while they would fit at least six people into the tiny space and still be happy and content.

Over the years in this incredible land, I have come to

understand what a different concept of personal space Indians have, compared to that of foreigners. Many Indians have never been alone in their whole life — let alone slept in a room that is there only for themselves! It might be another reason why the art of meditation was mastered and perfected in this country, as it is, at times, the only way to find any solitude at all.

The priest of the temple was a man in his early forties belonging to the Brahmin caste, the upper caste of society, which maintained an absolute monopoly over the religious landscape of India. The temple itself was a family affair, as the priesthood was handed down from father to son, one generation to the next. The priest himself was a kind and very practical man who treated his role just as any worker would treat their job. One day I queried him about how he was comfortable receiving such handsome donations from the poor village folk who came to worship at his temple. He looked at me with some bewilderment, puzzled by the nature of my inquiry and with the simple innocence of a child replied, "Sir, everybody must have some business, some work to do so they can live and support their family. My business is God business, very good business indeed!" He said it with a good and happy smile. I looked back at him; I really wasn't sure whether to laugh or cry.

I left it alone, for already then I realised that the difference between our outlooks on life was so vast, that it was pointless even to have a debate on the subject. In the evenings, he would go up to the flat wide rooftop and smoke a small clay chillum while he watched the sun go down over the desert sands. Often, he would invite me to join him and mostly we would sit and smoke in silence, both of us in awe of the marvels of creation, mesmerised by the hypnotic desert sunset as the red fireball changed its colours as though a dimming furnace across the horizon.

My days back then followed a predictable routine — long morning walks into the desert, followed by time spent at the cremation grounds on the edge of the village. On my return home, usually sometime around midday, just before the sun hit the earth with all her fury, I would go shopping in the market for my daily food needs. Cooking lunch was a long and elaborate affair and it was really my only meal for the day. I cooked on the veranda outside of my room in a small oven made from an old tin box covered with clay. I used dry cow dung for my fuel, as wood was scarce in those parts of the world. The menu was always the same; rice, vegetables, lentils or some other sort of peas or beans. In those days, I was a very strict vegetarian, it was before I understood that it is the same breath which breathes through all beings, and the presence of life permeates equally through all.

She walked in one late afternoon with a small pack on her back and moved into the room adjacent to mine. I didn't get to see her face when she arrived, though I did get a glimpse of her long, flowing black hair and the large colourful gypsy skirt she wore. In those days I spent most of my time in silence and solitude. I talked a few words when I was at the market taking care of my essential needs or when I stared at the expansive desert sunsets from the roof with the priest, yet apart from that, I saw no need for words, neither did I feel I had anything to say or give anybody. I avoided most forms of communication and was content to be in solitude, which began to feel like an ally and a most trusted friend. I was a wounded young man injured by a society that offered no sanctuary to anyone who attempted to ask questions of a different nature, or decided to step off the ever-growing tedious caravan of greed.

I didn't trust this structure that had bred me to be a cog in a wheel. There was no way I was going to support an invisible apparatus which its main aim was to enhance the production of material goods, increase the flow of capital into the big corporations and stimulate people to consume more and more products which were supposed to make them happier. In reality, nobody was happy. They had just numbed their minds with clutter. They had abandoned the world of magic for the world of rationality and, in the process, wiped the smile completely off their faces. Most people I knew had long lost their capacity to think with freedom in their hearts and turn their lives into a meaningful, creative, spontaneous journey.

In fact, the concept of a real spirit walk, a path originating from an inner illumination rather than from a borrowed doctrine, a journey which focused on principles unrelated to the material world; was deeply discouraged and never taught in their schools.

The society I hailed from was rapidly embracing commodities as symbols of culture. The whole purpose of education was to breed us to fit somewhere within the wheel of fortune. Myself, very early on in the game, well, I felt it to be all a load of shit. My whole being was screaming out loud, "We are being fooled, taken for a ride; life has something much more profound to offer us as guests on planet earth!" I needed to find out if life had any meaning to it beyond the crap taught to me in the houses of learning. What was truth, and was there any such concept at all?

I was twenty-four years old, and nobody—and I mean nobody—had ever sat me down and explained the real significance of our earth walk. Not my parents, not my teachers at school, nobody did. It was left squarely to me to wander and roam through the dark forbidden tracks searching for the place where the light came from. Yes, I was told that I needed to study hard, so I could get a job and work hard, so that I could make money and spend hard, so I that could support my family and . . . blah, blah, blah.

It took a long time before I understood the meaning of *presence*. I knew something was wrong. I knew that the *being* I was bred to be by a whole system was not an *alive being*; it was not grounded in sound principles or guided by an inspired vision. Basically, beyond all doubt, I felt it was just utter crap—some weird fantasy that humanity had conjured up over generations of lies and deceit by the powers that be; mostly religious establishments seeking to control the masses through the myth of a male almighty god. A ferocious god of right and wrong, originating with the so-called children of Abraham, spilling and spreading its fallacy over many centuries through different names and forms, a god that existed only in their stories. However, a god that could not be found in the love and giving of mother earth and creation herself. After all, how could god be a male anyway, when all creation is being birthed through the divine feminine principle? In reality I had no clue what God was, I only knew what he wasn't.

There was so much I needed to comprehend and understand as I first dared to venture out of the mould designated for me by the corporate and religious masters. The first step before I could undergo any meaningful change was to unlearn the whole myth that had been instilled in me so professionally and efficiently by people who actually believed in their tales of god, greed and separation.

The next day after her arrival, as I returned home from the market place, I saw her. She was sitting on the small, thin strip of grass in front of our rooms underneath the shade of a big Poinciana tree. She was leaning over a drawing book with a bunch of pencils and crayons, sketching the surrounds. Lifting her head briefly from the drawing pad, she greeted me with a silent nod of the head and a gentle, subtle smile. There was a slight air of aloofness about her. Her jet-black hair went all the way down to her thighs and her skin was white, very white; almost pale as though it hadn't seen the sun for a long time, yet there was a certain shine to it. Her brown eyes were slightly oriental; she must have some Asian heritage, I thought to myself, although there was definitely a European aura about her. I will never forget the beautiful embroidered white blouse she wore that day, to me she looked like an angel that had just descended from the heavenly planets, yet, at the time, it was all too much for my tortured soul to handle. She was beautiful, the most graciously beautiful women I had ever seen with my own eyes or in my imagination.

Strangely though, I didn't feel excited by her arrival, nor was I spellbound by the presence of her beauty. On the contrary, I felt really irritated by her sudden appearance. She felt like an invader, trespassing into the sanctuary of my solitude. There was danger in the air, this much I knew immediately. Choirs of alarm bells were ringing loudly inside my head. Was I ready to relate? Connect? Feel anything that might distract me from the journey I had chosen to undertake at this moment in time? I was also annoyed by the pattern I had noticed emerging in my life. The blueprint seemed to ever be the same, each time I started to feel settled in my journey and comfortable with my own path, somehow life ushered in a new challenge to disrupt the proceedings dramatically.

Walking into my room that day, I made a firm decision. I wasn't going to connect with her; if need be, I would move elsewhere. I didn't need any friends or lovers at that moment. It had been months since I had had a meaningful conversation with anyone; basically, I wouldn't know what to say. There was no language left in me, I was in hollow space, existing in no man's land. I had left somewhere, yet I still hadn't arrived anywhere. I was in the process of shedding a whole past; nonetheless I hadn't walked through any new doorways yet. Escaping the jailhouse, I hadn't yet broken the prison chains.

✼ ✼ ✼ ✼ ✼ ✼ ✼

The river keeps on flowing in silence as though she hasn't heard the news of the impending disaster and the changes which she is about to undergo. The massive dam upstream has burst and in half an hour or so, the whole valley will be submerged by a raging wall of water.

Back in time it was a greedy white man with a bible in one hand and a gun in the other who showed no respect to the circle of creation. Now greed, like any epidemic left unchecked, has spread to all corners of the earth. People have fought for many years to prevent the building of this dam; they protested, marched, fasted, organised, agitated – they did everything possible within their non-violent means.

Everybody knew the dam was being built in a high seismic zone, which had already experienced major earthquakes in the past. Even the Supreme Court weighed in on a couple of occasions, halting the construction on this and other grounds a few times. To the corrupt politicians, however, the dam meant a golden cash cow to be milked from the bribes paid by the massive construction companies involved in the project. They kept resurrecting the project each time it was about to die off. Really, it made no sense to take this beautiful fertile land – a pristine Himalayan valley that has been tilled for thousands of years by local mountain folk – and turn it into a dam.

The local people didn't need this dam; all their needs were met by the ample gifts that the glorious landscape bestowed upon them. The valley was fertile, water was plentiful, wood was abundant, medicinal herbs were everywhere and the small herds were healthy.

The dam, however, wasn't being constructed for their benefit, not at all. They didn't figure into the scheme of things. The architects of *progress* treated the valley as though it were vacant of human habitation. The word *development* does not take into account the lives of the simple, gentle people who live close to the earth and treat her as a living, giving mother. A mother they take care of, rather than enforce their will upon.

The dam was to benefit the city folk living far away

from the towering mountains where the Gods have their playground. These people didn't care at all if the mountains were injured and the locals ended up as refugees in their own country. As far as the modern people in the city were concerned, the mountain folk were uneducated and backward; it was of no concern to them if many ended up living a life of deprivation in city slums. "*Progress* always has a price," they said. It was just statistics, as long as it didn't affect them or anyone they knew.

More so, the city folk did not know the tribal people living in the high mountains. The two cultures vibrated on different frequencies and answered to different calls. One was attuned to the law of *love*, while the other worshipped the law of *want* born in the shadows of *fear*.

It wasn't the first battle the mountain folk waged to protect their land against the forces of greed; and it wouldn't be their last. For many years, contractors from the plains came and cut down the trees, slowly turning the mountains into naked, barren slopes, stripping their majestic mane. The trees held the fragile young mountains together and kept the water flowing. The trees made the mountain air rich with oxygen; they gave wood to build houses and supplied fuel for the cooking fires that kept the people warm in the cold nights. The trees were the centre of a whole community of plants, animals and people, providing shelter and sustenance to all. The trees gave and gave and gave, while, in return, the people looked after them and worshipped them as living Gods.

When the situation became desperate with more of these mountain Gods being cut down by the blind forces of greed, the people decided it was time to act. As the tree fellers came, the people hugged the trees to protect them. In the process many died or got hurt when the trees came down, howling in pain.

Most of the brave were women. It was a movement inspired by the feminine courage of the local mothers, who, like the mountains and the trees, embody deep within their core the essence of sustaining and nurturing life. After many casualties and a public uproar, the government yielded and the remaining trees were protected. Their action came to be known as the movement of the *tree huggers* and they inspired people to participate in the many environmental movements worldwide that emerged in the coming years.

However, times were changing at a rapid pace and people who chose to walk gently upon this earth and treat her as a living *being* were considered a nuisance to the architects of the blueprint of progress. They lived out of touch with the so-called miracle of *economic growth,* and cared for different things. The land that they had worshipped since the beginning of time, which in return gave them their daily bread, was useless as far as the people in the capital were concerned. What they needed was more and more electricity for the thousand and one gadgets produced to make their lives easier.

In fact, this is nothing short of material barbarism at the expense of the living creation. In the process, the hypnotised masses were left with no time to think or feel. When one really touches the world around them, they come to recognise that the inner journey may be far more relevant to their life on earth than the endless chase for momentary pleasures produced by material catatonia. Their perceived advanced modern lives left them with no space to take a deep breath and sight the flutters of a butterfly as the sun sets behind the majestic hills. Someone had robbed everyone of their time with life, thus leaving them with no time to listen to the frogs as they call in the rain or to watch the birds dance while being carried in the currents of the wind.

They became slaves, bowing in deep reverence and full surrender to the gods of *mammon,* saturating their beings with as much clutter as possible. They never had the time to look in the mirror of *self* and wonder about simple truths; who am I, and what is the purpose for my walk on earth?

Am I alive, or do I just exist? What am I contributing to by diminishing my being to a *human consumer*, rather than celebrating life as a *living creator*? The gods of greed have captured centre stage within society, while the culture of *give me more* has over-shadowed the spirit of *let's share what we have*. The idea that we must ensure that, seven generations from now, people will thank us for taking such good care of the earth we live upon, seems far-fetched to the ones making the rules.

Loving and caring for each other, while preserving the beautiful earth for the children and all creatures big and small, is termed a stupid ideology, the domain of dreamers' way out of touch with reality. Some have even started to label the ones who stand up for life as *terrorists*. You are either a cog in the machine of *economic growth* or you are banished as an outcast. How far has humankind gone from the core centre of *love* – have the fear gods established such a warm home within the hearts of the many? Why are we letting a bunch of self-centred, greedy lunatics chart an insane path for humanity, a course most of us seem to be happily or blindly accepting as the norm?

Looking around me, I realise it may be futile to ponder over these issues at the present moment, even if they are the direct cause of the unfolding catastrophe. In the distance I hear the sound of people screaming in panic, attempting to gather their few precious possessions and run up the hill for safety. A police jeep passed through the village just a few moments ago, announcing on loudspeakers the bursting of the dam. The people knew it anyway. The moment they felt the earth shaking, they knew the age of Kali was upon them. Turning around from the river I notice some of them grabbing what they can, searching for their kids and heading up the hill in panic. They know there is a bit of time left, nonetheless some of them may also realise it is a lost cause, as their personal survival will be challenged in the mayhem that will follow the great flood.

I choose to remain motionless by the river. There is no other option as far as I am concerned. No more escaping *what is*. I do not see any sense in running for my life or fighting the river anymore—I am content to watch and wait. At last I have reached a new sphere within my being, a stellar resolve—just be still. I am going nowhere: life is not going to make me react to the melodrama it is enacting. I am comfortable to sit and observe.

Bit by bit I become oblivious to all the commotion around me, immersing myself in the presence of the river. She feels so still, so quiet. Could it really be that in a short while she will turn into a raging torrent and wipe out everything in her way? Does life really change so radically from one moment to another in a blink of an eye? Is there anything else to do at the present moment other than keep still?

I have had my heart burned so many times on the stake of love, at the tree of honour, in the whirlwind of desire, for the sole reason that I have tried to change the reality of the moment *that is*. Yet now it all feels so different. The totality of my being is absorbed in profound stillness. I walked many a life and seen the story unfold again and again. I flowed with the river, danced with the wind and been consumed by the flames of tomorrow, to at last feel at peace with *what is*.

The last time she left she said she was leaving forever, yet I feel my love for her is as true and present as love can ever be. I am not going to chase her anymore, for she is forever living inside me, so deep, so alive, as though she never left. It is only my own illusion of separation that has felt her depart so many times before. I can hear her singing a sweet melody deep within my heart. She is always with me, separation is not an option and we both have known it all along—since the first moment we smelt each other's breath in the rat temple beyond the rose garden.

I couldn't sleep that night: I realised change was upon me and I was really agitated by it all. Yes, she was beautiful, really beautiful, so what? I went over to Karni, the rat Goddess, to seek an answer to my predicament. As a Goddess-Guardian of storytellers, I could hear her telling me to go back to my room and write.

Late that night, by the dim light of a candle I wrote my first poem.

> *You stripped me,*
> *My skin a memory of time*
> *The wind biting through*
> *The last of the shields*
> *Once held proud*
> *As a passage of faith.*
>   *Now there remains nothing*
> *But a shimmering hum,*
> *And the song of a line*
> *Drawn in the shifting sands*
> *Of a time*
> *Yet to be known.*
>   *Love, they say*
> *Will carry me*
> *Yet the chariot is unwilling.*
> *Love, they say*
> *Will free me*
> *Yet the chains are unyielding.*
>   *Tomorrow is a passing*
> *With its flutter*
> *That I may be.*
>   *Today I sing a song,*
> *Painting totems*
> *In yesterday's sky.*

"I have only just started the journey of working out what my life is all about and the last thing I need now is love," I thought to myself as I put my pen down. At the same time, there was another voice, a very subtle one, incredibly delicate, almost unheard, whispering in my ear that love would come and lift me with her trusted wings and carry me through this difficult passage.

I wasn't sure how much I believed this whisper, though in spite of this the next morning, moved by a force unfamiliar to me, I went and bought all the flower garlands I could find in the village market. My hands were heavily laden with marigolds and orange blossoms when I returned to the temple yard and knocked on her door.

I wasn't nervous, not even slightly apprehensive of how my gift would be received. Actually, a big part of me wished that she would throw me and my marigolds out, and move away from her room that same day.

She didn't, though. She opened the door, looked me in the eyes and then gazed down at the flowers. She didn't seem surprised at all; it was as though she had been expecting it all along.

It wasn't the fact that she was a princess, a priestess of the highest order, a queen from another faraway galaxy that fascinated me; it was the fact that she knew she was and felt so at ease with it. Looking back at me, she smiled. There was so much joy in her smile; the whole unimaginable beauty of the universe was present in the contours of her face. Her smile was a beam of light that said everything; there was no need for words. "She reads my mind," I thought to myself, "she knows I can't handle words at the moment." And she did, for she didn't attempt to strike up a conversation and drag us into a circle of meaningless awkward small talk. She didn't even say thank you.

We gently leaned in towards the other, precisely at the same moment, as though the script was already written and gave each other a long kiss — well, it wasn't really a kiss, actually. Our lips touched each other's in silence with no movement; we held the touch for a while and then let go. There was no passion in the kiss, just a sense of deep surrender. We both knew we had met before; we could taste it on our breath. I held both her hands whilst looking deep into her eyes. They felt like a magnet that slowly opened a doorway that sucked me beyond the stars to reveal the signposts of eternity.

From that day onwards she always kept the light shining in the circle of our dance, even when so often our physical bodies did not inhabit the same place on this earth. It was a simple twist of fate in a strange moment in time that changed my life forever. I can still feel her light with me by the river now, though it's been many moons since I last saw her in the flesh.

※ ※ ※ ※ ※ ※ ※

Qua... qua... qua... out of the blue I hear the crows cawing with great fanfare as they announce to the world at large that they are here by my side and intend to probe into my being. A warm wave of wellbeing rushes through me as my new mates affirm that they are here to keep me company on this epic journey with the self.

I feel I need them now by my side and I value their companionship at this moment in time. I can sense that they are true allies of mine, otherwise why would they be here by my side, when there are many more interesting things to do in the crow paradise.

Once they make their presence felt, I don't feel alone anymore; it is as though the whole web of life is present, offering me its guidance and protection. In honesty I am not really sure what I need protection from. Perhaps they shield me from drifting into a self-absorbed state where I could get lost in forever. Their presence reminds me that, somehow, I am not alone in this world and my obligations extend beyond the small *me*.

"So, what do you make of it all?" the most talkative of the three crows strikes up conversation again. I am curious to know why they left me and where they flew to for this short time, though I am not sure they would appreciate my probing into their own affairs.

"What is there to think?" I sigh, looking back at them with deep affection. "The river will come soon in all her might and fury and it will all be gone. Really, there is no place for thought anymore. You guys will rise up in the air, flying into another sun where the land is dry. Myself, I suppose, I will flow with the great river and eventually end up as food for the fishes in the ocean," I say with a voice devoid of emotion.

The crows look at each other, asking questions with their silence. I notice the two quiet ones staring at the one, which up to now has done all the talking. I sense they want him to continue this conversation, to say something more to this stupid human sitting aimlessly by the river while the whole world is on the move. By now I have ascertained that he must be an elder crow, of some standing in his tribe or a leader amongst them. At last he introduces himself with a deep, husky, gentle, croaky voice. "My name is Nobi, messenger of the bird tribes." He doesn't seem to be in any hurry to continue our conversation as we listen to the sounds of the majestic night together.

Some of the lights are still on in the village, however what strikes me is that, in all the commotion, people have left many of their animals behind them. A few people might have taken their pet dog with them, and apart from that, the rest were left to wait for the river and fend for themselves. As *feeling* beings, the animals are sensing the impending disaster and many of them are in a state of panic, crying out for help.

Anyone who has ever been to an Indian village or town knows how domestic animals, and some wild ones, share a very close proximity of living quarters with humans. There are always cows, dogs, goats, buffalos, pigs, chooks, sheep, and of course the marauding red-faced monkeys who delight in causing havoc. Now, the cows who are still tied up in their small sheds are desperately trying to break free, while the dogs are howling at the half moon in the night sky, as though to say, "Oh, great spirit, what have you done?"

I notice some of the men, after securing their families on higher ground, return to take their prized cow or a favourite goat. Then again, really, there is not much more they can do, for none of them want to be trapped when the river comes down in all her might and, with every passing moment, that wall of water is a moment closer.

It's a beautiful calm night and the air feels so still — disaster always seems to hit amidst the splendour of beauty. It is a pleasant warm April night. Not the steaming hot weather of May, when the monsoon is being conceived within the realms of father sky and the whole hemisphere is loaded with this full-on intensity; a certain barometric pressure that sends humans and animals alike, a bit mad.

The stars are twinkling, smiling at the earth below — an earth that is about to experience a major catharsis — yet the stars are still happy and will continue to shine their light and joy, no matter what comes.

The river is about to overflow with energy and bestow her might on the earth and its inhabitants. And although the river is connected and part of the *all that is*, it is still the river's journey, while the mountains, wind, sky, and stars will just be watching as an attentive audience sitting in the members' gallery. No doubt, they may offer their support and assistance if needed, whilst being aware that the journey is the river's and they will trust in her wisdom, since she is part of the great mystery, eternally aligned with the force that spins the wheel around and around.

Likewise, we humans all have a journey, which in one way is connected to everything, and at the same time, is our own personal path. This is one's individual outing with life, to be walked and experienced, felt and transformed and no one else can traverse the road for us. This passage is ours to navigate, and only then does it have the potential to uplift us from existing in an unconscious state of being, to be living as warriors who walk present with life.

I am watching the river, the sky and the stars while listening to the sounds around me. As I stare at my crow friends, a realisation dawns on me. "It does not matter how far my mind has been wandering, what truths I've contemplated or memories I've drifted to. In honesty, this is the only reality pertinent to the present moment. This moment *is* the totality of my life—a River, a Crow and a Man, while the winds of light are twirling amongst us of their own free will. Everything else is a fantasy conjured by a mind, which has not yet learned to be utterly still."

Nobi, the talkative crow, is giving me a long, hard stare. He is unhappy about something; I can sense he has a slight irritation with me.

Feeling within me, I realise I haven't been as open as I could have been with him, neither have I offered him my full trust. I consider sparking up a conversation again; instead, I close my eyes and drift back to the jasmine garden in the desert where I first met the woman who was to turn my life upside down.

We held hands and gazed into each other's eyes for a long time. It felt like eternity, though it didn't feel uncomfortable. After a while, she asked me if I would like to come in. I nodded in a silent agreement and sat on the mat. Her room, like my own had no chairs or bed in it. There was a straw mat, a rather new one that she must have bought at the village market, and a mattress stuffed with smelly old cotton. The room was painted with some pale blue whitewash and that, too, by the looks of it, was done a long time ago. There was a built-in shelf in the wall, like a window with no outside to it. In the far corner stood a small, low table where she had a couple of post cards of Indian Gods, a double-headed rose quartz crystal, and a couple of pieces of tribal jewellery.

She placed some of the flowers around the small table, while hanging others on old bits of iron sticking out from the wall. There were so many flowers and nowhere to place them. She just smiled, spread them all over the small room and came to sit by my side. She held my hands, sitting with crossed legs facing me, and asked me my name. She spoke with a strong French accent, which sounded like music to my ears.

"I am not sure what my name is anymore. The name my parents gave me feels so meaningless, so out of touch with who I am," I replied quietly, testing to see if my vocal cords still worked.

"OK, man, so then what shall I call you? Mr Nobody,' or Mr 'Waiting for his name to feel right,' or shall I just call you 'Nameless' until you decide what you name is?" she asked with the voice of a woman who knew everything she needed to know. I said nothing. She didn't press me for an answer, just kept a gentle smile on her face.

"My name is Void, I am pleased to meet you," she said, with a cheeky smile written all over her face

"Really?" I replied at last, offering her a smile in return, not getting the joke.

"Well, if you are nothing, then I am void. You silly, I am just joking, as I feel you may be. My name is Nulla." She gently let go of my hand, resting it on my leg.

"Nulla, that's a beautiful name," I replied, attempting to

be part of some sort of normal conversation.

"Hey, you don't really have to talk if you have nothing to say, it's alright to be quiet. I'm happy to do the talking for both of us, while you stay in your silence. I am a woman after all and I sensed your uneasy silence from the moment I walked into the temple compound. I can feel you are in no frame of mind for words and perhaps in not much of a mood to relate to me." Again she spoke with the conviction of a person who was utterly certain of the facts she was stating.

I was taken a back a bit by her opening speech. "Who is this woman, can she read into my mind? And what does she mean when she says *uneasy silence*?" She was right about some of things I felt, although not about everything. There was a part of me that did want to relate to her; I liked her, I mean, I more than liked her — I was almost consumed by her being from the moment she arrived. She fascinated me in a strange, weird way and, at the same time, her presence instilled a great calmness within my heart. A gentle, delicate smile started to emerge from within the recesses of my heart. Yes, for the first time in months, I felt a certain sense of happiness and an unexplainable wave of wellbeing. Something in this world made sense again. I suddenly had a relationship, but it wasn't so much about having a relationship with this women who I had just met, what I surprisingly felt was a fresh tangible rapport with the world.

Is this the reason why we all crave the love of another?

Nulla came and, out of the blue and most probably unknowingly, offered to be my bridge with the world, an anchor and a new reference point to life. All I had to do was allow a deep sigh of relaxation and accept the journey *that is*.

"My new friend," she addressed me again, with a tenderness that only women are capable of. "Not only am I a woman, I am a French woman and we French, we love to talk, so I do not mind doing the talking for both of us, hey." She lifted her hands in an attempt to tickle me. I laughed; it was a strange, unfamiliar sound emerging out of me. At that moment I realised I couldn't even remember the last time I had laughed or smiled or felt at ease with the world.

We sat in her room all afternoon: she talked when she felt like it and when she didn't she just looked at me or held my hand. I rested my back against the wall, immersing myself in her presence. Her father was French, she said and her mother Vietnamese. They met at the time when the French had given up their colonisation of Vietnam, although some French soldiers still remained in the country as well as some Americans. It was the mid 1950's and it was supposed to be the beginning of a new dawn for Vietnam as Ho Chi Minh emerged as a unifying charismatic leader. In spite of this promised new dawn, it predictably turned into a horrendous nightmare as America, reneging on the deals signed in Paris, supported a new war effort and backed the military dictators and the landed gentry of the South.

Her mother was a poor village girl and was sent to the city to work as a prostitute with the foreign soldiers, as her family was starving and needed food to eat.

Nulla's father, being one of her regular clients, fell in love with her, and decided to marry her and take her back to France when his tour of duty was over. She was happy to leave her country, for she never forgave her own father for sending her to sell her body to support her family back in the village. Nulla's mother had two children: Nulla was the younger. Her older brother died when he was only eight years old and she was just five. It was a freak car accident while the family were holidaying in the Alps. Nulla's father while negotiating a curve on a narrow mountain road, lost control and slammed into a tree. Nulla's brother, who was sitting in the back of the car with her, snapped his neck and died in the arms of his five year old sister.

Nulla was then twenty-two and had come to India a

month before in search of life's beauty and art. That was the way she described it. She had her own way of painting pictures with her words; she was an artist after all.

I was happy to sit and listen to her share her life story with me, while in return I had no words to offer. I stretched my arms and pulled her closer to me, she rested her head on my chest and we embraced.

❄ ❄ ❄ ❄ ❄ ❄ ❄

I could remain in this dream wonderland thinking of Nulla forever, or at least until the river comes and sweeps me away. Nobi, the talkative crow, has different ides about allowing me this quite space and demands my attention again.

"So, mister Runaway Buddha, or at least pretending to be one that has attained a state of silence, can you wake up from your slumber for a moment and acknowledge our presence by your side? Or are you just like the rest of them, living as though the world around you does not exist?" He suddenly addresses me with a commanding voice, asserting his authority as messenger of the wild.

"OK, Nobi, yes, we do need to talk. I mean, perhaps I haven't fully shared my heart with you," I answer him while somehow still jumbled by the two worlds splashing like waves through my inner landscape.

Nobi stares at me long and hard. "What do you mean you haven't shared your heart? Hey, man, maybe I spared you my fury, though no more holding back now, mate. The time has come for some straight talking, and I have been waiting for this opportunity for a long time."

The two other crows nod in agreement, hopping from one foot to the other whilst voicing their approval with a raucous "Qua… qua… qua…"

"So, what are you actually doing, sitting motionless by the river? Are you trying to be some sort of holy man? Are you attempting to imitate the ones who have found peace by retreating from the world, like the person you people call Gautama the Buddha?" He pauses for a moment to make sure his words are sinking in.

"Nobi, what are you talking about? What was wrong with the Buddha? He was one of the most amazing figures in history, a remarkable man that I admire. A man who found peace and silence that could not be shaken by any external circumstance. This is what I am attempting to do now, find a glimpse of this peace, and you keep snapping me out of it," I answer him, slightly irritated by his latest statements.

"You stupid humans, you are all the same, blind sheep led by the jingle of the bells, never really looking into the heart of matters. What did that man you call the Buddha *do*? Have you ever really thought about it, or are you just being a parrot to the accepted line trumped up by the prevailing *wisdom* of the day? You all seem to have lost the capacity to think beyond the tales instilled within you by the Manufacturers of Consent. What I am trying to convey has very little to do with the Buddha, since you are nowhere near the inner peace that man has attained. It has something to do with an ability to form your ideas and truth from your own direct experiences, rather than being a consumer of borrowed knowledge."

Nobi is enraged, he is on fire and I have little choice but to give him my full and undivided attention. "So, my human mate, here we go again. What did he do? I am waiting for some intelligent answer." Nobi speaks again, with an ever-demanding voice that commands that I think before I offer him a reply.

"What do you want of me, Nobi?" I hit back at him, annoyed by his persistence and by the fact that I feel he is being critical of a figure I've always looked up to.

"I don't want anything of you; I am asking you a simple question: What did the Buddha do?" He keeps on pressuring me, as I observe his intensity grow.

"Well, he went to many teachers in his quest for truth and searched for the meaning of life. Then one day, sitting under a tree meditating, he discovered the cause of human suffering and the way to liberate us from this inner torment. Rejoicing in his findings he proceeded to teach many others a way to find peace," I say, happy with the way in which I have described Siddhartha's conduct.

"Well, yes, this might be one way to look at it; however, have you ever thought that this story could be interpreted in a different way?" Nobi asks in a calmer, more solemn tone, although he is still determined that I take heed of what he is trying to convey.

"It's amazing, the myths you humans create around people whom you place on pedestals and how you always colour things up, painting the pictures you wish were true. Have you ever paused for a moment to think what actions the Buddha took in order to find the peace he was seeking? He left his wife, son and responsibilities to the world in order to pursue his own happiness. Has it occurred to you that, by doing so, he hurt the people closest to him? How would your own wife react if you left her for the pursuit of peace? Would she think you are a hero, a holy man, or would she be convinced you are running away from facing the challenges life has presented you with?"

Nobi gives me a long hard stare again, checking to see if I am getting the meaning behind his words. I am in no hurry to offer him a reply. I have to sit still and feel out the truth in what he is saying. It is the first time I have heard anybody speak of the Buddha in this manner. I actually feel a bit unsettled by his words, and although they are full of contradictions, I am starting to understand something of what he is trying to hammer into me.

"Hey man, this silence isn't going to liberate you," he

continues passionately. "You know, not only did the Buddha retreat from facing the challenges of the world, he then came back and taught his followers to beg for their food and needs. So while other people toiled all day, he and his disciples sat in silence in the forest. What good is this silence if it comes off the sweat of others, and what sort of peace is it, if it is found by escaping from the world?"

I take a deep breath, voicing a long sigh.

"This is no time to sit and sigh, mate," Nobi says. "Look at you and the so-called *children of light*. What have you done, what are you really doing to make this planet healthy again, to heal the suffering of creation? Hey man, what are you doing to stop the extinction of dozens of species every day? Come on tell me! Are you sitting and meditating and praying and hoping it will all just change like that? The future is already screaming in despair at your callousness!" His wings flap with rage and I feel that nothing I say can pacify him in this moment.

"Hey, Nobi, you know this is not totally true. In my opinion, the Buddha did not run away; rather he sat and faced the inner conflict. Perhaps, if more of us did so, we would be better equipped to face the challenges you are talking about. And, Nobi, still there are many of us directly involved with the struggle for a new earth, the quest to preserve the sanctity of life." I reply, not sure if my words are coming from the depths of my knowing, or are a reactionary defence.

"Many of you? Not many, some of you, very few, while the rest of you are in a selfish pursuit of your own happiness. And we need all of you, the whole of creation needs you to stand up and be counted. This is not the time for half-hearted measures. This is the time for all of you to reaffirm your commitment to the collective wellbeing of creation herself. This is not the time to sit and wallow in your small realities, of *me*, and what do *I need* to be happy. The moment has come for all of you, all of us to work together — before it's too late. If we don't, this beautiful dream of life on earth will turn into a hellish nightmare. And your entire search for personal peace and happiness is doomed from the word *go*, for each and every one of you is related to the whole and, if the great mother is wounded and crying, so will you all be."

Nobi stops talking and looks away. I notice a few tears flow from his eyes onto his jet-black neck as he moves his head in the direction of the river. Perhaps she will embrace his tears with deeper empathy than I am able to do at present. The other two crows stare at me with utter contempt and disgust, as though I am to blame for his suffering, for I represent the human race.

My thoughts are all over the place. Every word he spoke rang as a sermon of truth. At the same time I could just as easily walk a few steps further around the universal wheel of Truth and see it all from another vantage point, be offered another perspective. Maybe the new view would be an insight equally as powerful, maybe not. I need time to orientate my thinking, reflect and find my equilibrium again.

The whole pain of the natural world, the universe that is my home, is reflected to me through the crows' agony. Their pain and suffering is a direct result of human action or inaction, depending on your vantage point.

Nobi made sure I grasped the fact that I belonged to a race that was committing a mass genocide on a scale never witnessed before.

"And you must know," Nobi raises his head and continues to talk, "it's not the blind, stupid humans possessed by greed and fear that I am really angry with. No, they are just blind and stupid. It's the mob that can *see* and the ones that *know* what's happening and, in spite of this, still choose to do nothing; they are the real culprits in this saga."

I sense his rage is now slowly turning into deep sadness. The two other crows look at Nobi, yet he ignores them.

He stares at the water as the gentle ripples in the river are swirling around like whirling dervishes caught midstream.

So, it isn't human action that he is upset about—it is human inaction. On this I have to agree with him. The earth carers are few, very few. Many people are aware of what is happening, though in spite of this, few really care and translate that care into action. Some see confrontation as a *negative* thing, and don't want any negativity contaminating their pure, positive, spiritual existence, which is poisoned with judgements of right and wrong and anything in between. Others think the task is too big or feel inadequate to deal with it. There always seem to be incredible discrepancies between people's words and actions. Everybody has an excuse why somebody else should be the one to act, or why there should be no action altogether. Many say that it was just evolution and that species would die and disappear, while others will emerge. The majority of people, however, intoxicated with their ever-growing bubble of gadgets, don't even believe that anything out of balance is taking place.

A few weeks ago I read an article in a major daily newspaper. It was a small, insignificant page-seven news item; one that is not really meant to be read by many. The small headline read: "Pollution Wiping Out Three Species Every Hour." Now, do any of us really understand what this actually means? It means that bit-by-bit; we are destroying all of earth's support systems and basically committing collective suicide. It is shocking, and telling of the present human value system, that this appalling piece of information only makes it to page seven in the newspaper! I feel that, if the human race were sane, if we lived in a world where people cared for *real* things, this small piece of news would be the headline screaming out from the front page of every newspaper in the world. It would be the talk of the day, the subject on everybody's lips.

In fact, if we were a sane bunch, we would have never got

to this point where we are wiping out life on earth without even pausing for a moment to contemplate the wisdom of our actions.

How far we have strayed from the core of our being and how stupid and callous we have become! Don't we realise at all what is taking place? Three species of life every hour, gone forever! Our brothers and sisters in creation — seventy-two a day and there are 365 days in a year. Do any of us really fathom what we are talking about here? Do we really grasp the significance behind these numbers? I doubt it.

I do wonder though, how we humans would react if somebody tried to eliminate us off the planet. How would we respond if we were about to become one of the three species an hour being eliminated by the actions or inactions of another race? I have a feeling we would fight tooth and nail, with all means possible to ensure our survival and would expect all other species sharing this planet to support us in our plight. No doubt we would expect our extinction to make front-page in the crow media. Yet we are so stupid that we can't even see that, by destroying everything around us, we are actually destroying ourselves.

With all the trees gone, will money give us the oxygen we need to breathe?

With no fish left swimming in the ocean, will our stock market shares provide us with the food we eat?

With the earth turned barren and dry, will we grow food in our high tech laboratories?

With no animals roaming free, will we live on an earth void of the song of life, ready for the age of the robot?

I gaze at the river. There are no answers to be found.

The crows look away, staring at a horizon beyond my reach. Nobi has rocked the epitome of my reason for sitting still by the river. I feel shipwrecked, sad and alone — my perfect peace in tatters.

Needing a break, I drift back to the sweet memories of that day when I first held Nulla in my arms . . .

❋ ❋ ❋ ❋ ❋ ❋ ❋

"I am going to the land of love; and you know, one does not go to that secret far-away house of magic on their own. Would you like to come?" Nulla said, smiling at me playfully. It was close to midnight, we both felt in a timeless zone, the space we touch when we truly don't have a worry in the world and are happy for the present moment to last eternally. We just sat there on the mattress slumped against the wall, holding each other for all those hours. I stroked her long black hair gently. It was long, I mean really long, and each time my fingers opened to take in her beautiful mane, I felt like a merchant on a silk caravan, who had just scored gold. There is nothing more seductive and appealing than a woman's long hair and Nulla's hair was a jewel, so soft and welcoming to my touch.

"Where is the land of love, Nulla?" I asked her, still unable to comprehend the immense peace permeating every cell of my being.

"It is where the story of the Heart is told," she said.

"And what is the story of the Heart?" I asked her while gently kissing her forehead.

"Well, that's what we need to find out, don't we?"

"The land of love," I thought to myself, "what would I find there?"

We lay together on the single mattress holding each other silently, whilst slowly drifting off into the land of sleep.

The next morning, it dawned on me that life had changed forever. First light had just announced the arrival of a new day while Nulla still lay in deep sleep in my arms. I slowly lifted her off me and quietly got up. I stepped outside into the soft morning light and decided to take a stroll into the desert beyond the outskirts of the village. There I sat under the big tree, which overshadowed the burning grounds.

The burning grounds were like the local cemetery; a

66

place where the bodies were brought in to be cremated and returned to ash, to become one with the desert sands again. It was also the place where the Aghories went to meditate on the impermanence of all material phenomena.

The Aghories follow one of India's numerous spiritual roads to the divine. They are wandering seekers who dress in black and spend most of their time meditating in burning grounds. They often have human skulls as their drinking and eating vessels. They smoke and drink and partake in all the sensory delights life has to offer. They negate nothing, while embracing everything. Their quest is to walk through any open gateway and transform it, rather than avoid or deny anything the varied banquet of life on earth presents to them. In their pure form, they are true tantric seers; the core of their spiritual path is to walk through and beyond every human desire. They experience rather than reject. They indulge purely for the taste. It is their way to transform the clutches of craving. The sincere ones amongst them are true seers, attempting to use all available energy for the experience of the divine within.

Of course, many of them misuse their powers and abuse the path they are on, thus giving them quite a controversial reputation. They worship the divine mother, especially the goddess Kali, who is the destroyer of all illusion. They indulge in magic, white and black alike and are often sought after to cast or dispel spells. They are frowned upon by the more conventional approaches to spirituality in India, as many judge them as lacking the purity expected from seekers on the path to divinity. Some also fear them, as they are perceived to possess magical powers.

As I often wore black and hung out in the burning grounds, many people kept their distance from me, as they thought or suspected I was a "Kali Baba."

The burning grounds on the fringe of the village were one of my favourite places. It was usually very quiet, as most people kept away from the area and there also weren't

67

many Aghories around at that time of the year. So my only company was the occasional cow and a couple of stray dogs; the regular, a black one, which I named "Kalu."

In the preceding months, I would often go and sit there for many hours. The peace of the desert, magnified by the domain where life and death embraced one another, offered me a soothing and inspiring space for all my contemplations. There was also something very appealing to me about this path, which involved the constant company of the dead. I felt totally disillusioned by the sermons dished out by the preachers of good, purity, don't do this and don't do that, and you will be liberated and secure a berth in a future heavenly planet beyond the one we are living on right now.

I sensed that the world had been in the hands of the so-called "do-gooders" for a few thousand years and look at where it had led us.

I needed to feel what was happening inside me, the nature of my turmoil, all of it—the shit, the garbage, the fear and the twisted desires. The anger. Yes, all the suppressed rage I had with the world. So many times it felt like I had gotten off at the wrong planetary stop, and earth was not really where I was supposed to land on.

All of it, my whole inner tapestry needed exposing. It all needed to be felt, experienced, understood and comprehended if there was any chance for me to step forward from the place where I was bogged.

If I lived in denial and affirmed only the light, what would happen to all the rest? Would it be swept under the carpet, hidden in a dark corner of my soul to later erupt one day as an uncontrolled monster out of shape?

Already, in those early days of seeking, I had a great aversion to saints. There was something unreal about them as though they lived in great denial of the world we live in. They had a very calculating nature. To me it felt that for them it was all about earning good points for a front row seat in the theatre of the afterlife.

Feeling the world around me, I sense the river as part of my being. We are both in deep surrender to the mystery embedded in the silence of the night. Most of the commotion has shifted up the hill, where people scrambled to higher ground in the hope that it will offer them safety from the impending deluge.

Some seem content to find a safe place where they can still watch the river when she comes in her might and fury, while others keep on climbing across the hills; getting as far away as they can from the approaching calamity.

I can run to a secure place if I choose to; I can just walk, there is plenty of time left to clamber up the hill and be a witness to it all. Why am I staying by her waters?

I don't really have an answer to this question, though I have *a knowing*.

I have to stay here. There is a story, a tale, something in life's chronicle, narrative, that will only reveal itself by staying where I am. Sure, my body will survive, at least a short time longer if I move and walk up the hill; yet, at this moment, I feel way beyond the body, gazing into a realm I am yet to fathom.

I close my eyes, my whole attention focused on the essence of my breath. In—out—in—out . . . it meanders as it gradually slows its pace to a point where it seems there is no more inhalation or exhalation, just the one constant movement, a subtle hum. I can sense the breath of all things permeating through me; a quiet, deep resonance, the sound of an ever-playing drone: it feels like the breath of creation.

We come into physical form with our first breath and leave with our last. During our life we undergo many physical changes, spiritual transformations and emotional upheavals; still the breath remains the same. It is the unchanging song, the ever-present melody; the force of magic that carries us from one moment to the next. So often we forget to give it any attention. Why is it that we give so little consideration to the essence that is our life? Breath is the core, the heart of who we are and the force that sustains us through life. We can go days without food or water, possibly weeks; nonetheless we cannot sustain life for more than a couple of moments without the presence of our breath. It is our closest and most trusted ally.

In truth, it's much more profound than this. When we are present with our breath we are one with the *all that is,* the source where life emanates from. Lacking this awareness, we just exist; survive, though we never go beyond.

And then there is love, the force that compels us to die again and again in her presence; the power that uplifts us and nurtures us through the mosaic of life's numerous experiences. I felt that flower bloom within my heart twenty-five years ago in a small village in the Indian desert and it has nurtured me ever since.

"It came at the wrong time, though," I muse, as I drift back to the temple by the jasmine fields.

❋ ❋ ❋ ❋ ❋ ❋ ❋

"The land of love," I thought to myself as I sat quietly amongst the land of the dead. "What would I find in that land?" It was probably the oldest unanswered question in human history. So many stories had been told about the riddle of love, though none of them had really shed any light on the moment and place where she is born. One thing is for certain though; the continual resurrection and dominance of this powerful emotion in shaping human evolution.

Wars have been fought, borders crossed, songs sung, books written, no other subject throughout time has taken a more essential role than the question and quest for love. Rivers of blood have been shed in her name, torrents of tears have flowed, while they all still call her love and seek her company. What is the *real* story of love and why, in the passageway of life, is there nothing greater we desire than being held safe within her all-encompassing embrace? Is it because it is the place where miracles are born, the space where the soul soars and kisses the lips of the divine presence, even if just for a fleeting moment? "What will the journey to the land of love bring," I pondered, "and why doesn't one journey to that land on their own?"

I was twenty-four years, young or old, either way; how many times had I been to that mysterious land, if at all? I'd been to the land of desire, climbed the hills of passion and each time it had been the same story, pleasure followed by pain and expectations shattered by disappointments. Would a different narrative be drawn in the land where love lives?

I wasn't sure, I'd seen so much of the thing called love around me and it always seemed to sing the same songline; a fairy tale followed by a nightmare. "So has Nulla offered me a journey to hell?" I pondered as I gazed at a couple of stray dogs quarrelling for possession of what seemed to be human bones left over from the funeral pyres. Why does the story of love more often than not go pear-shaped?

If love's birth is always such a deliciously illuminating time, perhaps we humans have a fundamental flaw in the way we conduct ourselves. We always pay so much attention to the point where the journey begins, whist neglecting to focus with awareness on the journey itself, and then we act surprised when the flower wilts away again and again. Any gardener knows that a flower needs water, sun, nourishment and space to grow. Have we lost the art of tending the flower garden of love and dancing the art of life?

Still there was something else that puzzled me even

more than the pulsation of the movement of love. Why was I feeling such a deep calm after months of inner turmoil? Was it the thing we call love or was it something else, something which I had no words in my vocabulary to describe, an energy that lived in a space beyond conceptual syntax?

I had only known Nulla for a day and a half, yet was I sensing a shift beginning to take place in my inner axis? Was there something different about my encounter with this woman? And if there were, how would I know? I really didn't even know if I had ever known love. For want of a word I'll have to call it *love*, for I too, have some right to misuse the most overused and abused word in HisStory.

I had just spent the night in bed with Nulla for the first time, and felt very little sexual desire towards her. She was stunning, attractive, lush, as beautiful as I could imagine a woman to be, though I only wanted to hold her, listen to her breath and take in the moment of magic she offered. To be still and at peace was a miracle for me. A sensation so foreign that I had to pinch myself a few times so to make sure I wasn't dreaming, that it was actually happening. And why had she taken my hand and asked me to go on a journey, I wondered, a walk that could end anywhere or last forever, when she doesn't even know me? There was a part of me; a deep silent knowing that whispered, "All these questions are just inner chatter." She knew me, she felt me from the moment we met and our breaths touched.

Nulla often dared to venture directly into the eyes of truth, where I was still timid to act on my knowing. In the years to come, this would be a pattern that would almost destroy me as a finder on the path back home, and us as eternal companions on this earthly walk.

"Then, again, this stillness, the serenity I was feeling, where was it born?" I kept asking myself, like a scratched broken record, hoping the spirit of the dead would offer me some insight.

"Is every woman an embodiment of mother earth—the land, the water, the trees and the butterflies while man, being a reflection of the sun, has no reason to shine without the earth ready to receive its rays. Is a man alone like a sun shining on a hollow galaxy where there is no one to embrace or use his gifts?"

My mind went on and on, consumed in a self-absorbed inner babble until I noticed two Aghories walking slowly over the hill. They were dressed in black robes and adorned with numerous necklaces, chains and rosaries of little beads with skulls carved out of bone. They held large brass vessels in their hands, like small pots with a handle, in which they would carry the offerings they'd received of milk or food.

They sat on the other side of the big banyan tree, while one of them immediately started collecting twigs to make a fire and the other cleared the earth to make a little camp. There wasn't much to the camp they made, other than a small fireplace and lots of the ornamentation they had brought with them, an array of symbols to invoke the different energies they believed were the guardians of their journey. They stuck a Shiva trident in the ground, chanted mantras in Sanskrit and lit incense before they proceeded to light the fire.

All this time they seemed to be completely ignoring me, although I was just forty feet away. Perhaps they were surprised by my presence in the burning grounds, which they took for granted as being their own private domain.

They placed a little pot on the fire while one of them waved his hand at me to come over. "Chai pyio?" he called. My Hindi wasn't that good, still I did understand their invitation for chai. Somehow, I was reluctant to go over, for I could anticipate their next question. Nevertheless, I picked myself up from my comfortable sitting place and walked over to their little camp.

"Hari Om, sir, how are you?" the elder one of the two asked me in what seemed to be reasonable English. Over the years that I have spent in India I have come to learn that many of the nomadic holy men were people who had held some position in society before they decided to leave it all and live the life of a vagrant seeker. There were ex-lawyers, teachers, government workers, and so forth. On the other hand, there were also the lawless ones who, in an attempt to escape prosecution, robed themselves in orange, black and white to become invisible to the eyes of the law.

"Do you have some good charras,[2]* sir," the Aghorie turned to me again asking exactly the question I anticipated, which was their main purpose in inviting me over

"No, I am sorry, no charras with me," I replied, with a voice not used to speaking.

He looked very disappointed and mumbled something in Hindi to his friend. They were probably questioning the wisdom of wasting a good cup of tea on a foreigner who had the audacity to hang out at the burning grounds without any charras.

I really had nothing against smoking, except for the fact that I felt my being was on such a fine edge that any mind-altering substance would shatter what was already a very fragile psyche. I decided not to hang around with them, for I did not want them to feel obliged to share their precious chai with me while I had nothing to offer them in return. I turned to the elder one with the big burning eyes who spoke English, "Baba," I addressed him with the deep respect deserving of one who had walked way further down the path of self-realisation than I had, "I have one question for you before I go, for I must go now, I have been here for many hours and I can feel a friend is waiting for me," I said. He looked away at the fire and I wasn't sure if his gesture meant I could continue, yet I did in my quiet voice. "Would you tell me what is love?" I asked in almost a whisper.

2   * Charras - Indian word for hashish.

He kept gazing at the fire in silence as though the answer was present in the flames. After what seemed to be an eternity he lifted his eyes and looked at me. His gaze almost threw me off balance; there was a deep knowing in this stare from a man who I sensed had ventured into many parallel realms of existence.

"Love is death," he whispered back at me, while signalling that it was time for me to leave them alone.

※ ※ ※ ※ ※ ※ ※

Love is death. The words the wise Aghorie spoke to me many years ago in the desert, still ring as a truth in my ears today, as I sit awaiting the river to overflow with emotion. I have heard many descriptions of this most miraculous phenomenon in existence, though no portrayal seems more precise. It penetrates into the heart of the matter more clearly than any other depiction.

Love, true love, fearless love, is death — it must be. For love only lives in the complete annihilation of the ego. It brings our illusions and fears to an end. At least temporarily, as most of us, once the spell eases a bit, seem to close off and stand in the way of love's alchemical magic.

At the same time, what have we as a collective been doing to the spirit of love? We have narrowed her infinite bandwidth to a place where she hardly has space to breathe. We have confined her to the walls of desire, passion and possession. We have made her exclusive to the one, rather than all-inclusive. Have we forgotten that love is the air we breathe, and the forever presence of life permeating everything around us? Love shines at us from every mirror offered in the tapestry of life, if we just allow her to!

So why have we strangled her and put her in a little box? Why are we so afraid to smile at the stranger in the street? Is it because we really believe it's a stranger, rather than know it's a brother or sister we just haven't met yet? Is the idea of separation responsible for this morbid fear of expressing our love whilst touching the universe around us? Have we failed to see that all nature is a dance of love? The tree offering us peace and shade is singing her sermon of love in silence, yet we fail to listen. The flower shines her love at us; do we ever thank her, stroke her or take a moment to offer her our love in return? When is the last time we hugged a tree in gratitude? When is the last time we hugged each other, just for the sake of touching love's limitless song?

The crows seem to be a bit despondent due to my constant drifting away into memories beyond time and space. They want my full presence with them, a presence I am unable to offer at this very moment. Nobi wants to talk of the destruction that is taking place, and I want to feel the whole of creation dance within me. Then again, I may not be seeing the whole picture here. Creation and destruction are of the one source, and Nobi is endeavouring to reflect a truth that so many of us are running away from. He sings the voice of the earth and he speaks the language of the divine mother, a dialect still foreign to me after all these years.

At last he lifts his teary eyes and looks at me. Creation is crying in my face, his grief is total. It is all too much for me to handle. I need to look away to avoid his pain, lest my own suppressed grief bursts open from where it's been concealed for so long now. My stomach is in knots; I feel that any moment now I might start sobbing. For the first time ever, I *really* feel the pain and despair the great web of life is going through and how related it is to my own personal agony.

"I have a question to ask you, my dear human friend," he addresses me with great tenderness for a change. "If a certain species were in the process of annihilating creation, the flower garden of God, including exterminating humans off the face of the earth, wouldn't you expect us crows to do everything in our power to stop it? Wouldn't you expect us to put our lives on the line to save you guys? And when some of us say, this is just negative stuff, part of the great cosmic play; would you accept this as a valid answer?"

I look back at him, tears flowing down my face. We are both crying now together. "Do you really want me to answer you, Nobi? Or are you just stating the obvious?" I say with a voice filled with tears. He looks back at the river in silence, both of us staring at the shadows where wisdom is born. We are in deep prayer; appealing to the face of eternity that she may grant us the courage to be.

What is the source of existence? It's the crows, and me, and the river, and everything that breathes life in whatever forms that breath may manifest. The rock has its own breath, perhaps not apparent to our conditioned human mind, yet it is still alive and part of the source of creation. Everything in this planet, in fact in this galaxy and beyond the great void, breathes its own breath and circles through a cycle of evolution and dissolution, expanding and contracting into being and out of being. The cycle may take millions, trillions of years, yet the movement is of the same nature.

Our planet is a small tiny speck in this great cosmic Lila, yet it is a unique one, inhabited by a myriad of life forms, all sharing this small and magnificent space. As far as we know now, and we are probably wrong, only one planet has consciousness out of millions of galaxies and trillions of planets. It is the small and precious earth we live on.

In the beginning, before the illusion of time created an inner schism within us, the song of love must have permeated all things, whilst we all shared this planet in a spirit of give and take. Everything had its role, which was part of the whole. Then something strange must have happened, when the spirit of love was overtaken by the shadows of despair and sorrow. Is this why the state of life on earth is where it's at? Have we become so out of touch that we have even made the birds cry?

When did this state of human confusion first emerge, and did it sprout from the idea of separation? It seems humans feel as though they have to make the choice to swear total allegiance to *human society,* and forget and neglect the needs of the natural world they hail from — thus, always living in a fragmented reality.

What are we first, humans or animals? Of course, we are both: we are a human that has lost all animal instincts of oneness, unity and trust and have decided to go it alone, leaving behind all our relations who share this planet with us.

Except, going it alone is futile, for even a kid knows that for humans to go it alone means a very simple thing — a quick and effective suicide for most life forms on earth, definitely for the human one. All of us on earth, all possible life forms, share the same divine source, while only we humans refuse to embody this truth as a light guiding our walk on earth.

My thoughts and memories of Nulla dominate the landscape of my mind more and more. I miss her dearly and wish she were here having this conversation with Nobi. She would handle it much better than I do, I am sure of that. However, she didn't always deal with things so well and definitely at times she could be quite self-centred as far as my take on things was concerned.

Walking back from the burning grounds after the first night we spent together, I kept on thinking of what the Aghorie had just said to me. Still, I was unable to fully comprehend how these words were pregnant with the fact that, in time, I too would have to die within, in order to fully experience the taste of love.

Leisurely, I strolled back to the temple through the small market place, smiling at the shopkeepers and vegetable sellers. Some of them must have thought I had gone mad, for I never even looked at them in the past, let alone offered them a smile. I used to walk looking at the ground six feet ahead of me, totally oblivious to the world around me. I was lost in my own caged universe. That was until the day I met Nulla.

Arriving at the temple compound, I walked straight to her room to say g'day. Instantly my blood went cold; I felt as if my chest was going to collapse into my stomach. The door was open and the room was empty.

"She is gone," I heard a voice behind me. It was Pradip, the temple priest. "She left a couple of hours ago."

"Did she say where she was going?" I asked him, with a sense of panic creeping into my voice.

"No," answered Pradip, his voice sombre and sad. He knew how I felt; he had to.

He had watched me transform in the two days since her arrival at the temple. He must have noticed how, all of a sudden, I started to awaken from my deep, long slumber. How I was attempting to climb out and emerge from the dark hole I lived in, to acknowledge the presence of life again. And, anyway, in India everybody knows everything. It's the land of no secrets.

"She said something about wanting to go to some place with you, and you didn't answer her. Baba, I didn't really understand what she said," he added with affection, and then left. Often he called me Baba, which was a sign of his warmth and respect, as I was a recluse and lived a life that resembled that of a sadhu.[3]*

"What does she mean, I didn't answer her?" I felt really

---

3   *Sadhu—seeker, holy man.

angry. She came disguised as a gentle breeze, turned into a full-blown wind, twisted my life upside down and then she disappears the next day. "What a nerve this woman has! Hey, wait a minute," I paused my mind. "I didn't really give her an answer. I didn't say, yes I will come with you, Nulla, to the land of love; I just asked her what would I find there. Even so, this definitely is no reason to run off just after we've met." I felt confused, utterly shattered, my head was in a spin. I opened the door to my room and threw myself on the mattress, covering my head with a pillow.

After an eternity of almost choking on my silence, the tears started flowing down my face, and in no time they turned into a raging waterfall. I was sobbing uncontrollably, my whole body shaking and convulsing. It was the first time I ever cried as an adult man and my spirit was letting loose a prisoner who had just got his first taste of freedom. I didn't care anymore. "The whole world can watch and laugh," I thought to myself.

Nulla triggered the pain, yet what was pouring out of me had nothing to do with her. It was an overflowing dam, waiting for years to burst, and it only took a mild earthquake to shatter the wall holding it all in.

The whole pain and inner torture that I had bolted up for so long was bucketing out of me, and there was nothing to hold it back anymore. It felt as if I was a part of a larger body of pain that had been growing in us all for a long time. If I had to put one word to this pain, narrow it down to one single emotion, I would call it *abandonment*. Of course, there was an array of emotions, nevertheless the feeling was of total abandonment, of being in separation from the source of life; the inner acknowledgment of this truth had at long last broken me down.

From the first moment I entered the crusade of life on earth, I was abandoned. First by my mother, who immediately handed me over to the hospital staff the moment I was born. They then proceeded to give me Nestlé's milk formula.

In the sixties, after humans have been breastfeeding for hundreds of thousands of years, Nestlé embarked on an aggressive marketing campaign to convince mothers worldwide of the virtues of baby formula. They focused their campaign in developing counties, emphasising that it would make your baby healthy and weighty, as being chubby was a sign of prosperity. Of course, the baby's health and emotional needs were secondary to the profits of the mighty multinational corporations. It was baptism by the fire of greed and an induction into the ills of the world. As babies feel the reality around them and respond to them in kind, I was forced to close off to the world before I even had a chance to open up to it.

Total treachery to life's natural flow was my first experience of my walk on planet Earth — a rejection by one's own mother in refusing to offer her own nourishment to her child. The whole of society had abandoned its connection with the spirit of the great mother, and my ever-sensitive soul never felt at peace within this fragmented reality.

It felt as though every step of the way, from the moment that I was born, I had been betrayed. My essence, my pure innocence, my roaring, free spirit was suppressed from the breaking of the first dawn. This caused me continual untold agony and turmoil, until that day in the desert when the wind came and offered me a gift of love and nourishment, and then blew it away before I could even take a deep breath.

I am not sure how long I lay there in that hysterical state. When my tears did eventually dry up, a thought surfaced within me: "I must go and find her."

Life involves a fight, a struggle, a quest and an ability to face things as they are whilst endeavouring to change our circumstances, if we wish to do so. "I am not going to just lie here, sobbing till the end of time, for anyway I will eventually run out of tears." I got up and walked over to the washbasin situated on the other side of the garden, just outside the bathroom. I gave my face a good splash and tried to offer myself a smile while staring at my red eyes and the story they told in the dirty mirror.

I rushed out to the village market, trying to piece together some sort of search plan in my mind. There was only one person in the village I knew in a personal way, apart from Pradip; it was Suresh, the chai seller. He made the sweetest, most delicious chai I had ever tasted. He was a teenager about sixteen years old — a very handsome desert boy, who always had his black hair heavily oiled and combed back: "Looking like movie star," he used to say with great pride. I hurriedly walked in the direction of his chai stall.

"Hey, Baba, what is going with you? I never see you walk in such big hurry, you are walking like some big devil come inside your bones," he said, while greeting me warmly as he always did.

"Suresh, I have a very big problem, you need to help me, have you seen this girl, very long black hair, you know, hair like Indian woman and face a little bit like Japanese?" I asked him.

"Oh this girl," he answered me with a twinkle in his eyes, "very beautiful girl indeed, I would like to make girl like this my wife, wouldn't you?" He gave me a long stare, wondering what had come over me and then gazed back at the boiling pot of chai, holding it in one hand, swirling the sweet milky drink around in the pot while adding some cardamom to it with the other.

"Yes, I see her before two-three hours. She come for cup of tea. She tell me she meet some weird man that don't know how to talk, then I think of you, Baba," he said with a smile tinged with the pride of being the one man in the marketplace who knew me.

"Chai, chai, garam chai," he announced to the world that his delicious brew was ready to be served while shifting his attention back to his business. I wanted to go through this all a bit faster, though I knew that the more you try to hurry an Indian, the more they will take joy in slowing down the dealing of the matter at hand. It was as though they really wanted to take their time feeling out the heart of the issue before they offered their support.

"So, Baba, what is it with you today, you are talking more than you do in the last six months, maybe Baba not feeling so good?" Suresh gave me his attention again.

"Baba feeling tik hai," I snapped back at him. "I need to know, if you have any idea where this girl went and I need to know this as soon as possible," I asked with a more demanding voice. I was getting frustrated with the long-winded conversation and in the process I was wasting precious time.

"Ahhh, Baba like this girl—oh, this is big problem for Baba," Suresh said as though he possessed the wisdom of an elder.

"Please, Suresh, don't worry about my problems now, I have only one and you can help me solving it. I need to know where this girl went to!" I pressed the subject again, adding more intensity to my voice.

Suresh was busy serving his fresh pot of chai to the four men that sat on the wooden bench by his stall and he wasn't very impressed at how I was trying to grab all his attention. Of course, he could have answered me yes or no immediately, then again that wouldn't have been enough drama for him, and Indians thrive on a good story.

"Of course I know where she goes. You know, Baba, in India we all know everything, no hiding," he smiled with one last culmination of suspense. "She went to bus stop, she say she is leaving today. Though Baba doesn't have to worry; no bus before evening and sometime bus come very late. So now Baba can relax, have cup of chai and afterwards slowly walk to bus stop and get his girl. Plenty of time, Baba," he said with a reassuring voice.

"Thanks, Suresh," I patted him on the back and rushed off.

"Baba, no hurry, shanti," I heard him call behind me, yet I was already gone.

❀ ❀ ❀ ❀ ❀ ❀ ❀

Emerging from my dream state, I open my eyes to see the crows staring at a horizon beyond my reach, perhaps they too are reminiscing on the journey that has brought them here to this moment in time by the river.

I gaze at the river that only a brief moment ago seemed so calm: ripples are becoming visible as I stare into the night's reflection in her waters. Am I merely a mirror image of this great river? From one moment to another, life changes: is there anything to do but surrender? Does another option exist, other than yielding in peace to the inner ripple while it meanders through me?

Should I endeavour to change what is taking place within me, struggle with it or am I just here to be an observer, watching whatever moves through me, as the waters of this mighty river keep on flowing by? It's the same river, renewed every moment it flows. Does the river ever offer resistance to changes bestowed upon it?

My breathing is calm again with my choice to embrace the reality of the moment as it is. Change seems to be the only unchangeable principle governing us, the only solid universal code. Is transforming space and time a mere surrender to the eternal flow?

The river Ganga owes its birth to the land where the towering White Mountains meet the silent embrace and cool breath of father sky. She is born as daughter of the mountains, and with time she changes to become mother of the plains. According to one legend, she commences her flow out of Shiva's locks so as to soften her impact on the earth. Shiva is the destroyer, the one that comes and gives us a good shake up, so we awake from the world of illusion and embrace the eternal reality of the oneness of creation. Thus, the river flowing endlessly through his locks has again and again acted as a vehicle of transformation for me, as I dared to venture out of the small self and its petty concerns into the embrace of the all-encompassing *I*, that is all that I am.

I took my first Ganga Darshan[4]* around twenty five years ago and since then spent many a moon sitting by this river, receiving her numerous blessings and teachings while observing how much both of us changed over time.

I have listened to her in ferocious floods, when her sound was deafening and her colour murky brown as she pushed her way in anger and rage, washing away anything that came in her path, cleansing herself in the process.

I have watched her as she flowed in serenity while her blue-green calm waters reflected nothing other than her eternal tranquillity, peace, and a voice of a heavenly soothing *Om*.

I observed how at times she almost dried out, withdrawing her giving, contracting, with not much more to offer than a dirty trickle of water and the tears of millions of villagers.

Aren't all our lives a river, a flow that keeps changing according to the condition of the world around us and the song of the universe within? And how much say do we have in it all? As much as the river has in directing its waters . . .

4   * Literally, Darshan means "to see," and it also means "to be in the presence of the divine."

❋ ❋ ❋ ❋ ❋ ❋ ❋

The bus station was situated at the far end of the village, about a two-kilometre walk from the marketplace. Well, really, to call it a bus station or a road would be an overstatement. An old tar road passed by the high end of the village; over the years the road's surface had almost returned to the desert sands, and what still resembled a road was riddled with potholes.

Actually, there was no bus stand at all; just one chai shop and a small food stall by the roadside, serving mostly very spicy samosas cooked in oil that looked as though it could be as old as the road itself. One night-bus connected the village to the capital of the state and a couple of local buses passed through during the day that would only go as far as the next market town. There was no clear timetable though; it was just go to the bus stop and wait. The occasional camel cart passed by, the pace of the camel reflecting the timelessness of the desert sands. Waiting is something at which desert folk are very adept, it's as though the aura of the desert takes all the hurry of the human spirit away and places it in a timeless realm. Such a serenity did not engulf me that afternoon, I was in a great rush and the two kilometres, that usually would take a half an hour at a leisurely pace, disappeared under my feet in a mere ten minutes.

She was there, sitting on the sand behind the tea stall with her small red pack lying by her side. Some kids were playing around her and they were all laughing out loud. She lifted her head up. "I was waiting for you," she said, smiling peacefully and reaching her hand out to hold mine. The kids giggled and whispered something to each other. They probably thought it looked like a love scene from a romantic Hindi film.

I sat on the sand by her side. She was calm and seemed

happy. What does she mean, "I was waiting for you," I wondered? She had just run away, for what, so she can wait for me in the bus stop? Is this the way French women enact their dramas?

"What are you doing, Nulla?" I asked her with an agitated voice of a dejected lover.

"What do you mean?" she replied, with the innocence of a little girl.

"What do you mean, what do I mean?" I snapped back, feeling the fire igniting within me. "Why did you leave like this, without saying a word after just the night before inviting me to walk with you to the land of love, I mean, I thought we were starting something together," I said in a very anxious tone.

"Oh, you thought that?" she looked at the desert sand, her voice sounding a bit more serious. "So, Mister No Name and No Speak, you didn't accept my invitation to go to the land of love. You just asked me what was there for you."

"C'mon, Nulla, you knew I was coming, didn't you feel the energy between us?" She looked away far into the desert. She wanted to say something, yet the words weren't coming.

"Hey, Mister, this is the first time I spent the night with a guy on the first day I met them. I've only been with couple of guys in my life. I am not the type of girl that just jumps into a man's arms. Being a daughter of a woman who was forced to sell her body hasn't necessarily made me feel comfortable with my relationship with men. In fact I've never been with a man, they were just boys and maybe you are just a boy too." She paused for a moment, as though she was anticipating a reaction. Still, I was numb. I had mastered the art of masking my feelings a long time ago and perhaps I wasn't sure what to feel.

"I woke up this morning to find out you had disappeared from my room. You didn't even say anything; you just vanished at the crack of dawn! What did you want me to believe? I thought this was your way of telling me it was time for me to go. You really hurt me," she said.

"But, Nulla," I was getting more emotional, "you are the first woman I ever . . ."

"Ever what," she snapped back at me.

She was a sensitive woman, very sensitive, as I would learn in the years to come, and I was so often lost in my own world, with my prime concern usually being the world according to me. I didn't pause for a moment to consider how it would feel for a young woman, as wise and mature as she was, to be miles away from her home and to hook up with a confused weirdo like me. And yes, by all accounts of normality, I was a strange one. It didn't even occur to me that there was something wrong in disappearing before she woke up. I was so utterly absorbed in my own drama that I failed to recognise that my actions might affect somebody else.

We sat by each other in the late afternoon sun, the time when the desert starts to dish out its feast of sunset magic. We were two young bodies with old, very old souls, who had jumped the ship in search of a pure ocean to swim in. Yet, she was a woman and the way she approached her new journey was vastly different to mine.

"You would stay here in this desert village forever in your attempt to escape from the world, if it was up to you. Wake up, man, I don't want to take the journey to the land of love with a wilting vegetable! I want to walk with a true warrior." She talked again with determination in her voice.

A warrior? That was the first time a woman had addressed me in this way. It felt complimentary and challenging at the same time, though I'd never thought to use this word before. "I thought I was some kind of warrior to take the stand I was taking." I answered with a meek voice reflecting insecurity, contradicting the statement I had just made. "What do you mean a warrior? Do you mean I am not one?" I said, suddenly feeling offended and confused by the whole developing scenario.

Nulla sighed, "A warrior, wow, have you ever heard of a warrior who is running away from the world, who can't even give a clear answer, one who just sits all day and gazes into the abyss?"

"I am not running away, Nulla, I am trying to figure out something! Maybe something which is beyond your understanding," I started to wish I had never met this woman and had followed my original intuition to ignore her when first she arrived at the temple. I wanted life to return to the peace and surety it promised just a couple days ago.

"Oh la la!" She was starting to lose her cool or maybe she was just being theatrical, I wasn't really sure and the fact that I couldn't read her clearly bothered me.

"So, big man, what are you trying to figure out, the colour of the desert sunsets? How many cracks there are in the ceiling of your room? Life is so beautiful, there is so much art everywhere, so much magic and you sit all day long feeling sorry for yourself, man! Do you think blaming the world is going to get you anywhere? Ah!" Nulla was on a roll.

I sensed it would be utterly futile to continue this conversation or offer a response to any of her accusations. We were both hurting and the pain went way deeper than what we were ready to face at that present moment. It had nothing to do with the other. It did have something to do with a society that bred us in the myth of fear and separation. We both made a choice sometime in our lives to reject this fallacy; however, we had to learn how to walk on the new road before we could run up and fly. It took time to release the shackles of the past, and even more time to learn to trust again in the abundance and miracle of life.

I got up and offered Nulla my hand; smilingly she accepted it and lifted her body off the desert sand. She lifted her pack up and, when I offered to carry it, her smile grew wider while she gently stroked my belly. We walked back to the temple in silence as the sun was preparing to go to bed and give way to the stillness that lives in the mystery of the night.

No time in the desert is more awe-inspiring than those moments when the sun has already set behind the eternal sands and an array of her hypnotic lights still linger. It was the daily celebration of the family of light and colour.

When we finally reached the temple, it was already dark. I suggested to Nulla that it would probably be wise to ask Pradip for her old room again.

"I am moving in with you. You know, a whole Indian family lives in a room the size we have for ourselves. We can live in the same room, it will take us beyond the *me* world, into the *our universe*."

"Welcome to the cave of no return," I gestured to her theatrically to enter my room. She accepted my invitation and walked in, just as a princess enters her palace of dreams.

❉ ❉ ❉ ❉ ❉ ❉ ❉

The river is moving in circles, many little ones, whirling together like a troupe of dancers rehearsing for a gala show. She isn't quiet anymore and in her movements there is a hint of something else brewing beyond the façade of the moment. The serenity that was my companion just a mere moment ago is starting to fade away. The memories of Nulla, the conversation with Nobi, have all stolen me away from the present moment. Or perhaps I am wrong, maybe this is the present moment; for it is *present* in this *moment* even if it does not fit my set of expectations of how being present in the moment should feel like. Possibly, a resistance is simmering within me to deal with the new challenge the moment has brought forth.

I can recall the advice a friend shared with me many years ago when I first started exploring the possibility that life had more to it than the current program on offer. At the time, around the age of nineteen, I was working in a bar in the seedy part of town. The place was a launching point for bands in the beginning of their musical careers. Much of the music was folk/rock with strong anti-war themes and I always enjoyed listening to it as I wove around the crowded bar, picking up glasses. The bar owner liked chatting with me at the end of the night and often would offer me his take on life and the mistakes he had made. In a way, he was a wise old man and I did value his advice, as I didn't have a clue in which direction I was willing my life towards and the consequences of moving into a new matrix.

"Never get off the boat, if you are not willing to go all the way to the shore, and make sure you don't freak out every time you are taken out of your comfort zone" he said to me one night when we were cleaning up, hoping I would heed his warning, or rather listen to his advice, so I may be firm in my commitment and find the resolve needed when one walks in a different direction to the herd.

Well, I did get off the boat, well and truly, and for the first time I wonder how far I have really travelled? I may be halfway through my life, while some of the questions, feelings and enquiries are as raw as they were twenty-five years ago by the jasmine fields. And a few moments, a mere few moments in time, have turned my universe around from being perfectly at peace to a storm of emotions.

And I missed Nulla, as I have done so many times before.

Nobi is staring at me with moist eyes, his being overwhelmed by emotion, just as my own is. I can feel he actually needs me, too, at this junction of life, as much as I need him. This recognition humbles me deeply.

"So, are you finally back with us, mister 'lives in his head'?" he asks me with a heart soaked in sadness.

"Yes, Nobi, I am ready to talk again. I don't really see

where this conversation will take us, when in a short time it will all be washed away. Really, all I want to do is find a circle of peace in my heart," I plead with him.

Nobi looks at me, he isn't angry anymore, he just wants to understand us humans a bit better. He did say he had been waiting for this conversation for a long, long time. "You know, mate," he proceeds to talk and I can feel it is going to be a long one. "You say many of you work with the wellbeing of creation guiding your heart. That many of you strive to save this beautiful planet, the sacred mother earth and restore the sense of a caring community within all circles of life. This may be true, I am not sure. Though, if you say so, you must know something that I don't. Nevertheless, it's not the numbers which really concern me here, it is the purity and integrity of the intent," he says, while pausing for a moment to look at the river, giving me time to reflect on his words.

"Some of you folk do work to save the whales, the forests, the climate. More often than not I hear you use a very strange language. You talk in terms of concern for economy first, whilst you ignore the spirit that moved you to be part of this circle of life. Have you gotten so accustomed to the nightmare of economics that life on earth has become that you have forgotten to dream big?

"You have bought into the language of the system that is enslaving you all, and have overlooked the fact that words make thoughts and they in return create your reality. The words you use pave the way for the purity of the intent behind the actions that follow. This brainwashing has turned you from a species that used to love life, to a people that love things! Do you get what I am saying, my human brother?

"Why is it we never hear you guys talk of the spirit of unity, the magic, the life force, the whisper of the leaves, the kinship of all life! Are your brains so shattered by an overload of borrowed information that you have lost your capacity to touch the world around you with words that vibrate with the truth you are trying to affirm and express?

"What are the earth lovers afraid of? That the plain truth when spoken clearly will freak people out! Why do you always seem to be somehow holding back? Maybe you are underestimating the intelligence of the people at large. Perhaps they are craving for their brethren to stand up and finally speak with some clarity. Everyone is so tired of listening to this endless, meaningless, gibberish being thrown at them from the idiot box and all other forms of media. They are craving to hear something new which is as old as time itself, words that will touch their minds like the caressing of the fresh autumn breeze. Once spoken, their own cellular memory will recognise these words as a vibration that has long been forgotten, the reality that creation is a song of unity. By continuing to function within this limited framework, you are attempting to eradicate a symptom whilst leaving the disease untouched."

Nobi's words resonate as an unshakeable truth in the very fibre of my being. Meaningful change will only ever be possible when fear and calculations have been thrown down the drain of past illusions.

"Do you know why they are working so hard to numb your brains? Because a young mind that has not totally conformed, recognises immediately that even the people who seem to advocate change are censoring the real truth — the truth that the whole story of life has nothing to do with money, nothing! That it is about love. It's about love and care for one another, love for all life, care for all your relations and the silent worship for the celebration of the life that is. Only when you finally roar the pure call of the wild, sung from a clear heart, will the sleepwalkers finally be awoken."

I look at Nobi, he is eager to continue with what seems to be turning into an epic speech rather than a conversation with his human mate by the river. "And the naked truth is, at this very moment, the biggest mass extinction of species in history is taking place, mainly due to habitat destruction. However it must be stated loud and clear; it is human action, not nature that is responsible.

"The naked truth is that Himalayan glaciers, which feed all the major rivers in Asia, are disappearing at such a rate, that in twenty years they may be no more. These river deltas are the food basket of over two billion people.

"The naked truth is that you are fishing the oceans at a rate, that sooner rather than later, fish will be something you only see in an aquarium, rather than a *being* swimming freely in the sea.

"The naked truth is that you are killing the oceans, killing the forests, killing the rivers and killing three species of life every hour.

"The naked truth is that you are systematically eliminating the last tribal cultures on the earth, content only to save them as museum exhibits, while remaining a silent uncaring witness to the destruction of their ways of life—a way that could hold within it the key to your future.

"The naked truth is that the god of *economic growth* is stripping the biosphere of its life support systems while depleting the planet of her riches. If the god of economic growth was measured in real terms, of the real cost it exacts, it would be a losing god, deep in the red.

"The naked truth is that every moment you continue to accept these crimes with the same eerie silence you have done for years, you become the perpetrators of this mass genocide, the biggest slaughter ever to be witnessed in our Milky Way and beyond."

Nobi is on a roll; he looks deep into my being to make sure I am really hearing what he is saying.

"All of a sudden the plight of the earth is making some news headlines. However this is not real heart talk. This is not a conversation in truth. They talk of climate change alone and how it would affect our economic and future prosperity. Fuck the economy, how loveless has the human vision become? Do you need science to tell you that you are totally out of balance; that life on earth has become a journey of exploitation and greed, rather than a walk of silent worship and deep gratitude? You are not faced with climate change, you are faced with a total global meltdown on all levels and the sooner you recognise this, the better. The planet is heading towards a major short circuit if you don't do something right *now* to alter your *consumption centred* way of life."

He takes a deep breath and stretches his wings to give them a flap, though I can sense he hasn't finished.

"If you really want to know the naked truth, the pure song, go and talk to a child. You cannot fool children; their innocent minds haven't been fully corrupted by the prevailing lie guiding the human race.

"Go and tell a child that the European Union keeps dumping tonnes of butter in the ocean every year to keep prices up, while children the world over are malnourished. That child will surely feel you are cruel.

"Go and tell a child that the Indian government lets wheat rot in its warehouses for the sake of stabilising prices, while millions of children in its villages go to sleep crying in hunger: that child will feel you are a criminal.

"Tell a child that the butterflies and the bees are dying everywhere because one seed company wants to control the future food supplies of earth — that child will cry for her relatives, the gentle winged ones.

"Ask a child if it makes any sense to cut a tree that took a thousand years to grow and make toilet paper out of it; the tree gives us oxygen, water, medicine, shelter and much more. At the same time you can make all paper from hemp, which grows in a few months except you don't do this because of some stupid out-dated law.

"Tell a child that forty thousand of his brother and sister children die every day from hunger and preventable disease, while half the riches of the earth are dedicated to instruments of war. That child will know you are a murderer.

"And tell a child that for years now you have been destroying the planet, and most probably its own children will not have an earth to live on. Do you think for a moment a child with its pure uncorrupted innocence would think there is anything sane in a system governed by principles as these? NO.

"A child would not think, a child would *know* that only evil people let others go hungry, while they throw away food. That only insane men run the world if their prime concern is their margins of profit reflected in the *casino royale* subsequently called the stock market."

I feel speechless, though Nobi certainly isn't.

"So, how come it is that you *grow up* and learn to accept these callous actions as *normal*? I am convinced that your term *grown up* is actually a fallacy. You don't grow up; you turn stupid, heartless and numb." Nobi is on fire. I feel he has bolted these words in for a long time and feels relieved he can finally share them with a stupid human such as myself.

I do suspect he does know we are on the same side and I agree with every word spoken, though he also knows something I have been denying for many years now, that I wasn't doing my best. That I wasn't total; that many of us were doing something, however, hardly anyone was doing their best.

It seems that most of the time, even when faced with truth, we find it difficult to act upon it. We are eager to conform within the walls of the known, rather than live in what we are led to believe are the margins of society. Maybe we sit in the margins at this very moment, yet this is always the place where change emerges from. Every meaningful transformation throughout history has been initiated by outcasts that only later come to be accepted as the torchbearers of the future.

We must at last make our voices heard and actions felt, until sanity prevails and balance is restored. It would only take a handful of us, being total, fully present earth/human lovers with pure heart, clear intent and a stellar resolve to really set this chariot in a direction to where all things find their balance and rightful place under the sun.

I look at Nobi and feel the deepest of love for him. This time we are in agreement and, more so, we sense our kinship. I feel he is a true brother to me and actually cares about my wellbeing. I slowly close my eyes to find some peace and solace in the memories of the precious woman I love so much.

❊ ❊ ❊ ❊ ❊ ❊ ❊

"Where did you go to this morning? I freaked out when I woke up and you weren't there. You have to understand, you don't live alone in this world. It's not always about your feelings," Nulla said as she pulled her belongings out of her bag. She folded her clothes in a neat pile in the corner while placing her drawing pad and pencils on the small table. In a matter of ten minutes she rearranged everything in my room and my small hermit's pad transformed into a temple of love.

"If there is beauty around us, it will help the song within grow," she whispered. She was happy, as though no drama had happened between us. That's how she would always conduct herself in the years to come; she would put the past behind her as soon as she let it go, and never mention it again. I wasn't always sure if she avoided looking at things, or if she had really mastered the art of living in the present moment.

"I went to the burning grounds, Nulla, to contemplate

what the word *love* means." I answered her; still somehow bruised by her sudden escape, wanting some acknowledgment of the hurt she had caused me. An acknowledgment I was never going to get, as far as she was concerned.

"And what did you find there, in the presence of all those ghosts this morning?" she asked with what I felt was a hint of sarcasm.

I sat on the mat and lit a stick of incense, placing it on the altar by the picture of the Goddess Kali, the destroyer of all our illusions.

"I discovered that everybody must die and nobody is ever dead," I said.

Nulla gathered her long flowery skirt between her legs and sat down with her knees up, leaning against the wall opposite me.

So many times over the years I have tried to find words to describe the fantastic beauty that emanates from this woman, and I've never found any that would do it justice. It was more than perfect grace; she embodied within her a total serenity that was woven with an ever-alive passion. There was a hunger and stillness in her, and a shy cheeky smile that never failed to disarm me, even in my darkest moments.

"You know, Nulla, in all the time I've spent at the burning grounds, one of the deepest insights I have had, has been that the dead are not really dead. The body may be long gone, merged with the desert sands, yet they are still here with us in some sort of formless form, at least some of them. It never really feels silent there amongst the dead, as though all these spirits are hanging around, still unsure which world they belong to. It feels like they are yearning to sort out all their unfinished business on earth; broken hearts, family disputes, things they wished they said and things they wish they didn't. One of the most profound revelations I have had in these months is how important the end of the journey is. We pay so much attention to the birth of a journey; sometimes we give a bit of thought to the voyage itself, while most of the time, we fail to close the circle properly. I can constantly hear the echoing voices of unclosed circles at the burning grounds."

Nulla looked at me. Her eyes were sad. "I agree with you. People don't close the circle, or if I were to use different words, I would say they just don't let go. They hold on, to good and to bad. Some family feuds have lasted for generations, though the people involved don't even know why or even recall the names of the original people involved. It's the same with nations still trying to settle scores over disputes that occurred a long time ago. You know, my mother, she will never let go of the anger she has towards her father for sending her to be a prostitute. She burns daily in the fire of living consumed by the pain of his actions. She will die and be reborn with this anger.

"Myself, I would love to meet my grandfather and understand the pain and despair he was living through, which brought him to the point of sending his own daughter to sell her body so he would be able to feed his other starving kids. His soul must still be crying in eternity. I often wonder if he is still alive and I long to tell him that, if my mother never forgives him, then I will. You know, how can we ever really judge the pain and suffering that compels people to act in certain ways?" She spoke with deep sadness and longing that reflected in her beautiful eyes.

I moved closer to her and held her hands. She leaned her head on me with a tenderness only known to women who have touched the heart of sadness. We were quiet for a long time, both very comfortable with the silence, which became an integral part of our communication. In silence we could really listen to each other.

Months later, Nulla would tell me how she never really meant to leave me that day; nevertheless she needed to concoct a plot to shake me up from my narcissistic self. She wanted my presence with her immediately; she didn't want to wait for it.

* * * * * * *

Nobi is silent while he stares at the shadows reflected in the river.

His two companion crows flew away while I was absorbed in my memories of the time I met Nulla. Now it's just the two of us left to gaze at the river in wonder, both pleading that she guide us with her ever-growing hum.

At the same time an unseen yet tangible energy permeates the sphere around us. The heart of the universe is making its presence felt, the force that guides the river through its meandering journey to the sea, the energy that illuminates all our journeys on earth, especially in the times when this place can be so inhospitable to a sensitive human soul.

I reflect on what Nobi said to me just a short while ago, *we aren't doing our best.* Few, very few were doing their best and this is reflected in the reality we are living in; these weird times where nothing seems to make sense and everything, almost everything taking place is out of touch with the rhythm of the cosmos.

How many of us are really willing to go all the way! How few of us are fully committed to personal and global transformation?

History has shown again and again that only people who are willing to give it all, to sacrifice everything, to be total in their quest and actions; only these sorts of folk ever effect change within society. It is with this type of commitment that we will make the world around us — all creatures great and small — smile again.

At present, none of us are giving our best effort, none

of us! Thus we are abdicating our responsibilities to future generations whilst betraying the self and the ancestors. How many of us have really transformed, crossed the river, dared to go beyond all fear and illusion to the land of the brave?

When we don't serve the circle of life with passion, we are mediocre with the self; they go hand-in-hand, in and out of the one loop. The world around us is a creation of the universe within, and this is what is reflected to us at the present time — life out of balance. The whole of creation is waiting for us humans to awaken from our slumber; will it have to wait forever?

At present, the equation is simple. We have a system — a culture based on lies, therefore we have no reality. We are indoctrinated into mediocrity and encouraged to be content with it. Living in this sick illusion, we are lost like a ship that has broken its anchor and been left to float forever in the sea, at the mercy of its currents.

Nobi is staring at me; he is ready to talk again. I can feel he wants me to share my thoughts with him rather than drift away. By now, we have developed a kinship of two beings that care for each other. We notice when each one of us needs silence or relating. It seems he bounces from one leg to the other and slightly opens his wings and stretches his jet-black neck when he feels the need to speak.

"You know, mate," he addresses me again, "we didn't really conclude our conversation about the Buddha and his ways. What I often wonder is, since so many of you have chosen the path of finding the self — meditation, the peace within — how come so few of you have attained it? I guess it's for the same reason I mentioned before, you are not doing your best and any path you choose in life requires your totality. Do you understand me? It's not really that I disagree with the Buddha's teachings, not at all; what I don't like is the way his followers have turned into worshippers rather than seekers of their own truth, and you should know that I totally admire the totality of his quest. This is the reason why so many look up to him. Do you get it? He was total, and that wholeness reflected in his quest, has made him such a beacon of light for the past two thousand years," Nobi said, his voice quiet and peaceful. His latest statement confuses me; it seems to contradict his original rave on the Buddha. Though I do agree with him, how inspiring it is when we come across a rare being that is doing their best — a total being!

"Of course, I understand you, Nobi. Why do you think I am sitting by the river now instead of taking myself to the safety of higher ground? So many times in life I walked with a commitment that lacked totality. I felt I was giving it all, in reality I wasn't. There was still a fear, a doubt niggling somewhere in the inner chamber of self. The notion that I was supported by the world at large rang as a truth, though it was still difficult to embody. No more of this for me, mate. I will sit still as this rock below me does, even if my totality of presence is only lived for the last ten minutes of my life. It doesn't matter how long I have left, it's better to be late than never arrive." I said this, feeling that I may have at last explained the rationale behind my choice to stay put by the river.

He stares back at me with hardness in his eyes. "So finally you have found some resolve in your being and you are going to run away with the river? You are a wimp, like all of them, a fugitive escaping responsibility lest your presence be challenged by the forces of time. Why don't you take your new-found resolve and insight and carry it into the world?" He speaks his words as though he is shooting arrows at me, the friendliness of a mere few seconds ago replaced by sheer disgust.

I recall how often Nulla urged me to act, make my presence felt in the world rather than sit silent in retreat. "I will never accept anything less than your best, my love," she often said to me, and, my oath, she was a very demanding woman.

Nobi is right and wrong at the same time; at least, this is my perception of the situation. I could go up the hill and maybe find a way back into the world with my new found insights; though in the process I might lose a valuable lesson, a satsang[5]* that awaits me on the banks of this holy river as she slowly gathers her waters ready to unleash her fury.

※ ※ ※ ※ ※ ※ ※

"Everybody wants love, craves love, so how come this world is such a loveless place?" Nulla was half asking, half stating a truth as she gently rested her head on my shoulder.

We lay together on my single mouldering mattress that had become our royal honeymoon bed. It was though there was no longer her or me anymore, just a single body lying on the tiny mattress, one being with four legs, four arms and two faces, sharing the one love, with the innocence and the purity of a moment just sparked into being.

I was silent for a while, thinking over what she just had said. "Why is love so hard to come by in this world when everybody constantly talks about it? Perhaps it has something to do with what the old Aghorie told me: *love is death*. So, while we are all so fearful of death, how can we ever pray at the altar of love? For love lives when the ego dies, and the death of the ego is harder to embrace than physical annihilation, for it requires the self to empty itself completely of lifetimes of garbage, to completely let go. So we seem to want the rebirth without the death, the purity without the cleanse, and life as a rule does not often offer us any short cuts."

---

5   * Satsang literally means to be in the company of

I could feel Nulla's warm, sweet breath caressing my neck as we slowly drifted away into the in-between lands of wake and sleep. "You know, everybody wants love, but it feels like a bargain, they give only once they receive."

I wanted to listen to her more, to bathe in her words, the music that was her sweet voice, the poetry that was her being, yet my world of words was tiring as sleep was higher truth opening its welcoming doors.

If I had ever prayed for a miracle, I had received one. Its name was Nulla, and by allowing her in, the presence of love was growing between us, as a song is born out of the sounds of silence.

"Good morning," Nulla whispered in my ear. It must have been the crack of dawn as I could hear the bells ringing in the temple. The morning puja was in progress while the rats were being served their breakfast at the altar.

"I love you, man. I've been waiting for you for a long time." Nulla had her arms on my chest with her chin resting on her folded hands. Her hair was open wide and renegade strands were tickling my arms and face. She looked into my eyes. I wasn't sure if she was expecting some sort of reply to her grand statement. I'd never before told a woman that I loved her, I wasn't sure I knew how to do it. These words *I love you* seemed so unoriginal and clichéd. I felt that this statement would almost degrade the enormity of what I was feeling at the present moment, the seed of promise that was being conceived in my heart in the presence of this woman.

I remained silent. Nulla kissed me on the lips. "Let's get up and go and make our offering to the rat Goddess, thank her for this beautiful miracle that is unfolding for both of us," she said.

Nulla was full of energy while I was still emerging from the twilight zone of sleep. She got up and offered me her hand to rise. After a quick splash at the hand basin we walked over to the temple where the priest and his family were ringing bells, waving incense sticks, which were thick with an overly-sweet aroma, and throwing breadcrumbs to the giant rodents – all this whilst reciting mantas in Sanskrit. It was rat party time and it happened every day, twice.

Really, if it wasn't something you were used to; the daily happenings at the temple to the rat Goddess could be interpreted in the wrong way, as some sort of macabre, weird insanity. There was something fascinating, though, about this rat worship. Here was a creature, reviled and feared by most people, being worshipped as a living Goddess. She was being honoured in her rightful place under the sun. Everything is divine, including our cousin the rat, and every illumination has its own energy and gift to offer us.

When I first arrived and Pradip told me the temple was in honour of the rat Goddess, I thought he was pulling my leg; I really didn't think he was serious. During the months of staying there, my perception about many things changed, including my relationship to rats. These cheeky rodents were a catalyst for changing many of my fixed worldviews. Well, if the elephant God and the monkey God can be worshipped, then why not the rat Goddess?

Pradip gave us both a handful of breadcrumbs to offer to the rats. He was delighted that we had come to the morning puja. It was not often that I joined him in his ceremonies, especially not the morning ones. I would normally wake up and walk with my head down to the desert sands for solitude. However, there was nothing normal anymore about my life, for the being of yesterday had died and was in the process of being reborn by a lush desert oasis called Nulla.

Pradip liked Nulla from the moment she arrived; he could feel the deep respect she offered his culture. She always wore long skirts and covered her shoulders. She was interested in the world around her and asked lots of questions. She walked softly on the earth, as though not wanting to disturb anything in her way. He was also delighted by the positive change he saw in me and I knew how much he cared.

Pradip's wife, Shruti, joined the morning ceremony and Nulla moved close to be by her side. Nulla put her hand on her shoulder and they started chatting as old friends do although they had never met before. It always amazes me the ease with which women embrace each other and feel comfortable in sisterhood. We men are different, we take our time; we are not so open. We are more solitary beings. Perhaps we are, after all, just reflections of the animal world. The females of the species usually hang out together in groups, while more often than not the males of the species live a solitary existence. Nulla and Shruti were giggling and chatting away as though they had been friends for a long time. Perhaps they had.

What I really liked about this temple was that they never took the ceremonies too seriously. It was a family affair and a rat feast.

Pradip chanted the last mantra and turned to talk to me. "Today Karni Ma is very happy," he said.

"Why is that, Pradip?" I answered in amusement.

"Well now, Baba has been with us almost six months, and Baba never look happy. Today, Baba look happy, then Karni is feeling it and she is happy too and also me Pradip very happy to see Baba with peace in his face. Sometimes I worry much about Baba and what is happening in his mind," he said.

Years later when I visited Pradip and his family again, he shared with me how concerned he was with my mental state over those months. He did many offerings for my well-being he told me, and even asked the priest in the main temple to pray for me. Some people in the village were afraid I would totally lose it and cause trouble. These people wanted to hand me over to the police, he added. He however assured them that I was a good and sincere man, a western sadhu on a quest for truth.

I never really knew this, how much Pradip and the villagers were caring for me. Talking to him many years later, I realised that the whole village was willing my transformation. It is an incredible thing about Indians, how pure their love is and how much space they allow you to grow. I did sometimes judge Pradip for his priesthood in the early days I stayed with him, though through it I learned not to judge things I didn't understand and to see him for what he was: one of the most loving and caring human beings I have ever met. My personal experience with him was impeccable. During the years since we met I have thought of him a lot. On one hand, he was willing to take the last coin off a poor villager who came to get a blessing at the temple, a coin that could see their kids deprived of their next meal, and on the other hand, Pradip was a remarkably generous man.

The complexities of our beings never cease to astound me. There seems to be a killer and a lover in all of us, with the most dangerous culprit being our judgements.

❋ ❋ ❋ ❋ ❋ ❋ ❋

I shift my legs around to change sides in the half lotus position I am sitting in. Nobi is silent, staring into space. He is somewhere else, a place unknown to me. I reflect on his words concerning Gautama the Buddha, the person admired over the past 2500 years as being a beacon of peace and understanding, a figure that I myself was inspired by as I first ventured into the realm of spirit. I often wonder if the Buddha were alive today; would he be happy with the fact that a religion was formed after him? Would Jesus be happy that a religion was formed after him? I sort of doubt it. I have a feeling if the Buddha saw all the golden statues erected in his name and Jesus looked everywhere at his image suffering on the cross, they would both somehow feel sick to the stomach. After all, what did they teach us? They taught us to look within, whereas within organised religion we have become worshippers of externalities.

For some reason, all religions, in the course of time — regardless of the sincere intent with which they were formed — have come to resemble political organisations and the priests are the politicians.

Religion, no matter from where, or in the name of what God, comes to teach us the way of peace and love. So how come more blood has been spilled in name of god and religion than any other cause in HisStory? The source of all religion is so pure and inspiring, so what happens, where does it get corrupted? The sickness, as far as I am concerned, rests with the concept of organised religion, with an establishment, a hierarchy, a place where power is centralised and with the course of time, eventually corrupted.

This of course does not mean that within organised religions we don't find remarkable personalities. I think of the Dalai Lama, the Buddha of compassion living amongst us today, showing us that even to his enemies, who have stolen the land of his people, he will show only love. Is this love supporting the suffering people of Tibet? Unfortunately at the present moment their despair is often growing into anger. Is this love teaching the privileged ones in the materially developed world another way to deal with adversity? If they listen, it does. Nothing is black and white. No one is a saint or a sinner.

There is another thing that makes religion click with the masses. Religion takes away the need for us to be responsible. It hands it over to someone else; conveniently to someone that no one has ever met yet. Religion is actually anti-God and pro-priest, that's how it manages to survive. And who are the priests? They are shrewd businessmen, soliciting clients with the promise of heaven. It is strange how every other concept, idea and human invention, is subject to the law of change and in time evolves or gets replaced by a new idea. Yet religion is the one truth that seems to be written in stone and cannot be challenged to evolve and transform.

They are all the same. I have been to many houses of worship of many faiths and it has always felt the same, the priest has an agenda, and it isn't necessarily the good of his flock. Yet, there was Pradip, a man with a golden heart; I liked him, there was goodness in him. So, to every rule, there must be some exceptions. Or perhaps he was nice when he was not being a priest. I cannot really tell. To me, he was a friend, a good one that saw me through one of the most challenging times of my life.

Still another agenda exists, a more insidious one. The priest and his master, *the almighty god*, always seem to be male. The feminine principle of God has been suppressed a long time ago, since the birth of the children of Abraham.

And how, just how, can we benefit from the worship of an almighty god somewhere out there unknown amongst the stars, when we forget the divine mother, the giving earth, the ever nurturing Goddess which sustains all life? The worship of god as a male, a single almighty entity, seems to have changed the course of humanity for the last few thousand years. In the pre Judaeo-Christian era, there were so many Gods and Goddesses; a great party took place in the heavens. All the deities had a direct relationship with nature and life. There was the sun Goddess, the moon Goddess, the tree Goddess, and many others; they all had divine consorts to celebrate with. The natural forces, the elements, the unseen spirit and the life manifest were worshipped and revered, while humans saw themselves as part of an awesome universal circle which encompassed all things, just another insect in a big web. The ruling principle was feminine, magical, giving, nurturing, transforming, seductive and full of trickery. The name of the game was a constant seeking of harmony within all things.

Then a new idea came to birth around six thousand years ago. The idea that god was a male, that there was only one god and he was awaiting each and every one of us on judgement day. Thus life was transformed from being a celebration of the present moment to a promise of tomorrow. And more so, this almighty god gave man total dominion over the earth mother and all of creation. Thus started man's domination of women and all *life manifest*.

It was late afternoon. Nulla and I were sitting at Suresh's chai shop enjoying a cup of hot, sweet, milky tea. It was my favourite time of the day in the village, the occasion when the sun gradually moves to meet the earth and allows the desert to exhibit its enchanting charms, as though it was a work of art on display. The heat gives way to the welcomed evening breeze and the whole desert world takes a long breath out. Another day of extreme heat passes to make way for the relieving evening shadows as everybody ventures out from their midday hiding places to enjoy the spectacle of the low-lying sun reflecting its rays over golden sands. It is also the occasion when the market is bustling with energy again and the chai shops fill with customers ritually enjoying their intense sweet milky hit while sharing conversations, musing on the happenings of the day.

The centre of the market place was the meeting point for all the village inhabitants; humans, cows, monkeys, dogs and pigs alike. They shared a common purpose—they were all after the essentials necessary for their survival. And while humans mostly purchased it, the others had to somehow score it, steal it, beg it, or use any means at their disposal to acquire it.

The vegetable vendors were at the front line of this battle, constantly harassed by the cows and monkeys. The monkeys usually would make a hit and run grab and disappear before they could be admonished. The cows were more persistent and kept coming back as they were shooed away again and again with large bamboo sticks. Eventually they made a score and the vegetable seller smilingly accepting his defeat. For after all they are considered holy, and sharing food with a cow will always add merit to one's actions of the day. It is incredible what a contradiction this country is, and especially how the people who find it hard to make ends meet are ready to share with all their relations.

The village was dotted with cows all over. I could never figure out how many were actually owned by someone and how many were just free rangers. Most of the local village people made some sort of daily offering to the cows. Many of the roaming bovines were bulls who, due to the advent of farming machinery, found less work in the fields, and were thus retired to the streets in a country where eating beef is mostly taboo. The good nature of the bulls always amazed me. In my own country, if I strayed into a cow paddock with a bull inside, I would most likely have to run or be torn to shreds. Most male cows in the west are castrated anyway, and could not be considered males anymore. In India, huge male bulls roam the streets and coexist with the rest of society in a peaceful and serene manner. Why have we instilled so much fear into our cows? Is it because we never talk to them and only consider what they can give us?

One huge Shiva bull named Nandi would roam the street every day and command the respect of the entire village. He was so big, he towered double in size, over the rest of the bulls. At the same time, he was an embodiment of peace, almost unaware of his immense power. Food was not an issue for him, since he was always fed the best food around. What he was after, though, was affection and he would always stick his head out in an attempt to secure a good neck rub and, if you passed by without doing so, he would watch you with a slightly annoyed look on his face as though it was not only his loss, but yours as well. The cows would usually congregate in the evenings and lick one another, in what seemed to be a pure sharing of cow love and affection, with the bigger ones sheltering the smaller, more vulnerable ones.

Suresh, as always, was delighted by our presence in his chai shop. For him, the coming together of Nulla and Baba made for the perfect Bollywood script, whilst at the same time he could take some credit for our union.

"I tell Baba. Don't worry, Nulla will not go," he said to the vegetable seller next door, while pouring cups of tea into the small glasses on his workbench. He was twisting the truth, though not really by much, he did reassure me that I would find her and he did tell me exactly where to look. It seemed that the whole village was thrilled by our togetherness as from everywhere came the greetings, "Namaste Baba, Namaste Nulla."

Most probably, it was a normal phenomenon; nonetheless, this was the first time I was ready to relate to them. My heart had emerged from its narcissistic centre and at last I could notice the world around me and accept the love it had to offer. It was a wonderful world, my village in the desert.

I had lived amongst the villagers for more than six months and each and every one of them knew about the weird, silent foreigner that stayed at Pradip's temple. And now, finally, after all that time, I was ready to say g'day. Of course, they knew love was in the air and without a doubt it made them even more exited. Indians, like all people worldwide, worship and adore the Goddess of love.

"Baba look like coming from the dead," Suresh said, having a dig at me. "Maybe now Baba stop going to burning place and sit with Aghorie. They are not happy sadhus," he continued his friendly assault, whilst smiling at Nulla.

I laughed at him; we were all in a good mood. "Suresh, what happened, you are afraid of the dead? I thought you are big hero, like movie star," I shot back at him.

"Arrey," Suresh snapped back at me. "Before, Baba don't talk, now Baba talk too much."

"No, Suresh, he doesn't talk enough," Nulla joined in the conversation. Nulla liked and trusted Suresh from the first time she met him. He was honest and there was a fire in his eyes that looked to challenge the world around him, and at the same time he was funny, adding humour even to seriousness.

"So when is marriage?" Suresh changed the subject and got to the part he was really interested in. "What do you mean marriage, Suresh? We've only known each other for one week!" I replied, bemused by his question.

"One week long time, Baba, we Indians marry then meet. You are lucky couple, you already meet one week," he said.

"Maybe he is right," Nulla turned around, brushing her shoulder against mine. "Maybe we should get married, that could be fun," she said, winking at me.

I wasn't sure if she was serious or was just pulling my leg. "What does she mean, 'fun'? Marriage is not a joke," I thought, slightly alarmed.

Suresh smiled at Nulla, sensing victory, as though together they had conspired to make me tie the knot. It all seemed a big laugh to them. "Hey, Baba getting married to Nulla," Suresh yelled over to the lassi[6]* seller on his right. There was nothing I could do now other than surrender to this news. Of course, I didn't intend to get married, though I knew that by tomorrow morning, everyone in the village would be in on the knowledge that there was a wedding in the air. Mohan, the vegetable seller, walked over and

---

6   * Lassi—yoghurt milkshake.

ordered a chai from Suresh. There was hot gossip going around and he wasn't about to miss out on the action.

The wedding is probably the most important event in an Indian's life. From birth, parents groom their kids and raise them with the intent of finding a good marriage. If the family is not well off, it means extreme sacrifice on the parents' behalf. They will have to work hard in order to get their kids a good education, hoping that it will lead to a good job and increase the prospects of finding a bride or groom of status. Of course, to the rich, status means different things than to the poor. Marriage meant a new family and a family is one's anchor, roots, and reference point to the rest of the world. An Indian's life revolves around their extended family. A friend once said to me "We Indians are never alone, not even when we sleep." Indians share everything with their kids; therefore a twenty year old would assume that whatever the family has is his own. There is no such thing as having to make it alone, on your own in this world. We westerners have become very insular people. We've lost our tribal instincts. We are very protective of our personal space and our individuality. Indians share their life; we in the west control and protect ours.

"Baba," Suresh looked me in the eyes almost pleading. "Baba."

"Yes, Suresh."

"Baba."

"OK, Suresh, you said Baba three times already, what do you want?"

"Why is Baba not wanting to get married? Baba knows that he will never find woman so beautiful like Nulla. Look at you, Baba. You are a different person now. All the village is see what love make for you, what Nulla do for you," he said while raising his hands as though he was asking the Gods to put some sense into my head.

"Well, well," I thought to myself, "from being a quiet recluse wandering the desert sands, I have become the talk

114

of the village."

"Suresh, in my country, it is not the custom to get married one week after meeting," I tried to make him see some reason.

I am not sure Nulla agreed with my last statement, as she frowned at me while pulling the hair away from her eyes. "Since when are you so attached to the customs of your country? I thought you said the society you came from was full of shit. I think you're just afraid, man, you would put off everything forever if you could." Nulla joined the conversation in her typical French passion. "So, Mister Great Warrior, in your country how long does it actually take to recognise the eyes of love when you first look into them, if a week is such a short time for you? I do wonder why you bought all the flowers in the market and brought them to me the other day? Were you planting a garden?" she smiled, while elbowing me in the side. The crowd around us was growing and they were calling over anybody they knew to come and watch the next act in the foreign love story. All that was missing was the camera crew, as it would have made a perfect Bollywood romantic comedy.

"Do you know why you brought me the flowers, did you ever think about it?" Nulla continued her loving assault on me.

"Why, Nulla, what's your take on it?" I said with the voice of a man who knew he was fighting a losing battle.

"You brought the flowers, because for a moment, for a brief moment in your life, you dropped your shields, you put your mind aside and just flowed with your natural instincts. For once you acted, rather than dwelling in your tormented mind. I don't really care if you don't want to marry me, man, what I do care about is that you are so afraid to listen and see what the universe has given us," she said with defiance. Nulla was right of course, yet I still felt overwhelmed by what was happening.

Throughout my life, acting from a deep inner knowing had always been a positive for me. Getting bogged in the mind and trying to forever analyse things seemed to lead to a constant question mark. And life is not a question – it's a quest. We have to figure out our calling and then walk head on into the journey. We may walk on many crooked roads. We may walk out the same door we've just walked in. It does not matter; it's all learning. We must make many mistakes in order to know which path is the highway of our soul's design. The secret is to make new mistakes, rather than to keep repeating old ones.

"Nulla," I took her hand and held it with both my hands, "let's get married."

❋ ❋ ❋ ❋ ❋ ❋ ❋

Life is a circle within a circle within a circle within a circle," an old tribal elder from my homeland, once told me, his people on the brink of losing forever their traditional ways. "The first circle is the self. The next one is one's immediate family. The next one is the tribe, and the outer circle is all life manifest."

So perhaps the Buddha wasn't abdicating his responsibilities, I think as I reflect on my dialogue with Nobi a few moments ago. Possibly Nobi is not totally right. Yes, the Buddha left his family; he didn't stay to take care of them. He abdicated his conversation with the world to delve into the source. He honoured the self and the eternal yearning to search for meaning. Yes, it was done at the expense of his family; in truth every meaningful action we ever undertake exacts a price. In doing what he did, he touched something that benefitted humanity and changed its course. Or has it really? Has there been that much change? Is there less suffering in the world since the

Buddha walked on earth?

Nobi is quiet as we are both consumed by the presence of the river. "Nobi," I address him affectionately. "Maybe the Buddha wasn't a culprit like you claim he was. His family might have suffered, yet in the process he found a way for us all to break free of suffering," I said, sensing that I had won the argument. He remained silent for a while, in no hurry to reply.

My breathing is calm again, the inner storm that a moment ago seemed to consume my being has, for now, turned again to a deep sense of serenity.

"Well, yes, he may have found a way out of suffering. In fact, I am sure he did. At the same time, I had to shake you a bit so you stop accepting everything you are told as truth. There are always many ways you can look at the same thing, depending on what lenses you use. The Buddha may have found a way beyond suffering—it was *his* way. If it were true for all of you, there would not be so much anguish in the world today. No one can find the path for anybody. Each one of you has to do it. You have to fight your own battles and discover the truth that brings peace to your heart. Nothing, and I mean nothing, can ever replace direct personal experience," Nobi says. "And let me add something here, my friend," he continues immediately, as though he forgot to mention an important point. "I am really sickened by how you have managed to package and commoditize everything in this age of greed. Even your spiritual quest has become something you go and shop for in the market place. And the realisation of truth is not something that is cheap; it cannot be attained by purchasing it from another, never!"

I sense that he is right. Nothing can ever substitute for personal experience. The Buddha may have said anger is bad for us, and we may understand it within the realms of thought. We won't, however, translate this truth into understanding until we ourselves see into our own anger and walk through and beyond it. Suppressing it is no good; it will fester, to erupt another day as a disfigured monster. Following anyone is a sign of defeat — a telling mirror that we need a crutch to walk through life. And that is exactly what religions have offered us — a crutch to lean on. The Buddha himself dropped all his teachers — left them, for he understood that one must discover truth through his or her own inner vision. There are no short cuts in life and it cannot be handed over from one to another. Something else can be shared, though, and has been, when humans were still in touch with the *way*. What can be passed on are the songlines, the stories, and the visions of where we aspire to go with our inner venture in life. Yet the path, the discovery, the joy, the agony, the success and the failure are still our personal domain to experience.

A warrior charts her path and knows that she, and only she alone is responsible for her walk. He does not detest the people who obstruct him, for all is his mirror and reminder to refine his impeccably. She always walks with compassion and leaves punishment in the hands of the gods.

"Mate," Nobi turns and faces me. "You know, some of your religions talk of *God* and others don't. Either way, they degrade the enormity of the Presence you refer to as *God*. I'd rather not use this word as it has so many connotations attached to it. Let's just say that there is a force that by its Pure Emanation guides all universal movement. This force, this Great Spirit, this Great Mystery, is forever guiding and protecting you, for you have chosen to embrace life and seek truth. Trust that you are a child of the universe and are cared for by forces beyond your comprehension!"

I feel moved by Nobi's statement. I want to say something but my voice chokes on its words. Nobi looks at me with a love so pure; I stretch my hand out and gently touch his shining black figure. I feel as if I am touching creation herself. His feathers are so soft, as though they are made from the highest quality silk.

In truth, I don't know what I would name the thing we call God. Mother? Father? No, nothing like that. In fact, I don't feel that we are even close to comprehending, let alone understanding this energy, so how can we attempt name it? Though, if I had to call it something I would call God *the Greatest Lushest Lover*. And to be that She must be greater than what we are able to touch at present.

❋ ❋ ❋ ❋ ❋ ❋ ❋

We married in an Indian desert village, at a Rat temple by a garden full with jasmine and roses, three weeks after we met. Pradip wed us in a traditional Hindu ceremony, a tribe of rats as our witnesses. I felt it was appropriate that the rats, which are considered to be the incarnations of storytellers, were present at our wedding, for stories are like desert tracks while storytellers weave their tales through the wilderness. A new path was being drawn on the canvas of life for two souls amongst the desert sands.

It felt like half the village was there, though probably not. The village must have numbered close to a thousand people and a couple of hundred of them were present at the wedding, mostly invited by Pradip with some people showing up just out of curiosity. Pradip's wife, Shruti, oversaw the preparations and the usual Indian wedding banquet was served, consisting of a variety of delicious spicy, oily vegetarian foods, and very special sweets unique to the area.

The ceremony itself lasted six hours, with Pradip guiding us slowly through the elaborate rituals. He recited the prayers in Sanskrit and then translated them into English. He was a well-educated man and spoke perfect Indian English, a language that could at best be described as Hinglish.

Nulla wore a bright red sari with a blouse in a deeper shade of red. Her hair was in a long plait, with jasmine flowers woven throughout. She looked as though she had just descended from a heavenly planet, a glowing goddess in the pale shades of a reflecting desert. Due to Pradip's insistence, I wore traditional Indian dress as well, a white kurta pyjama set. "Black is no good for marriage, Baba," he told me and I just accepted. We both had thick marigold garlands draped around our necks.

The whole wedding story was a process of letting go for me. It was as though I had no say whatsoever in what was happening to my life—I handed it over to a force I can best describe as surrender.

A few days before the wedding I offered Pradip two hundred dollars to cover the wedding expenses. He declined, and at the same time I felt that he was a bit insulted by my offer. "Pradip, it is my wedding, you don't need to pay for it," I said to him as I tried to shove the money into his hand.

"Baba, you are our guest and it is my honour to marry you and Nulla. From now on you will be like my children," he said, unwilling to enter into any further discussion of money. I didn't really get it; nevertheless, he wouldn't take the money and while I still felt uncomfortable that he would incur the cost of my own wedding, there seemed nothing to be done about it.

I talked it over with Nulla and she thought it was all cool. "You know, with love we must learn how to receive, it makes us more open and vulnerable," she said, while excusing herself to hang out with Shruti as they planned the wedding reception together.

I did try to press the issue with Pradip one more time, since I still didn't feel at ease with it. He just smiled and said, "Baba, this is not about money, it's about love," and dismissed me. Well, it was a kind of love I had never experienced before or knew much about. I was a westerner, humbled by the immense giving nature of the people of this land, their constant desire to share the experience of life with the world around them. It was love in its purest form. There was nothing I could give Pradip in return, nor did he expect anything of me on any level.

It wasn't the type of love that was like a subtle bargain; it was giving in motion, by a heart that has seen it all. "Does the presence of so much suffering around us, refine our love and our willingness to give of ourselves?" I wondered.

It was not the last time that this country humbled me with the purity of her love. It made me appreciate how out of touch the so-called developed world was from the essence of true love. With time we had become very calculating; we needed a rationale behind our actions; we couldn't allow ourselves to be guided purely by our instincts and hearts alone. And more so, this love came from a priest, the people I disliked the most. And I loved Pradip. Time and again, life has proven to me the absence of any one absolute truth, and once more the reality that *is,* had blown into the wind any judgements I held.

Life is the movement that *is,* no more and no less. It is not a judgement; it is an experience with the now.

Suresh, who was drunk to the hilt, was disappointed there was no band playing music. The wedding was a bit too quiet for him. Pradip did suggest he hire one of those bands with which we would move in a procession through the village; however, this was where I put my foot down. It was just one step too far for me. I was happy to marry in an ancient Hindu ceremony; still I didn't want the kitsch of modern India. It was Nulla's and my special day, we were both very quiet and reserved people, or at least that's how I perceived us to be at the time.

Late that night we lay in our bed, which was still a small single mattress. Three weeks ago I was hermit, walking the desert sands, lost in my world of wonder, which was mostly painted in shadows. My only companion was a small bamboo flute that I would play when I sat at the burning grounds; I thought it would soothe the spirit of the wandering souls. Now I was married to the most beautiful woman in the world — at least to my eyes she was — and an entire new songline was about to be played out. I didn't have a clue where this journey would take me; nor did I wish it to carry me to any particular place. A seed was growing within me, sprouting a song of hope in my heart; if I allowed it, I sensed that it might blossom into a flower called trust.

Men become what they dream; I didn't have a particular dream, except I knew I had to invent one. I turned to Nulla, wanting to talk to her; however she was already deep asleep. Myself, I was too charged from all the day's events and couldn't keep still in our small bed. I got up, put on my clothes and went for a walk to the burning grounds. It was late in the night, with trillions of stars dotting the luminous desert sky. A half-moon was shining her light low over the horizon. The burning grounds were quiet and deserted. There were no Aghories camping there and even the usual resident dogs had gone to seek some companionship and adventure elsewhere.

"I am a married man now, what does it really mean?" The last three weeks moved as though a greater power was in charge. It felt like I was being carried through some sort of dream spell, as though I was sitting on a chariot with an unknown driver holding the reins. I had no clue in which direction we were moving; yet somehow I trusted the invisible hands that were guiding the journey. Embarking on this path, I hadn't paused for a moment to reflect on what getting married meant to me. Nulla and I hadn't talk about it much. It was just "let's flow in a space of trust and see what happens." Well, it happened, and I was a husband to a mysterious Goddess, whom, in reality, I was still to meet.

Suresh did say to me that Indians first marry and then

meet, and that's exactly how it felt; I married a woman that I was about to know. Little did I realise at the time that knowing another person, really knowing them, is an ongoing process, which actually never ends, and the secret mantra called *change*.

At a distance I heard a pack of dogs having their usual nightly disputes and paw wows. "If love is death, I am definitely in the process of dying, for love has touched my heart." Lying on the cool, welcoming sands, I slowly drifted off into sleep.

✳ ✳ ✳ ✳ ✳ ✳ ✳

By the river the night feels calm and warm. The presence felt in the flow of water always seems to enhance a deep sense of tranquillity and surrender. The commotion-taking place doesn't seem to affect the great river. She maintains her flow, as though nothing unusual is occurring around her. She is not touched by events, neither by the fact that she is going to change in the moments to come.

The river is present in the moment, with no concern of what is about to take place, and this presence of being is gradually infiltrating every cell of my being. Just to be, what will come will come, because it *has* to come, when it *has* to come.

I may change, the river may change, it all may change; still there is no reason for me to move from where I am. I have no idea what the change will look like until it *actually* occurs.

Feeling comfortable and at peace, the crows stare at me with a sense of bewilderment in their eyes. Many things can be said about our dear relation the crow, other than that it radiates peace and tranquillity. Or is it that the crows, living in such close proximity to us since time began, have been rubbed by our ways of blab. They always seem to come and ask questions, probe for information and tell us what's happening at the world at large.

It is Easter Sunday according to the Gregorian calendar.

I recall the life of the man who, according to legend, resurrected on this day, the great warrior of light, Yeshua of Nazareth. He was a Son of God, as we all are, no more, no less, born of the same divine spark we all hail from.

His presence was burning with love and care for his fellow beings, reflecting an earth walk centred on surrender to Great Spirit.

He, too, was a desert man like so many truth finders living through times and legends. It's as though the desert, projecting an aura of infinity in its forever space, compels us to look beyond the confines of our small minds and egos, into the spirit of all things.

And there is the silence too, and perhaps it's the stillness in silence that propels us to listen to the sounds, songs and symphonies played by the endless orchestras of elves and fairies whilst it remains unheard by our physical ears.

The desert warrior Yeshua chastised us for worshipping the gods of greed, fear and separation. He called us to walk a path of sharing life's abundance, with compassion, forgiveness and understanding. He pleaded with us to be content with taking what we need, while resisting the temptation of want, for in the garden of infinity there is abundance for all creatures to satisfy their needs.

He lived, loved and was a full on rebel, refusing to toe the line and live by the accepted paradigm of his day.

Societies have always detested the ones who dared to challenge the prevailing status quo. They make people look at things they would rather avoid, thus they are perceived to be dangerous in the eyes of the ones that seek to control us through the instruments of fear and separation.

The light warrior Yeshua was a dangerous man, for he offered people a way that was threatening to the rulers, a way that might lead them to question how they live, and dare to seek their own empowerment.

He was a freak, a free spirit and a revolutionary of the highest order.

The warriors of truth and seekers of love have been crucified from the moment that *man* decided he is the ordained universal overlord, for they pose a great threat to the powers that be. They are feared and reviled by the privileged ones, for they offer people something nobody can control or take away, and that's the gift of freedom.

The power of a free man or woman rests in the fact that they can never be subjugated, manipulated or threatened, for true freedom is a state where fear has lost its gripping power of control. And how can anybody ever be controlled without the cunning instrument of fear?

Yeshua, who in reality may have just been a legend, a parable, a good story to reflect man's quest for a higher truth, has been worshipped in the last two thousand years as the Son of God by so many. Ironically, always by the same multitudes that are happy to crucify anyone who resembles him in their quest for truth, love and freedom.

Really, how dumb has human civilization become! We worship legends, stories, something that we feel we can touch with the limited senses we are aware of and at the same time we lead lives that are contradictory to the teachings of the Gods we claim to adore. We always seem to want a tangible God, preferably with form and name and by doing that we just degrade the enormity of the intelligence that continues to spin the galaxies around. We crave something that we can touch with our mind rather than trust in our heart. This is why we keep on handing over our power to others. We want someone else to solve the riddle of life for us, and no one will ever be up to the task. It has to be felt and lived. It has to be experienced and it can never be borrowed.

✳ ✳ ✳ ✳ ✳ ✳ ✳

I felt a hand stroking my face; it was Nulla. "What are you doing here, you run away from your wife on your wedding night, don't you ever learn from your mistakes?" she said lovingly.

"No, Nulla," I smiled and pulled her over to give her a kiss. "You fell asleep and I felt really charged, so I took a little stroll; I did intend to come back to the room, though I must have fallen asleep, it feels late in the morning already," I said while wiping the sleep off my face.

"You know, My Love; I wonder what type of husband you will be?"

"A good one" I smiled back at her. "I love you Nulla," I said holding her eyes within the space of my own.

She knelt on her knees in front of me and held my hands. It was the first time I had told her that I loved her, and I meant it with every cell of my being. A few small, delicate tears trickled down her cheeks. If I could ever freeze a moment in time and make it last forever, it would be that moment in the desert on our first day as husband and wife. Perfect love. Total presence. Absolute surrender. All I ever would be, could be, shall be; was present in that precious moment.

"Is this the landscape of enlightenment? Is this what the sages call the deepest realisation? How long am I able to make this moment last, and will it ever come again?" I questioned myself.

"I love you too, man. I have loved you from the moment you stood in front of me with a mountain of flowers and nothing to say," Nulla said with a smile of a Goddess enjoying the divine moment.

Is love the key to the land where time stops still and desire is no more? Does the flowering of our deepest desire lead us to a space of no desire?

126

We sat there together underneath the huge banyan tree, which graced the burning grounds with its life.

"So, Nulla, this is the first day of our honeymoon and we're being blessed by the spirit of the dead." I was in a good playful mood and so was Nulla. It felt really special that she had come into my world with the dead. And the burning grounds were without doubt one of my main anchors to life during my time in the village.

"You know, you may have been silent in the last six months, though really, you are a bit of a storyteller. I feel this silence of yours is just an exterior mask. Your inner world is full of chatter," she said, and she was right. Still I never pretended to be anything else.

"We are both storytellers, Nulla, and what we are attempting to whisper is part of a new tale that humanity has been waiting for. Many of us are part of this new narrative being sketched, and we are extra lucky for we live in the rat temple, the abode of the storytellers!" I said.

"Hey, where are you taking me for a honeymoon?" Nulla changed the subject. Slightly bemused I looked back at her; I wasn't sure if she was serious or just being playful. She did continue to press the subject "I think I would like to go to a deserted palace on a cliff overlooking a vast desert horizon, a place where the maharajas use to live. I'd like to go there and feel how a princess feels. Just sit and stare out the window while you brush my hair," she said, and she wasn't joking. I did learn that about Nulla, she always meant what she said, even if it was said in jest.

In the years to come, brushing and combing Nulla's hair would become one of my meditations. Often, when she would sense a bit of friction in the air or some misunderstanding between us, she would grab a chair, sit by a window and hand me a brush or wooden comb. We would never talk while I combed her hair; it was a kind of sacred ceremony that wove a rope bridge across the divide of her and me. It had a hypnotic effect on me, and even in my most agitated moods, once I touched her hair I would feel calmed. Nulla's hair was really long and quite thick falling all the way down to her waist; it seemed only right that I would offer my services to such a silky mane.

"Nulla," I looked deep into her eyes. "Yesterday in the ceremony, did you feel comfortable with all the words Pradip spoke?" I asked her.

"Yes, they were really beautiful, it really touched my heart; he spoke the essence of what I myself feel marriage should be." She smiled softly with a question in her face, "Didn't you feel comfortable?"

"I did, I just wondered, when he said about your duty to serve and follow your husband . . ."

She stopped me mid-sentence, waved her hand and chuckled. "Didn't you hear the other half of your duty to serve me?"

"I did Nulla, but you know women these days are very sensitive to this type of talk," I said.

"I am not a radical, fanatical feminist" she said, a cutting edge in her voice. "I am a woman and want to be one. I am the earth and the river and the lakes, and I expect you to be like the sun − giving and present!" she stated in her usual poetic manner.

It took me a while to realise what a strong and powerful woman Nulla was and to understand that only in strength could we live in surrender to the other. It is usually weak people that try desperately to hold onto a sense of a separate self; they cling to it, since they are scared that they may lose what is not really theirs to begin with.

We got married in India where people are always depending on each other for survival. And from day one, our walk together was an interdependent dance, two song lines woven together into one symphony of love.

✳ ✳ ✳ ✳ ✳ ✳ ✳

Every journey in life is conceived in a lullaby of promise. Yet the river always changes its course. Ours, like the voyage of any river, experienced deep turbulence.

Sitting by the river now, I recognise that without the trouble, pain, and conflict and despair that Nulla and I shared at times, we wouldn't have grown to be who we are today. They were like springboards, edging us to new levels of conscious awareness. We both left each other a few times, sincerely doubting that we would ever meet again. Yet we would both cry our hearts out in longing when we were apart. We made the mistake more than once of taking on the other's inner pain and struggle as a reflection of their diminishing love. And we also needed space to grow. We had to pull apart from the assurance given by the other and find our own personal melody, the innermost circle of our being.

Darkness is a friend, too, when lived as an internal process of working out our demons and fears. It has to be lived in our own time and space. It is very difficult to journey through the shadow-self with a companion by our side. The night is the womb that holds within its confines the promise of a bright day still to be born.

With the river as my final reflection, I can honestly acknowledge that my whole life has been a quest to hold love in my heart. To feel love permeate through me and to earn the love of the divine Goddess. My whole purpose for walking this earth has been one—to share my love with the world around me. Love has been an oasis for my wandering soul, a sacred pool to quench my thirst and fuel my longing to touch the divine spirit beyond the constant dance of opposites.

In the final analysis, I might have failed, for I am sitting by this river alone, readying myself for the final chapter of this crusade called life while Nulla is alive in my memories, although she is nowhere to be seen.

I do know, though, in the depths of my being, every person walking this planet is seeking love, just as she said to me all those years ago. Every mirror that has offered me a reflection through my journey on earth has spoken this unshakable truth to me as well.

I know beyond all doubt that the darkest of criminals, the most vile of men are still in the quest for love. The worst killer, murderer, rapist, torturer are all crying out for the calming grace of love; a love they have not found within their being, nor found on the outside, for they were never nurtured with love by the world that brought them into being.

In the core of the most horrendous human act is a yearning to touch love—a cry, a scream, a howl that love has somehow been denied due to one's upbringing and circumstance. It is my inner most conviction that everything that is nurtured by pure love and freedom, like a flower, will grow to blossom. A heart that has not been deprived of love, which is the essence of life, will always walk this earth with balance as their guide. So how come, when love is the essence we all crave, the absence of it is the most common telling mirror to greet us in the corridors of life?

Hence, this is why so many fall between the cracks and abdicate the caravan of goodness to seek love and acceptance in the most warped ways the human mind can imagine. Then, when caught, they are punished by society; a social order that never really gave them a chance in the first place—neither will it ever give them a second chance. And punishment without love and healing is sure to be condemnation to eternal damnation.

Years ago, I read a quote in the daily "sacred space" column of an Indian newspaper. It read: "the hands that feed the poor are better than the lips that pray to God." In that instant it dawned on me, that one of the most profound ways we find the presence of love — is in action. Love is not the word *love*; it is the actions, which are usually silent. It is the being, the giving and the serving of the other. The allowing to be; that makes the flower of love bloom . . . for love without the action and intent, is like following a God while cursing creation, or quenching our thirst in a spring of poisoned water.

All the true masters and teachers throughout time had one message, just one call — love. Love all, unconditionally, for a heart filled with love will never fall into the stinking pit of hate, revenge and fear.

So how is it that the so-called followers of the one almighty God, like the ones who worship the love baba Yeshua, have killed and maimed and tortured more people than any country or organization in HisStory? And they still do, in the name of their god, wage war. It is usually the more devoted fanatical followers of any religion that are raring for the kill. How come? Are they deaf, have they really listened to the masters they claim to follow?

Obviously they have not, for the world of religious orientations is all about the politics of power. There may be some sort of weird god involved, though there is definitely no godliness.

Nobi gives me a long stare: "What are you thinking about, mate?" He finally decides to snap me out of my mind's chatter and bring me back to the present moment.

"Well, I was thinking about love — although then my thoughts slipped to the absence of it."

"Ha!" he has a bit of a sarcastic chuckle. "Love: this word all of you use all the time, yet so few of you live by."

"That's exactly right, Nobi," I give him the thumbs up. "I think I underestimate your insight into the human condition," I say, while he chooses to ignore me. Nobi looks away, staring at the river.

"It seems that all of you humans underestimate the wisdom of the natural world. The fact is that all *life manifest* carries its own consciousness; that everything is living in relationship to another; and everything is affected by the actions of the one. We always try and build a bridge to you guys, though seldom do any of you pause to listen. If you did, you would feel the life surrounding you and you would harness the immense power and support offered to you.

"The warriors of truth and love are not alone. Still, even they forget that we are here, all of us, the whole myriad of creation, everything is in full attention to support and nurture the forces of light, the movement towards the one."

✻ ✻ ✻ ✻ ✻ ✻ ✻

Often, when we envision a desert, the picture painted in our mind is that of a barren, desolate landscape. Frequently we make the mistake of thinking that deserts are places devoid of the melody of life and without the general commotion that takes place when creatures, be they flora or fauna, dance together in the cycle of evolution and dissolution. In reality, deserts are far from that. Some deserts are dotted with vegetation, while others require a deeper and longer attention span, in order to observe the life permeating throughout.

The desert around my village was a meeting point of shifting sand dunes, a lush oasis and an endless horizon of dotted thorny shrubs that even the goats stayed away from.

Amongst the thorny trees, which provided reasonable shade and firewood, were a variety of cactuses and other plants. They all shared one thing in common; they all had some form of protective mechanism to make them unappealing to the palate of the small herds owned by the desert folk, thus ensuring their survival in this hardly hospitable landscape. Okay, I have to take back these words "hardly hospitable" since it is unfair to the warm welcome deserts all over the world have offered me throughout the years. Let's just say she offers a different kind of welcome, a more subtle and seductive embrace, rather than flaunting her full colours to the prospective lover upon his arrival.

Nulla has been my desert princess from the moment we first met. Like the tweak of a magnificent sunset over shifting dunes, she drew me in, tempting my curiosity with glimpses of her magic. Slowly she allowed me into her world, yet never revealed all her secrets to me, always leaving some mystery for the coming of tomorrow.

"My friend and love," Nulla held my hand. "Why do we need to wait until we die to reincarnate or to find out if reincarnation is even possible? We can reincarnate in this life, in this moment, right now. I feel that we can and we must rebirth ourselves into a new way of being, it seems to me that it's part of our sacred duty on our walk on earth. I mean this is what both of us are doing. We are dying to the stupid self we were bred to be and being reborn into freedom. We are rewriting the story of our life. To wait for the promise of a next incarnation is just another delay mechanism we are all becoming masters of."

It was late in the afternoon. Nulla and I had spent most of the first day of our marriage at the burning grounds. We had talked a bit and then fallen asleep for a while under the shade of the banyan tree. We could talk forever, or keep silent forever, it didn't really matter; we were definitely broadcasting on the same frequency.

"Yep, I suppose you are right. Maybe that was the real meaning behind the Aghorie's words when he told me that 'love is death.' I do feel like a child being reborn, there is a certain fragility, tenderness, wonder that has been ignited within me, something which I had forgotten while *growing up*." I said. Nulla laughed. It was a gentle laugh, actually more of a big smile.

There are two types of love in this world. One that is

instant, at first sight, and one that grows with time. They both need the essential ingredients of trust and surrender. Our love was a bit of both - instant recognition and a love that never stopped growing. At times the growing pains were severe, however, on that first day of being married to the most amazing woman in existence, life did seem to ride a wave of perfection.

"Hey, man," Nulla addressed me again. She wanted to talk and I was comfortable in silence. "What did you do before you came to India?" she asked me. It was the first time Nulla attempted to probe into my past, something which she had not done up to now.

"Nulla, now that you are my wife, you feel the right to ask me about my past. You know I don't like talking about the past. It's irrelevant to the now. It's just blab blab to fill empty space. Have you lost your comfort zone with silence, girl?" I said, a bit irritated by the constant barrage of words.

"I don't agree with you, the past is what shapes us into who we are." So there we were again. We would often sit for hours and have these philosophical discussions. Nulla enjoyed them more than I did, however I did get into the spirit of things at times and she knew how to hook me in. She wanted me to contemplate the ideas that were spinning around in her head. I on the other hand felt more comfortable keeping my inner chatter to myself.

"Yeah, the past may shape us in some way, still for that reason exactly, it's the past that we must drop, destroy, annihilate in order to walk in total freedom in the now." I sounded very convincing I thought, though I wasn't sure I had totally experienced what I was stating as truth. Totally letting go, being entirely present in the moment, was a fleeting notion for me, however when touched it felt like the space where truth abides.

✳ ✳ ✳ ✳ ✳ ✳ ✳

By the river another truth is making itself known. The river is flowing, with an ever-growing hum, gathering some energy in her movement while both Nobi and I are sitting by her fragile banks, transfixed by her presence.

Life is a miraculous journey that continues to unfold and the changes, inner more than outer, never cease to amaze me. Inner movement is a constant renewal of the spirit, an ascendance, propelling us ever nearer to oneness — the source from where all life emanates. And every river is a perfect reflection of this continual ever-changing movement.

Where does the river birth itself? At her source, while she continues to renew herself along the way as she heads to the sea. With time she changes her course, she breaks her banks, she even dries up to emerge sometime later. With all the detours, obstacles and surprises offered to her on her way, she always moves in the same direction, to the sea. And there she merges into the *one* - and her journey does not end there. It begins again as the sun's rays gather the moisture for the clouds that will rain and snow at her source and commence her flow again.

Aren't we all a river, always moving towards the source that gave us birth and spins us on the wheel of life again and again? Aren't we all an ocean, which is a river itself, with no beginning and never ending?

Nobi and I are sitting in silence on a deserted ghat; a set of wide steps, descending into the river, at the northern end of this village. The stairs are about ten metres wide and they usually serve as a space where locals and pilgrims alike come to take a holy bath while they perform various rituals. It is a relatively quiet ghat on normal days, mostly used by the locals for their daily bathing rites and also utilized by a couple of laundry men who beat clothes upon the smooth stone surface. We two, man and crow, are sitting on a small concert platform perched a few feet above the river.

It is a place I often would come in the evenings for meditation and contemplation whilst visiting in this part of the country. Frequently, White Socks would come and sit by my side, demanding my attention. White Socks was a local street dog with whom I developed a strong friendship over the years of visiting her turf. She was a sook for pats, especially long belly rubs. I named her White Socks since all her four legs were white while the rest of her body was the normal pale dusty brown, the colour that seems to adorn millions of Indian street dogs.

In all my adventures and travels across the globe, I have never come across a more loving creature than the roaming, pack orientated Indian feral dog. They inhabit every town, city, slum and village all over India. They number in the millions, and they look as though they all share the same grandparents, which one might assume was a close relative of the Dingo. It is quite remarkable the unconditional love these animals have shared with me over the years and how I have come to rely on them in my times of need for silent love and affection. They seem to especially like the company of foreigners who often offer them care, food and touch, while the locals commonly fear and shun them for dread of diseases like rabies.

White Socks enjoyed a good stroke from whoever was willing to offer it and always greeted me with a 'hand shake'. She had a habit of putting out her front leg as a greeting. At nights I would buy her a sweet bun and cut bits off to throw in the air, while she in great delight, caught them before they landed, savouring the victory and the munch.

Where is she? I wonder. Has she run up the hill with the rest of the people? I would so much enjoy her company here now for a few moments. White Socks may be absent, still Nobi is here by my side, eager to talk again.

"You know, mate, there is great sadness in my heart, in the hearts of all my brothers and sisters, the winged ones. We have watched you guys for a long time now lose touch with the essence of life, though we always thought that sooner or later this trend would be reversed and some meaningful change would occur. We thought that people would wake up and with their passion and purpose, chart a new course for the human race and all life on earth.

"And, yes, there is a small awakening taking place at present around the world. Some of you are attempting to touch the wind again, though it's a bit late, half-hearted and slow. Everything in the universe operates at the speed of *now* . . . there is no time for delays when truth reveals itself to you. And the truth is that *now* is the time to restore the balance to the universal heart!"

Nobi is gazing into the night. He needs to talk, and he isn't really talking to me anymore. His body is by my side; nevertheless he seems far away. He is talking to humanity at large, his words a prayer and a plea that we all open our hearts to the calling that emanates from the place where all rivers meet.

"Do you think the earth is angry when she makes herself shake and the river flood? No, she is not; she is overflowing with compassion. This flood is the earth extending her unconditional compassion to you people, so you may wake up from your folly and sort out this mess you have created with life on earth." He continues talking, while now and again pausing for a moment, allowing his words to flow downstream into the ears of the unseen listeners.

"You know, there was this man, the one that was voted to be the president of the United States, before that Texan cowboy stole it away from him. Anyway, this dude has been speaking for a long time now about how the climate is changing and how earth's life support systems are in trouble. He is not a freak or a hippie or a mad scientist, yet nobody listens to him.

Even when he presents all the facts in the language spoken by the powers that be, many of your leaders and their followers ignore him. Why is that? He is actually one of them, they should at least trust the people who are still in allegiance to their system of government," he says.

"Yes, I know, Nobi, I agree with you. On the other hand, look at what is happening. Now that some are finally listening, all that they are doing is squabbling over money and how a profit can be made from the impending calamity by trading the rights to pollute. So even when they agree to act it's all about money again and it all seems to be too little too late." I reply with a sense of sarcasm.

"Nothing is ever too late," Nobi snaps back at me. "You must always offer a positive action, an alternative, in the face of adversity. To say it's too late is just another form of escaping from the challenge and responsibility life has dished out for you. At the same time you must realise there is a deep problem with the whole message of this man and many other so-called mainstream environmentalists. Human civilisation has converted nature into a resource as though it was given to them to exploit and destroy. Nature has become a property with no rights, the open mine of the corporations. Only once it becomes your friend again, could some momentous change be possible."

Nobi pauses for a moment, as he always does, when he really wants me to focus my attention.

"This guy is speaking of a climate crisis, yet the crisis is so much deeper than that. The climate changing is just one of the many symptoms that are showing up, a sign of a long lasting chronic disease festering in the human heart and mind, the disease of separation and superiority to the life that surrounds you," he says.

"I know, Nobi, he is still a man of Babylon," I reply in haste.

Nobi gives me a ferocious look as though he is going to eat me up. "What's happened to you my friend? Forget about Babylon and Zion and all terms of separation; these sorts of divisions are not signs of a healthy or balanced

138

mind. There is only one human race and it's you guys. There is only one creation and it's all of us together. Yes, this man may have a limited vision; still at least he has one.

Of course it's not the climate that's in crisis, it's the human mind and heart that has long lost its affinity with the circle of life; and as long as it sees itself as a separate entity then all talk of change is futile," he concludes.

I am fired up by Nobi's talk. I am amazed at how he seems to have walked with us all along as a companion. All the World Trade Organisation protests, the forest blockades, the peace marches, the pro and anti-actions; now I understand that we were never really alone. Nobi seems to be aware of everything. How can it be? He did mention that we are always supported . . . *wow*, we always talked about it, and in spite of this did we ever really trust it?

And of course, he is right, nobody can solve the climate crisis while the economy is still the worshipped god and terms like *growth* are seen not only as desirable but necessary. What makes the modern concept of economic growth destructive is that it's an unnatural phenomenon. It has caused every living system on the planet to be in a state of decline. Where is our promised sustainable future?

If the economy was growing at a pace level with the growth of human population, that would have been a natural process, still challenging, though possibly manageable. Every mouth needs more food, everybody needs more clothes to wear, thus as we grow in population the economy expands as an interrelated entity, not some separate reality dreamt up in the boardrooms of multinationals and executed in the *casino royale* of Wall St. By continuing to export and popularise the current ideas of development we are leading humanity to mass suicide and the planet to extinction.

Humanity needs to change its reference point and take a deep breath. We need to question how we measure wealth and ask if there is a different more profound way to measure our wealth. Then and only then might we finally get it, that it's not about money — it's about love.

✻ ✻ ✻ ✻ ✻ ✻ ✻

Well, love was definitely present in that time back then in the desert.

Our first few weeks as husband and wife were somehow uneventful. We spent our days in a quiet, peaceful routine, gradually getting to know one another and becoming familiar with the other's presence by our side. I still went most days to the burning grounds as I did before I met Nulla, for I valued the space to be by myself, contemplate life and play my small bamboo flute. All the same, there was a contrasting quality to my visits now; my heart was no longer a well of darkness, hope was in the air and an enthusiasm vibrated through my cells as I eagerly anticipated what life had in store for me next.

Nulla spent her days creatively; she learnt embroidery patterns from the local women in the mornings and then would draw and paint in the afternoons. Generally, she would stop in at the market after her embroidery sittings and then the two of us would prepare the food she brought home and share our lunch together, although at times we deviated from this routine and instead went out for lunch at Govinda's. In my pre-Nulla days, the only person in the village I exchanged a few words with, apart from Suresh and Pradip, was Govinda. On certain days I just didn't feel like cooking, it felt like such a long mission that would often last almost two hours and at the end of it, it only took ten minutes for it to all disappear down to my stomach. The alternative was Govinda's. Govinda had a small space, which almost resembled a cave. You had to walk down a few steps and then venture into a dark room. Since Govinda was only open for lunch, it was the perfect place to serve it, away from the scorching desert midday sun. There was no menu at Govinda's, the fare was the same every day; dhal, vegetables and chapatti. The vegetables changed occasionally throughout the year, though in cold season it was always potatoes and cauliflower. Govinda's food was really tasty, much more appetizing than the lunches I managed to scrape together back at the rat temple. For the honour of being served food at his place I paid three rupees — this, too, was unlimited. I could eat and eat until I was stuffed, though in truth, at the time my appetite was quite tamed.

A couple of weeks after our wedding, Govinda was struck by a bombshell. After making his lunches for seven years and supporting all his extended family from his modest business, the landlord had decided to evict him. A cloth merchant from a neighboring town had come and offered more money for the premises. Govinda was a proud man, as most desert folk are and both Nulla and I could feel how desperate his situation was. He had two sons and two daughters to support as well as his mum and dad. He was a man of honour and had managed to send all his children to school, including his eldest daughter, who was going to the high school in a neighboring village. Usually, at the first sign of financial stress, parents would pull their girls out of school. A lot of parents felt it was a waste of money, since the daughter would be married away to another family one day. Govinda had other ideas, though, and he was very proud of his daughter being an exemplary student in her high school. We met him one evening for a chai, while he told us of his new idea. He was planning to buy a cart with four wheels, a small flat table on which he would deliver goods around the village by foot, since the village had no vehicle access. He would pick up goods from the place where the trucks dropped them near the bus stand and deliver them to homes and businesses. I wasn't sure how he would make enough money to support his family from this venture, though since he owned no land or livestock, there weren't many options open to him.

The cart would cost sixty dollars, since Govinda felt he needed good wheels to negotiate the sand and the twisty village lanes. He told us he managed to save thirty dollars from his lunch business, after paying off all his family's debts, some incurred by his grandfather to a loan shark a long time ago. At once we offered to give him the thirty dollars he was missing, and some more money to advertise his new venture. After some cajoling he agreed to take the money, though as a loan and not as a gift.

I met Govinda twenty years later. He was still wheeling the same cart around. As the village grew there was more and more demand for his services. All his children had finished high school and his two daughters had graduated from university. His eldest daughter was a doctor, which made him the proudest father around.

I asked him why he didn't let his children support him now. In his fifties he was as fit and strong as an ox. "Baba," he said to me affectionately, "while I can work, no one need support me. I am happy for my children." He then pulled out the equivalent of sixty dollars and handed it to me. "This is for the thirty dollar loan and the interest for twenty years." I laughed and handed him back the money. However he wouldn't hear of it, and insisted that he must pay back the loan. We negotiated for a while until at last we found a solution. Govinda would give the money to a poor family in order to support the education of their daughter. Who knows, perhaps there is another lady doctor in the making, from the village of smiles in the heart of the Indian desert.

In the afternoons we often went to Suresh's chai shop for a late afternoon chai and chat. Suresh loved it. We had quickly become celebrities in the village. After all we were the first foreigners to get married there and in a traditional

Hindu ceremony at that. Suresh felt it gave his chai shop extra status, the fact that we always had our chai with him. He would often yell "Baba! Nulla!" across the market when he spotted us heading towards his premises. He wanted to make sure no one in the village missed his special connection with us. I enjoyed the times with Suresh, there was always a good laugh in the air, and it was a kind of a social club cum story-gossip-telling corner.

Bit by bit we started making new friends in the village, especially Nulla. She loved the company of the local women and engaged herself in learning all that she could of their traditional gypsy crafts, while teaching them a bit of drawing in return.

It was on a particularly oppressively hot afternoon when we headed to Suresh's chai shop that something seemed weird and out of character. Suresh didn't yell our names out before our arrival as he usually did, announcing to the world that we were coming for his chai. Instead he seemed in a sombre mood, and avoided looking us in the eyes.

"Namaste, Suresh," I greeted him with the deep affection I always felt for him. Still he kept silent and didn't even look my way. "What's the problem Suresh, is everything alright with your family?" I asked him with some concern. Now and again he would talk about them, however, it wasn't his favourite subject; in this regard we were very similar. I knew some bits and pieces about his family, he did tell me his dad had had tuberculosis for some time now, yet he still continued to smoke biddies all day.

"Everything alright with family, Baba," he replied, again avoiding eye contact. It was the first time I'd experienced Suresh in this type of mood, and I knew beyond all doubt that something wasn't right.

"Are we still welcome to have chai in your shop, Suresh?" I said trying to lighten up the mood.

"Baba, there is big problem," he finally looked my way.

"What is it, mate?"

He didn't seem in a hurry to answer, as though he needed to figure out the right words to break the bad news he was holding back. "Baba, today police coming in my chai shop, asking about you and Nulla," he said and as he did so he seemed relieved he had found the courage to speak.

"So what is the problem, Suresh? We are doing nothing wrong," I said while putting my arm around his shoulder, pulling him closer to me to affirm our friendship.

"They ask about your visa, Baba," he continued.

"No problem, Suresh," I smiled back. "Pradip has the details of my passport and visa, so if they ask him they will see that everything is thik hai." Sitting down next to Nulla, we both continued to offer Suresh our reassurance that there was nothing to be concerned about.

"Suresh, don't worry, this man does not need a visa, because he is a commonwealth citizen and I have a visa. It's probably just a routine check," she said with her warm smile.

Suresh wasn't convinced by our words and remained in his sombre mood. "You don't understand, Baba, when police start to ask questions, it is not good sign. They say you have been here very long time. They are also angry with Pradip that he marry you in Hindu ceremony in temple." Suresh continued his rave. I assured Suresh that I would talk it over with Pradip that evening and let him know tomorrow what light could be shed on the matter.

That night, after reflecting again on what had transpired at the chai shop, I couldn't fall asleep. Nulla had asked me to talk with Pradip when we came back from Suresh's, but I wasn't in the mood for it. I knew the police must have paid him a visit too and if he had something to say to us he would do it in the morning. Nulla was in deep sleep while I sat leaning against the wall stroking her hair and counting the cracks in the decrepit ceiling. My heart wasn't calm; I sensed a new challenge in the air. I got up, put on my waistcoat and lungi and took a stroll to the burning grounds, to seek the wisdom of the dead.

There is something about the carpet of stars adorning the desert nights, that always brought me closer to the source, the infinite soul we are all a part of. And at that moment I needed the wisdom and comfort of the foundation that life springs from.

I sat down by the big banyan tree, which by now could probably recognise me just by my scent. Tears started to blur my sight and wet my cheeks. Kalu came over and put her head on my lap, reassuring me that I was part of her universal story. Stroking the dog eased my spirit a bit, yet I knew beyond all doubt that big changes were about to take place. My sweet life in this small timeless paradise was all about to come to an abrupt end.

I didn't want it to be like this. In my dream world I envisioned Nulla and me growing old together in this place; having our children roam free with the pack of village kids while we enjoyed our freedom in the timeless zone which life in the desert offered. I even started to contemplate ways of making a living by exporting village crafts to the west. Essentially my reality and life were focused and centred in this village. It was here I had met Nulla, here I had found love, here I had begun exploring the meaning of being present with life, and I didn't want this present moment to ever come to an end.

Life however, often has different ideas than we do and I felt that a new journey was upon us. "Am I ready?"

I wasn't really sure what I was prepared for, and I was aware of a profound change within me over the weeks since I'd gotten married. Suddenly I had a responsibility for another person. And what did this scary word *responsibility* mean? Perhaps responsibility is my ability to respond to any given challenge that arises. I did not have the luxury anymore to sink into my narcissistic self and wallow. I had to stand up and shine the light on the earth just as the sun does, even at times like these when doubt and uncertainty polluted the air. Are any of us really ever ready for change when it makes itself known or is there always a sense of trepidation when we are called to move on from the soporific comfort zone of the known?

In the weeks that passed I noticed how my awareness was gradually transiting from my ever-babbling mind, to the actuality that I live in a body. It was as though I had suddenly remembered that I had a body, a complete encyclopaedia of knowledge that could answer any question I could ever imagine to ask. As I became more aware, my thoughts dropped anchor in the source that shines a light in the desert night sky. Hearing my breath humming through the silence, I felt aligned with the movement of all that is. When hearing my breath I am present with it, thus a soothing balm is applied to the mad monkey rampaging through my mind.

And then there was love; a flavoursome combination of my deep growing affection and awe for this mysterious woman called Nulla and an unfamiliar sensation of this new self-love tickling the trillions of cells dancing within me.

I heard the voices of the disembodied homeless souls drifting around the burning grounds, buzzing in agreement with me. I listened to them as they whispered not to follow the roads they had walked, for they still felt unresolved with their journey's end.

"Always walk with love in your heart; and never allow fear to be your guide. You must trust that within you all answers abide." I heard the whisper of an unseen desert knight blowing in my ear as I got up to leave this populated ghost town. I walked back to the small room that was my home, where my divine goddess lay blissfully asleep, completely unaware of my wonderings amongst the land of the dead.

✳ ✳ ✳ ✳ ✳ ✳ ✳

Net Universal Love, Gross National Happiness, Net National Health, wouldn't it be nice to measure our evolution and accomplishments as a race in terms such as these. Wouldn't a change in definitions and goals, mark a shifting point in the way we experience life on earth!

The river reflects her light through the half-moon shining in the sky, voicing her silent agreement with me. At the moment, we humans measure our growth and achievements with the catch phrase *Gross Domestic Product* as our guiding light.

How many of us have ever paused for a moment to reflect on what a load of bullshit this is; surely only a few of us, the rest of us have the wool pulled over our eyes. We seem to blindly trust the *wise* words dished to us by our corporate masters. How the hell is growth in our domestic product supposed to ever make us a happier, healthier, wiser human race? How is it going to craft our walk on planet earth into one that is sustainable, joyful and in balance?

Nobi is keeping quiet by my side, allowing me the space to drift away and be present. I can sense he is delighted with the inner rage he has managed to evoke within me, and wants me to work my way through it.

Who does it really benefit, this growth in domestic product? Does it benefit the small farmer who toils in the fields from sunrise to sunset? Does it put more food on her table? Does it bring her clean drinking water to quench her thirst at the end of a hot day?

No, of course it doesn't, for the so-called *brave new world* was never meant to take the toiling masses on the bandwagon of illusory prosperity.

Actually, growth in GDP most likely means her clean river, which for generations provided her and her family with crystal clear water, has dried up to make way for an intricate dam project. Now she has to walk five kilometres every day to fetch drinking water of questionable quality to quench the thirst of her family.

The river that was her lifeline for generations has been dammed to make ample electricity available for the sweatshops, owned by transnational companies. This is so that the country may increase its GDP and thus be in the good books with the World Bank and International Monetary Fund. And let us not forget that this electricity will be provided at subsidised rates, so that the multinational companies feel the country has set up an *investment friendly environment*. Of course anybody who dares to resist the process would be suppressed and silenced with the most draconian measures, while being painted in the local media as *anti-development* or even as a *terrorist*.

So why is it that we continue to use terms and concepts that only benefit the few rich and powerful, I wonder, while the masses have been robbed of the access to the basic necessities of life? Are we stupid enough to accept exploitation as a just and necessary reality that we need in order to sustain life? Are we really content to see the GDP grow while the space and opportunity around our own lives shrinks?

Nobi is absolutely right; the whole human race is being manipulated into this weird nightmare, *the fantasy of economics* — a horror movie conjured up by the few rich and powerful and supported by our eerie silence. It seems that we have grown and adapted actually to be fond of horror movies, at least some of us have.

Take this for a scene in this sick Hollywood production; in 2009 the world spent one thousand and six hundred billion dollars on arms, half of this is by the United States alone. Just a fraction of this would ensure that no child ever goes to sleep hungry again, another fraction would ensure nobody dies from diseases which are easily curable and then there would still be plenty of change left over to provide basic health care and education for all.

So, why is the current horror movie so popular with the masses? Are we all so cleverly manipulated that we have become willing or unwilling participants in this nasty production? Look at some of the terms they use to convince us of their economic fantasy. For example, the term, *free market*, is one of the key catch phrases around our brave new world. If we examined it for a moment, what would we discover? Has there ever been a time in history when the market has been so *un*-free?

A few giant transnational octopuses control everything.

Where is the time of family owned stores and vibrant family farms? That time of a real free market has gone? Now the market is free to play between a dozen or so huge corporate houses, and all of us are fooled as they laugh all the way to the bank, which subsequently they own too.

And it's not only our money that they are after in this so-called freedom dance where nothing is free; it's complete and utter control over every facet of our lives. Of course, if you oppose or expose their lies and deceit then you are a terrorist.

Nothing has ever undermined democracy more than the so-called *free market*, controlled by the corporate globalisation forces. It is a process where the gap — between those who make the decisions and those for whom the decisions are made — is growing by the day, to the point where the two have lost sight of each other.

Nobi is staring at me and I know that not for a moment does he think that the blame rests with these few giant manipulators. He places the responsibility squarely with us, the ones that seem to know and can see what's happening, and choose to do very little about it. What have we done? We have basically surrendered our rites of passage on this earth, and in the process abandoned all our relations.

Then again, hey, why am I thinking of all of this, why am I allowing Nobi to pull me out of my silence and contemplate his agenda, when all that I am after is a perfect moment of peace?

Wait a minute, where is my mind really slipping to here? This is not Nobi's agenda; it's just the wrong time for us to have this conversation.

"Nobi," I address him again. "What's the point of discussing all this when you know the river is coming so very soon? This is not what's important for me now; it's irrelevant at this time, when only a few moments are left," I said, determined to return to the silence I had been drawn away from.

Nobi looks off. "Then what is important to you, man?" he asks me with a tone of disgust.

"Well, to sit in a state of perfect peace, to be totally present in the moment and observe what is happening within me," I answer him meekly.

He is in no hurry to reply, as though wanting to give me time to hear the folly in my own words. "Well, this is what's happening in the present moment, I am here, and I am annoying you, for I won't let you slip into your self-centred world, while you think you are about to embrace eternity; your perceived heroics are pure escapism. Actually, this is what's happening with all of you, you are all sitting and doing nothing while waiting to be swept away. This is not the way, man. Each of you humans comes into this world in order to bring your gift as an offering at the feet of creation. Do you feel totally satisfied that you have offered this beautiful mother all that you can? Have you shared all your gifts and presents with her that you think you have nothing more to give? Or have you surrendered to accepting the shit around you as a reality, like everyone else has done?" he says, shouting into the night with a voice that is losing all patience with this human stupidity sitting by his side. Again he leaves me speechless; actually, this time he floors me.

Nobody has ever presented reality to me in such a way.

In the final analysis, in my last moment in time, what would be the impression that would define the authentic song of my life—my actions in the world or my ability to sit with utter silence in my heart?

I felt so delighted by the fact that my inner universe had found a deep reference point of stillness, that it was the only angle I was using to define my purpose at this juncture; to find the silence within, while readying myself for the coming of the end of time. And now Nobi comes and opens a vast new playing field that I thought I had left behind, yet it is equally relevant to man's quest on earth.

We come on this journey called life to reconnect with the silence, the source we emanate from. At the same time we come to compose a new melody, a fresh song and offer it at the feet of creation. We pray that she receives our offering and that it goes into the big basket of jewels, which paves the way to the new dreaming; cycling through the continuous movements of rebirth.

Life is a paradox, on one side deep silence; on the other we have to make our presence felt and count. We must roar for the jungle to take heed. How will I be remembered once the river comes and sweeps me away? What will people say when they speak of me? He planted a few trees; he understood the folly of the world; he did a law degree, but chose not to practice. He found silence a moment before the river swept him away. What would they say? Would there be a big *wow* in it, or just the ordinary niceties?

And does all this really matter? It does and it doesn't.

If I had a dream and didn't walk it, then it does matter, for I have taken the energy of life yet offered none in return.

If I had a dream and walked it, then I lived and loved and left something in the collective basket. And if I found perfect silence, than that's the dream I may offer to the circle.

Well, I am now ten to fifteen minutes away from being swept away by the current that *is*. Have I walked my dream to its realisation? Did I dream big or was I timid, going for what I thought was possible and risk free? Did I really dare to walk with heart, with my head held high, embracing the magnificence that I am?

Perhaps. I am not really sure, though what I do know is that I would somehow like to feel that I made some sort of difference in this world, that I added something to the lullaby called *life on earth*.

※ ※ ※ ※ ※ ※ ※

I urgently need an answer to this pressing question. I feel I am starting to run out of time. Somehow I sense that, by reliving these times in the desert when I first met Nulla, I might come to a point of clarity. It was a pioneering time for me then, when my soul was breaking the shackles confining it and discovering its wings.

The next morning after the sombre afternoon in Suresh's chai shop, Nulla and I joined Pradip and his family in the morning puja. After feeding the rats and singing the devotional songs, Pradip invited us for breakfast.

We sat in the yard behind the temple enjoying freshly deep-fried flat breads with a chickpea dish. On one side of the courtyard the rats squabbled over the remains of their breakfast, their squeaks not the nicest music to the ears; on the other side the mustard coloured desert shimmered with heat before us. As I watched, I started to understand how one could see an ocean mirage.

Pradip looked at Nulla and me, "I am sure you know the police were here yesterday," he said with a smile on his face.

"Yes, Suresh from the chai shop told us, he was really worried. What was it all about?" Nulla replied with a question. She needed to know if there was anything to be concerned about. She loved being here as much as I did; we both didn't want things to change.

"There is nothing to worry about; they just want some baksheesh[7*] from me, since I am renting you a room without having a guesthouse licence," he said, attempting to put our minds at ease.

"Everything is alright," Shruti joined in on the conversation, and the more they tried to reassure us that all was well, the more I knew that the time to leave was not far off now.

"Never go against your instincts, never," a friend once told me when I first hit the road.

My instincts were telling me that neither Pradip nor Suresh were sharing with us the whole truth. At the right moment I would have to talk this over with Nulla; we would have to leave soon. It was time to make a new dream live, walk through a new doorway. I didn't have a clue where we would go or what we would do; yet I knew that if I sat still long enough, really quietly, a new vision would make itself known.

The moment we got back to our room, Nulla held my hand and looked at me. "You didn't really believe Pradip, did you?"

"Nulla," I looked into her eyes. "It's not that I don't trust him, he probably believes things could turn out alright, still I sense we should leave soon. I am not sure when or where to, and I'd rather we didn't talk about it for a couple of days. Let's just feel what's happening and allow for some guidance to whisper answers into our ears," I said.

"You never like talking about anything, do you?" she said with disappointment in her voice.

"Come on, Nulla, you knew from the moment you met me, I am not big on talking, let's trust. You're the one who taught me how easy it is to trust. I choose to explore the

---

7　　* Baksheesh—bribe.

world through your eyes now. Talking about it is not going to change anything. Why don't you go and enjoy your time with the women, I am off to the house of the dead." I said, picking my flute off the small table.

"Be careful you don't get stuck in their world!" Nulla huffed at me as she left the room without her usual goodbye kiss.

At the burning grounds, the world was as silent and welcoming as always and even the resident dogs had deserted the place in the search of somewhere cooler to hide. Only one cow remained resting under the shade of the big tree, marooned there by the sun's intense heat. It seemed that, every time I entered this place, my being changed its axis point and I crossed the threshold of the body and entered into the world of spirit; a place where answers made themselves known and visions arose. I must have liked the company of the dead, for I felt so peaceful and at home amongst them.

I had lived seven months in the village now. For six of those months I was a silent, weird recluse lost in the desert of my own universe — and the police, well, they didn't even so much as bat an eyelid at my presence. There were a few other foreigners, half a dozen or so, though I noticed most of them only came for a few days, took some photographs and then left. The police knew that I lived at Pradip's temple all this time and, in spite of this, they never really bothered to ask any questions. It was as though I was actually a sadhu, a seeker of truth; and according to their own cultural norms, they offered me the space and respect, which they would give to any local spirit man.

However, the moment I got married and changed my social settings, they suddenly became interested in me. Perhaps they saw it like this; the moment I *disrobed* in their eyes, I lost my immunity and became a man like everyone else. They may have also felt that Pradip had crossed a deeply entrenched line by marrying two foreigners at a

Hindu temple in a sacred ceremony. I wasn't sure if that was the issue, I would somehow have to ask Pradip about it when the time was right.

It did occur to me, though, that as a married man, I was now part of the biggest flock of birds and subject to a new set of embedded rules. I had left the exclusive club of the lone ranger and joined the largest club on earth. For a moment I started to question the wisdom of getting married. Yet I couldn't let that thought linger for too long, as I was married to a beautiful woman whom I loved, and I would have to face the new challenges posed by the outside world as I discovered my new role as a husband within this dance of opposite polarities.

In the years that followed, I began to understand why so many so-called spiritual seekers renounced the world to attain enlightenment.

Living in the world presents us with a constant flow of challenges and we have to face the music. Being in a relationship is like looking in a clear mirror, though it's not easy to see one's self all the time. It's confronting. Living with a woman is by far a greater challenge than retreating to the Himalayas.

In relationships, in love—we have to die. Only then can the true flower emerge and the split dissolve.

And death is scary, really scary, for finally we are called to live . . .

I am about to die. The staggering realisation dawns upon me, that in a few moments I will be no more. I watch the river, my soon to be executioner, building momentum in her flow. Am I ready to die, what am I sitting here for, am I on some sort of suicidal quest? Why was I so peaceful up to now, in such deep acceptance of my impending death?

It strikes me that prior to this moment I had not used the term death for what I am anticipating will take place by the rising of the river. Without the word death ringing in my ears, a term I have been bred and conditioned to fear, I was feeling at peace with the unfolding of events. Thinking of it as a passage, a journey, made me feel comfortable and at ease with the mystery we call death.

Though now as I change the terminology into one of finality, a numbing fear grips me. Is this why we all fear our impending death, for we cannot conceive of being no more? Yet how can anything be finite in a universe graced by infinity and endless possibilities? A universe that transcends forever, for no one has even contemplated or dreamt its end. The more dense and fragmented our beings have become, the more we have grown apart from the multi-layered universe we abide in, and thus we have come to fear the ending of our journey on earth. I can hear my breath again, its soothing sound a balm, calming my sudden panic.

"Nothing ever ends, it just changes." Nobi says, while reassuring me with his nod that he can hear all the inner chatter raging in my mind. His words ring as truth in my soul. My life experience has been to witness continually the law of change. Why would a different law govern death? It's all part of a cycle. The river dies to be reborn again and again and again; am I unlike this mighty river? Does a different law govern my life?

Death could actually be a magical, mystical land, the home of the never-ending. The abode we journey to after our contract on earth is terminated, a transit point, to continue our expedition through infinite galaxies and possibilities. Okay, so maybe death is cool, I do wonder if my spirit will journey in peace or will it be like the wandering souls at the burning grounds, with all their unfinished business and things they wished they did and things they wished they didn't.

Have I completed everything I needed to do and closed all the circles I opened? Have I walked my dream to its realisation and am I left with nothing more to give, no more dreams to walk awake? Do I really have no more songs to sing?

There is no easy or clear answer, still more and more questions. All this talk with Nobi has thrown into the equation a different perspective than just the quest for total inner silence. My state of stellar resolve with where I am heading has been replaced with a new enquiry into the *now*.

Nothing is a coincidence and Nobi's presence is a gift I have to recognize. Of course there is more I can give this world. Then again, do I need to? Is it my destiny to do so?

I often wonder if fate is the way the dice rolls, or a preordained story, written in the records of time and truth. How much choice do we have in it all? Is it my destiny, to sit here by the river with Nobi by my side, or is it a choice I made in a moment in time? Where do destiny and choice overlap? Do we really have free will in our walk through time and space?

Perhaps we can choose our destiny. Still the question remains, could we choose another? I really don't have a clear answer, other than the reflection the river has to offer me.

How much say does she have in her flow? She is continuously connected to the world surrounding her and her flow is affected by a plethora of conditions: the melting of the snow, the rain at its tributaries, the pumping of water, the dams, the sun's evaporation, soil erosion, constant deforestation, the list goes on and on.

And so is our voyage through life affected and charted by a myriad of external affairs which all have their bearings on the flowering of the song within. So maybe I am just part of a movement, being swept along by the wheel of changing seasons, though I can still choose my relationship to *what is*.

I can still choose whether to smile at my fate or curse what it has brought to me. I can choose every moment to be present with life or sit on the fence watching it. This much I know, and this choice is, I believe, where destiny truly finds its meeting point with free will.

❋ ❋ ❋ ❋ ❋ ❋ ❋

Back then, in my lovely home amongst the ever-shifting desert sands, I wasn't contemplating whether it was the hand of destiny that dealt Nulla and me the new set of circumstances we had to face; I just felt, deep below my belly button, that it was time for us to leave. My latest hunch, though, had distracted me for a while from being present with life; I found myself retreating into my shell again and not seeking to relate with Nulla much.

We had been married for almost a month now and life was rolling by like a sweet lullaby. Well, that was up until the moment Suresh told us that the cops were snooping around, asking questions about our presence in the village. From then on, I drifted back to my self-absorbed universe in an attempt to figure out what the next step in life would be, instead of remaining open and accepting that when the moment came, everything would reveal itself to me.

What I discovered as the years passed by was that life, as a rule, doesn't stay idle for long. It always presents a new challenge just when everything seems smooth, as though it again wants to inquire into the present state of our being, confronting us with the question: Do you really think you have found peace . . . okay, let's see how you handle this new challenge?

Life has its own independent wisdom and perfection and is governed by a clear set of principles. There is an impeccable, unshakable law amongst this great chaos. Life will never dish out more than we can handle, yet it will always usher in a new challenge. That is the nature of being on a quest for freedom and once we affirm to the universe our desire to grow and evolve, it gives us the tools to do exactly that. Life plays with us; and yes, at times, it may seem like a bit of a bad joke. However, with the new realities it presents us with, it poses the query: Are we willing to act rather than react? Thus enabling within us the process of self-transformation.

The self will never be transformed whilst living in a status quo.

I withdrew to the solace of the burning grounds during the days, since I really didn't have a plan, nor had I concocted a new dream of where my life with Nulla was heading. I had never really thought beyond living at the rat temple, and now I had to. I needed to talk it over with her. Still, I didn't know what I would say. I sought to have some vision, insight; a story to share with her of where I felt our next step should be before I asked her where her dreaming was at.

A man without a vision is like a river without water. It heads nowhere and quenches no one's thirst. At the same time, I wasn't sure if Nulla fully agreed with me that we had to leave. I sensed she felt I might have been overreacting to the situation at hand.

In the distance, I saw a person approaching over the hazy sand dunes and immediately Kalu, who was sitting by my side, went into a barking frenzy, while she made sure I noticed how good a guardian she was to me. Stroking her gently, I calmed her down; she was my good canine mate. She, like me, enjoyed the peace of the surrounds, which offered solace from the village milieu. She was an old dog and didn't really like much company, animal or human alike. It took Kalu some time to trust me, after sussing me out for a while and with the help of quite a few biscuits, she agreed to form a friendship. She realised we were both after the same thing, the silence and solitude offered outside the centres of human habitation.

As the person got closer I noticed that it wasn't an Aghorie. The man was a local which was an unusual sight; for normally the locals shunned this place for fear of the bad luck they might incur by hanging out with the spirits of the dead.

"Namaste, sir," he folded his hands in front of his heart in a traditional gesture of respectful greeting. "Beto," I motioned him to sit by my side. At first he was hesitant to sit down for fear of Kalu who was still humming and ahhring. I assured him that she was my friend and would cause him no harm.

"Thank you, thank you, sir," he smiled as he took out his handkerchief and neatly made it into a little sitting mat.

He wasn't dressed in the traditional white clothes and turban of the local desert folk; rather he wore the *modern* Indian male fashion of poly-cotton trousers and a collared shirt. I didn't recall seeing him before, then again I was so absorbed in myself in the time before I met Nulla, that I don't think I had registered the faces of more than a handful of locals.

He seemed to know who I was, as most of the locals did. "I have been wanting to talk to you for some time now, sir, you are living in Pradip's temple for long time now, sir," he said.

"You speak good English," I complimented him while attempting to put him at ease as he seemed very nervous in my presence.

"Oh no, not very good, sir though this is what I want to talk with you about. I am the teacher in the village school and I want to ask you if you can come and teach English for the local children and tell them about how life is in foreign countries. They will be very happy if you can do this, you know, only for a couple of hours a day," he said, offering me the insecure smile of one who is not sure what answer to expect, or if it was even right to ask in the first place.

His request left me speechless. I wasn't really sure what to say, though in an instant it occurred to me what a joke life was, a theatre of opposites with its continuous unfolding and ever-changing drama.

A short moment ago I was contemplating leaving this place, while now I was being offered a job. Well, not only a job, more so, a purpose to stay here.

Life is so volatile, moody, we just have to take a step back and pause for a moment, before we push our *will* onto it and it is bound to show us a *way*.

I realised right then what this would actually mean to us. If I taught English in the school, the police would have to look at our presence in the village favourably, for the villagers would be irate if we were harassed in any way. There was something else here, too, something that had been nagging at me for some time now. For seven months I had lived here and in more than one way was supported by the whole community around me. They gave me so much. They gave me a new lease on life and now I had the chance to give something in return.

It dawned on me that everything is in a state of fluctuation; even intuition can be a momentary thing that changes from one moment to another. The last moment's 'gut feeling' is not necessarily this moment's truth. A new intuition was making itself known. The universe was throwing us a lifeline to hang onto if we wanted to stay here. I knew Nulla did; myself, I wasn't sure anymore.

My head was all over the place trying to figure out what the message was in this sudden twist to the story. I knew I couldn't teach these children; I didn't have what it takes to relate to kids—the inner joy and playfulness one needs to captivate the heart and mind of a child. I still needed my aloneness; I couldn't project my darkness onto the happy, innocent souls of these kids.

"I am sorry, sir, I don't think I have what it takes to be a teacher. Still, I know somebody who does," I replied kindly.

His eyes looked a bit surprised. "Who, sir?" he asked with a quiet voice.

"My wife, Nulla. I have a feeling she would love to teach the kids. She is French, she studied two years in England, her English is very good," I said.

So here I was volunteering Nulla without even asking her, *knowing* that she would love to do it. "We don't have to leave anymore," I thought to myself. Life had rolled the dice again with a new number on it. Fate doesn't seem to be a finality inscribed in stone - rather a line drifting with the ever-shifting sands of time.

❋ ❋ ❋ ❋ ❋ ❋ ❋

"There are a few places left on this earth where man doesn't rule the roost, where his heavy foot prints haven't altered the natural rhythm of life." Nobi snaps me out of my past, his voice soft and directed at the river as much as at me. I did affirm to myself that I would give him my full and undivided attention. He is a messenger and a friend sent to me by the forces present behind the veil of mind, a curtain that has been blinding many of us for a long time now.

"When you happen to visit one of these places, what's the first thing you sense, what's your first impression, mate?" He asks me whilst giving his wings a bit of a stretch and flutter. I look back at him, the regal old crow that he is. His piercing eyes set deep in his jet-black face. Slowly he starts to endear himself to me. It feels like I have known him forever; that we have always been by each other's side, even if I only met him a mere ten, perhaps fifteen, minutes ago.

"Silence," I reply. "My first impression when I step into

the marvels of nature is a profound calm."

"That's right, you feel silence, and isn't it amazing, for nothing is quiet there. The birds are chirping, monkeys calling, lizards running around, the leaves rustling, the frogs singing, the rain falling, creeks cascading, the forest is nothing but quiet. And you feel silence, because there is *harmony*, and where there is harmony there is peace.

This harmony is so much missing in the world you guys have created, and ever-present in Great Spirit's world. For in God's world there is no ruler, just all of us sharing a space. Each species takes what they need to live, no more than what they require. There is no greed in the natural world. Greed is a sick human invention born of a mind imprisoned by the shadows of the fear and anticipation of tomorrow."

Nobi speaks what few of us know or are willing to face. Humans have lost their natural instinct, the real natural flow of life, and are running on fear. And where there is fear there is want, and where there is want there is greed. I want this and that and more of this and more of that, way beyond our needs to sustain a happy existence. The result is that life on earth has tilted out of balance.

What have we been doing in recent times to the harmony of life? We have killed a hundred million of our own species in the last one hundred years, in acts of war alone. We are continuing to inflict unimaginable cruelty and suffering on each other and on life on earth. Is life meant to be this loveless, endless toil for material possessions? What good is our ceaseless quest for the *material* if it does not make us happy? If it makes us kill one another and destroy the world we live in? Is there ever an animal, living amongst the majesty of the forest, which is unhappy? Yet our minds have been imprisoned to the point that one million people a year, our brothers and our sisters, commit suicide. We are all depressed, even the children have often stopped smiling. What are we doing that we have even made an old crow come to tears? We used to love life, now we love things!

I often wonder if there is actually a conspiracy to destroy the earth, or is it just pure human stupidity. I feel the latter may be closer to the crux of it, though I am not totally sure. Really, how stupid have we become, are we really that dumb as a collective entity? We are inventing more and more *things* to distract us from the *now* and the still space of *presence* and have completely lost touch with the world around us.

There was a time, not far gone, when kids would find a few stones that were similar in size and play numerous games with them. They would collect these stones and take care of them as though they had found diamonds, treating them as magical articles manifesting many wonderful games.

I can't imagine a kid nowadays in the so-called developed world, being satisfied playing with a mere few stones. From childhood we are led to become gadget junkies, wanting more and more toys to stimulate our senses. In the process, we have killed our sensitivity to the world around us, and the call of the wild.

"Nobi," it's me calling back his attention this time. "What's the use focusing on all this stuff? I agree with you one hundred per cent, do you really see any solution? Do you believe meaningful change is possible? Perhaps there is really nothing else to do other than find the peace within—the unshakable space, untouched by any external circumstance life confronts us with?"

"Look," Nobi sways from one leg to another, giving his wings a bit of a shake before he talks again. "I am not saying to focus on these things; still to be aware is important, so each one of you can choose to take *right action*. And being a positive dynamic force in the world is no contradiction whatsoever to exploring the silence beyond all words, on the contrary it supports it.

More often than not—it is by focusing your attention

outwards — by serving another, you heal yourself. Perhaps too much focus on the self makes it bigger, whereas focusing outwards shrinks its importance. Do you get what I am saying?"

There is a lot of passion in his voice, or possibly he is starting to realise that time is running out.

Something in me wishes that we could just sit by each other's side in silence and await the river, listening to the sounds of the story unfolding around us. It's seems that so often in life we desire a different story to the one present; we wish *things were different*, that the moment should unfold in a different way, and often life has a dissimilar idea from the one held by our ego.

For me, in this moment, a different tale is unfolding by the river than what I originally perceived and put out for. A bird tribal elder is holding his reflection clear beside me, and I somehow still wish the process were different, that I could sit here in silence with nothing to distract me from the presence of the river.

The difference between living or existing seems to be dealing with the challenges life offers us in the moment, as opposed to avoiding them, pretending they aren't there. It's our ability to respond to the moment that defines the quality of our life and the richness of our experience.

Truth is transitory; the moment is real, for the only truth is the moment.

We stayed in our sweet village in the desert for three more months. Nulla spent her mornings teaching in the school, and most afternoons she hung about with some of the village women, who by now had become her circle of friends. During the days I hardly saw her and when we did get to spend time together, her favourite subject was talking about the children. It was another reason why she enjoyed being with the women so much; they would talk endlessly about the kids while doing their traditional crafts. I felt excluded from Nulla's new world.

Some of the women had their own children in the school and treated Nulla like a living Goddess. On her part, Nulla loved what she was doing and could somehow find the uniqueness in each and every one of those children. They were all special to her, individuals with their own unique story to share with the world around them.

"Each child is a universe of its own," she said to me one day when we had our dinner. She felt she had to find the gift in every child and nurture it. She didn't really teach them English; she just loved them and talked to them in English and some French, while at the same time they taught her the local Hindi dialect. Of course as a painter, she went and bought heaps of drawing materials; paper, pencils and crayons, and encouraged the kids to express themselves through art.

Nulla never studied a day beyond her high school graduation; in spite of this, I am not sure if these kids ever had a better teacher. It has nothing to do with what we do, it has everything to do with how we do it and Nulla did it with love, and that love became a song in the children's hearts.

Gradually, I came to realise why I was so afraid of teaching these children — they had to be loved, unconditionally, each and every one of them, and I wasn't sure what this truly meant. I didn't fully love myself.

And maybe unconditional giving comes more naturally to women, while we men still need to learn to cultivate the hidden undertones of the heart.

About a month after she started working in the school, Nulla asked me one evening as we were taking our stroll through the flower gardens, savouring the beauty and aroma emanating from jasmine and roses: "Hey, don't you feel the time is ripe for you to change something. I mean, if you continue to go daily to the burning grounds, you'll eventually turn into a ghost." She wasn't pushing me, neither was there was any frustration in her voice. She was happy, still she knew I wasn't, and it weighed heavily in her heart. Nulla's life was in full bloom; from morning to sundown she was busy with so many things that made her happy.

I had the spirit of the dead to keep me company and the echoes of my own silence. I knew I needed to change, except I wasn't sure in which direction.

I hardly saw Nulla apart from in the evenings and I slowly started to drift back into the grey tunnel of my narcissistic self — my pre-Nulla existence.

"Why don't you come one day and play with the kids in the school, they would love it. You can teach them some woodwork maybe?" she said lovingly, while brushing the hair off my face.

"Nulla, it's a desert here, there is hardly any wood, it's not a skill they need," I answered, proud of the good excuse I had found.

"You are a stubborn man" she replied, "I am sure there is something you can do with the kids. The child spirit will pull you out of the vortex you are in. Why don't you come and play cricket with them?"

"Okay Nulla, I get the point, just let me think about it for a while." I tried to change the subject which was gradually making me uncomfortable.

"Hey, man, you think too much and do too little," she said with a sense of irritation creeping into her voice. Well, that said, I went silent, I wasn't going to continue the conversation and turn it into an argument. An argument I could not win, for I knew Nulla was right.

A couple of weeks later, I finally gathered the courage one morning to join Nulla at the school. "Nulla, I am coming with you to school today," I said with a bit of fear still lingering in my voice. In fact I was petrified and I wasn't sure if I did a good job at hiding it.

"Really?" Nulla jumped on me. "Are you serious or are you just pulling my leg?" She pinned me to the wall and started kissing me all over. "What are you going to teach them?"

"Relax a bit, Nulla, you are over the top. I'm just coming to watch you and see what you are doing, and if I feel comfortable I may play with the kids a bit."

The school was situated halfway between the temple and the village bus stand. It comprised of a big thatched hut with some mats on the floor and a small blackboard. Outside was a sandy yard where the kids would play between classes. There were kids of all ages. The only teacher the school had was Mr Soni, the man who had come to see me in the burning grounds some weeks ago.

It was a poor village, economically poor; nonetheless the people were not desperate. Everybody had enough food to eat and their basic needs were met. It was the kind of poverty that leads to cultural richness. It was a village of smiles. They were not hungry, neither were they overfed.

Often I wondered why it was that poorer, simpler people were so quick to smile and be happy, while the richer and more sophisticated ones always seemed so serious, stiff and tight.

"Good morning, sir, I am very happy to see you here." Mr Soni greeted me warmly on my arrival.

"I am glad to be here," I said, offering him the traditional Namaste greeting. And I was happy. I felt that by going there I had managed to jump over a really high wall that had pieces of glass stuck on top of it to prevent thieves. Of course, the wall was all in my mind, yet that made no difference. More often than not, the walls in our minds are harder to climb than the physical obstacles life presents us with. I still felt a bit apprehensive about how the kids would react to my presence.

Nulla had been volunteering almost every day for six weeks, she talked about the kids all the time, and I felt I had little choice. I had to step beyond my self-created boundaries.

The moment I finally did step into the classroom, a mini riot ensued. In no time, the kids were all over me, wanting to show me their drawings, the special sticks that they played with, their makeshift cricket bats, and so on. Nulla didn't bother introducing me or going through any formalities. They all knew who I was and they wanted to relate instantly.

Mr Soni was responsible for the serious study time and kept the discipline, while with Nulla it was free-playtime, which she somehow managed to control with the magic and love she wove by the total attention she gave to each individual. We drew and wrote letters in English. We played cricket in the yard and built castles in the sand. I laughed and hugged and laughed like I never had before. When it was time for Mr Soni to take over, I hugged each one of the kids while they asked me to come again the next day.

I didn't. Not because I didn't enjoy my time with them, actually I was overjoyed, and my whole being was rocked to the point that I was finally broken.

It took a bunch of simple desert kids four hours to do what I couldn't do for months on end. They did it with the overflowing pure love and boundless joy they shared with me. The children managed to do what I failed to in all the months at the burning grounds. They finally destroyed who I thought I was.

Seeing how much Nulla loved the kids and how easily she related with them, I realised for the first time that we were going to have a family. Nulla was a universal mother. What I didn't know then was that the universe can also be a cruel place, dishing out the most painful of lessons to the purest of hearts.

"Did you enjoy your time today?" Nulla stated the obvious while we were lying in bed that evening. "Nulla, I have never experienced so much happiness in all my life as I did today. The kids are so pure, so present; they have no past, no future, and no questions. They are just there, making the most of every moment. I feel your school kids have floored me. I don't even know who I am anymore. I know I need to change this story with my stupid ego that keeps feeling sorry for itself, maybe I do need to hang out more with kids."

"I love you, still even more than that, I trust in your process." Nulla said as she drifted off to sleep in my arms.

It was her total, unconditional trust that gave me the courage to push my boundaries again and again in the years to come.

❋ ❋ ❋ ❋ ❋ ❋ ❋

What I would do to just touch your love one more time. What I would do to just touch your love again in this life. I would climb the ladder to the stars and above if need be, or swim across the ocean of eternity for the promise of your love. Every morning I wake up with the joy of your love. Every night I go to sleep with the pain of love that has gone wrong.

Where is she these days? I wonder as I stare at the river. It's been months on end since I've seen or heard from her. Does she still trust me unconditionally, or did I somehow fail to sustain that trust? Was I being my best self or did I drift again to hide behind my protective shields when we were last together?

Nobi seems lost in his own world. Perhaps I am betraying his trust as well by not being present with him at this very moment. Is there something I am attempting to conceal from him; like the fact that his words are having a much bigger effect on me than what I am letting him know? It seems that, throughout my life, I have mastered the art of disappearing into my shell and shutting out the world at large, especially in times of uncertainty.

The Sufis believe that as long as we live within the confining walls of the *I* and *me* universe, we merely exist in separation and are controlled by our egos. It's only once we transcend the focus of our world into the *we* and *us* universe that we start to touch the essence of life.

I recall the time when I first arrived at Pradip's temple; how I judged him harshly for his priesthood, especially when he took money from the poor villagers. What I didn't understand then was that Pradip had transcended the separation that was distorting my perception at the time. Pradip did not perceive himself to be disconnected from the villagers in any way whatsoever. He never asked them for anything and would offer the same prayers for the ones who gave him money and the ones who didn't. When they made an offering to him, he received it with a smile and thanksgiving, thus supporting the universal vibe of giving and receiving. He once told me that if he refused an offering, he would be offending the giver as if questioning the spirit and integrity behind their generosity.

The world is a cycle and the more we give, the more we eventually receive. Therefore, by accepting with grace, we support the giver to be a generator of abundance on planet earth — all hands together in a deep embrace.

✳ ✳ ✳ ✳ ✳ ✳ ✳

Sitting at the burning grounds one morning, I realised that the time had come to leave. Every cell in my body buzzed with that knowledge. Nothing was wrong, neither was there a problem with the police; on the contrary, things were going really well. I went to the school a couple more times and had as much fun as I did the first time. I helped Pradip give a fresh coat of paint to the temple's courtyard and made some new flowerbeds in the garden for more jasmine and roses to be planted in the coming monsoon, which was now just around the corner. I played my flute a lot and generally pulled myself out of the hole I was stuck in. Nulla worked at the school for those months and her enthusiasm was as high as ever.

Then again, this is the time to leave; when life is on a high. Leave because it's the call of the moment, not because life has become unbearable. Life is so good; overflowing with deep contentment, yet the calling has come to walk into a new experience to further our growth.

After living in the village for ten months I finally felt that I needed a change; my spirit required me to face new challenges. I wasn't sure how I would relate this to Nulla or how she would react.

The police not only accepted us being there, they had even visited Nulla at the school one day to give their blessings to her work. The village was a warm home full of love and acceptance for both of us. However it was still time to go, I *knew* it, I felt it in my body.

When Nulla had finished work at school I went to meet her outside the classroom and shared with her where I was at. To my surprise she accepted it with a smile, "I understand. I feel we stayed these extra three months for me. You were probably ready to leave when I had just arrived. It's okay, I am happy to go. Have you thought where you would like to go next?" she asked while looking at some of the children's drawings she held in her hand.

"Well, I still haven't taken you for our honeymoon to a deserted palace, why don't we do that?"

She smiled, leaning her head on my shoulder, "I would love it; it's your call. You make the plans, I am just coming," she said.

There was no actual strategy; I was always really lacking in the planning department. "I thought we'd take the night bus to the capital of the state and from there I heard it's another three hours' drive to an old deserted castle on a hill, overlooking a vast desert tract," I said.

"Cool, I'll let them know at school tomorrow, and you better break the news to Pradip." With that said, Nulla left to meet the women in their craft circle. I wasn't really sure if she was happy with it, or if she was just putting on a brave face for me. Her life in the village was full of so much purpose.

Two days later, we held a big party at the school. Everybody was there; Pradip, Shruti, Suresh, Govinda, the mothers of the children, some of the fathers, and, of course, all the kids. We hired a caterer to provide a feast for everybody and we decorated the hut with balloons, colour strings and drawings. When lunch was over the tears started to flow with the goodbyes. We both cried and cried and cried as each kid came and hugged us with tears in their eyes.

Pradip came over and sat by my side. He was in a quiet mood, unusual for him. He handed me a big envelope and hugged me. "You know, Baba, we will never forget you, everybody in the village — even the people you never met. You and Nulla changed something in this village," he said. I gave him a big, big hug.

"And this village has changed us too, especially you, Pradip, you are like a father to me now." I replied in a choked voice.

"I hope you and Nulla don't forget us and come to visit soon with your children," he smiled, squeezing my cheeks as though I was a little boy.

In the late afternoon we walked to the bus stand with Pradip. When we passed Suresh's chai shop, I greeted him warmly and put my hands around his shoulders. "Last chai, Suresh," I said.

"No last, Baba; never say last, you will have many more chai here another time," he said, visibly upset, not bothering to hold his feelings back. I loved Suresh, he was a true friend; the type of mate that would do anything for you once his heart had met yours.

We drank the chai in silence, all of us too emotional to talk. I handed Suresh money for the drinks, he refused any payment for the chai and just left his shop to join Pradip and us on the walk to the bus stand.

Arriving on the old desert road where the buses stop, I couldn't believe my eyes. All the kids where standing there as a sort of guard of honour shouting out, "Nulla and Baba zindabad! Long live Nulla and Baba!" and waving their hands in excitement. I laughed my head off and was moved to tears at the same time. It was the type of chant you heard usually in political or patriotic marches.

A couple of the girls put garlands of marigolds around our necks, and then came another surprise. The kids handed us a little wrapped box. "This is, so you will never forget us."

Nulla hugged the little girl who handed her the gift, while I could see she was holding back a river of tears, ready to burst into a torrent. "We will never forget you, never," she assured the little girl, while stroking her hair.

We all sat on the sand together—Suresh, Pradip and the kids—and played games together for two hours until the bus finally arrived. Before boarding, Pradip held my hand and looked into my eyes. "When you feel life is too much to handle, too challenging, always remember that there are people with greater suffering than your own, and they still know how to smile. Always keep in mind how lucky you really are."

"We will return soon, Pradip." I looked at him, while really reassuring myself.

I didn't know then that we always have one plan and life has another, and it would be many years before we would return to visit the jasmine and roses field in the desert.

We took a seat at the back of the bus, while Pradip boarded the vehicle to have a chat with the driver and the conductor. He basically ordered them to take good care of us.

When the bus finally left, we kept waving until the lights of the village disappeared out of sight. We then collapsed into each other's arms and sobbed uncontrollably.

❋ ❋ ❋ ❋ ❋ ❋ ❋

It took me many years to appreciate what a profound influence Pradip had on my life, what an evolved and supportive person he really was.

And possibly, only now by the river, at what seems to be the end of the road, I at last recognize what Pradip really did for me.

In many ways he was my guru, guide, guardian angel in a phase when I most needed support. Pradip was my host during one of the most difficult times in my life. In the many months I lived in his temple I was like a wandering lost ghost. I didn't talk; at times I didn't eat, on other occasions I never slept. I hung out where most locals dreaded to go, and associated at times with people they considered black magicians, and feared.

Yet he never, not once, interfered with my process. He could have said to me many a time things like "snap out of it," "get a grip on yourself," or could have offered me some sort of advice on how to change myself. He was wise enough not to do so.

All he ever did, and that *all* was the universe for me, was hold the space for me to change. He put a ring of protection around me, a circle of love, while trusting in universal intelligence that I could sort it out myself. Nobody had ever given me such deep unconditional trust before and that trust opened to me a universe of possibilities — to choose to be who I truly was, rather than drift into the flock of sheep, walking blindly down the road of life.

When we walk with our eyes closed, as a cog in the machine, taking the word of others to be gospel, we take every day a step closer to death.

When we open our eyes, to the way of the warrior, the finder, the brave-heart, we walk with a sense of responsibility and awe, which in turn guides us every moment closer to life and eternity.

Isn't it amazing what transpires when, instead of being told that what we are doing is wrong and destructive, we are guided in silence with love and trust. It works like magic, where all *proper* guidance is sure to fail.

Freedom and trust are the cornerstones of love. Yes, at times even the freedom to destroy ourselves, if this is what we need to do, to learn a lesson in life. For a phoenix rising from the ashes will fly high on the air currents of infinity.

Two hours after we boarded the bus it stopped at a roadside *dhaba* so that the passengers could have dinner and chai. The journey to the capital would take around twelve hours and this was the last food stop for the night.

The bus was packed way past its capacity with people

sitting in the aisle on top of their belongings and scrambling for every inch of free space. The vehicle itself felt like it was from another era, a bygone time, long ago. Not one glass window was still in place and only the iron bars remained.

The view inside the bus was a feast to the eye - colour and ancient beauty; as the desert folk, woman and man alike, were loaded with an exquisite array of ornamentation for the world to see. Most nomadic and semi-nomadic people wear their wealth on their bodies, especially the women.

The men wore their traditional coloured turbans, which comprised of eleven metres of brightly dyed fabric rolled on their heads. The women were adorned with magnificent massive skirts in different patterns and colours according to their village or group. Each one of them had thick silver bracelets on both, hands and ankles, the latter draped with jingling bells that tinkled with every step they took.

Consequently, when the people alighted from the bus and sat by the old wooden tables to order their dinner, they attracted everybody's attention. There was no roof to the *dhaba*[8]+, apart from where the kitchen was, so the night desert sky shone its light on the diners.

The chapatti[9]# maker was working full power, rolling one after another, sticking the flat round pieces of dough inside the hot tandoor. The tandoor was made from a 44-gallon drum lined with clay. For most, dinner was dhal and chapattis with some ordering extra dishes of vegetables. It was a striking array of humanity, reminiscent of a time when grace, beauty and valour dotted the desert sands. Above us, the magical night wove its spell, as all nights do under the immense desert sky.

Both Nulla and I weren't really hungry; we were still overwhelmed with emotion, fragile and tender with the sensation of leaving our *home*.

---

8   + Local restaurant.

9   # Indian flat bread.

We ordered chai and walked a short distance away from the crowd, to enjoy the scene and smoke a biddi.[10]* We sat in silence on the soft sand gazing at infinity in the sky above us, pleading with the stars to grant us some solace and soothe our delicate emotional state. Nulla's eyes were still red and moist from the overflow of sentiment she felt. We had left our home and really we didn't have a clue what to do or where life would take us next. In truth, I wasn't even sure if the palace one of the villagers had told me about really existed, or if it was just a figment of his imagination.

About half an hour later, the driver boarded the bus, turned on the engine and started to honk the horn with great energy and impatience. We boarded the bus again and took our seats in the back, while the passengers who hadn't finished their dinner, cursed the driver while scrambling to eat their food, pay the bill and get on the bus. Ten minutes later, once the conductor made sure all passengers were present, we set off into the night.

After driving for some time, I noticed more and more vegetation as the desert slowly made its way into more fertile country. Nulla was already asleep with her head on my shoulder, while I was lost in memories of my life in the village. The burning grounds, Kalu my dog friend, the rats, Suresh, Pradip my mentor and friend and the intoxicating aromas drifting in the nights from the jasmine and rose gardens. It was such a blissful existence, an actual dreamtime which had come to an end. Where would life take us from here? Why did we really choose to leave? I wondered, as I too drifted into dreams, whilst resting my head on Nulla's.

It must have been some hours later that I woke up to a commotion taking place; the bus was stuck in what appeared to be a massive traffic jam. People were screaming

---

10 * Hand-rolled Indian cigarette using leaf instead of paper

and shouting while the sound of explosions echoed in the distance. Some people were running frantically around with burning torches in their hands.

I woke up Nulla, who usually could sleep through anything, and grabbed both our bags down from the luggage rack. Half the passengers were already off the bus and running into the night. People were banging on the bus with large bamboo sticks telling us, or rather threatening us, to leave the bus at once. "Hurry, get off fast!" I heard a passenger who had just jumped from the bus yelling at us as he ran off into the night. We held onto our bags and one another and managed to push our way out.

Once off the bus, we looked at each other in utter bewilderment as to what was happening. We didn't have time to be afraid or to register what was actually taking place. In the distance I noticed the bright yellow of mustard fields and we chose to run in that direction. With no time for words, I pulled at Nulla's shirt and off we shot, clambering with our packs as fast as we could.

Once we reached the fields I heard a big explosion. Looking back, I saw that our bus was on fire. I also noticed that Nulla's face was bleeding. "Are you all right Nulla?" I asked her while we kept on heading into the dark, deeper into the fields.

"Yeah, I think it's okay, it's just a cut from a bit of glass from the front windscreen of the bus, I guess. Let's get the hell out of here and then have a look at my face," she said in a whisper, so as to not attract attention to us.

We half walked, half ran for another ten minutes before, unexpectedly, we heard a voice calling out to us in English from the shadows of the night. "Are you foreigners over there?" I looked at Nulla, wondering if it was wise to reply.

"Yes! What's happening here?" she asked the voice in the dark.

"I'll tell you the story later. We have to get further away. There is big trouble in the air, just follow me." A figure of a man appeared and he signalled to us to come towards him.

"My wife is injured, we have to stop for a moment," I said. He walked over towards us from where he was hiding in the dark and we both inspected Nulla's face. There was a cut, though it wasn't deep. I grabbed a t-shirt out of my bag and got Nulla to hold it against her face to stop the bleeding.

The man spoke very good English and had a worldly manner about him. He must be an educated city man, I thought. "We have to continue walking," he urged us again. I took Nulla's bag off her shoulders and we followed the stranger into the night.

We must have walked for at least a couple of hours before the first signs of dawn announced the impending arrival of day. I felt utterly wasted; having carried both our bags while Nulla nursed her wound. I asked the man if we could stop and have a rest and he assured me we would do so soon.

After some time we came across a big tree in a field and he decided that it was finally time for us to stop and rest. I was glad to have the two bags off my aching shoulders. I had one litre of water with me and we all shared a drink, after which I inspected Nulla's face again, there was a deep cut on her forehead and a superficial one on her nose, the one on the forehead was deep enough to leave scar. We used the rest of the water to wipe the dry blood off her face and clean the cut. We were all too tired to talk or ask questions. We spread out our shawls and lay beneath the tree for a rest.

The sun was already high in the sky when I opened my eyes and saw the man talking with three young kids. He said something to them and they ran off. "Good morning, did you have a good rest?" he greeted me, with a warm smile on his face. He must have been in his mid-forties, of medium build with short greying hair. He looked like a good man. He wore black-rimmed thick glasses and his eyes had the appearance of those that had spent a lot of time reading.

"I sent the kids to get us some chai, biscuits and water. There is a village about two kilometres away, they should be back in an hour or so," he said.

"Thank you," I replied. I still wasn't sure if it was the right time to ask him what was happening, maybe I should wait until Nulla woke. She was still curled up in deep sleep.

"Did I make a mistake by leaving the village, my heavenly abode amongst the rats?" I wondered. "Is this some sort of weird sign? Is God playing some dirty trick on us? We are supposed to be on our honeymoon now, not running away from a riot and a burning bus!" I felt dejected by the hand dealt to us from the deck of cards in the relentless game called life. In our first journey together I failed to fulfil my role as husband and protect my wife, one of the duties Pradip spoke of clearly when he married us in the temple. It was a vow I spoke out loud at the wedding; that I would always ensure no harm would come my wife's way. "Will the scar that Nulla may carry forever on her forehead, be a constant reminder of my shortcomings as a husband?"

I got up and walked a short distance to have a piss. We were in the middle of a mustard field and the beautiful shades of yellow wove patterns like a big Persian rug. In the far distance I noticed rolling green hills thick with tree cover. It was so different to our village in the desert. The signs of life created a different symphony here. Nature had a different story to tell, the song had more words infused in the music. I watched our friend collecting some sticks for a fire, and went for a little roam to stretch my aching body and forage for something to burn as well.

When I returned to the tree, our friend had already lit a small fire and Nulla was gone. "Where is my wife?" I asked him.

"She went to find a place to go the toilet, she must be somewhere in the field." I put the sticks down by the fire and folded my shawl, my nostrils acclimatizing to the smell and taste of green for the first time in a while. The desert offers a different scent than that of green fields; it doesn't tickle the nostrils.

Nulla returned and we all sat together around the small fire, allowing the flames to tell their story and calm us from the events of the night before.

"My name is Rahul," the stranger joined his hands in a traditional greeting. I introduced myself to him and so did Nulla. We felt comfortable in his presence; still, I wasn't sure what to make of him.

"So, I suppose you want to hear the story of what took place last night?" he said.

"We sure do," I answered him while adding a couple of branches to the fire.

"Well, it's basically a story that has been told countless times throughout the makings of HisStory. It's the chronicle of exploitation and abuse of the poor and vulnerable by the rich and powerful." He talked slowly in a calm voice laced with conviction; a voice of a man who knew his dream and was walking in its direction.

"Some years ago, the government had decided to dam the river. Tribal people inhabit most of the rolling hills you see in the far distance; these hills lead to the river. The tribal people here are called Adivasis. They are the most marginalised people of this country, with few rights and no political voice. In fact, this is the untold story of India, its hidden dark shadow. India has the biggest tribal population in the world and everybody in power wishes they would just disappear into thin air. What the world doesn't realise is that there is an ongoing revolution taking place on over twenty-five precent of India's land mass. People are seeking a redress to the wrongs done to them." He paused for a moment, allowing us time to absorb his words. He wanted us to really *hear* what he was saying.

"Of course the tribal people oppose the dam because

182

it will flood their lands and displace them from their ancestral homes. They have held a non-violent campaign against the building of the dam for three years now, and nobody is paying attention to their plight. Yesterday, they held a big march at the district headquarters. There must have been at least two hundred thousand people. The march was peaceful until the police attacked the protestors with bamboo sticks. Many were injured and some of the protestors started fighting back with stones, sticks and anything they could get their hands on. The protesters outnumbered the police and so, fearing for their lives, the police started shooting at the protestors. Four people were killed." Rahul stopped talking for a while as though he was offering the dead respect with his silence.

"When the bodies were brought back to the tribal villages later in the evening, their grief turned into anger. In India, when people are angry with the government, they set out to destroy government property. So they went out in large numbers to the highway to stop the government vehicles and burn them. The bus you were travelling on was most likely a government bus, therefore a target," he said.

"So why did we have to get so far away from there?" I asked him.

"You know when a man is angry he doesn't recognise friend from foe. Also the police were sure to arrive, and they would just start to shoot into the night at anything that moved or made a noise. The bullets of those old British guns travel a long way."

We looked up and could see in the distance the children returning. They held a metal container full of chai, three clay cups, two packets of biscuits and a bundle of puries[11*] with a handful of sugar to sprinkle over them, wrapped in newspaper. They also brought us a container of water. Rahul invited the kids to sit with us while he poured the

---

11   * Fried Indian flat bread.

chai into the clay cups. They were shy, though; it was surely the first time that they had ever met foreigners in the flesh, and preferred to watch these ghost lookalikes from a safe distance.

We were all ravenous with hunger and got stuck into our breakfast with gusto. The chai was sweet, maybe the sweetest I had ever tasted. It was basically a breakfast of sugar, which we all enjoyed and probably could have eaten more of, had the food not run out so quickly.

Rahul got up and said something to the kids; he then looked back at us. "I am going to the village with the kids to see if they have any news of what's happening and I'll return soon. You guys just relax for a while, you're safe here."

That said, he took off with the children while we stayed beneath the tree in the mustard field, looking at each other, not sure what to make of it all. We moved away from the fire and sat down, leaning on the big tree while stretching our tired legs. "So is destiny having its upper hand over our free will?" I wondered. "What are we doing here caught in a conflict that has nothing to do with us, when what we had intended to do was go on a peaceful honeymoon to celebrate our love and discover a new path. Does life always have to play jokes on us? Is the saying, 'The gods laugh when they hear our plans' really true?"

I looked at Nulla and gently stroked her face. "I am really sorry it turned out like this. This is not how I envisioned our honeymoon," I said softly.

She rested her hand on my leg, "Don't be silly, what are you talking about? You are not responsible for this mess. And anyway, let's see what this is all really about," she smiled; reassuring me that she was ok.

"Hey, do you have the envelope Pradip gave you?"

"Yes, I think I do, it was in my small shoulder bag." I got up and walked over to the bags, the envelope was still there. I opened it; it was some sort of certificate just like the one a doctor hangs in the waiting room of his surgery. I showed it to Nulla. It was in Hindi and we both couldn't read the language. "It looks like an honorary citizenship of the village or something like that," I laughed with her. "After your work in the school, you definitely earned a special place in their hearts," I said affectionately.

"Hey, they love you as much as they love me, for different reasons — the same love."

Nulla knew that there was a lingering feeling nagging me from within that I took more than I gave in my time in the village. We had talked it over a few times. She tried to reassure me that my presence in the village offered something special to the locals, just my way of being a unique individual. Myself, I still wasn't sure exactly what I gave them or how I made the village richer by my presence. Perhaps I had to put aside my pragmatic mind for a moment. Possibly we can give in many ways and perhaps giving is not always a tangible act. It could be that at times we give just by being totally who we are in the moment.

My life had changed so radically in the months since I'd met Nulla, that gradually I'd become interested in the world around me. I was concerned how that world felt and what my relationship to it was. Whatever change had taken place; I did endeavour to make my presence on this earth a more meaningful one. I had no idea how to go about it, though I intended to find a way.

In the distance I could see Rahul's silhouette moving towards us. I wondered what news he was going to bring. However, the first thing I wanted to know was what was this piece of paper that Pradip had given me?

"It's a marriage certificate," he said, while holding up the document with the cheeky smile of a village announcer. "It states the day and the time of the moon, which you were married in, and the priest who wed you. Did you get married in India? That's so cool. I knew there was something special about you guys the moment I noticed you." He looked at us with great joy in his eyes.

"Yes, we got married four months ago, in a desert village, at the Karni temple." Nulla answered him with pride in her voice. I never knew Pradip recorded our marriage with the registrar in town. He didn't even tell us. The more I thought of him since we left the village, the more I loved and missed him.

"Congratulations!" Rahul kneeled over to shake our hands, trying to be humorous, although it didn't come to him naturally.

"You are the first foreigners I've met who have tied the knot in this way, I can sense a bit of the rebel in both of you. That's good; you will need this energy in the days to come." Over time, I would understand better why he liked the rebel aspect he saw in us, and that maybe, just maybe, it was the main reason why he endeavoured to cultivate a friendship with us.

"So what is the news, Rahul? When can we go back to the highway and continue on our journey?" I asked.

He was not quick to answer or maybe he was just unsure what to say. "Well, they heard on the radio that there are clashes between the protestors and the police on the road, still. That's all we got, no more details," he said.

I wasn't sure if he was telling the truth, and my trust in him was far from complete, he was a stranger after all. I felt it was time to get out of there.

"Could you give us directions to the highway and we will start walking back," I said with determination.

"I don't think it's a good idea. Emotions are volatile everywhere at the moment and the police might even think that you are supporting the protestors. We need to go to Nandini, which is a few hours walk that way. It's a small village, which serves as the headquarters of the struggle against the dam. In a couple of days, after things quieten down, somebody there will walk you back to road." he said, while getting up and gathering his small cloth bag.

"Hey, wait a minute, man! I am not sure we are coming with you. There is something I don't like here, something doesn't smell right." I said, in defiance of the leadership role he had assumed over us.

"And what is it, sir? What doesn't feel right for you?" he said smiling.

"Well, this is not our story and never will be, and every step we take with you is a step in the opposite direction from where we are going," I said.

He was a very patient man, this Rahul, and he wasn't perturbed by the anger I was displaying towards him. Rather, he sat down again and continued to talk softly. "That's what I used to think too; that unless something wasn't directly related to me, then it wasn't my story. Then again, life has taught me that everything that takes place on this earth is somehow my story and is related to me. That's the reason I left a successful business in Delhi to support these tribal people, to give a voice to the voiceless. It may appear to be their struggle, yet it's not only theirs—the struggle is ours, all of us; every human being who cares for life on earth. If you want to go back to the road, I cannot stop you, though honestly, I don't feel it is safe at the moment," he concluded, leaving the decision up to us.

I looked to Nulla for a clue of what to say or do; she ignored me. She always did this when it was time for a hard decision; it was her way to make me stand in my power. I knew though that if I moved in a direction that she didn't like or trust in, she would step in and stop me with all her power.

My head was in a spin: "Do we go with Rahul or return to the road?" Each direction was an unknown and fraught with danger.

I walked over to my bag and picked it up. "We are coming with you, Rahul, it would be nice to spend a couple of days in a tribal village, we are due for a new experience," I said.

Nulla smiled. It was what she wanted to hear, so did Rahul.

With the passage of time, I would understand that the decision I made that day in that mustard field, gave our lives something which is called a greater purpose. My free will met my destiny again and they danced in perfect symmetry.

❋ ❋ ❋ ❋ ❋ ❋ ❋

"If you reach a junction in the road, and you are not sure which way to choose, always walk the direction of your biggest fear," a wise grandmother advised me some years ago. I am not sure if I was aware of it that day with Rahul and Nulla, in truth, both directions held their share of uncertainty and trepidation. There was one difference, though. If I chose to go to the road where we left the bus, I would have been tracing my steps backwards. And I had never liked that notion since I was a kid, so I chose to walk forward.

I gaze at the river. Seldom do her waters turn backwards and even when they do retreat, it's just for a brief moment before she turns again in the direction of the great ocean. Often when we walk back on our tracks we negate life the opportunity of unfolding in all her colours. Water never stops in its movement – it just alters its course at times. When it reaches an obstacle, it finds a way to flow around it and continue on its journey with the least friction possible.

Nobi is silent and still; it's as though he is completely oblivious of my presence. I want to tell him that I love him and cherish his company by my side at this juncture of life — at the same time I am not sure I know how to do so.

How many times in life did I want to tell people that I love them and didn't? How many times have I left words and feelings unsaid and unexpressed? Would my spirit yearn to descend back to earth after my death to deal with all my unfinished business? Some of it can never be said again, for time has vanquished the moment long ago.

Never, ever miss an opportunity to say that you love, for regret is the mother of sorrow and leaves a bitter taste that lingers in the mouth for a long time.

Never miss a chance to give thanks and praise, for in the process you praise creation herself and all life manifest.

The ripples in the river are reflecting the light of the moon and stars above, millions of small sparkling lights dancing on her waters. It is the language the river speaks as she offers her thanksgiving to the force that nurtures her life.

The brilliance of life unfolds whilst paying equal attention to all things big and small. It is this awareness that defines our being, and shifts the matrix of life from an ordinary one to a profound walk on earth. It's the spontaneous smile on an evening walk at the stranger crossing our path that could change their lives forever and definitely transforms ours. So often we tend to miss the *little things* that cross our path, for we are so lost in the confinements of our small worlds.

It is in one of these almost unnoticeable subtleties that we could find the key that opens the doorway to infinity.

A warrior holds no special magical powers. What characterises her is her total *presence* with life.

It was late afternoon when we had our first glimpse of the river. We must have been on the move for four to five hours without saying a word. We walked by the side of rice and sugar cane fields and along irrigation canals. On the way, we passed two small villages and in both we stopped for a drink of water and a short break. Rahul exchanged niceties with the locals, and probably asked them for news about the situation, before we continued on our way.

She flowed there, nestled amongst the rolling green hills, a deep blue body of water, snaking her way through a narrow valley. The mosaic of colours was breathtaking. The desert always seemed to project itself through the numerous shadows of red, while the aura of the river embraced all imaginable shades of blue green grey and brown.

The hills visible in the distance were adorned with all possible modes of green, with the gentle early evening light sparkling in their midst. Amongst the finely crafted terraces along the hillsides were shades of yellow, white, pink, golden brown and more, all reflecting the colours of the different crops planted and the few wild flowers still in bloom in the pre-monsoonal heat. The valley and adjacent hills reflected a pictorial dreamtime of lushness. If God asked you to create a Garden of Eden, She would surely send you to this place for inspiration.

We stopped to take a rest and savour the enchanting views. No words could ever describe the beauty that emanated from the perfect natural harmony of colours and contours. It was nature on song.

"We should reach the village of Nandini in an hour or so." Rahul spoke after a while as he sat down to rest his body against a rock.

"Have you heard of the Ganga?" he asked us.

"Yes, of course we have, is this the Ganga?" Nulla asked him in excitement.

"No," he smiled back. "However, as you may know, according to Hindu belief if you bathe in the Ganga, you cleanse yourself from past karma and receive a blessing. This beautiful river is not the Ganga, the locals call her Devi, which means 'Goddess' and according to legend you only need to set your eyes on her to get blessed. The flow of this sacred river is being destroyed by the forces of modernity and greed." There was no anger or frustration in his voice, just a stating of the facts. "Anyway, for me all rivers are sacred and should be treated with the same respect and reverence." I wasn't sure what to say, or if I had to say anything. I just stared at the mesmerising view in front of me and savoured the moment.

What I didn't know then was this moment spelt the beginning of a long relationship with the River Goddess, wherever she is present on this earth, a relationship that would see me face the eyes of death on the banks of another holy river, so many years later.

"Rivers are like the blood vessels of the earth. They nurture her body and sustain her life as they flow freely through her in numerous shapes and forms." Rahul spoke again. "We all know what happens when the flow of blood is blocked in our bodies even for a few moments. Why do we think we have the right to do this to Mother Earth?" he said.

"So why are they building the dam?" I asked him.

"Well, we'll have plenty of time to talk about it all later. Now we better get going if we want reach the village before dark." He got up and started walking off slowly; we gathered our packs and followed him along the narrow trail.

It was pitch black when we finally reached the village. Some people came and greeted Rahul and he walked away with them, engrossed in passionate conversation. They seemed taken aback by our presence and I wasn't sure if we were welcome there. We took our packs off and sat on top of them, watching the scene around us.

The place was a hive of activity, like some sort of scout camp. There were people sitting in circles talking, while others were preparing food in huge pots under a makeshift tarpaulin roof. The place was lit with kerosene lanterns, oil lamps and by the odd fire. There was obviously no electricity in the village, and the smell of smoke was felt everywhere; a sweet smell of fire lit by good dry hardwood from the forest. A few people stood and stared at us for a moment or so with a sense of bewilderment, yet nobody approached us, as they seemed to have more important things to take care of. There was a sense of purpose in these people's eyes, the fire you see when people are united and connected to a power greater than their egos; eyes that have seen through the veil of separation and into the heart of unity.

Around half an hour later Rahul returned with a grim look on his face. "You will have to wait here for some time, while the people decide if you can stay. You see this is the headquarters of the struggle and, therefore, could be the target of a police raid soon. Some people are concerned that if the police or media find you here, there will be talk that the anti-dam movement is a foreign conspiracy to block *development* in India," he said.

"What?" I snapped back at him. "What are you saying exactly, Rahul? We walked all the way here with you and now we have to walk all the way back at night?" I felt the fire inside me rising. I was furious with him. "Why are we here?" I wondered, "I mean if the police catch us we will be deported. Fuck the dam and the foreign conspiracy story, that's their story, our story is our honeymoon," I thought on the inside.

"Don't worry," he assured me, unfazed by my aggression again. "I am sure Shanti will come up with a wise solution."

"Who the hell is Shanti?" I continued with my rage.

"Shanti is our leader and our inspiration. She was a professor at a university before she quit and came to support the tribal folk in their struggle. She is the voice of the movement and the mother of our vision. Shanti is guided by the ideas and teachings of Mahatma Gandhi and in turn she inspires us. She is one of the main reasons why I am here. Her living example gave me the courage to leave the rat race and change the paradigm of my life. Come with me, I will show you a nice place where you can sit comfortably and rest while we talk the situation over in our circle," he said with a calm voice and a smile on his face.

I was going to say something to him, but before I could, Nulla grabbed my hand and stroked it gently in an attempt to pacify my growing anger.

Rahul took us to a shelter by the riverbank, it was a makeshift thatched roof supported by a few poles without any walls. "Sit and enjoy the river, I will be back soon with some news," he said and rushed off, as though he wanted to leave before I could say anything more.

"Everything will be alright," Nulla said as we stretched our legs and looked at the water.

"That's what you always say, Nulla, even when things aren't," I grumbled.

"Well, isn't it better to put out a good vibration to the wind, so goodness may return, rather than fill the air with stress and worry? Come on, man, they are good people here. Let's trust that whatever happens is for our best." Nulla expressed optimism in every situation, even when she didn't really believe in what she was saying. It was her way of dealing with stressful circumstances, and most of the time it worked.

The night was warm and temperate and we were both utterly exhausted. The river was quiet and it looked as if she was standing still. I could not detect any movement in the water. A while later a woman came over with two cups of chai. She couldn't speak a word in English. She proceeded to put down the two cups and said something I did not understand; she offered us a shy smile and left. The chai was good. It actually wasn't the normal chai we were accustomed to, rather some sort of sweet herbal brew. We drank it in silence and then went to freshen ourselves up in the river. We didn't bathe; we just splashed enough water on our faces to take some of the dust and sweat off.

"Nulla, I am really exhausted, we both are. Why don't we

spread our shawls out to have a rest and when Rahul comes back, he can wake us up and tell us what's happening. We will need all the rest we can get if we have to walk all night again." I didn't wait for her reply. I opened my bag to get my shawl and a couple of shirts to use as a makeshift pillow.

Lying down with the stars twinkling through the thatched roof I didn't know what to feel. There was a void inside me. I wasn't angry anymore with Rahul; neither did I know if we would be back on the road in an hour or so. Nulla lay by my side holding my hand and before we could say a word to each other we were both in deep sleep.

Feeling a hand stroking my face I woke up. Nulla was sitting by my side with her hand on my forehead. I was shivering cold, though the night air was warm. A thick silence permeated the night. The entire village seemed to be fast asleep. There was no light to be seen anywhere, just a few trails of smoke reaching for the sky. The night was lit with the stars and their reflection in the water. I was covered with Nulla's shawl. "You have a fever, you've been shivering for some time now," she said to me in a whisper. All of a sudden I realised I was totally drenched in sweat.

All this time in India, I'd never been sick. The food and water seemed to suit me and I didn't have go through some of the body trials and tribulations that other foreigners often had to endure. Except now I felt sick as a dog. My body started shaking uncontrollably. Nulla grabbed the shawl I was resting on and covered me with it also. I was thirsty, I needed a drink of water and we had none. "Nulla, I need to drink something, my throat is hot and dry," I said pleading with her. She looked at me with deep care and a tinge of fear visible in her eyes.

"I'll have to leave you for a moment and go and look for some drinking water. I don't know where I'll find some, I'll have to wake somebody up, it feels like everyone is asleep," she said. She took a big skirt out of her bag and laid it over the shawls; I needed all the warmth I could get.

A while later Nulla returned with three people. One of them was Rahul. She found somebody awake and, although they didn't understand what she was saying, they could feel the alarm in her voice. They went over to wake up Rahul — by now everybody knew he had brought the two foreigners with him. After giving me a drink of water, Rahul asked me how I was feeling.

"I feel shit; I don't know what's happening."

He gently laid his hand on my forehead. "You have a fever; it must be from the exhaustion of walking all day in the sun. You could also be sun-stroked. I will get a mattress for you and some more blankets and in the morning the village healer will have a look at you." He said something to the two men that stood by his side and they went off back to the camp. "You will be all right, don't worry," he reassured me with his ever warm-hearted voice. "I came earlier in the night to see you and bring you some food, however you were both deep in sleep." he said, while looking at Nulla, as I did too at that instant. I could see she was worried, and as always she somehow managed a smile. I learned with time that Nulla would never, ever, express worry or fear; somehow she would always manage to mask it with a smile, denial, or a positive word. Perhaps it was her unique way of dealing with fear, and I've learned to respect and love her for it.

About fifteen minutes later the two men returned with a thin cotton mattress and a couple of heavy woollen blankets. They made a bed for me and immediately excused themselves to return to their sleep, which must have been disrupted by this foreigner who had fallen ill upon his arrival. I lay in the makeshift bed with Nulla sitting by my side. Rahul stood up and announced he was going back to sleep. "Try and get some rest, if you need me, don't hesitate to wake me up again." That said, he slowly walked off into the night. Nulla lifted my head in her arms and made me drink some more water.

My head was on fire; the world around me didn't seem to make sense anymore. Nulla's voice and form felt as if they were coming from a great distance away. A big blur and strange, unfamiliar sounds engulfed me while I was being sucked down a vortex into the centre of the earth by a force so great that resistance was futile.

I arrived at a place encircled by big, looming mountains. No sooner had I registered the presence of these giant mountains, they all started to collapse down around me, just like a set of Lego crumbling apart. I ran for my life down a river valley with a woman by my side. Everything was falling apart—the earth around me breaking up. Every step I took, the ground that I had stood on a moment ago disappeared into the void. The woman by my side suddenly vanished too and I was running alone.

The whole earth was disintegrating under my feet. After running for what seemed like an eternity, I was pulled up by a powerful vortex into space, a place void of gravity. I rested suspended there for a moment, allowing myself to take in a deep breath; but the respite did not last for long. Again, a force I was powerless to resist carried me to a land beyond time; a quiet space with unfamiliar terrain.

I heard the beating of drums; the rhythm was hypnotic. A large fire burned at the centre of this island in space and was surrounded by lots of people. Their bodies were painted up in white and black shades, covered in holy iconography; crucifixes, Om's, stars of David and half crescent moons. Their faces were smeared with ash. Everybody was dancing. Gradually the rhythm became louder and stronger. Following the rhythm, my body started moving involuntarily, of its own accord. In no time, I was dancing with the rest of them. However it wasn't really *me* dancing, something was moving through me and the dance was just happening. It was as though I were possessed. We must have danced in this state for hours, for days, for years, perhaps, when all of a sudden the drums stopped and we all sat down in silence facing the fire.

Gradually, as the flames grew smaller and smaller, a circle of twelve crows appeared out of nowhere and surrounded the fire. The crows were golden and they glowed in the night; each one of them with a different unfamiliar symbol marked upon its forehead. They were humming softly, when unexpectedly what appeared to be a giant eagle emerged from the centre of the fire. She was standing amongst the flames — untouched by them.

At once the people fell to the ground as one, covering their faces as though to shield themselves from the eagle's gaze. The man beside me tried to push me down to the ground, still I was immoveable. I was lost in the eagle's gaze and there was no force in the world that could move me from where I was.

"I am that I am," the eagle broke the silence with a voice encompassing all the vocal chords of the universe.

"I am the no beginning and never ending.

"I have been here before time and I will be here after time.

"I am life and death. I am the sun, the moon and stars.

"I am the wind and the rain. I am the question and the answer.

"I am the song and the singer, the dance and the dancer.

"I come and I go.

"I am fire and water.

"I am mother earth and father sky.

"I am always moving and forever still.

"I am tears and laughter, agony and joy.

"I am you.

"Dance children, for in the centre of the storm there is stillness.

"Sing your hearts out loud for in sound rests the core of silence.

"Breathe children, for the breath is your rhythm, the beat that governs your being.

"Your life has a purpose and meaning and you are here because you *chose* to be here."

The eagle's gaze and voice transfixed me. Everybody around me was still lying on the ground as though a bombshell had fallen.

"Do not fear to look at me," the eagle continued, "for in me you will see yourself. And the time has come for you to do so at last. Lift your heads up, all of you!" she said with a commanding voice.

Instead, the people around me started running away into the bushes and in no time at all I was left alone by the fire, with twelve golden crows standing in perfect peace, circling the fire, and a massive eagle staring right through me.

"They fear me for they fear their own selves. They are slaves to their so-called traditions, steeped in fallacy and judgements and they believe that by looking at the face of truth they will touch the hands of the forbidden. What fools they are, how long will they continue to worship separation?

"I am the voice of infinity and I am always with you for I am you.

"You do not fear me, for you have taken the first step on the journey to see what lies beyond the illusion of separation. Claim your rights of passage and be rid of the doubt that our unity isn't for real.

"That you and I are one.

"Stand up and be counted in the chronicles of time. The moment is ripe for all of you to lift your heads up high and hold hands together again.

"It is a very special time in the evolution of the *all that is*. A time where everything is changing rapidly, yet the world seen by your physical eyes is still blinding to the realm of the senses.

"Sense your oneness with all creation; feel it and you will know it. Then fear will be a thing of the past and trust will become the song of the present moment.

"Once you truly trust the reason why you are on earth, your life will become a feast of miracles; the impossible will all become real.

"The dream spell will awake.

"The negative will dissolve to laughter.

"Desperation will shift to hope, and life on earth will heal from the dis-eased form it has taken.

"Separation is the source of all that is sick about humanity.

"Embrace the oneness, and you will never feel alone again.

"Trust the oneness and you could never harm another, for then you harm yourself.

"Every silent whisper in a quiet night vibrates through the heart of all that is. The more you celebrate the song of life, the more life will celebrate itself."

Suddenly she turned silent, her eyes like faraway galaxies. The crows were like light beams guarding the sacred fire.

"Remember these crows, little one; one of them, one day, will meet you again and guide you in the space where life overlaps vibration."

Then there was silence, an eerie calm permeating the night.

I felt dizzy; the fire started consuming the eagle. It gave a deafening screech that shattered me and made me collapse to the ground. I was petrified, screaming my head off as I watched the eagle completely disappear into the flames.

"It's alright, it's alright, calm down," I heard a voice calling my name and felt someone holding me in her arms.

"Where am I, who are these people . . . hey . . . where has the eagle gone?" I was drenched in sweat from head to toe.

"It's alright; it's me Nulla, your wife. Don't worry, you are just having a high fever and might have been hallucinating for a while. It's cool now, just relax, you are over the worst."

I recognised Nulla's face again. The sun was blinding

my eyes and I could feel many people around me. For a moment I thought they were the people from the dark space.

"Who are all these people, Nulla, can you tell them to go away?"

"Relax," she continued to stroke my face. "They are here to help."

"I don't need any help, Nulla, I just want everybody to go away," I cried, pleading with her.

A man said something to the people around and most of them walked away. I held Nulla close to me, as close and as tight as I could, and collapsed into a fit of hysterical crying and howling. I cried and cried and cried until the tears ran dry and all that was left was emptiness. I felt as empty as I never had before. I could see Nulla's eyes were moist with tears too. She put my head down on the makeshift pillow and gave me a drink of water. I drank more and more as though it was liquid gold.

Rahul approached me with an old woman by his side. "How are you feeling?" he asked with great care in his voice.

"I think I am alright," I whispered to him in return.

"This woman is the village healer, I want her to have a look at you," he said. A beautiful old woman squatted by my side and held her hands over my body. She had her eyes closed while she whispered something again and again in a language I didn't understand; it sounded like a calling of a bird. After a while she took a ring of eagle feathers from her bag and started fanning me with whilst singing softly. I had never felt so good in my entire life. It was as though my whole past had been erased. I didn't really know who I was anymore. I listened to my breath, it was real, and so was the total peace that pulsated through my body.

She continued to sing a soft melody for some time and then stopped and rose up. She said something to Rahul, and before she left she laid a beautiful tail feather of an eagle by my head. Rahul came over and sat close to me. "She said you would be alright. The fever has passed though it made you touch the song of the nameless one. You need to rest and eat while you come to terms with what has happened to you she said. In the evening she will come again. I will leave you now and in a couple of hours someone will bring over food and chai for you. And yes, the people have decided that you two are welcome to stay. They recognise both of you as a brother and sister of the one."

❋ ❋ ❋ ❋ ❋ ❋ ❋

I look at Nobi while tears stream down my face. It is only now after reliving the memories of that day in the tribal village when I was kissed by the lips of death, that I recall the words the eagle spoke to me when I floated in the space between the worlds.

"Nobi, Nobi, we have met before!" I pronounce with great excitement. He looks back at me and flutters his wings. The two other crows who left us a while ago now, appear from nowhere landing in a full *qua, qua, qua* chorus by Nobi's side. All of a sudden, the three of them are very still and for a moment they glow with a golden hue.

"So it's not only Nobi, it's the three of you that were there that night many years ago." Nobi looks at me, his eyes burning with light.

"It took you some time; I am glad you can finally *see* us. Of course we have met before, many times and we will meet again. There are no accidents in this great plan. I told you before, you are never alone on your walk and all of creation is holding hands with you, eternally. Will you at last trust it?" he speaks with a plea.

So, is trust the key; the code we use to reveal the secret to this entire puzzle? I can remember that day when I had the journey into the world in my state of fever, I knew it was real; I knew I met the eagle, yet did I trust my knowing? Obviously, not in total, for if I did, my life would have never known separation again. Nevertheless, that experience did have a profound effect on me and transformed me in more than one way. I recall my elder sharing with me a dreamtime story of the eagle roaming freely the skyways of eternity. Then one day when it had a message to pass on to the earthlings below, he came across a hawk and whispered something in his ear. The hawk went on his way and after some time met a crow and requested her to pass the eagle's message down to the beings without wings. Thus the crow became the bridge maker between the earth and the sky.

Nobi looks at me again. "You see, many of you get signs, messages, visitations from the great void, except you don't hold onto them. You don't embody them deep within your beings. Rather, you treat them as sensory delights, experiences you brag about, nothing else. When you at last know it's for real — once you do so — this whole system you live in of exploitation, destruction and subjugation will collapse like a house of cards.

"You get reminded again and again of the connectivity of all life. In spite of this, you still live as though you are separate, insular, engrossed in your small lives. You hand over your power to the ones who crave it, as vampires feed on blood. Be the glory that you are, for life is a grand show, the greatest circus in the universe awaits your reawakening."

That said, Nobi and the two other crows take off to be airborne, they circle above me, and as I look up I can see that they are glowing with the same shine as the stars above me.

So, what is the crux of what Nobi is telling me? Maybe it is that life really begins when we finally trust in the fairy-tales we so knew were real before the time we *grew up* and our minds were corrupted.

✳ ✳ ✳ ✳ ✳ ✳ ✳

Many years ago in a tribal village in the heart of India, I started emerging from being what I was bred to be — small and insignificant. It was at that time that I first glimpsed the reality that within me exists a great power, a strength that abides within us all; and it is the ability to effect change within and in the world at large.

Following the night of the high fever I stayed resting in the open hut by the river for three more days. Nulla fussed over me, although there was not much she could do, save to let me relax and integrate the events and visitations of the last days. The village healer came to see me a couple more times and brought herbal concoctions for me to drink. Her toothless smile was as wide as the universe. I trusted her more than any graduate of a medical school, for her eyes reflected the healing powers of the earth.

As well as the village healer, Rahul came to see us every day. He didn't say much. He just enquired about my wellbeing while in return I had neither the energy nor the desire to ask him any questions. He made sure that food, water and chai were brought to us regularly, and apart from that he seemed to have more important things to attend to.

Three days later Nulla thought it was time for me to get up and have a bath in the river. I stank from all the sweating the fever had induced and I still hadn't fully washed myself since we left our village in the desert almost five days ago. Nulla had used a wet cloth to freshen up my face and hands every day, however, my body needed a proper wash, a scrub and a full clean up.

I felt weak and peaceful, as though a massive storm had passed through my being, cleansing it of lifetimes of garbage. Immersing myself in the slightly cool waters of the river, I felt a happy murmur snaking through my body. Nulla smiled with joy and gave me a big hug. She had been married to this strange man for four months now and I am not sure if it were what she ever dreamt her marriage would be like. Perhaps she did, I never really asked her.

Early that evening, Rahul arrived with a woman by his side. They brought with them a pot of herbal chai and a plate of delicious dried fruits and nuts. The woman held the palms of her hands together in the traditional Namaste greeting and introduced herself as Shanti. Shanti was in her late forties or early fifties with long silver hair. She wore a simple white cotton sari. Her face was pale and her eyes were radiant. She walked barefoot as though she was an integral part of the earth she trod upon. Rahul introduced us to Shanti while she leaned over and embraced us both.

We sat together enjoying the chai and snacks while she spoke. "Welcome to Nandini, it is a very special place and I am sure you will learn a lot here. You are welcome to stay with us as long as everybody here feels it's the right thing for you and for us. The village healer tells me you have gone through a very powerful experience. The locals call it a 'sacred purification', which all of us have to experience if we wish to live a meaningful life. Myself, I have gone through it more than once." she said with her quiet and commanding voice.

One of the first impressions I got from many of the people here was how softly they spoke. There is no need to raise one's voice to be heard. On the contrary, speaking softly opens the listener's ears wide in attention to the sounds emanating from the speaker.

I couldn't fail to notice how mesmerised Nulla was by this woman, much as I was, I suppose. I had never met anyone like her before. I recalled Rahul saying she was an inspiration and I had to agree with him on that. She was like a magnet of goodness, a lamp glowing in the dark light.

"We endeavour to live here by Gandhi's principles of truth and non-violence," she continued to talk to us. "A heavy feeling and a certain sense of failure has been pervading the camp for the last three days, for as you experienced on your bus ride, some of us chose to turn their anger into violence. We have now decided to observe a time of introspection in silence in order to discover our shortcomings," she said.

"Hey, but you had a right to be violent, the police attacked you first, didn't they?" My fiery side emerged out of its closet for a brief moment.

"We never have the right to be violent," she looked back at me with her blazing eyes. "Nobody has. We may have a rational reason, though we never have a moral one. What would we ever achieve through violence? We are just adding more fear to a world that is already saturated with it. We must resist any wrong doings by another with the power of love, thus aiding in the transformation of the other. That's what makes us in truth a force of change in the world. Resistance has to embody a solution within its struggle, and the answer is love. If not, we are just reacting, fighting, and wars, well they have only losers."

I can't really say that I agreed with her in that moment, I could feel that Nulla did. It took me some time to understand the power that is held within the hands of love. Maybe it's a truth more easily accessible to the spirit of the feminine. Shanti gave us some time to absorb what she was saying. She sensed that these concepts and ideas were new to us.

"The village is usually a very quiet one with three dozen families living here, though now we number almost a couple of hundred people." She continued to talk to us. "We chose this village because it will be one of the first to be submerged when the dam is complete. The village is now like an ashram[12*] for us, where we all share the workload. So if you want to stay with us for a while, you will have to do some work too. There are local tribal people here, who have called this place home for many generations; as well, we have people from neighbouring villages, farmers

---

12   * Spiritual retreat, hermitage.

from downstream who will be affected by the dam and also many activists from the city — students, lawyers, teachers, doctors, lecturers and journalists.

"We are all united by a common vision here, a vision that another world is possible, a different paradigm for development and growth — a vision that supports all and enhances the human spirit. We are not talking about growth that is measured in monetary terms, rather an evolution that brings people closer to each other and to the source of being.

"This is why we shun violence, for how can the goal be separated from the journey? How can we fight for peace, for justice? It is a contradiction in terms. We must show that a different way is possible; it is not only the end result which we strive for, in fact, what is most important is the way in which we get there. For once we reach that place, life will offer us new challenges, and again we will have a choice to make."

I was drinking in Shanti's words like a man who had walked in the desert for days with no water and had finally arrived at a lush oasis. A voice within me commanded that I pay full attention to every word this woman spoke.

"At last I've met a teacher worth listening to. Why don't they teach us these things at school?" I wondered to myself. "Why do they just fill our minds with rubbish, which is totally irrelevant to our walk on earth? Isn't there much more to life other than just being groomed to be accumulators of material fortune? As human beings, isn't it about time that we all affirm as a collective that our lives have much more of a profound value, other than just being manufacturers and consumers of goods." I knew that, if we were in touch with what Shanti was saying, we could never go on destroying the planet and causing harm to one another.

Shanti got up and said it was time for us to come and join everybody for the communal dinner. "We brought you food over here in the last days, because you needed time to be alone; however, now it is time for both of you to come join the circle. We cook and eat together. After dinner you will be assigned your service for tomorrow," she said.

"What do you mean by service?" I asked her with some bewilderment. "Service is the work we do, although we don't call it work, for in the action we take we serve each other and life on earth. Anyway, let's get going now; you have had enough words for one day. We will have more time to talk later. And yes, for the time you are here, this little hut with no walls will be your home; you will get a lot of inspiration by staying so close to the river." She gestured to us with her upturned hand and we all stood and walked have to dinner with our new family.

Dinner was a silent affair. We sat in two circles facing each other, while the servers moved around with brass buckets dishing out the food. The plates were made of wide leaves stitched together. The food was much plainer than the local food I'd eaten elsewhere. Dinner comprised of rice, dhal and vegetables with a glass of buttermilk to wash it all down. After that Shanti stood up and spoke for a while, Rahul sat next to us and translated the gist of what she was saying. She spoke of how we needed to uproot all anger from our hearts in order for these violent reactions not to reoccur.

"The demons live within us, nowhere else, and that's where our struggle is at the moment. Once we clear our hearts, our message will be received by more hearts," she said. Apparently there would be no political activity or planning for further actions until this time of self-enquiry was complete.

"How long would it last?" I asked Rahul.

"As long as it takes for us to change, the inner challenge is as crucial as the outer one." He spoke softly so as not to disturb Shanti's speech. Before retiring back to our hut, we were assigned our chores for the next day. I would help in the kitchen while Nulla would weave materials collected from the surrounding forest to reinforce the roofs before the impending rainy season.

Later that evening we sat in our open air hut, marvelling at the magic of the serene night. We had been given a clay vessel for drinking water, a couple of cups and small tiffin for food. Nulla rested her head on my shoulder. "You know, this is the most beautiful honeymoon I could have ever envisioned. It's going to teach us how to live meaningfully. I feel it will prepare us better to handle the challenges of life and the trials of walking together as man and woman," she said.

So there was Nulla again, seeing the good in all, whilst living in surrender to the moment. Myself, although I was glad we were here, a part of me still wished we had made it to our planned destination.

All the same, life is not a mission to be executed, rather it is an intent that we put out into the universe and in return she either accepts or rejects our requests whilst guiding us to her destination of choice.

"Nulla, do you really think that if somebody comes and attacks you, it's right just to do nothing?" I asked her softly while lying down on a straw mat we had by the thin mattress.

"Man, she wasn't saying we do nothing. She was saying we do something bigger, more profound, and unexpected, it is the same as what Jesus said; *love thy enemy*. I feel what she said is that everybody is human, and we all possess our own weaknesses, so if somebody comes to us with anger, we offer them love in return," Nulla said with the conviction of a woman who knows she is the earth. I am not sure if I really grasped it in that moment or agreed that the concept was humanly possible.

It was only some years later when one of my elders and a good friend of mine said to me, "You have to love everybody, you don't have to like everybody," that I got a better understanding of what Shanti was sharing with us then.

I really had to work hard to embody what came to Nulla and Shanti so naturally. As I was falling into sleep a profound sense of wellbeing engulfed me. I felt safe in this world. I was exactly where the universe intended me to be.

✳ ✳ ✳ ✳ ✳ ✳ ✳

Sitting by the river now, anticipating the coming of the big waters, I sense the same feeling as I did that night in a tribal village by a different river.

I am where I am meant to be, life will take care of the rest.

A river is a perfect reflection of a human life.

All rivers are conceived and then come full circle in the great ocean.

All rivers owe their birth and dissolution to the same source.

All life forms mirror the same river, the movement of being from the source, to the source, with the source. The whole natural world lives connected to this flow. It is only we humans that have lost contact.

How is it possible that an ant, with no access to satellite weather reports, knows there is a storm coming three days prior to its arrival as she moves to find shelter much in advance? Does she possess some supernatural magical powers? No, she doesn't. She knows, because she feels the world around her and is one with the source of her being.

How is it that an albatross can navigate across thousands of miles and arrive on the same small island year after year? And this she does with no radar or fancy computer navigation systems. In fact, she will find exactly the same wide rock she nested on the year before after flying thousands of miles for weeks on end with nothing other than a mass of blue below and above.

The albatross can do it, for she does not doubt creation; she is just present with the source of life, she knows she is guided by it and she trusts her knowing.

And so it is with all creatures big and small.

All life forms experience their forever oneness with the nameless one.

Yet there is one small, hardly evolved life-form resembling a parasite, that long ago lost its knowledge of being present with the one — we humans, the most poisonous blood-suckers to have ever inhabited the earth. What has made us so inferior to the rest of the natural world that we cannot even conceive of feats like the ones performed by the ant or the albatross? Unless, of course, we are armed with a thousand and one gadgets and even then we lack the perfection with which nature discharges her duty.

When and why did this separation in human HisStory occur? When did we fall from grace? What was the cause, reason, motive, incentive or insanity, which made mankind sever its natural instinctive ties with the infinite source of love and wisdom?

Who was responsible for the horrendous crime that set man apart from the universe he hails from and made him dream this insane fantasy that he stands apart from all beings in this great cosmic play? When was this original sin committed?

Perhaps there is no answer to these questions, though the fact remains clear, that humanity at large is not living as *feeling* beings anymore. We are stuck in the mind, controlled by our thoughts and ruled by our fear.

So, how do we transform ourselves as individuals and as a collective?

Well, only one answer comes to me at this moment as I gaze beyond the stars. We need the courage to trust again. We need to stop the world just for a short moment and *feel* the knowing that rests within the arms of *trust*.

Trust grew within me in that tribal village, where people from all walks of life were united by one quest. The intention was to go beyond our perceived limitations, and walk with the power of the one love.

It wasn't always easy, yet who said that being wholly human was meant to be a cakewalk?

* * * * * * *

The first three days of participating in the activity of life at Nandini were somehow uneventful and allowed us time to observe our new surroundings without the burden of verbal communication. Since the leadership called for a period of introspection, most people observed silence. As Shanti mentioned, the real demons we had to battle were the ones that abided within us all.

Shanti asked everyone to shift their attention away from their anger at the brutality of the police. She said we must be aware of the fact that the birthplace of violence is fear, and thus we must exercise compassion towards the vicious ones. She wanted us to focus on our own fear and raging violence that live, albeit dormant, in the hidden corridors of our hearts. "This is the point where we change the world," she said, "by transforming ourselves first." She wanted a movement anchored in love and compassion, in action rather than reaction.

The period of silence and introspection was observed more by the outsiders while the local tribespeople carried on with the sound of their lives. The rhythm of living had to carry on; there were fields to till, animals to tend, and children to look after.

I worked in the makeshift kitchen on the morning shift. My job was to chop vegetables, wash huge cooking pots and participate in serving the midday meal. The kitchen was the heart of the camp and a constant hive of activity. The large shelter, which housed most of the outsiders, was at the far entrance to the village. It was an intricate bamboo structure covered by big green and blue tarpaulins. Some of the outsiders camped there, with their bedrolls rolled up during the day; others who had been there longer had their own makeshift huts.

This time and space for introspection made me feel peaceful and at ease. In fact, I was really delighted by the general silence, for quietude had been my trusted companion and dear old friend. I also needed more time to integrate the experience I had on the night of the high fever. Everywhere I looked I could see the eyes of the massive eagle gazing at me, haunting me, prompting me to live in the awareness of a truth perceived by a few. The awareness that the world seen by our eyes is a mere blip in the grander scheme of things, that numerous parallel realities are alive and breathing all around us, and the way to touch them is to stop the noise within and focus our gaze inwards. Of course a big fever or some other sickness or catharsis seems to kick-start the process of awakening.

Nulla's days had a bit more chatter in them though. She wove materials gathered from the forest; to be used to replace the old thatched roofs before the arrival of the monsoon, a job she really liked. Most of the women in her group were local, and she would share with me stories of constant laughter and song amongst them as they worked together. I enjoyed talking to Nulla in the evenings when we had our private space in our hut by the river. I didn't think any rule should be taken too seriously, and I was no stranger to silence; I knew very well that it had a dark side, too.

And, last yet not least, I was a rebel after all.

The village of Nandini was nestled on a gentle slope that descended downhill to the river, a river that appeared like a constant flowing stillness as though the water was comprised of stable sheets of glass moving along in unison; tricking the eye to believe it was motionless. The huts were spread around the area, each one of them surrounded by an abundance of fruit trees, bamboo, home gardens and a flourishing green understory. Most huts had another shelter adjacent to them, housing animals such as cows, goats, pigs and water buffalo. Chickens ran amok everywhere, constantly chased by the village dogs, whom sometimes took a beak to the snout in retaliation. The fields were small, mostly terraced and cultivated mainly wheat, millet, maize, mustard and seasonal vegetables. At the edge of the fields stood a thriving green forest that swallowed the bright sunshine and transformed it into living and breathing shade; providing the locals with many of their necessities such as building material, firewood, rope, wild fruits, bamboo, medicines, etc. By the riverbank stood a small shrine dedicated to the River Goddess; it was made from soft stone which had been so smoothed and polished by years of constant unwavering worship that it appeared to shine like gold in the fading twilight. Our hut was situated between the shrine and the sacred body of water. For a moment in time we were the gatekeepers to the river. And she in return was our guardian.

The local tribal people owned collectively a few small wooden canoes carved from the heart of big trees in the forest. They would take the canoes out in the lilac early mornings and throw wide round nets from them to see what fish would come up for them. The catch was shared by all, and provided a healthy addition to their diet. The river was relatively narrow at this point as it meandered gently through the curvature of the hills. There wasn't an abundance of fish in this place, although in certain seasons there was enough to go around.

After three days, the official silence was over and we were assigned a new service. I was to work with a group of people on devising new strategies to spread the message of the struggle to the outside world, with my kitchen duty shortened to washing the big blackened pots after lunch. Most of the people in my group were city folk, who spoke English. We would sit in a circle and formulate ideas, write letters and press releases and brainstorm different options as to how to make the world aware of what was happening. At the same time, we looked at creative ways to spread awareness; that there ought to be a different way to do things. A new approach to *development* was required; a process that *actually* benefited the masses.

Nulla worked in the art department with other talented crew in creating images that reflected the essence of the movement. It was in these days of endless talking, brainstorming and learning from these very committed sincere folk, that the earth warrior in me was conceived. It was there that I first really grasped what an insidious crime was committed daily, every moment, against the earth and against the quiet, gentle, happy people who live on the margins of the so-called civilised human establishments.

Gradually, I have come to recognise how in a cruel and systematic manner we have wiped most tribal cultures off the face of the earth in the last few hundred years. We are now effectively completing the job, destroying the remaining intact tribes by displacing them from their ancestral lands, which are the backbone of their tribal existence and the source, inspiration and foundation to their culture.

Often we would sit late into the night by a small fire, downing herbal teas and dreaming up a new world within the kaleidoscope of our vision—a rebirth of intelligent innocence. It allowed us to see the world with pure eyes again and discard the pseudo lenses installed in our brains by the ones who have propagated the myth of separation for the last few thousand years. A myth many of the tribal people still refuse to believe in. Nulla would join our group at night, contributing much enthusiasm to the passionate debates. When the people tired of talking, they would turn their voices to song. I learned over the years that every Indian is a natural born singer and dancer; they love both the film songs as well as the devotional chants.

Bit by bit, I started to comprehend what this story was really all about. Rahul patiently took the time to explain to us the intricate net of exploitation that was running the machine in his country and how it was interlinked with the world wide web of dragons of greed. This was apparent even before India decided to officially join the festival, where the goodies owned by the many were dished out to the party of a few.

The local state Government decided to build a colossal dam that would generate electricity for the city folk whilst diverting water from the fertile tribal lands to the more arid lands, where big industrial farms of mainly sugar cane crops were located. Since independence, large dams had displaced more than thirty-five million people across India. By some accounts, that number was closer to fifty million. Most of those displaced were tribal and marginalised people, who rarely received any meaningful compensation of land promised in return for their displacement. It was simply a matter of taking from the poor and giving to the more financially secure mainstream. Robbing the ones with no political voice and awarding it to the ones with full blown political clout, destroying the marvels of diversity to feed fields of monoculture cash crops.

Big dams are obsolete; this is a fact that has been gaining acceptance worldwide for some time. Consequently, in the so-called developed world, many big dams are being decommissioned. There are better ways, more sustainable, ecological and economical ways, to harness the power of water and distribute its life-giving force. More moral and democratic ways, which are socially acceptable ways to create power and harvest the waters locally for the benefit of the farmers, wherever they are.

And then there were the five hundred thousand people, of mostly tribal origin, that would be displaced due to flooding by the time this particular dam was built. What about them? Well, according to the lingo of progress, they were just a nuisance, an inconvenience, a pest which should just be ignored or, if need be, manipulated through the media in the best way possible. After all, they were backward tribal people who could find a better life in the city slums. They needed to be *reformed* from their *primitive* ways in the forest and learn to *contribute* to society. And contribution, of course, meant joining the mass consumer cycle. Or in other words, they too needed to line the pockets of the gigantic transnational corporations which weren't happy merely having the majority of the western world eating out of the palms of their hands; they had to have everyone, even those in a forest so far away from the centre of their materialistic existence. We were all becoming foot soldiers in the empire of consumerism, with the ones refusing to don the uniform being sent for re-education!

Well, these tribal people seemed to enjoy their so-called *primitive existence*, which was full of smiles, and had witnessed what happened to their brethren when they ended up in city slums on the fringes of plastic fantastic consumer paradise — the degrading poverty, the breakdown of the tribal circle, the disease, the exploitation and the utter deprivation. Often, the young women would end up as prostitutes, with the men forced into bonded labour to the brick kilns and similar work.

The people of Nandini decided they were going to stand up for their rights or be taken by the river, refusing to end up as refugees in their own land. They might have chosen a violent struggle like some of their kin in the southern part of the country, if it weren't for Shanti joining them early on in the movement. At first they thought her ideas were a bit strange, yet in a short time they understood that this is the only way for them to act without losing their own dignity in the process of resistance. If they chose to rise in arms, they would be awarding the biggest moral victory to their adversaries who wished to change their ways. By choosing a different path, they remained connected with the harmony, which was their home by the forest and river.

Late one night, Nulla and I were sitting at the shrine of the river goddess, enjoying her silent companionship.

"My dear man, I have never seen you so happy. You are radiating. You have lived so long within the confines of your mind and now you are finally out. You see, I told you it will all be all right. You really didn't know where that palace was, where you were taking me, and we ended up here. This is the most beautiful palace anyway, the best place I could ever imagine spending my honeymoon," she said while holding me close to her.

I loved Nulla. My body ached at times when I allowed myself to feel how much I loved her. She knew that if she waited long enough I would change, find a thread to pull myself up and touch the world around me again. She also knew that if she pushed me, I would stick with superglue to the hole I was fixed in when she first met me.

And she was right. I was happy, really happy. I was a rebel, a revolutionary who had finally found a cause in evolution. Or maybe a rebel is a term instilled in me by the powers that be, to alienate me from my true self, for all I was doing was getting in touch with the pure song of my own heart.

I was a soul lost in a world of shadows that finally had discovered that by giving and serving others, he was giving the biggest gift to himself. Nulla stroked my face and covered it with her hair. "Earlier today I came and thanked the river Goddess for your healing. I don't know if you are aware of how close you were to death that night. Not everyone was sure you would make it. You were boiling like the hottest fire in the universe."

"Thanks, Nulla, for reminding me how I always forget

to give thanks." I smiled back at her while acknowledging my shortcomings. She could have said it in a different way, she could have criticised me for my forgetfulness to give thanks, yet it wasn't her way. She was a river Goddess, a high priestess waving her magical wand over my life. Giving thanks is a key, an unshakable code found on the quest to become fully present in the moment. By allowing appreciation to pour out from our soul, life becomes full, overflowing and requires no more additions.

We walked silently back to our hut. I lit a candle and got out a pen and my writing book. I could feel a poem coming through me.

> *You waver in your emotions,*
> *Between time and mind.*
> *While trees are fallen,*
> *And rivers choking*
> *In the slime*
> *Of a system*
> *Drowning in its own greed,*
> *And suppressions*
> *Of freedom –*
> *Our birth-right*
> *From yonder ago.*
>
> *You stare at the forest,*
> *And see only mammon,*
> *Blind to a spirit*
> *With wings, full of song,*
> *Thine reflection*
> *You have not*
> *Come to know.*
>
> *Tears fall down,*
> *My mirrors of soul,*
> *As I listen*

To your heart's song
Die to the clock of Babylon.

There is no passing,
In this freedom,
But the knowledge
. . . that you are made of stone,
. . . of fires, mountains, thunder,
. . . of water, rivers, whales and shells,
    . . . of air, wind and roaring eagles,
. . . of earth, turtles and spiders too.

And, beyond all this,
Must be something,
Maybe a no-where
. . . a no-thing,
It has no place
Or life in time
    Earthward bound,
Not yet found,
It longs to touch your hand.

I put my pen down, folded my piece of paper and placed it under our mattress. I blew out the candle, closed my eyes and drifted off along the waters of a River Goddess called Nulla.

❋ ❋ ❋ ❋ ❋ ❋ ❋

Nobi seems to be somewhere else; this time it's him drifting away into a space unknown to me. I stare at the river and feel how alive her organism is. How she is a being in her own right. She is fully present with me, a companion nurturing me during this movement in time. It dawns on me how everything, no matter how negative it seems, is an offering from the Great Mystery, a gift that propels us to grow and find new ways to be and act. The river itself comes at times to a place where there is no passage. It does not offer resistance, rather it chooses another course to take, the one with the least struggle.

In the time we spent at Nandini, we were dealing with very destructive forces — forces that were about to destroy a river and the lives of many. However the challenge present brought us together, people from all walks of life and from many different lands. It gathered us to defend the sanctity of life and, at the same time, offered us a gift of personal growth and self-discovery.

If it weren't for this dam being constructed, we wouldn't have come together and conceived a movement that would eventually grow to be a global one, serving a very large circle of earth lovers, aligning their energy as one. It is in the coming together as a positive force that makes flowers bloom at the altar of creation, while offering a fitting response to a force bent on destruction.

The time with those people showed me the power that lay within commitment, action and unwavering solid intent. It revealed to me what happens when people come together and focus their energy on a cause larger than their small selves.

It was the realm where magic happens constantly, and our guardian angels are always present. It was a new way of being for most of us, and there were many failures. Though even failure is success, for it is a sign that life has been lived, a mark of movement, challenges faced, and new lessons learned.

In fact, really there is no failure or success, just experiences from which to learn, transform and grow.

If I had to choose between maintaining the status quo of my life or failing again and again, I would choose the latter, for that experience itself could hold the key that unlocks the doorway to my stairway to heaven and beyond. Isn't it true that most of us are afraid to venture from the known into the unknown, for one fear only—the fear of failure!

However, how can a child ever learn to walk without falling again and again? Aren't we all like children learning to walk in oneness again with the source that brought us forth to experience this passage as an earthling? As we form the *circle* there are bound to be many setbacks; they are only checkpoints to refine the process we have undertaken and sharpen our impeccability. It is my utter conviction and direct experience that it has been in the time of my total breakdowns in life that a new spirit took hold and resurrected me into realms untouched before.

Life is a great ocean where we constantly ride the waves, and forever rise and fall with the movement of the sea. A day came sometime in my journey, that I wasn't riding the waves anymore, I was learning to surf somewhere above them. I became less affected by the fluctuations of intensity presented by life and begun watching them as a cosmic flow of energy manifesting itself as an ever circling movement.

Life in Nandini was bursting with purpose. Everybody was focused on a common cause. There were two groups of people, from very different backgrounds. On one hand there were the activists from the cities who were in the process of discovering a new purpose for their lives and discovering the immense power that living close with the land provided. And on the other, there were the tribal people; they really didn't feel the need to discover a sense of purpose, for their lives were their purpose and reason for being. A life that holds no separation from the great web requires nothing other than being present with it. Hence, they weren't seeking because there was nothing to find. Life in all its diversity, connectedness and magic was their daily walk; the sphere they abided in. At times, they were even astonished by the endless philosophical discussions we held, chatting about the meaning of life and what is the finest way to explore this dance on earth.

Nandini had no electricity or phone. When a press release or communication needed to be sent, a messenger would walk for half a day to the road and then take a bus to the nearest town. We heard that calm had returned, though the police were still furious and a raid on the camp was a likely probability. It was decided that scouts would be placed an hour's walk from the village, and if they spotted the police they would fast-track back and inform us, so that the leadership could disperse and seek cover in the nearby forest. The police, for some reason, dreaded venturing into the thick jungle, so it was considered safe territory for the moment. Nulla and I would hide with this group when and if we were raided.

We talked it over one night as we sat alone in our hut; we contemplated if it would not be wiser to leave now, rather than to wait for the cops to show up in the camp. I felt we could be a liability for the cause if we were caught here. And, of course, we would most likely be deported from the country and never be permitted to return, a thought that petrified us. Nulla decided to have a chat with Shanti about it. After talking it over with her, she told me that Shanti and the others were delighted by our presence and would do anything to protect us in the event of trouble. Shanti reassured Nulla that the tribe's knowledge of the forest was second to none, and they could walk us all the way to the road if need be, without being detected.

Nulla had developed a strong bond with Shanti — they would spend a great deal of time together enjoying each other's company. Myself, I still wasn't sure what to make of her. I was in awe of the presence she radiated, yet I wasn't sure if I fully agreed with all her ideas, or perhaps more so, her ideals. Some of her ways seemed a bit unrealistic to me, the domain of dreamers, which didn't seem to suit the sometimes-cruel world we lived in.

It appeared to me that Shanti expressed ideas as *absolute truths* that couldn't be challenged. And we live in a world where truth is so often relative to the situation at hand; a constant dance of opposites. Many times I had witnessed so called *higher truths* used as a mere excuse to escape from cultivating our ability to respond in the world.

I really wasn't sure if choosing non-violence, as a reaction to being attacked with force, was a wise thing or a sign of fear. I could understand the moral power it held, though wondered if it was also some sort of collective righteous suicide. By choosing the so-called moral high ground, did we claim an award in a separate reality, which the world at large is not yet ready to embody?

Shanti came over to our hut on her own one night, when we were sitting in front of a small fire that we had made just outside the hut, enjoying the serene melody of the nightly insect orchestra and the choir of the divine river. The sky was full with trillions of stars reflecting their light on the face of the river. Nulla got up and embraced Shanti. They both sat down holding each other as we formed a little circle of three around the soothing flames.

"How are you feeling here?" she asked me with her ever kind and commanding voice.

"I am really good, Shanti, thanks for having us here. I mean, I am more than good; this is the most awesome experience I've ever had," I answered, wondering if Nulla had shared with her some of my doubts of the philosophy she preached.

"I think we all feel the same," she said while gazing at the fire. "For all of us it's a pioneering experience, a new frontier we are walking into, without really knowing where it's all going to lead us to," she said.

"So you are not sure of the non-violence story yourself," I interrupted her with some excitement in my voice.

"No, that's not correct, I am very sure that the only way forward in this struggle or any other, is the way of non-violence. What I am not sure about is where it will lead us. Then again you know we can never be sure about any outcome in life. It's as though the outcome is in hands greater than ours, while the journey itself is in our own hands."

This time I fully resonated with what she said. I myself didn't feel that my life's journey was in my hands anymore. There was a greater force controlling my life now, while all that was required of me was to watch as it moved me from one unknown to another. Since the day Nulla appeared in the village in the desert, my life was surfing a new wave, an unfamiliar current of being, and there was not much to do, bar allowing it to happen. I didn't feel I had much say in it anymore. Maybe it was the first time I trusted there was an invisible hand writing the story, one chapter after the other.

I looked at Shanti, she was shining with purpose and resolve, and some of it had rubbed off on me in this wonderful place. She seemed so sure of everything, while I still had so many questions. I wanted to get into a debate with Shanti, to challenge some of her concepts that she held as a sacred truth, but I couldn't find the words to do it. Silence, my old friend, was visiting again and I just stared at the fire while Nulla and Shanti went on talking about the different tribal crafts, and how the villagers could generate some extra income from marketing their craft as a symbol of the resilience and richness of their culture.

In the few weeks we had spent there my thinking had altered and I caught a glimpse of the world through a new set of eyes. It was as though I was finally removing the shades that were obstructing my vision. Contributing and learning from these amazing folk had given me some direction towards which to dream my life. Shanti raised her head to talk to us again.

"We've decided it is time for action again. Instead of waiting to see what happens next, we will make something happen ourselves. In a week we will march to the district headquarters, which is about a five days walk, we will stop in all the villages along the way to spread the message and gather people to walk with us. Marching was a tactic Gandhi used much against the British, and now the time is ripe for us to use it in our struggle with our own government. When we reach the town we will camp in the park and a group of us will embark upon an indefinite fast. I will be one of them." She stared at the fire and seemed to be lost in her own thoughts.

Listening to her words, Nulla gave me this look of, *you understand what this means for us.*

Shanti held Nulla's hand while she continued to talk. "This will be your time to leave us, since we are going to expose ourselves and provoke the authorities by our actions, albeit in a peaceful way. A couple of days before the march, some of us will walk you to a junction on the road and make sure you are on a bus to the capital. It will be a long day's walk; still the locals feel they know a good spot on the highway where your presence won't look too suspicious. Anyway, you have a few more days left here with us, so let's continue to enjoy each other's company and learn as much as we can," she concluded.

I noticed Nulla squeezing Shanti's hand hard in friendship before she got up and folded her hands in a Namaste before disappearing off into the dark of the trees. I didn't say a word to Nulla, I was just sure that she could feel that I didn't have a clue where we would go from here. Something in me was almost afraid to think of where we would head to now, lest I awaken the Gods of fate to have them laugh in our faces when we tell them our plans.

We lay by the small fire looking beyond the stars. I felt overwhelmed by a sense of nothingness, by how insignificant we all are. "What are these stars and where do they live? The words universe, galaxy; what do they really mean?" I contemplated. "It all seems so big, awesome; way beyond my comprehension. Each and every one of us is such a tiny, weenie dot within the grand scheme of things. Who do we think we are anyway, that we would be guided by an unseen hand, why should anything in this vast infinity be concerned with something as small and insignificant as a human being?" My mind was full of unanswerable riddles and all that the stars could do for me was to offer their light as a reflection.

I looked at Nulla; she was asleep by the fire, or at least pretending to be. It was developing in the usual way we dealt with the challenges life offered us. We would usually not mention it to each other for some time until we felt we were ready to talk it over. More often than not, Great Spirit would show us a way — in fact all the time, though we couldn't always see it. I covered Nulla with her shawl and gazed at the fire until it slowly died and I faded into sleep.

❋ ❋ ❋ ❋ ❋ ❋ ❋

It took me some time to come to terms with the fact that so many questions I've had throughout my life would go unanswered, and that was part of the magic, perhaps at times the real essence of it.

As I sit down by the river now, awaiting her catharsis, the stars are just as they were when I was a child, twinkling lights in the sky, that show up every night after the sun falls to sleep. And who says they are not just lights that God turns on to illuminate the darkness? Is it the wise mind full of borrowed knowledge, choked in the shackles of science?

So maybe it's the death of our innocence that severs our oneness with the source—the moment when we start to borrow our relationship with the world from others rather than feel it in its purity. How can a pure heart ever accept so much of what is happening in today's world as *normal*? It can't, no way, and for that reason alone from the moment we can listen and talk we are taught that the world is this and that. The this and that which moulds a mind to accept cruelty and exploitation, greed and domination, destruction and pollution as normal things rather than be utterly repulsed by them. For a mind in a pure state will always seek harmony with all that surrounds it. For a mind in a pure state will know that there is enough for everybody's need and none for people's greed. In living from the heart, we experience that we are all in this life together.

It was Adam's act of eating from the tree of knowledge that banished him from the Garden of Eden forever. Aren't we all Adams, eating the borrowed knowledge imbedded into us, being educated in the books of separation? So this might just be the crux of it. The road map back to the garden of infinity: dropping all knowledge and *being* again.

It was only after all that I held as so-called truths died and were buried in yesterday's sands, that a new freedom to *be* emerged within my being—the freedom to be a child again and view life through the lenses of magic and awe. The river lives in this knowing every moment as it meanders through the patchwork of landscapes offered to it. It tells a new tale with every corner turned, as though it has just been born again.

It was many years ago in a tribal village by a river with an uncertain future, that I was born again and found some purpose to my walk on earth. On the one hand, there were Shanti and the other activists, full of purpose and resolve, yet somehow lacking the smile that radiates from a being that is fully present in life. It could have been my own judgement; nevertheless, at times I found it all a bit too serious. I was a being emerging from the depths of many gloomy and introverted months, and all the reflection could have been just a bit much for me. On the other hand, there were the tribal people. Always laughing, smiling, ready to laugh, even at their own misfortune. They seemed to hold none of the tension the activists held, although it was their lives that would be adversely affected by the situation, while the activists would still be able to return to their homes in the cities.

We were lucky, Nulla and I, we had both mirrors to reflect upon, equally amazing groups of beings that together seemed to complement each other and form a formidable force of change.

It was mentioned a few times that once Nulla and I returned to the West we could dedicate our time to spreading awareness of the struggle that was taking root in Nandini. We weren't fully aware of how we were being used as tools in the hands of destiny then, or how the movement, which was being envisioned in Nandini, would eventually touch numerous hearts and inspire people from many lands to reaffirm their kinship with all life and rise up as a defiant voice and a power to be reckoned with.

There was an international twist to the proposed dam that we could exploit to try to effect change. The World Bank was providing much of the funding for the project and it was thought that, by raising awareness of how many people would be displaced from their ancestral lands, we could use the power of public opinion to force the World Bank to withdraw from the project.

During my time in Nandini, I learned that the World Bank was, for the most part, a scam and a sham; another misleading consent manufactured in the corporate media showrooms, using phrases it coins to realign our minds with its hidden agenda.

Contrary to public perception, there is nothing free or benevolent in the aid rich countries offer to the poor; rather, it's just another tool for them to introduce the way of capital into lands where the smile still holds its true value. They provide loans, which these countries will never be able to repay, and then force on them buzzwords like *structural adjustment* – interesting word, as though it was lifted from a chiropractic manual. And yes, that's exactly what is happening – a readjustment of the spinal cord of an entire country and its way of treating its people.

With *structural adjustment* comes the destruction of the indigenous ways of life in any country that is subjected to it. In reality, it means devaluing the local currency, so it's cheap for the massive corporations to come and buy up the country. This ensures that the existing local infrastructure is sold to the corporations for a fraction of its real worth. Once the country is virtually owned by its new masters, the government is forced to stop spending money for the benefit of its people, thereby ensuring the vicious cycle of oppression and repression keeps on circulating.

It was interesting, and more then mind-boggling, when I discovered that over half of the world's one hundred biggest economies are actually not sovereign countries, but corporate business houses, most of them based in the U.S. At the same time, I learned that the World Bank and IMF, despite their alluring names, were institutions controlled by the global elite and far removed from the benevolent creatures they are projected to be.

In fact, the World Bank has created more poverty than it claims to have alleviated, while spending on the poor has decreased in all countries concerned. It is the perfect instrument to prop up the capitalist ideals – because the donor countries themselves are enslaved too. And, of course, the contracts for these massive projects of pseudo development are granted to the multinational companies who virtually rule the governments in their own countries. What a scam! These realisations made me feel sick in the gut. Unreal, the money that was loaned to these countries never actually reached the people, and yet they have to pay it back, with interest!

The motto behind this insane way of thinking is clear — maximize profits, regardless of social and environmental consequences.

Nowadays, India is considered an economic miracle, while half of the children of this country are malnourished. More than half its population earns less than two dollars a day and lacks access to the basics, like clean water and sanitation. In many parts of the country, human rights are a bad joke; they only exist once you have money to exercise them and in the process bribe the right official. True to the laws of Babylon, it is stated by the World Bank and the IMF that India is an economic miracle unfolding!

So when the reality is that people still have no food to eat, and the economy is booming, shouldn't we pause for a moment and think; who does this economy really serve and who is really sharing in this unfolding miracle?

Is this the true face of the *brave new world* we live in? Our promised new dawn where the richer the corporations get, the happier our lives are supposed to be? Or is this a world where lies and deceit, manipulation and subjugation reign supreme?

It was just before the crack of dawn a few days after our talk with Shanti that Rahul came to our hut, saying "Wake up, guys, fast and pack your bags," with much urgency in his voice. "The police are on their way, we got word they would be here in about an hour, so be quick, I will meet you in the kitchen in ten minutes!" That said, he scurried off into the still dark.

I got up to rummage for a candle, though by the time I found one Nulla already had her clothes on and was gathering our things in the hut.

"It will all be okay, Nulla," I said to her, wiping the sleep from my eyes.

She smiled back at me. "Hey, man, I love it how you always say things to me while you are actually talking to yourself." She was right, I was affirming to myself that all was well, while Nulla always held much more trust that what was unfolding was always perfect and part of a divine order. Our small bags were packed in no time and we were off to the kitchen.

"Wait a minute," Nulla stopped. "Let's pay homage to the shrine of the River Goddess and thank her for our beautiful time here. Remember what you told me once about closing circles?" Of course I did, and I marvelled at how quickly Nulla embodied into her being what resonated with her heart, while with me much of it still lived in the realms of philosophy. We stopped at the shrine and sat in silence for a couple of moments in thanksgiving.

"Thank you, River Goddess for showing me that the Goddess within me, is alive and well," Nulla whispered, her hands folded in an offering of gratitude. We bowed in silence to the whispering river and then rushed off to the kitchen. Rahul was there with a tribal man and a woman activist.

He addressed us softly, "This man, Arjun, is our guide. He knows this forest like the palms of his hands. You have both met Radha before; she will also be coming with us. Now we have to get going quickly and we must walk in silence and with a soft footprint," he said.

And that was that. Off we went into the forest, no goodbyes or parting words with all the amazing people who had shared their lives and struggle with us over the last weeks. Sudden departures became, with time, a signature mark of the songlines I wove in my life. It could have been my sentimental soul, that wasn't able to handle the goodbyes, the constant letting go of the people and places I had come to love. And that love was always pure and present, for the knowledge that it was fleeting anchored it in the moment.

The sun's rays were twinkling through the canopy of foliage when we at last stopped for a break. We had been walking nonstop for at least a couple of hours at a relatively fast pace and we all needed a rest. We sat down in between the crevices of exposed roots belonging to a huge, shapely tree and shared a drink of water. My mind was full of questions that I wanted to ask Rahul. I thought the plan was that all the leadership would take to the forest once the police came, yet there were only four of us. I wondered if they were all scattered around in small groups in the forest.

"Rahul," I addressed him in a quiet voice so as not to disturb the atmosphere of nature around us. "What happened to the rest of the people who were supposed to flee when the police came?" Rahul kept silent, playing with a couple of sticks and drawing circles on the earth. He was in no hurry to answer me; perhaps he felt I had trespassed upon the quiet space we all had observed since leaving Nandini.

It was Radha who at last broke the silence to answer my question. "There was a change of heart. We held a meeting a couple days ago, late into the night and it was decided that the leadership would stay put. Shanti thought that the leadership running away would send the wrong signal to the movement at large and the authorities that wanted to suppress it. She realised that, by being arrested, she would offer a greater service to the cause. If all the leadership were taken to jail, a strong groundswell of support would grow, and this action would highlight the fear the authorities have of the emerging people power. It would be a blessing in disguise."

Radha smiled as she looked at both Nulla and me with great affection.

"It's just the four of us that left Nandini, of course we had to get you guys out of there, and as I am a journalist and writer I will go to Delhi and rev up media interest in the story," she said.

Like so many of the other activists, Radha had left a lucrative job with a popular weekly newspaper to join the struggle that was being consecrated in Nandini. She told us once, how she got tired of writing meaningless stories about superficial nothingness, to satisfy the editorial vision of the emerging modern India. She also had published a novel, which had earned much literary acclaim, and was quite a well-known writer who had won several awards. The money from these awards she donated to support the people in the forest and their struggle to save their land and life.

She felt much happier now, living a simple life and writing for fringe papers that were not afraid to publish the story emerging in the forest by the river. A story that, on the one hand changed her life and the way she related to the world, and on the other hand was a tale pregnant with meaning and vision that needed to be shared in these times when the status quo cast scorn upon anything that challenged the new world order of consume, consume, consume and be merry.

Arjun walked off to the forest for a few moments, returning with his hands full. He said something to Rahul and Radha and they smiled as he handed round some unusual-looking purple fruits. "They are wild berries," Rahul said. "They will give us the energy we need to walk all day. Arjun says that they have a very strong taste but you'll get used to it." I chewed on one slowly; it had a bittersweet quality and was quite to my liking.

"They taste really good," I said, smiling at Arjun, and

although he didn't understand a word of English, he seemed to get the gist of what I was saying and offered me a big wide toothy smile in return.

Arjun sat down and continued to talk with Radha and Rahul while looking at us; obviously he wanted to talk to us except he had to do it through a translator. Rahul took on the task of relating Arjun's words.

"He says that all the people in the village were happy to have you; you have become one of them. He hopes that one day you can come back and visit again and we will all enjoy swimming in the river and feasting on her fish," he said.

We didn't have much verbal communication with the local tribal people in the weeks that we were living amongst them, since only a couple of them spoke only a bit of English. Yet we related to each other in a language way beyond syntax, clear of the limitations of words. We shared each other's hearts and joined them in a circle of love.

Nulla wiped a few tears that were flowing down her cheeks; she was visibly moved by Arjun's words and the deep emotion he related. It took me a while to recognise that the presence of a couple of young foreigners in their uneasy times meant a lot to them. It was a small microcosm and our being there with them was as though the world at large was supporting their right to live their lives in harmony, which had been their songline since time began.

After a while, Arjun gestured to us that it was time to get going again. We strapped the packs on our backs and set in motion, weaving our way through the tapestry of the forest.

It was interesting for me for a moment to observe the two women amongst us. Radha was dressed in jeans and a long kurta, which is a long shirt, usually worn by Indian men. Her hair was cut short and she had a certain boyish look about her style. With that said, she was a stunning Indian woman with big brown eyes, high cheekbones and a delicate nose.

Nulla on the other hand was dressed in her tribal skirt and embroidered top and her hair was the length of Radha's kurta. It was as though one was affirming her right to be free of the shackles of tradition, while the other was celebrating her feminine core. They both radiated the light of the divine mother in her different shades and colours.

We walked most of the day, with a couple of stops for water and fruit. In both breaks, Radha sat with Arjun writing while she was conversing with him. I didn't understand what they were saying, and I could see by the expression on Arjun's face that it was important to him.

The landscape was mostly gentle rolling hills covered by a magnificent, thick, verdant forest. Often we observed red and black faced monkeys along the track. They were very curious as to where we were going and whether we were carrying any interesting foods with us. On the whole they didn't bother us, apart from a couple of times when they got a little bit too inquisitive and Arjun had to shoo them away with a stick.

By the late afternoon, the landscape slowly became flatter and more open as we ventured out of the forest canopy into green farmland of rice and sugarcane fields. We passed a couple of little villages that really were no more than just a collection of small buildings, where we stopped for chai and tried to find out information from the locals about what was the happening in Nandini. In both the villages we received a warm welcome and blessings for a safe journey.

It was about an hour after dark when we finally reached the road.

We arrived in what was a small junction with a couple of chai shops and a small eating-house.

Rahul looked at us with deep affection. "It is time to say goodbye now, friends. A bus should come within the next hour or so, Radha will continue with you guys. Arjun and I will walk back to the last village and stay there for the night before we continue back to Nandini," he said. He didn't have time for a long-winded farewell and I sensed it wasn't his style. He embraced us warmly, as did Arjun.

As they walked off into the dark night, Rahul turned around and yelled, "For the earth, and all life!" raising his hand with V for victory while slowly disappearing into the blackness.

We sat in one of the shops and ordered a chai, all of us tired and overwhelmed with emotion. Our presence in this junction did seem a bit out of place in the middle of nowhere. Still nobody asked any questions, it was as though they knew where we came from, and they were with us in spirit.

When a bus finally arrived Radha boarded it first, to have a few words with the driver before calling us over to get on. It was a typical Indian bus with two seaters on one side and three seaters on the other. There was a very small allocation of space for each passenger as though we were all meant to be small compact beings. "Indian bums must be much smaller then western ones," I thought to myself, although by no stretch of the imagination were Nulla and I big people. The conductor had to juggle a few passengers around to make a three seater available for us at the back, though nobody seemed to mind. Radha sat by the window while Nulla sat in the middle between us.

"It's a long way to Delhi, at least fourteen hours, so try to get some sleep," she said.

"Delhi? I didn't know we were going to Delhi?" I asked with a sense of bewilderment.

"You never asked where we were going," she answered matter-of-factly. And she was right, I never really thought where we would go to after Nandini, neither did I talk about it with Nulla. Life was so present by the river, that there were no thoughts of tomorrow.

Again, life played its own hand and by now I knew it was futile to resist. "We are going where we are meant to go; the journey will somehow reveal itself," I told myself. Nulla kept quiet. She had a soft smile on her face, as though she was reading my mind, anticipating with a subtle joy the story that the great unknown would have composed by the dawning of tomorrow.

✻ ✻ ✻ ✻ ✻ ✻ ✻

Nobi is staring at me. The expression on his face is wrenching my heart. I can't figure out if his rock-solid determination has turned into the deepest of despair. Has he given up, too? I wonder. Well, why am I asking this question? Is it because I have given up? Are my actions a pure sign of defeat as Nobi claims, rather than a resolve to be still with the moment that is?

Is this the heart of it? Have I lost the will and the faith, retreating to a space where the only demons I have to face are my own? Has Nobi been right all along?

"My friend," he addresses me again with a quiet and sombre voice. "My observation is that most of you have stopped thinking. You just accept whatever the media hammers into you, even if it doesn't make any sense and you know you are being fed lies. Its like thinking has become an uncomfortable notion and you'd rather someone else thought for you." Nobi speaks softly into the night, staring at the river as she flows by. By now we have both lost track of time. How long have we been sitting here? Perhaps twenty minutes, maybe more, possibly we've been sitting together for eternity, though only now, at this present moment, have I come to recognise Nobi's presence by my side.

"Look at your so-called patent laws, this new sick idea that you all accept as the ordained word of god. Have you ever really thought what a patent law means? It means that if you are the first in the patent office you can claim ownership on a form of life! Do you get what I am saying my friend?" Nobi pauses for a brief moment as he does when he wants to build the rage within me.

"Now, I can understand a patent being granted to one of you who works for years and comes up with a new invention, thus wanting to claim some award for it. However, when nature works for trillions of years, on a seed for instance; who gives the right to one of your giant corporations to go and claim ownership of it? And then there is tradition and culture, which evolved and grew from one generation to another, traditional uses of plants and herbs, etc.

"You remember the berries Arjun gave you in the forest that time? They suppress thirst and give you stamina. This, the tribes have known for generations. Now, one of these transnational companies with an army of top lawyers walks into the patent office and registers these berries and their traditional uses as their own. You see, these giant octopuses go and steal ideas of ancient cultures and patent them as though they have discovered something new. Outrageously, it's the same corporations that are at war with the wisdom of nature and the circle of life.

"Okay, mister, do you get what I am saying. Somebody, most likely someone very rich, thought it would be a good idea to let the corporations own all forms of life; that this would be another way to stimulate flow of capital. And all of you, and I mean *all of you* accept it as a norm. You have stopped fighting for your rights. You got cowed into submission by a corporate/state nexus, which is stripping you of your rights of passage on this earth. At the same time, you have been programmed to believe that anyone who roars against this brutal oppression is a terrorist!"

Nobi is quiet again. Of course I totally agree with him, though I am lost for an explanation of why we are letting this happen. Are we all scared, are we utterly hypnotised, really, who gives anyone the right to patent life? The more I contemplate it, the clearer I see what Nobi is getting at. We have all become stupid and submissive.

We have lost the plot, for we accept this insanity as a

norm.

"And friend," he's on a roll again. "Tomorrow someone will walk into the patent office and claim a patent on us crows! Really, how far are you guys going to let this story go before you stand up for the authentic right to *live* again? Corporations are totalitarian institutions; their aim is total ownership and control of the life around us. They are answerable to nobody and are run on the principle of maximising profit, regardless of any consequence.

"Life, on the other hand, is meant to be a celebration, a song, a sharing, and a place where the different dances meet in deep embrace of the unity that rests in diversity. So if you guys are going to do nothing, perhaps I'll have to call on the rest of the bird tribes to awaken you from your slumber."

That said, he takes off and disappears into the blanket of darkness offered by the shadows of a still summer night.

❇ ❇ ❇ ❇ ❇ ❇ ❇

We arrived in Delhi shortly before midday, to the greeting of an early monsoon shower. The humidity lay thick in the air, the type of stifling heat that adds extra weight to every breath and leaves you sticky with sweat and lethargy.

The central bus station was packed with taxis, buses, rickshaws, hawkers, food vendors, and countless people pushing and shoving their way through all the overwhelming noise and hustle. The air was filled with the smell of diesel fumes mixed with the aroma of chai and the scent of burnt samosas fried in what seemed to be recycled engine oil. For the last ten months I had lived in calm places with gentle people and this felt, literally, like Babylon running riot. Eventually we found a relatively peaceful corner in the big concrete monster of a building which must have been in an unfinished state for years, and sat on our bags. Radha kept her bag on her back as she was in a hurry to keep moving which was a surprise to both of us. It's not like Indians to be in a great rush; they usually treat time in a different manner from the way we westerners do.

"I must keep on moving, I have an appointment with a magazine editor sometime later today," she said, smiling at us through tired eyes. "So first I must go to a friend's place and freshen up a bit, so I'll look half decent for the meeting. Hey guys, the foreign tourist area is about twenty minute auto rickshaw drive away, you will find a cheap hotel there. All the drivers know it, so good luck to you whatever you do. Rahul gave you all our contacts, I would be happy if you contacted me to tell me what you ended up doing. And hey, before I forget," she scrambled in her pockets, got out a folded piece of paper, and handed it to Nulla. "I wrote this in our breaks while we walked in the forest yesterday. They are Arjun's words, which he wanted to hand over to you as a gift from his people." She placed her palms together and bade us farewell. We didn't really know Radha that well back then, though over the years we later became very close to her. Her commitment was second to none and her courage to challenge the establishment was a constant inspiration to me in my times of doubt and despair.

Nulla handed me the piece of paper left by Radha and walked over to the chai seller to get us two cups of tea while I opened it and started reading Arjun's words.

"To our brothers and sisters in the faraway lands, the friends we have not met, yet feel in our hearts always.

"You may not have known this before, that the country you call India has been inhabited since a long, long time by people who may have been the original people of this land. In fact the phrase used to call us, which is Adivasi, literally means 'original inhabitants.' Even in the language of the people we are acknowledged as the indigenous people of this land.

"From way before the Aryan or Dravidian civilizations came here; we the aboriginal people of India have walked the hills and swum in the rivers of this great land — ever since the time when the trees remember us sitting amongst them, and shielded us from the midday sun.

"Modern India calls us Adivasis in the newspapers, yet the people use many derogatory terms for us. We number many millions, some say close to 80 million, which makes us the largest tribal group in the world. There seems to be some worldwide consent of silence around our existence, our plight is never heard; it is as though we don't really exist.

"Since the birth of modern India and much before, we have been considered a nuisance, a backward people that must be assimilated into the mainstream and forced to adopt the ways of the majority. We often wonder why they find our way of being and living so disagreeable.

"We walk the earth softly and hold her close to our hearts with respect and reverence.

"We take what we need, no more and we trust that with the coming of tomorrow she will continue to nurture us.

"We see ourselves as part of creation and we do not seek to dominate her in any way.

"We care for each other and, within the circles of our kin, laughter is always the prevalent song.

"We treat our women with respect and they hold equal standing within our society. In fact, most of our healers, magic people, spirit guides are women. The land that we are custodians of is passed on from mother to daughter, as they are the givers and nurturers of life, as is the earth below us.

"We never infringe on the sacred space of another, nor do we offer them advice on how to lead their lives.

"The earth, of which we have been caretakers time and again, is still ever fertile and rich and our presence barely felt within the great scheme of things.

"Why is it, then, that the forces of modernity in this country find our lives so distasteful and offensive that they seek to destroy our way of being and force us to adopt their way? Do they laugh more than we do? Is a beautiful smile the ever-present song in the faces of their children?

"We thank you both for coming and supporting us in our time of struggle. You brought many smiles to our hearts and we will always remember you. The river and the forest have your melody within them now, for you have touched them with your presence and courage to be. May you always remember that we are all part of the one circle of life.

"Please pass on the call of the river to all the friends you meet."

Tears flowed down my face; I didn't feel deserving of Arjun's kind words. Nulla came over with chai in clay cups. "What is the matter?" she asked me. I handed her over the paper from Arjun and she read it in silence holding my hand, on both our faces a mixture of sweat and tears.

The conductors of the various buses roamed around the place announcing loudly their respective destinations and soliciting passengers to join their buses. One of them approached us with a big broad smile on his face, sparkling eyes and completely overlooked our fragile emotional state. He inquired as to where we were going. We told him we that weren't sure what we were doing yet.

"Come in my bus, going to Himalaya Mountains in one hour."

Nulla looked at me with smiling teary eyes, as though the story was already written and we were just turning the pages of the book again. We picked up our bags and followed him to his bus. The conductor was overjoyed, showing us off to the people we passed, as though we were some great score, adding extra kudos to his bus now that two foreigners had decided to joined it.

We took our seats in the back once again and secured

our luggage. The bus took another four hours before it left, since it only went when the driver and conductor were satisfied they had enough passengers to make the journey worthwhile. Still, it didn't really matter.

An unseen cord was guiding our fortunes towards a destiny written in tomorrow's chronicles.

❋ ❋ ❋ ❋ ❋ ❋ ❋

The time spent in Nandini had rippling effects that continued to surface in the years that followed. It was as though I finally discovered a role to play in the circus called human life on earth.

It must be said that it was much more than that. It was my first aware glimpse into a reality of being actually present in the moment as a way of being.

The people in that village were faced with the worst of calamities threatening their lives and way of existence on earth, and not for a moment did they complain, get depressed, or fall into the pit of helplessness and despair. That was saved for later, if and when disaster struck. It was not that they didn't act, not at all, they did, they gave birth to a movement and struggle that would last for many years and be a source of inspiration and courage for many. At the same time, they continued to live their lives with the same smile that has always graced their faces. Disaster doesn't strike until it does and, although it was important to rise up for their right to live, they did not succumb to the abyss of worry.

It was presence in the moment in motion, by a group of beings that have known nothing other than being present with life and celebrating its harmony. It was as though Shanti had the ideals and high philosophies, while they had the *way*.

Shanti's words resonated as truth in my mind, while the tribespeople very life vibrated as a song deep in the recesses of my heart. Shanti's non-violent ideas were a good strategy that fitted within the parameters of the time and allowed the tribal people to retain honour and dignity within their struggle. Beyond all doubt it was the tribespeople presence with life that left the deepest imprint on me, and is guiding me now in my final moments as I await the river of destiny, as she prepares to wash out the land standing in her way.

The river may come any moment, and until she does, I must remain present with life and all who are sharing this moment with me.

I reflect on Shanti's endless discourses on the importance of non-violence. Violence itself may be a judgement, or a relative point of view held in the eyes of the beholder, though there is no judgement in presence.

Living in Nandini also hammered the first cracks in my vegetarian mind, too. Shanti often spoke of how the Gandhian way is the way of non-violence; therefore, we should abstain from harming animals and should only partake in a simple vegetarian diet. On the other hand, the tribal people ate from the whole banquet around them, while harming none in the process. They ate fruits and vegetables, berries and nuts, chickens and goats, pigs and fish. They partook in all the feast creation offered them, and did not indulge in any of it. They did not separate one form of life from another; neither did they hold a judgement that one life held a higher vibration than the other. They gave thanks to all that nurtured their life and sustained their bodies, be it the green leaf or the red meat.

It did take me some time more to embody this understanding and to let go of the pseudo moral high ground held by a vegetarian mind.

The book of unity, rather than the fable of right and wrong guided the tribespeople lives.

Of course, it's the vegetarian mind and not the body

which is the real problem, for a body that can hold itself healthy and strong with a vegetarian diet, is a blessing in a world where we do not consume animals with the balance, freedom and thanksgiving as the folk did back in Nandini. Nor do we raise them with any sense of dignity. Rather we produce them in animal factories, through a life of degradation and torture and think that in return their flesh will offer us sustenance. How can it? Every cell of this animal's body has been imprinted with sadness and fear. The livestock in Nandini smiled while they lived and occasionally, not regularly, one was taken to offer nourishment and power to the people.

The river is full of ripples dancing in unison, moved by a force that is soon to make itself known.

I think again about how life is mirrored through different degrees of intensity. Perhaps it is more like being fully present every moment with the realm of infinite possibilities that really counts.

We'd been on the move for more than forty-eight hours and I felt utterly delirious, neither asleep nor awake. Every muscle in my body was screaming out for more space than what was afforded to my limbs on the cramped Indian bus built for people with shorter legs than my own.

The first night on the bus to Delhi with Radha I was so tired from walking all day that I managed to sleep through the night despite the lack of space. On the second consecutive night of travel, I was tired of sitting in the cramped narrow seat of the small bus fit to negotiate the narrow winding mountain roads. For the first few hours, the bus sped through the plains on its way to the Himalayan foothills. The bus driver seemed agitated at anyone who stood in his way, and continued honking his loud horn in an effort to remove all obstacles from his path. To me it always felt that most Indian bus drivers were kamikazes, perhaps incarnations of Japanese warriors on a suicide mission. The margin left for error by their manoeuvring through insane traffic on bad roads, was smaller than a space where a needle would fit. In order to succeed in their impossible mission, they all had elaborate altars to various Gods adorning the driver's cabins; for without the support of the Gods they would surely be doomed. A few hours later we started to climb, the bus huffing and puffing, its old body creaking as it struggled to ascend the steep road leading us up into the mountains. The exhaust must have had numerous holes in it and had the wheeze of an aging smoker, while it left a trail of black clouds behind it.

Most of the night I drifted in between sleep and semi wakefulness, observing how fragile my body became the moment it was deprived of space. For Nulla, space wasn't an issue; she could relax in any situation and was comfortably asleep with her head on my shoulder.

It must have been three or four hours after the bus started ascending the mountain road that the air slowly cooled down from the oppressive heat and humidity of the plains, making way for a welcome, refreshingly cool breeze. The first taste of cool air I'd had in over a year. Outside, the gentle rays of dawn were broadcasting the news of the birth a new day, while the scenery we were driving through was breathtaking in the surreal pre-morning glow.

Staring at the distance in my semi-awake state I could see the towering, majestic mountains reaching up into the sky, way above the clouds, adorned with a soothing cover of snow that merged with the hypnotic light to look like peachy pink garments dressing up the mountaintops. The immediate landscape that I could see in between all the folds of the land was dotted with small villages, surrounded by steep terraced slopes, which held the picturesque fields together. The presence of water was visibly abundant everywhere as we continually crossed numerous creeks and waterfalls, which had somehow made their way cascading down over or under the road.

I gently woke up Nulla so she too could savour the Eden we were entering.

I had never seen anything like it before, nor had I ever felt air so clear and crisp wash in waves into my lungs. I felt I could get drunk on this air and forever be soothed by the fragrant scent that infused every breath I inhaled with intoxicating waves of fully charged energy.

Nulla rubbed the sleep out of her eyes, "Wow, it feels that we are getting close to the home of the Gods," she said, while leaning over me to grab a drink of water.

It was never our intention to go to the mountains, nor did we have any plan really of what we would do after Nandini. The closest we got to discussing our future was one evening in our small hut by the river; we had talked of going to France and working on spreading the word of the tribal people's plight.

However, now it felt that we were exactly where we were meant to be — again. We smiled at each other with the inner knowing of how easy it is when you allow the universe to take charge, or rather when we listen to her whispers without being caught in the loud cyclone of our own minds. In truth, both of us were freaked out by the hassle and bustle of the big city bus station and it only took one friendly smile from a bus conductor to make up our minds that an hour in the big smoke was long enough for us.

The driver had been at the wheel for fourteen hours with only two short breaks, and there were still quite a few hours to go. Eventually, we stopped for breakfast when the sun was already up yet still veiled by the high mountains. The bus pulled over by a roadside teahouse, adjacent to a small waterfall cascading down by the side of the road.

We got out with the rest of the passengers and washed our faces in the crystal freezing water. It had the effect of making us fully present with the magical surrounds. All the passengers were moved by the presence of the mountains and freshness of the air and water. The sound of the small waterfall was a delightful change from the grizzle of the old bus, which was still ringing in my ears. We enjoyed stretching our arms and legs for a few moments and walked over to the teahouse to order some breakfast. This consisted of chai and long sweet dried biscuits that were only really edible once you dipped them in the hot, milky tea.

The driver was in a hurry to get to his destination and after only a short time the conductor gathered all the passengers back on to the bus and off we drove again. It was another three more gruelling hours of bumping along the steep narrow road before we reached a big village, where it was also time for another break.

This village had a couple of restaurants and a few shops; the conductor announced that this would be our lunch-break, even though it was only half past ten in the morning.

I walked over to the driver and ask him how long it was before we reached our destination; he said we would arrive there just before dark, which probably meant that we would arrive after dark, since all the Indians I'd met seemed to have a different take on time than us westerners.

My body was aching all over; it had enough of sitting in a cramped torturous space waiting to arrive somewhere. I couldn't comprehend how I could spend another seven hours on this bus. Every muscle and bone in my body was in pain and screaming for wide-open space and rest. I walked over to where Nulla was standing gazing in awe at the valley below and the river meandering through it.

"Nulla, how about we get off this crazy old bus and continue tomorrow? I am sure we can find a place to stay here. C'mon girl, it's obviously paradise here, we can handle a night in this place," I said, with pleading eyes.

Nulla didn't need any persuading; she was tired of sitting on the bus as much as I was.

"Okay, sure, let's get our bags and find a place to stay," she said happily. The conductor, however, was not so happy. He tried to dissuade us from leaving, assuring us that the driver would drive faster so we would reach our destination sooner, yet this only hindered his case. His pleas were to no avail; we had already made up our minds.

We dragged our bags off the rusting bus and walked over to a small general shop that sold anything from candles and cigarettes to cold drinks and biscuits and the rest. I asked the old shopkeeper if he knew of any places where we could stay.

"Yes, sir," he smiled, showing a mouth with more missing teeth than existing ones. "Mister Negi is having a couple of rooms in his apple orchard, which he rents to tourist," he said, and he happily left his shop and walked us the few hundred metres to the edge of the village where Mr Negi had his house, orchard and guest rooms.

Mr Negi was sitting on the small veranda out in front of his wooden house, gently stroking the head a young girl who was curled up on a thick blanket beside him. She must have been around ten years old, and her hands were rolled inward and she was moaning in a strange, strained, deep voice. The shopkeeper whispered in my ear that she was born like this. She seemed to have something like cerebral palsy, or a certain birth abnormality.

Mr Negi got up and greeted us with a warm welcome. The shopkeeper informed him that we were after a room and, having done this, he immediately excused himself to get back to his business. Before he left, he assured us that anything we might need during our stay we would surely be able to purchase in his shop. Mr Negi's dog, a big, brown, hairy mountain dog, came and had a sniff to make sure we had come in peace. It didn't take the friendly canine long to realise that two these two foreigners adored his species and he started demanding good healthy pats from us.

After engaging us in a bit of small talk, along the lines of: "Where are we from?" and "How do we like his country?" Mr Negi rose from his chair and walked us over to a small wooden cabin situated amidst the apple trees to show us the available room. It was a beautiful small room with full-size windows on three sides, which allowed guests to savour, from their cosy comfortable bed, the snow-capped peaks in the distance.

The room had a small iron stove, with a chimney pipe rising from its centre that was used in the winter for heating and cooking. Apart from that, there were two small single beds placed side by side to form a double bed, a desk and a couple of hooks on the wall. A woodchip stove was placed just outside the door and Mr Negi assured us he would light it every morning or evening according to our preference so we can take a hot bath. After agreeing on a price, which included our meals, we settled in, unable to stop admiring the place destiny had decided we needed to visit.

The apple trees were laden with small red apples still a couple of months away from harvest. The understory was speckled with purple clovers and small ganja plants that grew wild in this part of the world and also served as an excellent nitrogen fixer for the soil. In the wider spaces amongst the trees grew wheat, which looked as if it was just about ready to be harvested. Once we had unpacked our things into our new abode, Mr Negi's other daughter came to call us over for lunch. We sat down with the family on the small veranda of their home, enjoying a delicious feed of mildly spiced vegetables, dhal and chapattis – the usual Indian fare, which seemed to taste so different depending on which part of the country you were in. Over lunch Mr Negi shared with us the story of his life.

He had joined the army when he was nineteen, as many of the young mountain men do, as it provided a good secure job. He served as a sergeant in a supply unit for twenty years. With the money he got when he retired he bought some land, since his father's property had to be divided up between four brothers. He made his living from the apple orchard; a bit of milk he sold from the three cows he owned and the occasional tourist to whom he rented a room. He also had a small army pension, paid partially in whisky, which he mostly sold off, for he didn't like the way it made him think. The wheat grown amongst the trees was used to make flour for the family and so were the few other seasonal crops he grew as companions to his apple trees.

I wanted to ask him about his crippled daughter, then again, really, what was there to ask?

We spent the rest of the afternoon strolling around a narrow mountain path, which encircled the village periphery, savouring the uninterrupted environment. Nulla suggested we could stay there for a few days to relax and integrate the events of the last weeks. We were supposed to be on a honeymoon and life was keeping us at a high level of intensity, continually presenting us with life-transforming experiences with which we were still to come to terms with. Nothing in my life had been predictable since I'd met Nulla; it was as though we relegated the driver's seat of the vehicle we were on, to a force that had no name and came from nowhere, as a complete free form of motion. However, it did have a sound, an echo and a hum of a flowing river. This was the first time since we left our village in the desert that we'd had the time to just to be by each other's side and look at the being we had each chosen to be our companion.

Dinner was brought over to our cabin and it wasn't long before we were both deep in sleep, utterly exhausted from the long journey, yet at the same time exhilarated by our new home.

I wasn't sure if I was dreaming, the sound of some sort of motor revving infiltrated my sleep. I opened my eyes, it was early in the morning and Mr Negi stood outside our cabin with another man behind. They were spraying the trees with some sort of white poisonous cloud and the smell was awful. I woke up Nulla in a bit of panic and jumped straight out of bed. I went outside, without bothering to put a shirt on, and started yelling to Mr Negi asking him what the hell he was doing. However, I was clearly aware of what was happening.

"I am spraying the trees with fungicide, so the apples don't have any marks on them," he replied with a smile.

"So why the hell, didn't you warn us beforehand so we could get out of the room instead of being poisoned in our sleep!" I yelled again, furious with him.

"Oh, don't worry, sir, it is only medicine, I spray many times and nothing ever happen to me," he assured us. He and his companion wore no protective gear, apart from handkerchiefs tied around their mouths and noses. I didn't really know what to say, it seemed that he really believed what he was doing was harmless and didn't think of any reason why he should wake us up from our much-earned sleep to alert us to his actions. After I made my feelings known, Mr Negi stopped spraying the toxic chemicals, yet the noxious smell still laced the sweet mountain air for hours.

In that moment it was all too much for me, arriving in what felt like paradise on earth, then being shocked and jolted into the hell that reality can be at times. We packed our bags later that morning and headed back to the road to wait for the bus, which would take us further up the mountain. Mr Negi begged us to stay while stating how sorry he was for his oversight. At the time, I was too young to comprehend the tragedy that was his life; he and the rest of the simple people of the earth enslaved to the great oiled machine called *market forces*.

✳ ✳ ✳ ✳ ✳ ✳ ✳

Swells are visible in the river, while her energy is still. In no way is she agitated by the change in the rhythm of her flow.

I reminisce on my encounter with Mr Negi and how angry I got with him, when really I should have had compassion. He was a victim, another innocent casualty of a system that preyed on the good, simple people of the earth. Another nameless casualty of a ruthless regime that had no concern whatsoever for the wellbeing of the people as long as they continued to toe the line and be part of the deadly *wheel of fortune*.

Over the years, after participating in many campaigns relating to earth matters, I eventually came to comprehend the calamity that was Mr Negi's life and I wished I had not been so cruel as to leave his place in the manner that we did. At the time, I was a young man full of righteousness who did not bother to pause for a moment and ask questions before coming to conclusions.

The fungicides he was using to spray his apple trees are banned in the West, for they have been known to cause birth defects in newborn children. The fact that their use was forbidden in western countries did not stop the big corporations producing them, from rebranding them and selling them to third world countries. This, of course, was done with the conniving silence of the governments in power. The unsuspecting victims were the millions upon millions of small farmers worldwide, some of them illiterate, being played as pawns in a vicious chess game, to bring cheers of victory to the shareholders of their respective companies.

Mr Negi's daughter was, most probably, poisoned by his own hands before she even came into this world. She was one of the millions of anonymous sufferers of the cruel apparatus called the free market. Mr Negi was forced to spray his apples to make them look big, red, shiny, and uniform, or else the wholesaler wouldn't buy them from him. Nobody ever told him that there might be adverse consequences due to his actions or that he and his family could suffer as a result of using this fungicide. The poisons were marketed cleverly with pictures of smiling, happy farmers. The bleak reality is that more and more farmers are committing suicide because they just cannot pay the debts they acquired while embracing these new toxic technologies, which promised them the world and gave them misery.

So, when did this war against the earth we live upon, and the food that we eat begin? When did we sanction *modern agriculture* to be the established and accepted way of producing food for humanity?

Forever and a day, humans grew and gathered their food with no need to poison it. When did the approach shift and when was the decision made that it was time to wage war on the planet and destroy all that comes in the way of profit? They say that agricultural chemicals were first used after World War Two, when there were massive stockpiles of DDT left from the war, and some use had to be found for it. No wonder, any sane person can see that there is a war being waged against the earth – for we are using instruments of war on her and applying a scorched earth policy.

After years of researching the issue of organic versus chemical farming, Nulla and I both came to the conclusion, that chemical farming was one more of these scams, one of the manufactured consents we live in. The idea that the only way to feed the planet is by large-scale industrial farming is another clever mechanism, handing over the reins of growing food to agribusiness, in the process disempowering the masses that for many generations grew their crops by natural means and saved their seeds from year to year—thus allowing the seed itself to adapt to the conditions of the landscape.

Modern agriculture is another arm of the *mono* world a system designed to breed everything into a homogenised form, so it is easier to control and manage. Before the advent of India's green revolution and modern agriculture, India had two hundred thousand varieties of rice. Now it grows mainly twenty varieties and even this is on the decline. There are no profits in a diversified world. The corporations need to narrow the spectrum of everything in order to rule us easily. *Modern agriculture* is just another arm of the monster enslaving humanity.

The new buzz phrase going around *export-oriented agriculture* is another very clever scam. In fact, it's no different to the past slavery in the cotton fields of North America. I thought slavery was abolished a long time ago. Well, perhaps it has been in name, though in deed it's happening these days in the most insidious way and there are many more slaves than were ever brought to America.

The way this dirty game goes is, you get the farmers in the third world to grow cheap cash crops for you at their slave labour wages, and then you get them to buy food off you at premium prices! A well-organised scam orchestrated by the World Bank, the IMF, and the World Trade Organisation.

In the process, all traditional ways of farming are being destroyed. The small farmers are told that it's better to use the money from their cash crops to procure their food needs. Farmers who once grew a proportion of their land into their own kitchen gardens don't dare do so anymore, for fear of not making enough money if they don't utilise all their available land for cash crops. At the same time, the poor countries enslaved by the IMF's restructuring plans, are forced to cease subsidising their farmers while the rich countries pour billions of dollars a day to secure their own farmers; well, not farmers really, rather farm businesses. In the process, the corporations laugh all the way to the bank.

So, in simple words, the corporations get monetary support to produce food while the small farmers worldwide are left to fend for themselves. This is, of course, deliberately designed by the benevolent folk sitting at the helm of the World Bank and the IMF.

How far the big corporations have gone in their quest for total control is made evident by the new technology of terminator seeds—sold to farmers worldwide as superior seeds. Now, has anybody ever thought what terminator seed really means and the ramifications of cultivating plants that cannot reproduce their own next generation? First of course it's a mechanism of greed and control, forcing the farmer to buy the seed with every growing season, rather then collect it's own, thus shackling him in chains to the company enslaving him. And there is more: this technology is in total mistrust to the process of creation and evolution. Plants evolve season by season: they are also subject to the law of change as they adapt to new environments and conditions and the seed's memory encodes all this in it's cells. This GMO seed fantasy is another statement by the powers that be that man is superior to nature and must control it. I wonder when they will make us humans sterile, so we cannot reproduce of our own free will, thus forcing us to buy our seeds, with the selected genes likely to mark our docile enslavement to the company in charge of our future.

Some years ago, a farmer who contracted cancer from years of spraying his crops told me, "If people knew what was in their fruit and veg, there is no way they would eat them!" So how stupid have we become?

There is a lie that has spread like a bad virus amongst the masses that, without poisoning the earth and our food, humanity would starve. It is a sick and insidious lie. The truth is slowly emerging again, that by working in harmony with the earth rather than fighting her, we can grow enough food, of much better nutritional value, and in the process preserve the health of the soil, the water and the earth we all live upon. The other choice is untenable, for, if we continue in this way, we will soon live on an earth without butterflies and bees, as they are slowly dying from the poisons of genetic farming. And more so, with time and the advent of GMO crops, all our food chain would be contaminated by this devil – to the point of no return!

Every child knows that life is not conceivable without the song of the butterflies and buzz of the bee – have we adults forgotten these simple truths? In fact, the issue of Genetically Modified farming is the single most important issue facing us as a collective circle sorting out our relationship with the earth.

Climate change may shift things around a bit, however the effects of GMO farming will annihilate us before we will have time to understand what has happened. Environmental pollution may be able to somehow be tackled successfully if we act *now*, though genetic pollution will never be able to be reversed, no matter what we do.

We may have vanquished many species, while others have somehow survived, however the near future of humanity will be determined by how far we go with this insane nightmare called GMO farming – championed by a company that acts and sounds like the devil's stock broker. We are insidiously being led to believe that the genetic manipulation of plants, animals and fish, which is taking place at an accelerated rate, is done for our benefit.

So what makes this ruthless and distorted regime we are living under possible? What makes it click as a truth with the *silent majority*? Is it a mind that is not aware of its infinite nature, is it our beings that are never present with life, and ever distracted by anything and everything which sidetracks it from the moment that *is*?

Thus the world has taken a nightmare pill and each and every one of us is playing little monsters in a disturbed sleep. We need to wake up right now!

Martin Luther King, Jr. said in 1967, ". . . a time comes when silence is betrayal." He said it at a time when the horrors of war were the echoes bouncing around the sleepwalkers, while now the horrors are sprouting of the same root, and the war waged is against all of us — against the whole circle of creation.

Nobi is right; it is the ones that *know* and, in spite of this, keep quiet, who are the real culprits in this saga. We cannot live with this betrayal anymore; the time is *now* to sing the song of hope, while we make our voices heard in the four corners of the earth.

It was at the time of the seemingly negative experiences with the dam and the night at Mr Negi's farm, that my eyes opened to the folly of the world and at the same time compelled me to journey within, into a place untouched by the world around me. The place where the harmony *is* ever — ever was and ever will be.

It was those moments that instilled a resolve in me that I must act, though I was very aware that my survival in dealing with these negative forces depended on my inner peace.

We travelled on the bus until the last stop, which was the end of the road. From there on transportation was on the backs of sturdy mules negotiating the steep and narrow mountain tracks. The bus parked in a small hamlet nestled where the tree line gave way to the land of infinite snow. The landscape around us felt like a drawing from a fairy tale told by a choir of dancing Gods. The towering mountains seemed so close it felt as if we could reach out and touch them. They were like crystals, beacons of shimmering light, the snow reflecting the iridescent rays of the sun that were able to penetrate through the thick fluffy clouds.

We got off the bus and immediately were approached by a young Indian man around our age whom had travelled the bus journey with us.

"Are you here to see Om Baba?" he asked us in perfect English with a hint of a London accent. He wore the traditional white clothes of kurta pyjama yet had a very western manner about him.

"No, who is Om Baba?" I replied, while introducing Nulla and myself. He felt somehow embarrassed for approaching us without first introducing himself; the type of urgency I often observed people have when they are on a mission.

"I am sorry for being a bit rude. My name is Ashok. I have just arrived a few days ago from London where I am studying. I am on my way to see this great sage I heard about, an enlightened soul, who lives in a cave a few kilometres away from this village. They say that whoever meets him is instantly transformed once he gazes into their eyes," he said with a sense of excitement and purpose in his voice. "What are you guys doing here?" he asked us, while looking at Nulla, who I guess was more pleasing to look at than I was.

"We don't really know; we got carried here by the winds of fate with a purpose we have yet to grasp." Nulla answered him in her usual poetic way, fusing her French fervour with a tinge of a British accent that she had acquired in the two years she had studied there. She wrapped her shawl around her neck and rubbed her hands together, breathing into them. It was cold and we really didn't have many warm clothes suited for a high altitude climate.

"We need to get a room and then find if there is a shop to buy some warm clothes from. How about we meet in the evening in the chai shop and you can tell us more about this holy man?" I said to Ashok, while picking up my bag to make a move.

"Cool, that would be great, let's meet around sunset in

that small restaurant across the road," he said pointing over to the small eating establishment where half a dozen pilgrims were sitting around low wooden tables.

"Where would you be staying?" I asked him.

"Oh, I will go straight away to find Om Baba; they say that when he feels a special energy in you he invites you to stay with him in his cave, so actually, if you don't see me in the evening, then come over to the cave tomorrow. I assume that most of the locals will be able to point you in the right direction." That said, off he went in a hurry to find the enlightened soul he had come to meet from a long way away.

We were in no hurry, though, to meet any enlightened soul. Our beings were overtaken by the magnitude of our surroundings and the awe emanating from every particle of air present in this place.

We found a room in a small wooden guesthouse. Most of the houses in the hamlet offered a room to the few pilgrims who dared to venture to the abode of the Gods. The houses were all similar, made with thick wooden beams, wedged in amongst layers of stone. The roofs were constructed from wider slabs of stone and all the materials were sourced from the surrounding environment. The houses blended perfectly into the landscape as though they were an integral part of it. Once we settled in, the owner told us where we could buy some woollens to keep us warm.

It was a tiny village, more like a settlement built around the small temple in the centre. The temple was situated in a courtyard enclosed by ancient stonewalls which were ornamented with carvings of different gods. The carved stone looked old and it told me that the temple had stood here for a very long time.

Within the courtyard we could observe steam rising to meet the cool air, and to our surprise and delight we learned that inside the temple yard were hot, steaming sulphuric springs. There were two small bathing pools separated by a stonewall, one to serve the men and the other for the women. The temple itself comprised of a tiny shrine housing the resident deity, a Goddess-guardian of the hot steaming water, the giver of a gift of warmth in the land of eternal chill.

Thrilled by our discovery, we rushed to our room to get our sarongs and hurried back to the temple delighted by the prospect of taking a bath in the hot springs while the air outside was so close to freezing. Entering the small enclosure reserved for the men, I could sense again this ever-growing familiar feeling inside me, a knowing that I had arrived at a destiny guided by the angels pulling the strings of my journey and all I had to do was listen — holding deep attention to the whisper of the moment. I took off my clothes; it was late afternoon and freezing cold, especially to a body that had just spent the past year sweltering in temperatures usually hovering above forty degrees. As my feet met the water, I felt as though a fire was burning through me. The water was so hot it felt as if it was close to boiling, however the freezing cold air was enough of an incentive to garner the courage to dare to immerse my body in the liquid furnace.

There was one other man in the bath. He was an old man with long white dreadlocks and a very skinny body. He appeared to be in deep prayer and I wondered if he lived permanently in the land of the white glowing mountains, or was he just a pilgrim like myself, drawn here by the invisible hand of fate.

Bit by bit my body grew accustomed to the heat, while my breath slowed down to a faint whisper. I could hear it as it slowly and gently meandered in and out of my nostrils. Every now and then I lifted myself up to the ledge of the pool to cool down a bit before immersing myself again in what was gradually feeling like a welcoming womb in the heart of the majestical mountains.

Gradually, time and thought became one and melted

away as I was forced to pay full attention to the rhythm that held my being together in the sheer quest to keep breathing. The fire in the water robbed me of all sense of self, while the flurry in the mind dissipated. I was just a body engulfed by a liquid fire, which burned off all thought and desire, and all that remained was mere breath, presence, existence. For the first time in my life, I felt totally and utterly still.

It is interesting to note that in the language of this land, the word for yesterday and tomorrow is one and the same. It's not a joke; Indians use the same word for the past and future. Nothing reflects the reality of this land more than the truth of this oversight, or perhaps more accurately this great *insight*. It's all a game, there are no yesterdays or tomorrows, they are the same thing, illusions, fantasies; occupations of a mind wandering away from infinity's touch.

To be *here and now* was suddenly not a cool philosophical concept in this boiling bath, rather a hot emanating presence. Being in a timeless space, I failed to notice the passage of time. It was almost dark when I recalled we had a date with Ashok for dinner.

After drying myself and dressing while paying total attention to every move I made, I gave my homage and gratitude to the guardian and giver of this divine immersion and walked the short distance to the room to pick up Nulla. We walked over to the restaurant huddled together; feeling each other's silence and presence of being. Ashok wasn't there, so we decided to sit by a small table in the corner and order a chai while we waited for him to come and join us.

By the time it was pitch black we gathered Ashok wasn't coming. "The holy man must have liked him and invited him to stay in the cave. Let's order some food, I am really tired and quiet after the amazing bath. I wouldn't mind eating and going to sleep," Nulla said, while moving closer to me for the warmth the other always offers when the night is cold. We ordered the only thing on the menu, which was rice and kidney beans and ate our food slowly and in silence. The few other customers all seemed to be in the same mood, as though the fire/water had taken the gibberish out and replaced it with mindfulness. Following our dinner, we quickly retired to our room to snuggle under the heavy warm blankets. We lay in bed holding each other as close as we could. It felt that all separation, male, female, you and me, had been vanquished by the enchantment of God's playground. Lying next to my divine Goddess, I felt an enduring thanksgiving for the life that had born me manifest and the gifts it was constantly bestowing on me, namely through a woman called Nulla.

I loved Nulla, cherished her, admired her, liked her, enjoyed every moment in her company and trusted her more than I knew was ever possible. At the same time, it occurred to me that, while we had been married for more than four months, we had only made love about half a dozen times. Each time, it had been a blissful sensual experience, and at the same time I was not consumed by some burning desire for Nulla, nor did I have this constant urge to take her to bed, as I had done with women in my past. Was there something missing, or were our lives filled with a deeper love, surrender and constant stimulation by the intense experiences life brought upon us? I rolled over to ask Nulla how she felt about it, only to discover that she was already one with the angels, in a deep peaceful sleep. Closing my eyes I held her as close as I could without squeezing her completely. Our bodies were glued together as one. There was nothing wrong with our love - it was exactly what it was.

"I love you Nulla," I whispered in her ear, knowing that wherever she was, she could surely hear me.

＊ ＊ ＊ ＊ ＊ ＊ ＊

I do wonder now, sitting by the river so many years later, if Nulla can still hear me whispering "I love you Nulla," although her body is nowhere to be seen and it's been months on end, now, since we walked this life together.

Does love have any boundaries? Is it confined to space and time or does it live in an eternal land, unbounded by the realms of the senses?

Love can be warm at times—a tonic to the soul, like sipping warm mead on a cosy winter night. At the same time, when the heat is on, love burns, destroys, annihilates, floors us breathless, like a raging army that has just completed a search and destroy mission. We lay there at times, wounded in the battlefield of the heart, licking our wounds.

Yet with courage, insight and proper understanding of the procedure, we eventually gaze beyond the emotional bosh consuming us, to feel the divine fire that has just wiped our slate clean. Our spirit is renewed then, to merge with a heart much nearer to the core of where love in truth abides.

At other times, love freezes, withdraws, and beckons the cold winter of the soul. There is no giving or receiving; it just stands still. She instils within us the bravery to watch the *moment that is* and trust that, in her return she would, like wine, taste sweeter with the passage of the frosty cycles.

Love sincerely happens when the land of the brave is finally trodden upon. It has no demise, for its essence is death; it doesn't live in time, it abides in presence. Love reflects itself in presence and death, for they are one and the same.

"I hear you Nulla; I feel your song wherever you are. You can never be separated from me, for we have touched in the land where the earth mother is joined in unison with father sky."

I felt a beam of awareness infiltrating the numerous reluctant cells in my being, the organisms that were still holding on to the idea of *self* that day on top of a cold mountain. The fire in the water burned off all remaining resistance; to soothe my soul and empty it of all the accumulated junk borrowed from the world. Lifetimes of layers of shit stagnating within me were burned off, to be replaced by the celebration of presence.

With the passage of time and walking along life's winding roads, did Nulla and I hold onto our union too strongly? And holding onto love is like holding onto grains of sand. The harder we hold them, the quicker they slip away from our hands.

Did we continue to gaze at each other with the eyes of wonder that reach for the sky as we did on top of the snow mountain, or did we come to accept the other by our side, as some sort of divinely ordained birthright? When did I stop treating Nulla's presence in my life as a wonder of heaven? Was it the moment I began to expect that tomorrow would still usher in the same miracle as today?

The river whispers the prayer of change with every moment that it *is*. So is the story with life and love and all that dances between heaven and earth.

It was early morning; the fog engulfed the mountains as a mother protects her child with the warmth of her shawl, though there was nothing warm about this early morning mist. It was freezing, and immediately upon rising from sleep we hurried our cold bodies into the hot springs. The sun was still to make her appearance known behind the wall of mountains delaying her arrival. The people in the bath looked like shadows amongst the rising steam and prevailing mist of early dawn. The sulphuric smell of the water was half pleasant and half nauseating at first. There were a few men in the bath that morning, about a dozen, each focusing in on their own inner world. Some were in deep prayer, while others were just immersed in the bliss and silence of a body that could do nothing except surrender to the force of the steaming heat as it beat the early morning frost hands down. The moment my clothes were off, I submerged my body in the water until only my head was exposed, it too warmed by the clouds of steam rising from the bath. It was as though nature was challenging itself by offering this warmth in defiance of the frosty atmosphere.

Someone gently tapped my shoulder; I looked over and to my surprise it was Ashok by my side. "Good to see you, mate, how was the night in the cave?" I asked him in a quiet voice, in respect for the prevailing calm.

"I didn't stay in the cave. Om Baba didn't even talk to me. He let me sit by his fire for an hour or so and then told me it was time to leave," he said with a great sense of disappointment in his voice. "I am sorry I didn't show up for dinner, I felt like being alone after my meeting with him," he continued to talk in a soft voice, while staring at the steam arising from the water.

"How did you feel though, in his presence?" I queried him, not sure if he really wanted to talk about it anymore; he seemed somewhere far away.

"I am not sure, I am really confused now. I've come a long way and spent a lot of money to be here. I had great expectations that an amazing transformation would occur, and now I am just not really clear why I am even here at all."

I listened to him while my attention was divided between his voice and the sound of my own slowing breath. Expectations—don't they always lead to some sort of disappointment? What right did Ashok have to expect Om Baba to transform his life? It was strange, though, for me to observe the workings of my own mind. Up to that moment I had no interest whatsoever in going to see this holy man, and now somehow a curiosity arose within me. Those who spoke through their silence always intrigued me. For the same reason Ashok felt rejected by Om Baba, I suddenly sensed a certain attraction to meet this silent recluse.

"Did he say anything to you?" I asked Ashok, with my unexpected interest in Om Baba emerging.

"No, he just sat in silence looking at the fire, and then basically asked me to leave."

"Really," I thought. "What is there to say? Whatever can be said of any real value lives in a realm where words do not abide."

"I would like to go and meet Om Baba today, how far is the walk?" I asked Ashok.

"A bit more than an hour." The dejection still lingered in his voice.

"Look Ashok, he offered you something beautiful; he shared with you his silence rather than bombarding you, or worse trying to impress you with a chorus of worthless words." I tried to console him and offer another perspective to his meeting with the saint.

"Yes, I can hear what you are saying, nevertheless I thought he would offer me some guidance, give me some words of wisdom, something to take back home with me."

I left Ashok to his own space, while feeling the company of the heat melting me away. My mind traversed through memory lanes, the times in my own life when I had felt glum and abandoned by people who failed to fulfil the expectations I placed upon them. The times when I handed over to others the responsibility to fill the void within me, a task they were always bound to fail. As things stood, I was never much into holy men, really; in a way I had some aversion to them. Though something in the fact that this Baba did not offer Ashok anything other than his silence appealed to me.

Ashok had come halfway across the world to see this man, and the Baba did not oblige his expectations, he just stared at the fire. "Cool," I thought to myself, "I will go and see him today; I would love to feel this man who offers his wisdom in silence."

Once the three of us had shared a breakfast of chai and parathas[13*], I asked Ashok if he would come with us to meet the Baba again. He declined my invitation, saying he would rather stay in the village and think about what he was going to do next. He walked us to the beginning of the path that led to the cave. We walked slowly in silence amongst the majestic fir and rhododendron trees, the last few that managed to grow at these heights. They had a timeless aura and an intriguing quality about them, as if they could be the storytellers of these mountain paths.

After a while the track narrowed and we started climbing along a cliff that eventually led onto a glistening grass plateau. The scenery was breathtaking; a wide grass meadow above the clouds, strewn with wild flowers, surrounded by mountains as tall as the sky itself. The air was clear and cold; it tingled in the nostrils and tasted as sweet as ever. If the air we breathe could be categorized, this was the French champagne of air, the primo vintage edition.

There were a few shepherds around with small herds of hairy mountain goats and sheep. They came to graze these highlands during the summer months and left for the lowlands with the arrival of the first snows. The shepherds belonged to the remaining few nomadic tribes still free to roam on these tracks. They had been grazing these lands from the time man first made his presence felt in this part of the world.

We stopped on a big flat rock and sat down to savour the environs. Nulla took out her small sketching pad from

---

13   * Indian flat bread with more than one layer.

her bag and started drawing, while I sat down by her side and stared at the world around me. The sun's morning rays were reflecting on the white snowy mountains, with shimmering lights bubbling everywhere. The effect was a feast of floating rainbows that looked like drops of water in every shade of colour imaginable, with peachy amethyst pinks dominating this riot of colours.

My hand was drawing circles in the atmosphere around me, as I was trying to touch the fleeting mirage, which was as real as anything I had ever seen. Nulla smiled at me while continuing to draw with her more tangible thick black pencil. I noticed on her pad that more than the landscape; the amazing features of the nomadic tribal shepherds captivated her imagination. They lived so close with the land in this most inhospitable terrain and moved when nature told them that it was time. One could read the tale of cycles in the facial topography of these amazing people; their looks were illustrations of their lives. What made their features unique was that the story of their life was one and the same with the story of the earth they walked upon. It was a story of cycles, of change, of constant renewal while walking the pathways of old.

We sat on the flat rock for a while before anyone approached us. At last a young child about ten years old did. She was terribly shy in the presence of two white ghosts in the place where only the shepherds and the Gods tread. However, her curiosity was stronger than her wariness and she wanted to have a look at Nulla's drawings.

Nulla was used to shy Indian kids and it didn't take long before she disarmed her with her artful French charm, entwined with her Asian sensibility to cultural codes. Apart from that, she had a knack with kids, for she loved them utterly for who they were, and they in return adored her.

The young girl's name was Devi; it felt appropriate that she should be named Goddess while living in the land of nature's own temples.

The nomad's spoke their own language, so even a bit of broken Hindi was useless in these parts of the world. Through patient sign language Nulla managed to explain to Devi that we were on the way to see the saint that lived in the cave. A big white dog that hung out with the shepherds came over to suss us out and to make sure that we were being kind to the little Goddess who had graced us with her company of smiles. Dogs know everything about you immediately, and this one discerned that we had come in peace. In return she offered to be our guide and accompany us to see Om Baba. Devi wanted to come too, except we weren't sure if it was okay to take her away from where her family was grazing their herd. I suggested to Nulla that she could walk over and approach the two adults in the distance to see if it was allowed for Devi to come with us.

A short time later Nulla returned on her own, apparently permission wasn't given, or perhaps there was just miscommunication in the absence of any common language. The big dog, however, was still eager to go on an adventure and Nulla had already named her Angel — for she really looked and felt like one. We weren't sure if we needed permission to take her. On the other hand, it didn't feel as if she would listen to anything other than the calling of her own spirit as she continually sniffed the cold wind for clues of what was taking place on these high mountain tracks. We proceeded to follow Angel *knowing* that she would lead us to Om Baba.

Whoever has walked the great Himalayan Mountains must be aware of the amazing phenomenon of being escorted by a dog, sometimes for days, until they reach their destination. They appear like guardian angels and disappear as if they were beings from another world. The locals claim that Himalayan dogs are reincarnations of holy men who once walked the mountains and now come to assist and guide us, while they still enjoy the freedom and exhilaration of living amongst the Gods.

We walked for about half an hour on the plateau before the mountains formed a natural barrier and all what was left was a tiny narrow path only wide enough to be walked one foot at a time, as we held to the edge of the mountain overlooking the valley below. We stayed as close as we could to the rock wall, for the drop was a long way down. I was glad to have Angel with us and wondered why Ashok didn't tell us of the difficulties in reaching the cave. It wasn't long, though, before the path widened and in the distance we could see a trail of smoke meandering through the clouds. It was Om Baba's fire and we were delighted to have finally reached it. It must have taken us the best part of three hours to get there and I had to bear in mind how Indians always have a different take on time or timelessness than what we westerners do. "About an hour," is what Ashok had said, and really that could've meant anything. Perhaps if we walked with more purpose and gusto as he did, it would have taken us an hour to reach the cave.

Om Baba greeted Angel with great affection, as though they were old mates who had known each other for a long time. He sat at the entrance to his cave, cross-legged by a small fire, a picture postcard of how I always imagined a recluse in a Himalayan cave to look.

A long flowing white beard adorned his face and his hair was matted in perfect silver dreadlocks that almost reached to the ground. He was a bit chubby though, and I wondered where he got the abundance of food and sweets from to make him more than a bit overweight. For some reason I had always imagined Himalayan yogis to be skinny. It was hard for me to gauge how old he was, he could have been anywhere between forty and sixty years old. He wore an orange lungi with a matching orange jumper and sat on a magnificent tiger skin. His eyes were piercing with the fire of some other knowing, while he welcomed us warmly and motioned to us to sit down. A young disciple present with him quickly brought us a deerskin to sit on as we warmed our hands by the welcoming fire. The fire not only radiated warmth, it also emitted a delicious fragrance of a native Himalayan pinewood.

Om Baba, after making sure we are comfortable by the fire ordered his disciple to make us chai and proceeded to ask the usual small talk questions of, "Where are you from," and "What are you doing in India." His voice was calm and soothing and his English good. We told him of our life by the rat temple in the desert and our experience in Nandini with the tribal folk and the emerging anti-dam, pro-people movement. We learnt that he was from the southern part of the country where people didn't speak much Hindi; therefore his main way to communicate with his compatriots from the north was in English. He did learn some Hindi when he studied Sanskrit while at university and for a while he held a government job as a stationmaster in the Indian railways. He considered all this to be a past life within this incarnation, while now he was living his true destiny.

I couldn't stop thinking of Ashok and the promise of a silent Baba, for this one was quite a chatterbox, happy to natter away over a sweet cup of chai on any subject you like. I felt that this young foreign couple that had made their way up to the land beyond the clouds intrigued him. Perhaps when we expect silence we are greeted with words and when we want words we receive only silence. Does the universe always have to play the trickster?

The cave behind him looked comfortable and luxurious with many animal skins, rugs, carpets, an array of cooking utensils, and so on. It felt like a snug camp in the mountains. I couldn't stop looking at the magnificent tiger skin, his eyes staring at me as though he were still very much alive and pleading the case of his species. How many of these majestic creatures must have been killed to add extra kudos to the Babas in possession of one, and to add the extra power, which they perceived sitting in meditation on a tiger skin imparts? "Does the land of ultimate peace, internal silence, the place beyond the mind, depend on the death of a tiger?" I wondered.

Om Baba's company was soft and easy. He treated us as friends who had popped over for a visit. We just shared the uncomplicated small talk that people often do to pass time and get to know each other better. As I was a chronic sceptic of holy men, I kept observing him intently to the point that at one stage Nulla elbowed my ribs, as though to say, "Stop it and let the man be!" He was a kind man, who on one hand communicated aloofness and detachment, and at the same time was willing to interact with us ordinary mere mortals. It felt that whatever he was looking for in life he had found, and was at peace with the world around him.

The sun was already low on the horizon, somewhere unseen behind the high mountains and I felt it was time for us to leave if we were to reach the village any time before dark. I didn't fancy walking these mountains paths in the dark without a torch and only the stars light as our guide.

"I feel it's time for us to leave, it's going to get dark soon. Thank you so much for your hospitality," I said to him while rising from the deerskin and offering my hand to Nulla.

"Please, you are welcome to stay the night in the cave, it is just me and Krishna and there is plenty of space. I have lots of blankets to keep you warm," he assured us. I looked at Nulla for a clue of what we should do and although I knew she already knew what she wanted, she didn't let me in on it. It was her usual way and it pissed me off when I was in the duality of indecision.

"Yes, that would be nice. We will stay the night here if Nulla wants to do so," I said. Nulla smiled at me with approval. It really made me irate at times that she expected me to take on all the decisions in the world, although, of course, it had to be what she had already decided on in her mind. If I was out of sync with where she was at, which although wasn't often, she would immediately let me know of it.

Krishna, Om Baba's disciple and flatmate in the plush cave, cooked us a delicious dinner. We had dhal, rice, green beans, corn, yoghurt, and a dessert of sweet semolina halva. I asked Om Baba, "Where does all this food come from?"

He answered with a broad smile, "God provides." I learned in the coming days we spent in the village by the hot springs that *God* was all his disciples, who constantly made sure the cave was well stocked by sending in supplies with an army of porters. Om Baba wasn't a recluse in the true sense. He owned prime real estate overlooking the Garden of Eden, actually within the garden itself and he lived a comfortable existence within the perimeters of his cave. And as far as caves were concerned, it was unquestionably a five-star one. I didn't mind that aspect of Om Baba at all, in fact it somehow encouraged me to drop my guard and observe him for what he really was. He wasn't pretending to be some sort of ascetic living a life of denial, atoning for the sins of humanity, not at all. He'd found a good pad, peace within and enjoyed the fire constantly burning at the edge of the cave. Once a week he went to the hot springs for a few hours, he told us, though apart from that excursion, he'd been nowhere else for the last seven years.

He continually urged us to eat more until we were stuffed and then of course came the obligatory chai. I thought of Ashok, what he would have given to spend a night in the cave with this Baba, which he had come to see from halfway across the planet. We hadn't even planned to see him and happened to visit him because we were at the same place at the same time. There is some sort of universal intelligence and a law that states that in the absence of *want* we often receive unexpected gifts from the universe.

A hot chai in hand and our stomachs stuffed with food, we leaned on the fat cushions, enjoying the marvels of the night. An almost full moon adorned the sky. The moon was playing hide and seek with legions of clouds constantly drifting over its surface. The same was happening with the glowing mountain peaks, which kept appearing and disappearing as the clouds danced around them. The gentle breeze was cold, yet not freezing. I felt silent and at peace. The time in Nandini felt like the distant past at this moment. There was nothing I wanted to ask Om Baba or at least that's what I thought. I was happy that at last we were offered the promised silence Ashok had spoken of. We sat there for some hours in a timeless zone soaking in the presence of the mountains. The breeze made a gentle sound as it was whispering a tale of renewal and change. In the distance an owl hooted into the night; I wondered if this was the king of owls, the one living closest to the skyways above the clouds. A stream was cascading in the distance and I learned that it was Om Baba's water source, carrying to him the purest water on earth, direct from the mouth of the Gods.

We must have drifted off into sleep by the fire, as I felt a hand on my shoulder softly wake me up. Krishna had made our beds in the cave, two mattresses with thick woollen blankets to keep the nights cold away. Om Baba sat motionless in front of the fire. He was in deep meditation. Without a sound we walked over to our beds, snug in the cave that felt like nothing short of a safe womb at the heart of the mountains.

❋ ❋ ❋ ❋ ❋ ❋ ❋

Nobi arrives back with a great flutter of his wings, announcing his presence by my side again. His appearance snaps me out of my dream state and I feel a bit annoyed by the sudden interruption to my journey into memories of the days above the clouds. Nonetheless, I am glad he is with me again. I do wonder, though, where he has been in these few short moments.

"So, where is this wonderful woman you are so absorbed in dreaming about? How come she is not by your side, putting some sense into you now and walking you up the hill?" he says, half mocking me.

He has a good point, as he always seems to. Nulla would be utterly furious if she were here and probably would drag me by force. Or would she? I wonder. Why is she not here, then? What was our last senseless argument really all about? The stupid incident, which made me leave the woman I love and come back to the land that always offered solace to my soul.

I refused to offer legal support to some brothers and sisters caught vandalising property in a protest. Nulla was furious with me, to the point that it turned into an endless argument. I didn't want to support people who engaged in senseless violence; while Nulla felt whatever they did they were on the right side of the argument and deserved to be supported.

Yes, I did end up doing a law degree, though not to fulfil my father's dream, rather at the insistence of Nulla. She felt I had a mind, sharp as a razor and having a law degree would arm me with a valuable tool in the struggle for a new earth, though I am not sure if it ever did. I never took to the bar or represented anybody in court, rather used my knowledge to tackle the big corporations we were challenging and investigate whether they were breaking environmental or labour laws. On occasions I held it against Nulla; all this time I felt I had wasted getting a degree, which only made me understand a legal system that I did not believe in or trust.

Some people said we had to join the system to change it from within.

I don't credit anymore the validity of this argument. How can we change a system founded on rotten principles.

Any such change would be a cosmetic one, rather than a transformation of substance. We need to dream a new reality on earth, one that is inspired by ancient wisdom and pregnant with the freshness of a new dawn.

Both Nulla and I changed over the years. It was bound to happen - and how much each accepted the change in the other is reflected in where we are at today, worlds apart.

In our younger days I was the more militant one, mistrusting visions such as the one offered by Shanti and wanting to see more tangible action. Nulla was much softer and trusting. With time, Nulla became more radical in her views as we observed the constant evils of the system we lived in, while I retreated into my shell, seeking the light and peace within. I got disillusioned with the process offered by my brethren, which felt like singing half-hearted truths while still dancing to the tune of the mammon gods. In a way, I all but gave up on the possibility of meaningful change while Nulla got fixated, radical and determined. We both wanted the same thing, though at the same time we were viewing it from different vantage points in the circle of experience.

I knew it was temporary; however, this knowing didn't ease the ensuing conflict between us. At times I felt I really didn't want to see her again and I suspected she had the same feeling about me.

It hurt, really hurt, though there was nothing I could do to change the situation or at least that's what I believed at the time. Approaching our fifties we were as stubborn as we were when we met more than twenty-five years ago in the desert. The fact that we journeyed together all this time was a testimony to the most astounding love and care we had for each other—a love that no words could ever explain or define. A love that anchored its presence in our times in the desert village, in the tribal community by the river, and in the land where the mountains met the living room of the Gods.

✳ ✳ ✳ ✳ ✳ ✳ ✳

I woke at the crack of dawn feeling the freezing cold air bubbling through the cave. It may have been an opulent space; nonetheless it was open and exposed to the harsh climate of a mountainside over three thousand metres above sea level. I noticed Om Baba sitting motionless by the small fire in the same spot where he was when we went to sleep and wondered if he had been in that place all night.

Krishna fed the fire with some fresh wood, looking blurry eyed as though he had just woken up as well. I asked him if Om Baba was in meditation all night and he replied in the affirmative. He told me in a whisper, as not to disturb his master, that Om Baba rarely sleeps, he uses the still nights for meditation. He said that soon when Om Baba emerged from his meditative space he would prepare breakfast for all of us.

Breakfast was a delicious affair of sweet rice porridge cooked with raisins, almonds, walnuts, dates and grated coconut—it was not surprising than that Om Baba looked the way he did with the constant feast being laid out in his remote Himalayan cave. We ate in silence and washed down the porridge with the mandatory sweet chai. "No wonder India is full of sugar cane fields; these people have a sweet tooth like no other I had ever met before," I thought to myself.

Om Baba looked at us at length; all of a sudden his eyes felt piercing and threatening. He didn't feel like the friendly uncle he had projected himself to be the night before. At last he talked and I was relieved, for if he wasn't going to break the silence, I was.

"You know, young man," he addressed me as though Nulla didn't exist. "What you told me about your time in that tribal village where the dam is being built . . . " he paused to make sure I was listening to him, the way I observed many holy men talked; very slow, turning every story into a suspense thriller to extract maximum attention and command of the conversation.

"This anti-dam story is all a waste of time. There is nothing to be done in this life on earth; our only goal is to attain to the ultimate truth—nirvana, samadhi, oneness with the supreme. You will be a fool to be drawn into the plight of these people; whatever is taking place in that valley has nothing to do with you. It is their bad karma from the actions in previous lives and no one can help them. All over the world their time is coming to an end. This is Kali yoga, the time when the fire burns and the darkness prevails throughout the entire earth, it is a cleansing process that will go on for some time to come," he said.

He kept talking, although I was already somewhere else, my blood on fire: I wanted to scream at his prejudice. He wasn't a spiritual man to me anymore. In an instant he turned into a religious bigot, full of judgement and righteousness. Nulla squeezed my arm as she always did when she felt the storm brewing in me about to spit fire. It was way too late though. I wasn't burning—I was boiling over.

"What do you mean, it's their bad karma, you lazy hypocrite sitting up here in a cave, full of holy philosophies, with no concern for the welfare of humanity?" I yelled at him and could hear the echoes of my voice bouncing off the mountains. I noticed Krishna grab a big stick ready to defend the honour of his master. Om Baba gestured to him that there was no need to hit this stupid foreigner just yet. I stood up ready to leave that place which suddenly felt more like a disgusting den than a beautiful Himalayan cave.

"Relax, my child, what I am talking about you may not understand now, though one day you will," he said, attempting to bridge the gap. Being condescending, however, at the same time acting as though he knew something I didn't.

"I am not your child and never will be," I snapped back at him.

"How can we ignore the suffering of others?" Nulla joined the conversation, challenging Om Baba's truths, in a much softer way, a way that could actually be heard.

"Suffering is a relative thing and is connected to karma. There is nothing you can do to help these people or anybody else for that matter. You can only help yourself," he said as though stating a truth that could not be challenged. I wasn't sure what to say anymore. It wasn't the first time I met a holy man with this type of attitude and it wouldn't be the last. It felt to me more like the foundation of fascism rather than the doorway to a spiritual quest—words that would resonate like music to the ears of the likes of Mussolini or George W. Bush. The code of belief that another's suffering is not our business infuriated me.

I wondered why Ashok had come from the other side of the world to meet this man and felt that perhaps it was his own good karma that Om Baba had ignored him, lest he instil the idea into him of a separate self, of a self that is only concerned with one's own personal welfare.

"Sir," I addressed him with a much calmer tone, yet the inferno of indignation was still ablaze within me. "Aren't you a Yogi? And doesn't yoga mean union; that the entire universe is connected together on one thread?" I asked him.

He looked back at me and I wasn't sure what to make of his look. He didn't seem angry, nor was he in a hurry to answer me. Instead he ordered Krishna to make another cup of chai and feed the fire with some more wood.

He said he was off to freshen himself up in the small spring, the place where they drew the drinking and cooking water from, which was a ten-minute walk away. I suggested we leave for the village, while he insisted we stay and finish our conversation after a visit to the spring. He invited us to come with him and I surrendered, feeling almost powerless to disagree. We walked in silence whilst I wondered who this man was and what he offered his thousands of devotees that throng to him from all over the world. His walk was a bit clumsy and didn't reflect the solid stature he emanated when he sat in meditation.

It was good to breathe in the fresh crisp mountain air; it cleared my lungs and head after many hours of inhaling the sweet smoke of the fire in the cave. The small cascading creek had its source somewhere in the snows above. The water was freezing and delicious as I put my hands in to draw a drink from the fountain of the Gods. We washed our hands and faces and dried ourselves with the towel offered by Om Baba.

He wasn't a bad man by any stretch of the imagination, neither did I feel malice in him; definitely there was none towards us, even after my outburst in the cave. However, he was a religious man and at times this notion reflects a more dangerous proposition than anything else. He was aligned with his gods, his scriptures and his line of subjective HisStory. This was *his* land and given to him by *his* gods. The fact that people had lived here long before the Hindu civilisation arrived, meant nothing to him. The fact that they had their own Gods and a different set of beliefs was irrelevant. History and truth started with His Story, as far this holy man was concerned. Then again he wasn't alone; there were millions like him worldwide.

I had many more questions raging in me and I wanted to challenge his truth to make him see where I was coming from, still I decided to wait until we got back to the cave and had our morning tea.

Enjoying a sweet cup of tea again, I repeated the question about the union of all things. "You see my son," he started with his parental tone again, and I hated to be addressed as his son. He may have been older, nevertheless, his statement was surely patronizing, implying a right to some superior knowledge. "Union means to be united with the supreme, not with the illusion of the world. According to our belief, this world is Maya, an illusion, and a playground that is not real. It only serves as a vehicle to realise the supreme and return to the source which gave us life," he said.

I don't know why, it felt as though he was regurgitating borrowed knowledge, fancy words, that shone with some glimmers of truth, although at the same time it felt like the recipe for ultimate escapism.

"What about the Hindu belief, that serving others is a path to self-realisation?" I challenged him again, sensing I'd finally said something that could not be sidestepped.

"Yes, if you want to feed the poor there is some merit in it, yet it will not deliver you to the ultimate goal. At the same time, you cannot join and fight the struggle of these tribal people, their primitive days are over and it has nothing to do with you," he said.

I was over him. I could feel a bit of what he was saying, the bit of how important self-transformation was. In spite of this, the core of his philosophy seemed like the perfect formula to abdicate from the procession of life, and live as a separate self without a meaningful relationship to the circle. In truth, I did not feel that this Baba reflected the essence of Hinduism. Over my many years in India I have met more people than I can remember, whose sole life purpose was the service of humanity, the upliftment of the poor and the less fortunate; the ones dealt a raw deal by life's circumstances. All the volunteers at Nandini, who had left comfortable lives to go and support a struggle which was not their own, were a living testimony of the giving, unselfish nature, of many of the people of this great land. As I grew up a bit more and watched the workings of the world around me, I realised that holiness rarely resides within *holy people*.

We thanked Om Baba for his hospitality and left to head back to the village. Once we turned the first rocky outcrop corner, we saw Angel wagging her tail enthusiastically, ready to guide us again to our destination. We could hear her saying in dog language, "Welcome back to the interconnectedness; interdependent being of life on earth and beyond." We stopped to give Angel a serious belly rub and thank her for sharing with us the one thing that was so absent in Om Baba's cave—Love.

❋ ❋ ❋ ❋ ❋ ❋ ❋

It strikes me suddenly that I am talking out my memories aloud, allowing Nobi a glimpse of my inner dream world. It is clear to me, however, that he hears my inner chatter and knows everything he needs to know about what is going on inside me at the moment.

"You fool, you mister human. Can't you see into your own being? You have become just like that Om Baba, the one you have despised and judged all those years ago," he said with delight in finally hammering his point in, and winning one over me.

"I don't think so Nobi," I replied, feeling a bit hurt by the association he made. "I have spent the last quarter of a century serving people and working with earth matters, I feel I have earned the right to retreat," I said, feeling vindicated.

"Bullshit, you have just given up, lost stamina to walk the full journey. And very rarely did you really give your best, the totality of your being. A lot of the time you did it because it was the 'in' thing to do. Other times you had to be pushed into it by your woman, who from day one noticed your tendencies to run away from the challenges of the world," he continued his assault on me, showing no mercy whatsoever.

Have I really become like Om Baba seeking my own salvation over my commitment to the circle of life? I wondered.

"If you tremble with indignation at any injustice committed anywhere around the world, then you are a comrade of mine." These words of Che Guevara used to be like a mantra to me. What's happened, have I become a new age fascist concerned merely with my own liberation, comforts and peace of mind? Or have I seen so much suffering and destruction that I have become immune to it? Have I stopped trembling at the sight of injustice, and have I come to accept it as part of reality that cannot be changed?

It's amazing and utterly frightening, how quickly the human spirit adjusts to even the worst atrocities, if it is exposed to them long enough. I can still remember how devastatingly shocked I was the first time I walked over beggars with deformed limbs in an Indian railway station many years ago. When a local told me how many of these people were deformed by their own families for the sole purpose of making them into more successful beggars, I couldn't contain my outrage, I literally screamed. Over the years as I became a regular visitor to this country, I have gradually come to accept these things as *normal*, as part and parcel of life in this land.

How is it? What is it that makes our minds assent, even to the worst shit, to the vilest of human actions? What makes us lose our sensitivity to what is so offensive to the human spirit? Does constant exposure to shit numb our spirit?

Is this the reason why nobody is rising up about the plight of the earth and all disappearing life, which soon will be our own lives too? Have we come to accept a deformed earth, a cruel society and life out of balance as the norm? Has it been so long since any of us smelled the flowers in the garden of infinity? Do my past years of service hold any merit at all? Is life reflected in anything else save the calling of the moment?

These endless questions keep reverberating in my head. I feel as though I've been jolted by a jackhammer. My crow friend has wrecked me again, and I know he is my friend, as is the river.

What does she want of me *river-mother-divine* — my silence or my action? I feel I know the answer, except, perhaps, I am not brave enough to walk that bridge. I have come to rely on Nulla to act as a go-between for these two extremes battling for supremacy within me. Yet Nulla is nowhere to be seen and I only have a few moments left to come to an understanding as the river gathers its energy and starts spattering white froth, pushing and pulling away at her banks.

✳ ✳ ✳ ✳ ✳ ✳ ✳

We walked the track back to the village in silence, Angel escorting us most of the way home. An uneasy feeling filtered through into my being. It had little to do with our meeting with Om Baba; that really wasn't going to rock me, since it wasn't the first time I felt empty and disillusioned after being in the company of a *holy man*. It was something else that weighed on my heart, something that I dreaded even thinking of, lest my universe collapse.

We arrived back at the village in late afternoon and enjoyed a soak in the hot springs and then a rest before we went to have our evening meal. Ashok was there, sitting at the corner near the low stonewall, warming his hands with a cup of chai. The night was cold, freezing actually — as it always became the moment the sun disappeared behind the mountains and the cold air took charge over the surrounds.

Ashok was happy to see us and welcomed us to join him at his table. He seemed in a much better mood than the other day and I wondered if he had gone to see Om Baba in the afternoon. I guessed that was impossible, since we would have crossed him on the path. "Have you had your dinner already, mate?" I asked him.

"Yes, and it was delicious as always, I really like this hearty warm mountain food. You better order quickly before they run out."

Nulla jumped up to go to the kitchen to order two meals; she wasn't going to miss out on it, for she loved the mountain food too. "You know Ashok, we stayed with Om Baba in the cave last night" I spoke with some trepidation, thinking he might be hurt that Om Baba offered us what he was dreaming of.

"Yes, I know, the whole place knows, news travels quickly in these parts of the world" he said. "So how did you feel, did he say anything to you?" he asked us.

"Yes, actually he did. In fact, he didn't stop talking. You know the food was delicious and staying in the cave was an awesome experience, although he wasn't really my cup of tea," I replied in all honesty.

"Neither was he mine," Nulla joined our conversation. "You know Ashok, you may have received a gift from the sacred mountains being rejected by this guru of yours. I feel your sincerity is deeper than his, so is your devotion," she said while holding his hand to console him.

He didn't however seem to need consolation anymore; he was in a much different space than when we last saw him. It was as though the hot springs had freed him of the illusion with which he had arrived here, while offering him a gift Om Baba would never be able to bestow upon him.

"I am fine. I've had plenty of time to think and reflect. It was an expensive lesson and I had to travel half the world to learn it; nevertheless, I feel it was worth it. I don't have to look anymore outside myself for answers, neither do I need to idolise these holy men my culture has bred me to admire and worship as living gods. I am the master of my own life, as difficult as it may be.

"Anyway on the flip side, I get to see my relatives that otherwise I would not have seen for many more years. Tomorrow I will leave for Calcutta and spend the rest of my time in India there," he said with a new spring in his voice.

It was amazing how he changed in these two days. He was beaming with a light that only shines in the eyes of a man or woman who have decided to take charge of their own life and stop expecting others to walk the hard yards for them or to hand them the answers on a silver platter. Our food arrived and we got into it. Ashok ordered another chai to keep his hands and belly warm while he stared with excitement into the new horizons of his life. After our food and chai, it felt like the temperature had dropped again a few degrees. It was time to go and snuggle up in a warm bed. We told Ashok we would meet him for breakfast before he left, and bade him sweet dreams.

As I lay in bed that night, I couldn't stop thinking of Om Baba and Ashok and the whole story. Was Om Baba's behaviour intentional in order to empower Ashok or was it just universal intelligence making the arrangements known? I didn't feel angry with Om Baba anymore, either. I may not have been in agreement with him, but there was something in his words I did hear. I had to change myself first if I was going to change the world. Well, he never said I should change the world, that was my part. And it wasn't going to be one before the other, it was all going to happen simultaneously with my whole will and intent imbedded into this quest. With the passing of time I realised that the process was to go on forever, in different degrees of intensity.

I lay my head on Nulla's tummy and felt secure as though the earth was holding me in her womb. Outside it was cold while, in our small wooden room the universe felt as warm and welcoming as it can be.

We never saw Ashok again. When we went to have our breakfast the next day, the owner of the chai shop told us he had left on the early morning bus. I often wonder where his journey took him; he was a special man, a man who crossed the world on his quest and was brave enough to change his route the moment he realised he had taken the wrong path. Isn't it true that often in life we have to take a detour when we realise the door we have opened isn't going to lead us to our destination?

We spent the next few days relaxing in the small mountain hamlet, our gaze for the most part focused inwardly rather than on each other. It felt that for the first time in months we had time out from the intensity of experience that life had continually bombarded us with.

We walked a few times to the plateau where the shepherds grazed their flocks. We never visited Om Baba again; there simply was no need to do so. Nulla drew a lot and I spent my days in deep thought and contemplation, playing my flute and just running around the mountains with Angel, who by now had become our good friend and companion. She waited for us every morning in front of our room, ready for the next day's adventure.

I thought she would be in trouble for not looking after the sheep. Then I learned from the locals that she wasn't really owned by the shepherds. She was a free roaming mountain dog that joined the shepherds every year when they came to graze the highlands. Angel was a healer to me. She reconnected me with the ever-playful child within, the child without a worry in the world, just lost in the wonder that the moment offers them. At times, she made me race her on the plateau until I fell over with exhaustion and then she would come and lick my face, encouraging me to get up and have some more fun.

Nulla would watch us from her drawing spot on the big rock, she was happy to see me play and smile while she embraced the time for herself to draw. We all have a different ways to connect with the secret avenues of inner splendour; hers was drawing.

I would come to reminisce on these few weeks, up in the high mountains with the hot springs, as one of the best holidays I had in my entire life. They were true holy days where the spirit found rest and renewal from the eternal battle we wage with the self in the quest for transformation.

The first early snow brought delight to all. We ran around with the few kids, trying to catch the small white flakes which slowly floated down onto earth. We built snow castles and played around throwing snowballs at each other. It was just the beginning of autumn and by the next morning it had all melted away, replaced with wide blue sky. However, it was the first warning signal to the nomadic shepherds that in a couple of weeks it would be time to leave the summer grazing grounds and start making their way down to the lowlands. And the lowlands were the low times in the life of an ancient nomadic shepherd.

In the high mountains they lived free, while grazing pastures in abundance. In the populated lowlands, being a nomad was seen as a thing of the past and they were frowned upon. They had no place in the modern day of *capital,* for they didn't oil the wheel of fortune. They walked in tune with nature and consumed very little. If consumer sentiment were gauged by the lives of these people, it would read close to zero. If laughter and contentment sentiments were measured by their lives, then the stock market of happiness and love would go through the roof; we would all be happy shareholders, sharing the wonders of being alive on earth mother Gaia.

Often, when arriving at their ancient winter pastures on the plains, they were seen as encroachers, a nuisance, and were harassed by both the police and locals alike. Much of their pastureland had already been swallowed by the advent of so-called civilised society. Sure, they could sense the way of life they had enjoyed since memory began was coming to an end, sooner rather than later. Still for a brief moment, in the summers in the high mountains, they could continue to breathe in freedom, their birthright handed down to them from the spirit clouds thus forgetting the doom that tomorrow may spell.

Devi, the little shepherd girl, became good friends with Nulla and was always there when we walked up the plateau. They were slowly learning a bit of each other's language while hanging out together for hours on end. It's amazing what transpires when the language of love is spoken, how deep the human bond becomes, even if it's just for a brief moment in time.

I noticed how I hardly ever saw the shepherds in the hot baths and wondered why that was. Upon enquiring with the owner of our house, I learned that the locals looked down upon the shepherds, perceiving them to be dirty nomads who were not Hindus, and thus they felt they would pollute the holy water.

The silent agreement was that if they wanted to bathe they should come late at night and, even then, not too often. It made me sick to think of the aspect of this country, which was full of so many judgements, prejudices and gross hypocrisies. It is such a complex love affair I have with this land called India. At times it makes my spirit soar to a place that even the eagles cannot touch, on other occasions it makes me sink into the pits of hopelessness and despair while I witness how low the human spirit can stoop. Yet aren't all love-affairs complex?

With every passing day it got colder, the last snowfall taking more than a day to melt. "Winter must come early in these parts of the world," I concluded. One morning, Angel arrived at our room with Devi by her side. We were surprised to see her there, since we had never met her in the village before. Nulla embraced her warmly and ordered a chai and some biscuits from the boy running our small guesthouse of two rooms. She was dressed in a beautiful, colourful embroidered dress, not the usual rags she normally ran free in. Even her matted hair was clean and tied up with a bunch of wild flowers. After a bit of sign language and broken English, French and local dialect, we understood that she had come to invite us over for a meal. We were delighted.

Up until this moment, the shepherds kept a respectful distance from us and, apart from an exchange of shy smiles, they mainly left us alone. We felt deeply honoured to be invited by them and we told Devi we would come later, yet she seem to insist that she was on a mission and her task was to bring us over now. We felt there was some occasion in the air, so we dressed up in the best attire we could muster from our limited wardrobe. As we stepped out, I noticed the air was cold and the mountains around us had a thicker and lower cover of snow.

The shepherds welcomed us warmly and offered us a place to sit on one of the colourful woollen rugs spread around the fire. One of them, a young man around my age sat near us and communicated in broken English. Apparently, some years ago, he went to some missionary boarding school for a couple of years. He explained to us that this was the end of season feast, where they gave their offerings to the guardians of the mountains and shared a meal, before they started packing up for their journey down to the lowlands.

The food was delicious. They made big flat bread on something that looked like an upside down wok. I had never tasted this type of bread before. With the flat bread they served some tasty soft cheese made from the milk of their sheep and goats. In the centre stood a massive plate of saffron rice with chunks of meat in it. Maize was served boiled and there was a dish of spicy green beans that grew abundantly in the mountains in summer time.

More meat was being grilled over the fire and handed out, as it became ready.

I enjoyed the feast, except I didn't touch the meat or the rice, which was cooked with the meat. I was a strict vegetarian at the time. Nulla was a vegetarian too and, to my surprise, ate everything, which really shocked me a bit.

I looked at her while she smiled back at me with a piece of sheep in her hand. "Come on, man, make an exception, they are offering us something they have raised with their own sweat and toil," she said. But I didn't, I was an obstinate young man, who felt when he'd stumbled across the true way he had to stick to it.

Masjid, our interpreter, kept on nudging me to enjoy the meat, so did most of the shepherds. They saw Nulla eating and they didn't understand why I didn't have any. They were aware of the concept of vegetarianism, since many Indians are; yet they might not have thought of a foreigner being one.

Throughout the meal, I could sense an old lady staring at me with slight disgust. I felt that she might have thought that I didn't trust that their food was clean and fit for the palate of an *advanced* westerner.

For the rest of the meal Nulla got most of the attention, as she participated in the feast with all her heart, while I became a bit of an outcast. Dessert was a mix of sweet cream and dried apricots. It was delicious, although I didn't really enjoy it. In fact I didn't feel hungry anymore. Some strange disturbing feeling stirred inside me — the feeling that one gets when they know they have fucked up badly. The sensation that surfaces when you feel the whole of existence is disappointed with you.

We walked back to the village in late the afternoon in silence. For the first time since I met Nulla I felt she was disappointed with me. I kept to myself and watched Angel as she sniffed different rocks and shrubs on the way for signs of her canine relatives that might have passed through the area.

The eyes of the old lady kept haunting me, the hurt and disappointment that her gift, the circle's gift was rejected by me. I learned from Masjid, that they didn't eat much meat, only on special occasions, and this time they made more meat dishes since it was the first time they had foreigners as guests joining them for a meal.

We were ten minutes away from the village; I felt I could not walk anymore. I had to sit down; my head was in a spin. Nulla for her part completely ignored me and continued walking on. I slumped on the earth and begun sobbing uncontrollably. I was hurting like never before. I was hurt by my own stupidity, rigidity and lack of being present with life.

Why did I reject this gift offered with so much love? Had I joined the mass orchestra of modernity, who continually affirmed to these beautiful people that there was something wrong with their lives and way of being?

What did it mean to be a vegetarian? Did it mean we judge one life as greater than another, more precious; therefore we only partake in the lesser forms of life?

I was shattered, I wanted to run back to the circle and eat a whole sheep, just to show them that I love them and accept them, that they are living in tune with life and I am living only in theory.

I was no better than Om Baba, and that was precisely the reason I was so disgusted by him. It wasn't he that was a bigot; it was I.

What is purer and more nourishing to the body? An animal grown in the freedom and love with which the shepherds raise their flock, in tune with the cycles of nature, or a vegetable grown laced with poison chemicals by an angry farmer and shipped from miles away? I knew the answer, and the more I realised my folly the more inconsolable I became.

Nulla was way out of sight. I was pissed off with her for not giving me some support. Or maybe she did, by allowing me to face my agony in the company of myself.

Beside the point, it wasn't her style. She was ever patient; she gave me space and time to work through my "stuff." She also believed that I needed to face my shit on my own. Or maybe she just couldn't handle seeing me broken.

I lay there in utter misery, begging the earth underneath me for some solace and forgiveness, until it was almost too dark and too cold to be there for one moment longer. I walked over to our room to get a towel and proceeded to the hot springs, with a prayer that the mountains and their Gods would pardon me for the selfish, righteous bastard I could be at times.

For a few days we didn't speak to each other. I wasn't really sure if Nulla was still pissed off with how I had offended the shepherds, or was just giving me the space to face my inner music, which at that moment felt bitterly out of tune. I spent a lot of time at the hot springs in prayer and silence, so that I might cleanse myself of my own judgements and righteousness, especially where the spiritual ego was concerned — a very dangerous creature, that one — professing itself to be holier than thou.

For the first time since we met, I felt that I was unworthy of Nulla as my wife and a question mark arose in me as to why we had decided to take this journey together. We hailed from two different places, so far apart; did the future hold anything for us? Did I walk away from the burning grounds in the desert too soon? I recalled how when she first came to the rat temple, I felt I was just half way through my process of sorting out the inner mess churning inside. Was Nulla my Delilah, luring me to face a world I wasn't ready to deal with?

Gradually, with the grace of the burning furnace of the hot Himalayan springs, I came back to the awareness of my breath.

My inner debate was stranded for the moment. I pulled myself off the stinking pit of self-pity and returned to the beauty and wonder of the moment — a hot bath amongst the freezing mountains, all dished out by Mama Earth herself.

She really spoils us, this mother, and takes care of us. She always guides us and shines the light on our way. We just need to do one simple thing. Stop for a moment, just for a brief blip in time and halt that raging monkey running riot in our mind; just a moment, that's all it takes for us to reconnect with the miracle that we are all part and parcel of.

It was much easier to do this in the steaming hot baths, which on immersion, immediately took away the mind and forced me into presence. That's how it is, sometimes we are luckier than others and the universe sends us a prop to lead us back to balance on our two feet.

It took a few days before we talked again. We were no strangers to silence in our relationship, although the difference this time was that, for a while, the silence was loaded.

Our deep affection and love for each other was going to win out in the end, that I knew for sure. Really, there was no issue between us, the story was between me and my ego, and the fact that she made it her business for a while and chose to be disappointed, was her story, not mine.

It was late one night with a waning moon in the sky that I felt it was time to melt the ice and return to our circle of love and to nurture each other again.

"Nulla, there is something I have to tell you . . . "

"I know."

"How do you always know?"

"I am a woman."

＊ ＊ ＊ ＊ ＊ ＊ ＊

The sound of the river by my side is getting louder and louder as it slowly swells up from the massive amounts of water released by the breaking of the dam.

I remember these beautiful shepherds in the high mountains and wonder if they are still following the natural cycles of life, or if the forces of modernity have finally hijacked their will and forced them into joining the masses, bowing in fear to the evil god named mammon.

"If you are still there in the high mountains, where the rivers are born and the clouds dance, I hope that you can hear me now and accept my deep apology for my callousness as a youth who thought he knew it all. I promise you people of the clouds, that the day I refused the food offered to me from the depths of your heart, was a day that transformed me forever. Without acting in the foolish way I did, I may have never learnt the lesson of grace, the humility of surrender, and the vulnerability of receiving. I am sorry if my actions may have brought sorrow or the feeling of rejection to your hearts; at the same time I know that you were much wiser than I will ever be, to see through the folly of my righteousness."

The river taught me that through my biggest mistakes, in my most stubborn blindness, I learned the most beautiful lessons that eventually made me a better human being.

I have made many more mistakes since that day on the mountain and I hope that most of them were new ones. There is nothing more boggling to the growth of the human spirit than repeating one's footsteps and covering the ground we have already explored before.

We were leaving India; the sheer horror of this realisation slowly crept in, like a deadly snake meandering in and suffocating me through my veins.

Delhi Airport in the mid-eighties resembled something between a large warehouse and a small provincial airport. The overwhelming smell of phenol hung strong in the air. In fact, it was this smell that first greeted you when you arrived. I always associated it with a profound sense of wellbeing, since it was the aroma that welcomed me to the country I loved and which had nurtured me so much in return.

There was nothing well about my being now, however, and the smell of phenol almost made me sick to the stomach. The building that housed the departure and arrival areas showed serious signs of neglect or, more likely, contempt by the people who ran it. It was as though the various officials who worked at the airport would probably never afford a flight overseas themselves and wanted to make this statement: that if you were wealthy enough to afford a flight, you should at least have a taste of the real India while you entered and left.

Apart from the decrepit building, the whole administrative process took forever and, at times, it felt that the lines were stationary while the check-in staff were discussing the plot of the latest Bollywood film. The immigration crew, though, were possibly worse. For some reason, they enjoyed staring at your passport forever, as though they were professional photographers sussing out the quality of the photos and the techniques used to take them.

So, there I was, going to Paris, the land of my living Goddess and I had no idea what to expect. I'd never been to Europe, let alone France. It wasn't going there, however, that spun my brain into a total free-fall; it was the fact that I was leaving this amazing nurturing womb called Mother India. Her warmth and acceptance had nursed me for the last eighteen months and had become entwined as an integral, essential part of my being.

What is it about this country that makes her such a living being, an identity, a towering Goddess to always caress you in your hour of greatest need?

When I arrived in India, I was a mess, escaping a society that had nothing to offer me. A social order that had been approaching for a long time the gates of spiritual death, and that had embraced the trapped court of materialism and extreme subjugation as a valid emerging culture.

The accepted paradigm of normality and wellbeing was being narrowed to a very defined bandwidth called *consume and be merry*. India offered me a mirror, a reflection that held all the colours. She shared with me a fragrance that carried all smells far sweeter than the stench of total conformity and extreme materialism that was ruling the so-called developed world where I came from.

Why did I decide to leave? Does paradise always have to come to an end? Was I just following the footsteps of my divine woman, or did I trust an unknown destiny that would be unravelled by the winds of tomorrow? "Am I on a mission to spread word of the plight of the wonderful folk of Nandini and their brethren worldwide?" I wondered.

Nulla never asked me to go with her to France; she just said, "I *know*," when the realisation dawned on me. "Yes, we have to leave, there is some service we have to do. We need to repay in action the immense debt we owe the people long forgotten by the empire of greed." It was not a debt we were asked to pay back, but rather an over-flowing of love and gratitude we had to honour, and the growing resolve that our small voices and actions counted. Perhaps we were just two lonesome vagrants, and still we knew we could effect change in the world surrounding us.

Nulla was quiet by my side, savouring her favourite drink, sweet milky chai. I dared not ask her where her thoughts where at, in case I open the floodgates of dammed rivers held behind our eyes. We both didn't want to leave, and we both knew it was time to do so.

Airports worldwide are extremely sterile places, except perhaps not in India. Numerous cleaning ladies were patrolling up and down with their wide brooms, offering me wide-toothed smiles. The old lady who looked after the toilets, made sure to remind me that any spare local currency I may still have in my pocket should and ought to be given to her as a sign of appreciation for the clean toilets and the thirty centimetres of toilet paper she offered us to dry our hands with. There were still a few hours before we were due to board our flight. I slumped down into a chair and gazed out onto the tarmac, listening to the announcer repeating boarding calls to exotic destinations such as Tashkent, Sana, Bangkok, Dubai . . . and then our flight to Paris via Amman.

We landed in Orly Airport in Paris on a chilly autumn afternoon. It felt as though we were two fish who had just been thrown out of the ocean, attempting to swim on a surface strange to us. Nulla suggested we go and relax in the park before making our arrival known at her parents' home.

The park was beautiful and symmetrical, as city parks usually are; somehow when city folk go to the park, they change gear and slow down a little. People smile in parks for the momentary bliss of being reminded of and touched by the grace of Mother Nature, who can put at ease all the day-to-day worries, telling them that they can wait for a moment. A small canal meandered through, home to a family of ducks that were enjoying swimming gracefully in the water, while some children were trying to get their attention. The presence of autumn made the leaves change colour before they were shed for a naked winter. It is a scene we are deprived of in my subtropical homeland, and the array of reds, pinks, yellows and oranges presented a feast to my eyes. Although we were in the middle of a big city, the air felt fresh and crisp, inviting in a deep breath. I felt quiet and at ease, strolling with my arm around Nulla's shoulders, something we never did before due to the different cultural codes of Indian society.

A small enclosure with a few dogs in it and a sign I did not understand drew my attention. "What's over there with the dogs?" I asked Nulla.

"It's a dog toilet," she said, while pinching my tummy.

"A dog toilet?" I asked her with a bit of shock. I had

never seen one of those before. We didn't have them in the parks where I come from and still, more than that; I had just come from a country where two thirds of the people don't even have access to a toilet.

"Welcome back to the world you thought you left behind . . ." I heard a hidden voice whispering to me. I could feel it wasn't going to be easy and I had to hold back the trepidation that was slowly creeping inside of me.

❄ ❄ ❄ ❄ ❄ ❄ ❄

There are two qualities that make a woman into a living Goddess: total surrender and absolute defiance. Nulla was graced with both of these virtues. Whilst in India, the surrendered share of the living Devi came forth as the predominant energy emanating from her. It was as though she reflected the land she walked upon. The moment we arrived in France the goddess of defiance emerged, a part I had not experienced much in Nulla before. She wasn't Asian anymore; she was French to the core.

It worked well to support our campaign for the folk back in Nandini; it didn't fare too well when it came to our relationship. Luckily, over the next four years in Paris we were so busy and dedicated to the cause at hand that we didn't really have much time to focus on our relationship. Our attention was on Nandini and the dam. We managed to rock quite a few circles within the establishment, as we worked on raising awareness of the plight of the gentle tribal folk by the river.

At this moment, many years later, in my presence by the banks of another river, I have no one apart from Nobi to relate to. The village seems to have emptied itself of all its inhabitants, whilst the only action taking place is a river gathering its energy, ready to share a new narrative with the world surrounding it.

I feel the pain in Nobi's being as he avoids my eyes and stares away into the night. Fuck man, why do I continually assume it's his pain, it's my bloody own pain as well - it's all our pain! It's an accumulated collection of sorrow that has slowly been festering and mutating into a cancerous growth upon the face of the earth mother for a long time now.

It's the anguish of a whole circle of life that has gradually lost its balance and purpose over generations spent propagating the myths of fear, greed and separation. The grief of a distorted human mind which has long lost its ability to trust the intelligence that springs from the foundation of life itself.

I mean, look at where our so-called society has come to — if we can even call it by this name anymore, for society must mean that we are social creatures with the ability to care for each other.

We live according to the cruel design of a modern imperialist system that we have come to accept as normal. We have built a system, a society based on unsound principles of aggression, competition, greed, brutality, lack, and separation. First, we make people poor, then in their desperation, they revolt or resort to crime. The next step is we punish them for acting, rather than submitting to the fate we have designated for them. The matrix we live in specialises in the manufacture of poverty and despair as instruments of control. People live in deprivation rather than poverty. It is a deliberate and conscious act to enslave the masses. For, in reality, there is enough for everyone if we shared it in a proper way.

What are we spending most of our lives contributing to? The profits of the corporations! Isn't it time we make known the truth that the real criminals are the ones who create poverty in the first place — a poverty that is essential for them to run their caravan of greed.

Who is the real terrorist here? In my mind it's the ones who perpetuate the myth of terrorism, so as to advance their agenda and eliminate all open avenues of resistance. Half the world's population lives on less than two dollars a day, and without their misery and neediness, this so-called free market miracle is doomed. Do we ever pause for a moment to realise that prosperity achieved off the blood and tears of another is a sure doorway to hell?

Bit by bit, we are becoming a humanity of robots, the Yay Sayers whether we like it or not. There was a time when protest and dissent were seen as a sign of a healthy democracy in action, now they are deemed to be terrorist acts. There is no more dialogue, and the spectrum of diversity in ideas and cultures is fast narrowing down. We don't live in a democracy, we live in a media-ocracy, and the choice we have when we go to exercise our so-called democratic rights, is a choice between two puppets being pulled by the same set of strings.

We live in a world where half the global energy and resources go to support the military industrial complex. In plain language, half the money circulating around is spent on war.

Now our politicians are claiming to be fighting for peace, and has a war for peace ever existed? It is a contradiction in terms.

We are ruled by a bunch of schizophrenics, everything they do is the opposite of what they say, and we still buy into it. They fight wars for peace. They curtail our freedom to protect our freedom. Really, this lunacy is getting totally insane.

Have we ever tried to imagine for one moment one hundred per cent of human energy focused on love, health, education, and creativity? Why is it so hard to imagine? How far have we gone from the original mother, which sprang us into life on earth?

What is this *free market* delusion that we have embraced?

The free market is a clever and brutal mechanism of modern colonialism; it is total occupation of the land, people, resources, culture, rights and liberties. This is all done by a debt-based monetary system designed to socially paralyse us into submission—a modern slavery designed to empower the elite at the top of the pyramid of greed.

They tell us that we have evolved from being a tribal man, a Stone Age man, a forest dweller, a hunter and gatherer, to invent this wonderful idea of democracy — *wow*. It seems to be another one of these words with little substance behind them.

Is democracy democratic? Is it realistically possible to have a meaningful democracy in a capital-based world? Of course it's not—we are all hypnotised by the opiate of material gadgets and theatrical media.

Is there any big institution left in the world that is accountable to people rather than power? Our governments have become the instrument that the big corporations rely on to execute their agenda. Civil unrest, especially the one coming in the way of corporate profits, while they pillage the earth, has become a crime of terrorism. *Good investment climate* is usually the jargon applied to a place where human rights have been suppressed, so there is no opposition to corporate crimes. In fact, nowadays, anybody that does not toe the line is a terrorist. Human rights have become a nuisance, an obstacle to economic development.

What is normalcy? Is the accepted dictum of being normal really a sound, sane idea anymore? What does it mean to be human? We seem to live in a constant state of paranoid aggression led by the greatest bully in the world — the United States of America.

In the last fifty years, every year, the U.S has been at war, open or covert, with one country or another. At the same time, it calls itself a peaceful nation. Are they living in some parallel reality where they say one thing, yet act to the contrary? Why are we all being victimised? Is it so we totally submit and become eternally grateful for the few crumbs of life we are offered in return for our silent consent?

A telling fact of which most of us are ignorant, is that the U.S actually needs war for its survival. It is literally their biggest, most profitable business, which sustains their economy. Without war the U.S would go broke and the whole American dream would collapse. It is for this reason that it makes sense for them to turn more and more of us into an enemy, be it nations or individuals.

The accepted norm of criminal law is also shifting in most countries, followed by the leadership of the *Big Beacon of Freedom*. The presumption of innocence until found guilty is switching to the implication of guilt unless proven otherwise. Often the judges are hand-in-glove with the big corporations, suppressing any dissent that might stop the cheers in the greatest casino on earth, the legal one—the one called the stock market.

A study shows that a college student in the U.S can identify almost a thousand corporate logos and only ten local animals. Commodities have become symbols of culture. And the source of knowledge has become the media rather than the earth and the voice of the wind.

I look at Nobi, my head spinning out of control; I urgently need support from somewhere. Am I insane for not toeing the line and accepting reality as it is? I can recall some years ago my mother getting distressed by the fact that I had not found my place within the confines of normality. "It is okay to be a revolutionary when you are young," she said "although if you are still one when you grow old, you have not grown up."

So is that it? Are we all expected to grow up and accept the twisted reality we live in without questioning or challenging it? Is it our duty to sing hooray to the status quo or is there a moral obligation to challenge it?

"Nobi, what is there to do anymore, we are so deep in

the shit? Isn't finding the silence within the only thing left to do, rather than being trapped in the hopelessness of what is taking place? I feel in total despair when I think of what's happening on the planet." I'm pleading with him to offer me some piece of advice, though I am not sure what. He is in no hurry to answer, while I start to panic that I am running out of time and urgently in need of clear answers.

"The evil empire of greed will be dismantled eventually. Though, this is the heart of it: if force is used to dismantle it, it means you have left it too late. This is not the time to sit by the river, this is the time to go up the mountain and gather the people together, for it is you and we that can make it happen. Still, it must happen *now*, not tomorrow," he says, while still avoiding looking at me. I am irrelevant to him at the moment, or perhaps he is waiting to see if he would change my resolve. I am not sure I like the feeling inside me when I think of all the ills of the world, while I do like what takes place within when thought is absent. Can I find the same peace within while being an agent of change in the world? Is it possible that there is a meeting point between the passion needed for revolution and the silence essential for the continuous rebirth of the human spirit?

"Let me tell you something," Nobi finally turns around to look at me. "The ice on the poles is quickly melting. Can you ever imagine a world without the clumsy, charming walk of the penguins, without the grace of the seal or the magnificence of the polar bear? Is this the world you want to leave to the children? If you procrastinate and delay for even one more day, this is the world you *will* leave the kids!" he says with sadness, as though he too has given up on me by now.

What is it that makes me reject the notion that I am still part of the struggle for a new earth? What is it that has made me so disillusioned that I am happy to be taken by the river, rather than climb the mountain Nobi is talking about? Climb the mountain where the brave and committed gather to circle again—for this is the moment our ancestors have told us of, a long, long time ago.

Was it the years of grind, of continuous battle with forces so overwhelming, that so many times it seemed that the walls of ignorance and arrogance were too thick to penetrate?

When we arrived in France we were full of energy and purpose. The letter left to us by Arjun was always in my pocket as my guiding light, lest I forget the mission and purpose handed to us by the spirit of the forest and the call of the river. We joined a growing international network of activists with the goal of supporting the tribal people of Nandini in their quest to halt the building of the dam. Our strategy was to put pressure on the World Bank to stop funding for the project by convincing them that gross violations of human rights were taking place. We managed to apply enough public pressure so that, eventually, they withdrew their funding for the project.

We were overjoyed with our victory and felt the power of what we could achieve if we worked together as an international allegiance of like-minded people. Within a couple of months of our perceived triumph, the local state government decided to fund the project by itself and our hearts sank. It felt as if four years of hard work around the clock had gone down the drain. The whole thing was meaningless. It wasn't the last time I felt I worked for nothing, and eventually I couldn't see a purpose in any of it anymore.

With time, I realised there was a deeper change that needed to take place before we could effect change in the world. Yes, we have to change the whole system we live in from the roots up, and at the same time we have to transform ourselves. We have to *be* the change that we so desire to see, and the first step is to uproot all violence from our hearts, while still acting with power and determination.

The devastation of the planet is a reflection of our inner

decay; all of us to one degree or another are responsible. This decay has to be replaced by the spirit of joy, of trust. Our inner pollution creates the outer pollution. We are not taking responsibility for what is happening within us; therefore we are unable to respond to the need of the moment as far as the planet and humanity are concerned.

We seem to be waiting for some sort of a messiah to usher in the golden age and restore balance to an otherwise twisted state of humanity. Then again, the messiah is not going to come and all that we are doing is what we do best; waiting for someone else to sort out our mess, be it inner or outer.

Yet it's only us, with our deeds, actions and clear intent that can bring about the change we desire, be it a change within or the change to the collective wellbeing of all. We must at last walk away from the illusion of separation into the welcoming arms of the spirit of trust.

❋ ❋ ❋ ❋ ❋ ❋ ❋

The spirit of trust was alive and well within us when we first arrived in Paris. We lived in a small flat by a canal just off Rue 17. Nulla's father owned the flat and he agreed for us to have it rent-free until we got our lives together; we never did, and for his part he didn't pressure us for the money.

In reality, we never had any spare cash and the bit that we did have always went on the various expenses involved in what we did with our growing network of activists worldwide. This involved phone calls, faxes, letters, which all added up to quite a bit in those pre-internet days when being an international activist was not a cheap affair. And of course there were the various self-indulgent delights we consumed in our favourite coffee shops. Cafés have always served as hubs for revolutionaries; there is something about the intoxicating aroma of coffee that makes the brain function with greater clarity and ferocity.

To make money for these varied endeavours I acquired a newspaper run in the mornings; it was easy and fun. I didn't need to speak to anybody in my broken French and I got to cycle around the city before it awoke. It was the time when the angels and elves still made their presence felt. I liked that time of the day in Paris, especially on the cold mornings, when the smell of the baked delights and coffee from cafés in our neighbourhood would drift out onto the streets and into my alert nostrils.

By the time I completed my paper run around half past nine, I would have had already three coffees and several warm patisseries from my favourite bake-houses. It wasn't too long before I chubbed up, and Nulla started to wonder what had happened to the skinny wandering gypsy she married. Was he disappearing, or rather reappearing within the delights of French cuisine?

Nulla would usually greet me briefly when I arrived home and head off to her job as a model in an art school. Between our two part-time jobs and our free rent we managed to survive in an expensive city and position ourselves as a headquarters for revolutionary-minded people in need of a cause. An awesome group of people gathered around us; a few were Nulla's old friends, while most of them were new crew, attracted by the vision of supporting the oppressed and exposing the crimes being inflicted by the imperialist forces on the poor and vulnerable worldwide.

My French got better with time, although I never really mastered the language. I could not have imagined a better place to do what we did. Every French person is a revolutionary at heart and at any time the French are ready to take to the streets and stand up for social justice. In the rest of the western world we have become afraid of our governments and general strikes or a good riot seem to be a thing of the past. In France, it's the government that is afraid of the people, who are ready to bring the country to a halt whenever the government infringes on their rights as citizens. France seems to be the last bastion of active democracy in the so-called developed world.

Nulla's parents never came over to visit us; they basically left us alone. Every few weeks we would visit them for a Sunday lunch. They only lived a few streets away; yet they might as well have lived on another planet.

I never really did figure out Nulla's dad, nor did I ever come to know if he liked me or not. He seldom said much to anyone, not to his wife, nor to his daughter. Nulla's mom was a bit warmer — at the same time she seemed like the loneliest women I had ever met. She seemed to be constantly drifting in a sea of sadness. She had lost all contact with any members of her family back in Vietnam; she lived with a man who had stopped relating to her a long time ago, and her only son had died when he was a little boy.

Nulla never talked much about her big brother who died, or the car accident. I guess she was only a child at the time. The subject was taboo amongst the whole family. She mentioned her brother to me when we first met and it took many years before we ever talked about it again.

I did enjoy Nulla's mom's company and I loved her cooking. Her name was Luan and one of the reasons she liked me was my genuine interest in finding out what truly happened in the country of her birth. It was cool, as long as I didn't ask her about her family. I enquired a couple of times as to why she didn't go back for a visit and was met with a blank, almost hostile, stare. I could feel the pain that was laced with deep denial; like a bad smell that wouldn't go away and some of it was passed undetected as heritage to Nulla. It would take some years more before this silently festering wound would burst open to be offered finally a way of healing itself.

We worked day and night, and after years of hard

toil we had managed to get the World Bank to withdraw its support from the project. However, when the state government decided to fund the project itself and raise the wall of the dam even higher, thus displacing even more people, I became a broken man. I felt a lot of anger and frustration at the time, and I took some of it out on Shanti in a few strongly worded letters and confrontational phone calls. It was her suggestion that we focus our energy on the World Bank and its support for the project. In my opinion it was taking a crooked road that was never going to lead us to our destination. The real issue at hand was the whole paradigm of development. And it happened again and again as I watched activists go for pseudo targets rather than raising the truth about the issues at hand. This mantra of let's go for realistic goals made me sick to the stomach, and never sat easy inside me. I knew it was a sure way to lose the struggle. Things cannot be isolated; they have to be addressed in their wholeness.

When Shanti realised the dam was going to be built, she lost trust in the power of the people to stop it. She changed the mantra from "stop the dam" to "offer real rehabilitation to the people affected." In my opinion, she failed on both fronts. The dam ended up being built and the people were never rehabilitated properly. Some got a small amount of money, which didn't last beyond six months, while others received land that was worthless, the type of land that even their goats wouldn't venture to.

What I will give her is that she went for what she believed in and gave it all she could. I still love and admire Shanti in many ways, for she is still there with the people. I wonder though if sticking so strongly to a set of ideals was ever going to make the goal achievable. And in this case, the goal must have been to halt the building of the dam and save the ancestral homes of numerous tribal groups from being destroyed.

It brought back to me the issue of peaceful protest, as

opposed to violent revolution. We sat late many nights discussing the issue over endless cups of coffee in our small flat in Paris. I cannot really say we ever reached a conclusion as such; opinions and arguments were equally divided and equally convincing. The only thing I was sure of, though, was that whatever takes birth in violence will later be hard to convert into a peaceful, wholesome outcome. On the other hand, I was equally convinced that justice always came with a price, and without justice there can never be a society walking in peace and harmony. Disillusioned by the whole process and being encouraged by Nulla, I started my law degree by correspondence while looking at other alternatives to mainstream thinking that were making themselves known at the time.

There is a law that governs all creation, all life, all galaxies: life forms from the unseen to the seen, from the smallest atom and the energy that gave birth to it to the biggest, grossest hard matter. Man did not write this law. Once, not so long ago, we walked the earth in tune with this principle and led our lives according to the sacred geometry of the circle of life. It was actually not so many lives ago that our walk on mother earth was a celebration of the law that gave birth to our blessed life on this planet.

It is this decree that is whispering through the river now as she is about to burst open in catharsis and remind us that the laws we humans made are so far removed from the wisdom that governs life itself.

I spent some good years of my life studying man-made laws to come to a simple conclusion; there is no harmony in them, neither do they lead to peace or justice. They are just another instrument of control, another tool in the *he* made world.

The law that emanates from the heart of the universe speaks of harmony and connection. It sings the songs of all hands held together beyond time, space and the twisted realities we occupy at this present moment.

Watching the river, I can feel how connected she is with this law; in fact, it's not about connection, she is part and parcel of this law.

So, what is the surest way for me to meet this principle again, to become one with this universal wisdom? Can I slow my mind down to point zero, to the moment where life meets its eternal birth, allowing the moment to just be! Is this the instant where oneness is not an intellectual concept anymore, but a living fragrance?

"I got it, yes, yes, yes!" I punch the air in delight, while I get up from my sitting place and jump up and down like a mad man. Nobi looks at me with bewilderment.

"What's happened to you? Where is that stillness gone?" he asks and then takes off himself and starts circling around me, announcing to the river in his *qua qua* language that this man sitting in silence had finally got something. For a moment, I feel I can see Nulla's face in the dark sky above or is it Nukaya my love from so many lives ago, really I can't tell, perhaps they are one and the same.

"Thank you, river!" I shout, attempting to overcome the growing hum of the water struggling to break free of the immense power pushing it from behind. At last it hit me, the answer to the riddle of free will and destiny. It's so clear, so simple, as all answers are when they come from the well where truth holds its records in time. Why did it take me so long to grasp such a simple truth? It's all in the foundation of sacred law, which spins the universe around and around and around.

The river will always meet the ocean, the stars will always shine at night, the sun will always rise and my free will shall always meet my true destiny when I walk with love in my heart, with silence in my soul, and courage as my guide.

Everything is guided, governed and blessed by the same law, including our individual walk on earth. When we walk out of balance, our free will never meets our true destiny; rather it merges with its poor relatives called fear and hesitation. We then avoid our meeting point with destiny and are slaves to the clutches of time, fear and circumstance.

There is only one way to meet our destiny — to walk it, be it, live it, be our best selves, ultimate creators working hand in hand with God, as God creating God from moment to moment. We are all destined to love, be happy, be abundant, be warriors of light, creating new songlines and dancing with the eternal ones. When our life is filled with misery, it is not our destiny that we have met; it is our fear, neglect, and unwillingness to rise to the challenges of walking as one, with the one, in the one.

"Ouch!" A sharp pain pierces my shoulder. It is Nobi. He perches on my right shoulder and squeezes his claws into me. It hurts for a moment and then I get used to it; actually, I am overjoyed by this new closeness between us.

Rubbing his head against mine, he whispers in my ear, "Welcome to the land of unity, the eternal, ever flowing river of love." I smell the trees, river, air, flowers, grasses and rain in the fragrance of his feathers. The crow and I are one, subject to the same law, that answers to the eternal book of wisdom.

❋ ❋ ❋ ❋ ❋ ❋ ❋

It was late afternoon on a beautiful Parisian summer day when the perfect world Nulla and I lived in collapsed.

We had been together for more than four years and we never used any methods of birth control. Nulla was a natural born mother, as all women are; yet some embody it more than others. She couldn't wait to have kids. One day she decided to go for a check-up to see if there was anything wrong. There was. Nulla could not have kids: she was barren.

When she came home that day from the clinic, there were no smiles left in the world—her whole universe had collapsed into a tunnel of darkness. Entering our home that ill-fated day, she slumped against the wall, not bothering even to shut the door behind her. "Hi Nulla, what did the doctor say?" I greeted her, happy to see her, as always.

However, I did not need an answer. I'd never seen Nulla like this before; it was as though her whole life force had been zapped away, the whole power and stamina that moved her through life had been sucked dry. She was twenty-six years old and all of a sudden looked like a very old lady, exhausted of her life force by generations of suffering.

"Nulla, it's not the end of the world, we can always adopt children. Anyway, there are too many people on this planet," I tried to console her. I leant over to give her a kiss and a hug, and she pushed me away with a force I didn't know she had.

It felt like she was possessed. "I am the daughter of a whore and a whore myself. I am cursed, you better leave me before you are cursed too," she groaned in an unfamiliar voice.

"Nulla, don't talk nonsense, it's not the end of the world. Think of the suffering people we saw in India and remember how fortunate we are. What's happened to you?" I pleaded with her to see some sense and reason—that there was a life awaiting us, even if we couldn't have our own children. My words were falling on deaf ears. As far as she was concerned I wasn't even there. She wailed for hours on end and her tears never ran dry. Any attempt by me to approach her was repelled with more and more force. She felt dejected by existence and rejected by the force that brought her into this life to be a woman.

Around midnight, she finally ran out of tears; still her despair grew deeper. She walked over to the kitchen and drank a whole bottle of red wine in one go, a bottle that would usually take the two of us a whole evening to finish. This was the beginning of a hellish three months that almost killed my beloved wife and destroyed us as a couple—in a way it did and I often wonder if we ever really recovered.

Nulla wanted to die, she hated herself, and in an instant she became a different person to the one that I had lived with for the previous four years. It was as though the suppressed anger, hatred and pain that her mother must have felt when she was sent by her father to sell her body to the foreign troops, had been passed on to Nulla and had taken control of her. Her mantra became "I am a whore, god hates me."

Nulla retreated into her shell and I was at a loss as to what to do. She was my wife and I had to find a way to support her somehow, to lift her from the dark hole she was sinking deeper and deeper into. She stopped going to work and spent most days in bed staring at the ceiling and drinking bottle after bottle of cheap red wine. As far as she was concerned, I was just another bit of furniture. She stopped relating to me altogether.

I went over to see Luan and seek her support about what was taking place with her daughter. She stared into nothingness as she always did when I tried to talk about her family back home in Vietnam and said, "It's my father's fault; he cursed us all. Nulla is a daughter of a whore; you married into the wrong family. Maybe it's time for you to go home," she said matter-of-factly, as though it wasn't the wellbeing of her only daughter that we were talking about.

Gradually, I started to fall apart myself in those hellish months, though I knew I had no choice, I had to do whatever it took and endeavour to keep myself together. The morning newspaper run, which was always such a joy and celebration for me, became a chore I hated doing, yet we needed the money. Usually by the time I got back home, Nulla was already drunk and in her zone. Her hair, which was her feminine pride, hadn't been combed for weeks now and looked like a dishevelled mat. I approached her with a brush a few times, as she always loved it when I brushed her hair, yet she just threw it away and looked into space. She was actually going insane. Between the two of us, Nulla was always the stronger one emotionally. In a way, she anchored us both to the world, and to witness her in this state was certainly starting to rock me into a place of hopelessness.

One day when I felt all hope was gone I heard this subtle inner voice whisper to me, "Go to the cemetery." How did I miss this? The company of the dead was always the place where I sought solace and answers to the challenges posed by life, yet I hadn't stepped into their domain since arriving in Paris.

The cemetery was an easy fifteen-minute walk away. It was early one evening when I made my way there to seek the counsel of the dead, or rather to immerse myself in the peace and silence offered in their departure lounge.

It was a well-kept place with beautiful gardens and a comfortable, familiar calmness. The space was different to the burning grounds in India and the voices I heard were louder. "Perhaps putting the body in the earth rather than burning it keeps the spirit more attached to its previous earthly walk," I thought.

Nevertheless, it wasn't the voices and stories of the dead I was concerned with; my deep anxiety was centred on the fact that my living Goddess was slowly but surely killing herself at home. I found a small gravestone I liked. It said, "Here is buried a man who always loved." And this was the company I needed in that moment. I leant my head on the gravestone and drifted into a peaceful zone where answers have space to emerge. Around midnight it hit me like a rocket bursting into space, I had the answer I was praying for. I kissed the stone of the great-unknown lover and ran home as quickly as I could.

"Nulla, Nulla, guess what?" I said while I opened the door, "I feel we need to go to Vietnam," I stood there still catching my breath. She looked back at me for a long moment and then offered me a shy delicate smile in return; it was the first time she had related to me in months. I fell on the floor sobbing. I could finally afford to collapse. I didn't need to keep it together anymore. My wife and best friend was back from hell. We lay on the woollen carpet together holding each other for the rest of the night.

"Never, ever give up on anybody, especially the ones you love, even if they need more time than you think is adequate or appropriate." Nulla always gave me this space when I needed to change or work through something and I finally had the chance to return to her the gift of unconditional giving. We were going back to the scene of the crime, the place where the family's pain and agony was born and we were going to look it in the face and see it for what it was.

❊ ❊ ❊ ❊ ❊ ❊ ❊

Now and again through the journey we call life, we stumble upon moments when the core substance—the inner resonance of our being, gets challenged and rocked out of its comfort zone. In these instances we really get to gauge the strength of the mettle we are made of.

Our life's parable defines itself within these precious moments, when the voice beyond calls upon us to take a leap into the arms of trust and explore a road previously uncharted. The new pathway on offer is often frightening and fraught with danger to a mind used to habitual ways of being. It may totally alter the way we relate to the world, while *reality* as we know it is likely to acquire a new fragrance.

It seems that to be or not to be is a choice we have to make continuously throughout the flow of life. Some may call it a struggle between good and evil, except then we turn it into a judgement, and judgements never lead us on the path to freedom. The eternal tussle is between being a creative force in the world and surrendering to the clutches of circumstance.

Nulla was faced with making a choice of this kind many years ago when she slipped into the abyss of self-pity and despair. Yet the moment the universe offered her a rescue remedy, in the name of a trip to Vietnam, a journey to the place where her pain was born, she grabbed onto it without hesitation and never looked back.

The way we respond to the myriad of possibilities with which life gifts us, is intimately connected to the level of faith and courage present in our choices and will ultimately define our destiny. We are usually, at any of life's crossroads, offered a moment where our spirit stumbles upon eternity and hands us a gift, an answer, a solution, a miracle, a new love, or an unthought-of possibility.

The difference, between the ones who dance through life and the others who just crawl through it, is our response to these precious moments when that rainbow shines in our sky for a fleeting moment.

Do we hesitate, procrastinate, or do we grab it by the teeth in an instant and walk with a new promise tickling our heart? The moment never repeats itself. We have to act in a flash; delay is death. Life always offers us a very narrow bridge of opportunity, and if we don't seize it, it's gone. How many times in life have we sat down and thought, "Oh, I should have done this or that, I should have talked with him or her, I should have listened to the call of the moment." And we didn't. And worse than that, we didn't learn from our mistakes, for the next time the door opened to a spark of new possibility, again we missed it. Thus the universe might start looking elsewhere to shower its gifts on more welcoming hands. To truly *be*, to really *live*, to know *love*, we must act from the power within us, trusting in its infinite nature.

I never gave up on Nulla in her time of total breakdown; I just despaired as to how I could help her out of it. She needed to collapse that time, for it finally broke down the dam walls that trapped all the murk of the past within her. Yet the moment she heard me say, "Let's go to Vietnam," she knew, all her being knew, that it was enough. The purging was done and it was time for the phoenix to rise from the ashes and fly high again. And so she did. She was never one for delaying; neither did she tolerate the idea of not acting when truth is present. We never talked again of her breakdown once she snapped out of it. There was no need to.

My attention back to the presence of the river and my dear crow friend; I feel Nobi's gaze engulfing me with a serenity only known to creatures ruled by their presence. He sniffs out the gentle breeze and allows it to caress his wings.

Am I missing something here? Is there something in Nobi's presence or words that have offered me a new pathway I haven't yet fathomed? Are we all just addicted to the realms of the known? Is this one of our biggest limitations as human beings?

When living in the known, life only exists; yet it is celebrated, danced and unfolds within the unbridled playing fields of mystery. So why is it that we are so content to leave her story to the domain of books, movies and fairy tales; when at any moment, *this moment*, we can step into a new possibility we never ever dreamt was likely before. It is in this daring to leave the comfort walls of the known; that we offer life the assurance that we give it the trust it deserves.

We arrived in Ho Chi Minh City, the place formerly known as Saigon, on the 19th May 1990, while the whole nation was ecstatically celebrating its hero, Ho Chi Minh. Unknown to us, and as fate would have it; we arrived on the one-hundredth birthday of the father of modern Vietnam, its champion and its liberator from western colonialism.

The road from the airport was dotted with red Vietnamese flags, and the drive to the city's centre took forever as the taxi crawled its way through the multitude of people and the mass of bicycles that clogged the road. Everybody was dressed in their best clothing and the festive atmosphere of celebration was evident in the eyes of a people who had achieved their liberation through one of the longest and deadliest armed struggles in modern HisStory.

Nothing mattered to Nulla at that moment. She gazed out the windows, mesmerised. I could sense she was getting intoxicated by every small particle that caught her eye and by every sound that tickled in her ear. She was back home, in a homeland she had never known, and every cell of her spirit vibrated with it. She had arrived in the place where her body had first entered this world and her pain was born.

Nulla's parents left Vietnam twenty-six years ago when Nulla was just nine months old, and no member of the family had ever been back. Nulla spoke very basic Vietnamese taught to her by her father. With her mother, it was a different story. She spent the last twenty-six years of her life sweeping the past under the carpet and with it a bundle of pain that was slowly tearing into the very fabric of her being.

All that changed one fateful day when we came over to her apartment in Paris and told her we were going to Vietnam. She first looked at Nulla in utter disbelief and then as though a veil had been lifted, her face transformed and, looking out from behind tear-filled eyes, stood a fragile young girl again. She relinquished a sigh; a sigh that had been stifled for years and she collapsed into her daughter's firm embrace just as though their roles had been reversed and Nulla was now her mother.

They both cried and hugged each other as close as they could. I had been married into this family for more than four years and this was the first time I had witnessed mother and daughter have any physical contact. My dear mother-in-law, who had suppressed her pain since she was a teenager, was starting to crack. The dam was giving way to a torrent of tears held back for years by a survival instinct, that only women who have really been hurt to their core learn to cultivate by the sheer need to keep breathing.

Later that evening, while we were sitting in her lounge room, Luan shared with us stories of her beloved homeland, for the first time since I met her. She seemed like a new woman. Nothing in me ever anticipated that our going to Vietnam would be such a strong catalyst of change for her. After all, it was her daughter going, while she was staying behind. Then again, this is part of the mysterious bond between mother and daughter, the whisper of the unseen Goddess. It is stronger than blood and subtler than the tiniest of atoms.

Often in life, it is up to the offspring to walk the road that the parent would not have even dared to dream, yet wished they had in the silence of their hearts. Luan had broken twenty-six years of silence. She could feel what Nulla felt, the moment I suggested we go to Vietnam. She instantly sensed that maybe; just maybe, at the end of this trip lay a freedom-feather. Actually not at the end, just with the thought of this trip, a new liberty was unfolding within mother and daughter.

She walked over to her bedroom and came back with a small box wrapped in bright red velvet with a yellow line sewn through it. It hit me at once. It was the colour of the

Vietnamese flag. She opened the box carefully to reveal a bunch of dusty black and white photographs and a bundle of papers gone yellow with age. It was the first time she had opened the box since her arrival in France. Her hands were shaking as she dusted off the old photographs and shared them with her teary daughter. They were photographs of her family, her mother and father, brothers and sister, grandparents and some other relatives and friends from the village. There was one photograph that really stood out. It was of a man in uniform standing beside a stunningly beautiful Vietnamese girl dressed in traditional clothes and a wide straw hat. It was Nulla's mom with the foreign French soldier who later became a husband to Luan and a father to Nulla.

Nobi is quiet, though the river isn't anymore. The water is rushing by with great energy and rising with every passing moment. Nobi feels far away in deep silence and his black silhouette reminds me of Nulla's hair.

What is the true nature of these two forces swinging the pendulum within me? Is it action as opposed to peace? Or is it love versus fear — fear which may be disguising itself as a quest for peace! Is it my fear tempting me to stay put by the river, while Nobi is prompting me to continue with my quest for love? Is this really what he is talking about when he speaks of joining the band of the brave and climbing up the hill to seek the rebirth of the earth and perhaps my own resurrection as well?

In truth, love rarely resides within the neutral domain of peace, for if it did, how would she be an agent for growth, change, celebration and annihilation?

What is the core force that propels us to change, to

explore new frontiers, to break our boundaries again and again? It's love, it must be! Just a tiny word, yet the jewel in her majesty's crown. It is within love that we are forced to die, change and rebirth. It is with love that we embrace pain as part and parcel of life and that pain becomes an ally on our journey. It is love that edges us to better ourselves and refine our act in life.

Has anyone really ever transformed through peace, through equanimity of emotion! It's as if these are the moments when we pause and take a break from life's trials and growing pains: while the real evolution happens within the trickery that love offers us.

What is a revolutionary? It is a lover of the highest order, who is burning with love for his fellow human beings and is willing to sacrifice his and her own well-being for the betterment of humanity.

Who was Jesus, but a great lover? Did he seek his own salvation? No, certainly not! He wasn't afraid to act and rock the boat. He was up there for the challenge because he loved, not because he sought his peace and his own salvation.

So what the fuck am I doing here by the river seeking my own peace and liberation? Have I lost trust in the power of love?

There must be some sort of fighting instinct in all of us. If there isn't, how come our history is full of war and battles? Is it possible then to transform this warrior that abides within us all and to go and fight the good fight with love as our guide?

The use of force coming from hate is violence; the use of force coming from love is action. Isn't this what Krishna spoke about to Arjuna in the Bhagavad Gita! Perhaps it's okay then, to use force if it's coming from a place of love rather than hate. I am not sure. Though what I am sure of is that, if I had to choose between never loving again or forgoing attaining my peace, it would be a no brainer. I would leap into the fire of love any day.

❋ ❋ ❋ ❋ ❋ ❋ ❋

We checked into a small guesthouse in the old quarter of Saigon and went to roam the streets to join in with the celebrations commemorating this special man after whom the city was renamed. This was a man who sought peace and justice for his people, yet was forced by his adversaries to undertake one of the longest and bloodiest armed struggles in recent HisStory.

The streets were packed with people and we were both exhausted from the long flight. We ate a plate of fish and noodles in a small food stall just outside in the alley where our hotel was situated and then retired back to our room, to watch the celebrations from the small balcony. We ordered a couple of cold beers and sat back on the comfortable bamboo chairs. Nulla told me she wanted to make a move as soon as possible.

The following day Nulla was already busy making the plans to leave in search for her family. Nulla was born in this city, but at the moment she didn't care to stay and explore her birthplace. For the first time since we met, Nulla was in a hurry, a real hurry, and she was on a mission. She wanted to get to the village where her mother came from. She needed to find out if anyone from her family was still alive. If any of her grandparents were alive, they would be in their mid-seventies. Not unheard of in this country, not at all, though in between now and when Nulla's mom left her village over twenty-eight years ago, raged one of the worst wars humankind has ever known.

Fifty-eight thousand Americans and three million Vietnamese, Laotians and Cambodians died in the Vietnam War. The Americans dropped six million tons of bombs during the war and they lost; a war that was never theirs to fight in the first place. Had they ever apologised to anybody for the horrendous war crimes they inflicted on a peace-loving people? Had they ever apologised to us, a whole generation worldwide who were scarred growing up in the shadows of their war?

We took the night train to Da Nang and then a jeep back southwest and inland for a couple of hours. I held Nulla close to me all the way. I felt her inner being shaking. She was vulnerable, as a baby is when it is born into a world foreign to it, when it leaves the safety of the known to be confronted by a reality it may not have chosen to meet. Yet the choices we make are not always born of our own wish list, rather by a force invisible to the pen that writes the story.

Nulla didn't know what she would have to face, neither did she have a clue as to how she would deal with it.

The landscape around us was green with coconut groves, lots of tropical palms, which I didn't recognise, and rice fields that were dotted with people in wide brimmed straw hats working the ground. By midday we arrived at the village. It seemed to be a typical Vietnamese village with simple wooden and bamboo homes surrounded by endless fields of rice. In fact, it was a sea of green everywhere, the type of fluoro green you get from rice that has been sprayed with super phosphates. What really struck me, however, was that even amidst all this green there was a noticeable absence of trees in the village. In such a lush tropical setting, there is usually an abundance of native trees, even amongst the rice fields.

We handed the driver a piece of paper that Luan had given us with the name of her family on it. He asked the first person we came by and they guided us to a house at the edge of the village. Nulla was shivering, digging her fingernails into my skin. She wore a long green Vietnamese skirt with a black Chinese collared silk shirt, both given to her by her mom. Her hair was in a long plait and she could have easily passed for a local village girl. She was. That moment, she was French no more; she was Vietnamese to the core.

The house was quite large by local standards. It was perched about three feet off the ground. The rice fields almost touched the veranda. I noticed an old man sitting on the veranda that encircled the house. He was holding a small baby in his arms. He had a white goatee beard and once he noticed the car, he went into the house and came out again without the baby, squinting to see who the strangers were.

Slowly he walked down the three stairs of the veranda as Nulla got out of the car. They both froze at the same moment as though a silent voice from an unknown planet commanded their attention. There was no need for an introduction. As far as the old man was concerned, it was his own daughter standing there. The old man had been waiting for this moment for almost thirty years, wondering if it would ever come. He must have felt for weeks that the instant was approaching, as an animal hears the cry of their offspring even if they are miles away.

Nulla ran and hugged her grandfather. He was hesitant at first, as though he may have felt undeserving of the warm embrace. Gradually he allowed himself to stretch his arms around his granddaughter and hold her close to him. He was old, yet he looked strong and proud, the lines on his face telling a story that even a great actor would not be able to conceal.

He started crying; at first, however, the tears were hard to come by, as though he had forgotten how it is done. He tried to pull away from Nulla, but she wouldn't let him go. In no time the tears turned into wailing. He cried hard, really hard. He cried the tears of a man who had never cried before. He cried the sort of tears that had been held back for an eternity, however even forever has to come to an end one day.

I stepped aside to offer him the dignity of crying alone with his kin.

He cried not only for the loss of his own daughter, he cried for all the fathers worldwide who had lost their daughters to the crime of manmade poverty designed to break the will of the people.

He cried for all the husbands who had lost their wives to an enemy so spineless that it moves like a thief in the night dropping poison from the air on innocent people living as one with their land.

He cried for all the fathers who had lost their sons to an unjust war in an unjust world ruled by unremitting cowards, who would never dare do what they sent countless others to do for them.

He cried for his country, which had to pay the highest price possible for its freedom. A country still under attack, assaulted by an enemy more subtle and insidious than the one before, an enemy called globalisation, which slowly and surely was moving his country back to the turf of the enemy they fought so hard to be liberated from.

After a while, the tears ran dry and Nulla introduced me to her grandfather. He embraced me warmly and returned to hold his granddaughter close to him. He needed to feel it was really happening; that old age and longing had not planted a mirage within his sight, an illusion that would soon fade away.

They couldn't get enough of each other, each one of them nursing the other's pain and applying the balm of love on it, a universal magic-cure that never, ever fails to heal.

We sat on the veranda all afternoon with Nulla's grandfather, sipping endless cups of green tea and rice wine while he shared the story of his life with us. He spoke perfect French and a bit of English. I was okay at understanding French after four years of living in France, although my speaking was pidgin at best.

327

Nulla's granddad name was Hung. he lived together with his only remaining son who was married to a lovely woman. The son's daughter and newly born granddaughter were on a visit from the city, thus four generations of this brave family were there to greet Nulla, a granddaughter, niece and aunt they had never known. Nulla's granddad liked to talk. We sat there for days on his veranda savouring each other's company and that of numerous Vietnamese cousins, while he shared with us the sad story, the real story of Vietnam. The story our *free press* or HisStory books never tell us.

Prior to the arrival of the French in the mid 1800's, most Vietnamese peasants owned their land. It was an agrarian country comprising mostly of small land holdings. By the mid 1930's, seventy per cent of the population were turned landless and two and a half per cent of the population owned half the country's land. Thus, in less than a hundred years, the French managed to create a new paradigm of Vietnamese life, a paradigm that made it easier for them to rule and control the jewel of their colonial outposts. The French were finally defeated in 1954, and were soon replaced by the Americans.

The Americans entered Vietnam to support the rich in their struggle against the poor, the landed against the landless and of course, also to make a buck. They had done this in many other countries throughout the twentieth century, always hand in glove with a brutal military dictator. Always to protect *American interests* and *freedom,* a freedom that at the time was not even granted to their citizens of a different colour back home.

It was strange, though, because first it was the Americans who stood by Ho Chi Minh in 1945 when he declared independence from the Japanese and then they betrayed him . . . it was all sounding very familiar, as though history kept on repeating itself.

Later on, the New York Times published a report called

the "Pentagon Papers." The report revealed that former US presidents lied to the public and congress about Vietnam. That sounded familiar too. It was as though Nulla's grandad wasn't telling me the story of Vietnam alone, he was sharing with us the many told and untold crimes that took place along the second half of the twentieth century—the stories of Chile and Nicaragua, of Palestine and Indonesia, of Iraq and El Salvador and many more countries that fell victim to American imperialism. In 1973, the Americans were finally defeated. It took another two years, though, until the South fell and in 1975 the bloodiest war since World War II finally ended.

I was amazed by the well of knowledge that poured from Nulla's grandfather and I kept on asking him questions. It seems to be one of the by-products of a just revolution; the peasants educate themselves to look beyond the manufactured tales into the truth of matters. For the first time I also realised what Nulla's father was doing in Vietnam. He was a French officer advising the Americans on how to reconquer the country his own nation had lost, though the hurt pride was still there.

Over the next few days we learnt of the tragedy that Hung's life wove during the war years. He had three sons and two daughters.

All of his sons fought with the resistance against the Americans, though it took time before they joined in the act of war. As a family of devout Buddhists, they watched the maddening violence around them grow; in spite of this they chose only to participate in the passive resistance movement. However, all that changed one fateful day, when the American planes came and sprayed Agent Orange on the nearby forest, while Nulla's grandmother and aunt were out collecting firewood. Within days both of them died an agonizing death and within weeks, a forest that had stood since time itself can remember turned into barren, desolate land.

That was the turning point for Hung and his sons. The four of them joined the resistance and by the end of the war, Hung had lost two of his sons to enemy fire, his wife and one daughter to enemy poison, and the other daughter to the ravages poverty inflicted on his family. I was astonished he was still able to stand as tall and proud as he did, with two sons and two daughters gone, and also his beloved wife.

However, the survival instinct is strong within the heart of the brave, and every new smile awarded in their *Via Dolorosa* is a celebration to be treasured, like the arrival of his granddaughter who brought endless smiles to the face of this courageous old man.

After a while, it occurred to me that three days had passed and he had not spoken a word of Luan, his own daughter. Neither did Nulla mention her mom's name nor was there any passing of regards on from her to him. I stayed out of it and relegated myself to being a silent observer as far as family matters were concerned. I was intrigued, though. Were they both savouring this moment of bliss before they ventured into the closed dark corridors of the painful past, opening up old wounds when no one knew in what way they would fester? It was Nulla who finally raised the subject. "Grandad," she addressed him with a tender love that came from years of longing. "Mom wants to talk to you, is there a phone in the village we can use to call her?"

Initially he didn't say a word. He just stared into the rice fields, perhaps wondering what he would say to a daughter he had forced into one of the most vile forms of slavery. A daughter that he loved so dearly — still, with five kids facing starvation a sacrifice had to be made. A sacrifice he had regretted for every day of his life on earth and wished he had never made.

"How is my dear elder daughter, Luan?" he asked, at last breaking the silence.

"She is good. She was very happy when we decided to come to Vietnam, she asked me to tell her family that she missed them every single day since she left and her only wish in life is to see them again," Nulla said, while holding her granddad's hand with her own.

Nulla never told me what message her mom sent with her. Then, again, it didn't come to me as a surprise, from the moment I met Luan I noticed the wounded little girl in her that was still lamenting over the harsh card fate had dealt her so many years ago.

There was no phone in the village and we would have to go to the nearest town, which was more than half an hour's drive away to make a call.

The next morning we all took the bus together to the nearest town; Hung showing off his newly acquired granddaughter and grandson-in-law to his village acquaintances also on the bus. When we arrived in the next town, we walked over to the local post office where international calls could be made. Nulla dialled the number while her granddad stood by her side.

"Hi, Mom," she spoke, her voice quivering. "Grandad is here to talk with you." She handed over the phone to Hung who stood there with moist eyes. Nulla stood by my side, holding my arm with her two hands. We noticed the tears flowing down Hung's face as he finally spoke to his daughter after thirty years of unbearable pain.

❋ ❋ ❋ ❋ ❋ ❋ ❋

The river is starting to wobble all over the place, as though the force of water behind it is creating a sense of confusion with the direction it is heading. I recall the tragedy of Vietnam as a whole and the family of my beloved wife.

Some years ago during a time when Nulla and I were researching the insidious ways of GMO farming and how it is being spread around the globe, I finally came to understand how the poisonous tentacles of the octopus were often coming from the one source. At the time we were looking at ways to expose the fallacy behind the disgusting technology called terminator seed. We could not fathom how anyone would give consent to a company to market seeds engineered to become sterile and consequently enslave the farmer into buying seed from these companies year after year; rather than collecting their own seeds at the end of the harvest season, just as they had done since the time humans first settled and became farming communities.

We didn't see any reason for this new invention, apart from a wish to control and dominate the future food stocks of humanity. There is no benefit in it for anybody, apart from the company that is producing the seeds and propagating the technology. At the same time, this company is patenting life forms that have been created by a force they are at total war with — the force of the divine mother.

What really came to me as a shocking surprise was that this company, which claims to care about our future wellbeing, produces two of the most toxic substances known to man; polychlorinated biphenyls (known as PCBs) and dioxin (Agent Orange). In both cases we were told they were safe to use — until the truth emerged much later. When the truth finally emerges about the effects of GMO crops, it will be too late for all of us. Genetic pollution is something we will never be able to reverse and the way we are accepting this technology is as if we are intoxicated gamblers who have lost the will to live.

One afternoon when I was sitting in our lounge room in Paris reading about the history of this corporation, the realisation finally dawned on me; the same company, which produced the Agent Orange that killed the forests of Vietnam and my wife's grandmother and aunt, was now producing seeds that had no life in them and in the process was killing the butterflies and the bees worldwide. I was outraged by my findings and more so by the fact that not only are they allowed to operate freely as though they are masters of the land, they are also welcomed worldwide and worshipped by some as saviours of our future. How can they ever claim to be the guardians of the future of food? Can we really believe for one moment that these merchants of death, concerned only with their future balance sheets, really care about our wellbeing and the future of our children? Of course not! Only a fool or a morally deranged person would believe such a fallacy, yet one government after the other is opening the doors to this company and welcoming them to take charge of the future of our food — our life.

"Nobi," I address my dear crow friend. This time it's me snapping him out of his dream state. "Do you really feel there is any chance we can reclaim our future as a collective, is there any possibility that the sleep-walkers will ever wake up? Why is there a conspiracy of silence over what's happening?" I ask him. He fixes his gaze on the river, as though to point out to me the domain where all answers make themselves known.

"Do not worry about the sleep-walkers. Divorce yourself from negativity. Be concerned with your own actions. Claim your own future now and the rest will follow. The seed of a collective awakening is within your own heart this very moment and in the heart of anyone who can really hear the whisper of the river, the call of the mountain, the thunder of the cloud. We can't wait anymore for everyone. Be the one, as many others will be their own one, and the small circle by the force of gravity will draw more and more into its vortex. However, be utterly total, absolutely committed, fully in the knowledge that you hold within yourself, a power beyond your wildest dreams. Be aware of what is really happening here. The butterflies and the bees are dying because of this new devil that is spreading its wings throughout the earth. We all know that no child will ever smile again when the butterflies are gone and not much will grow at all without the hard-working bees. Don't mince your words anymore. State the truth as it is and if they don't listen, tell them to come and talk to Nobi, King of the Crows," he says while staring at the river and shifting his attention to the vastness of the night and all that lies beyond it.

"I am Nobi, King of the Crows," he calls the night into his attention. "Don't you all know that nature has never designed seeds which are mixed with the genes of fish and animals? Do you understand what GMO's really are? They are cell invasion! This insidious experiment is bound to breed monsters. Let us all not forget for a moment that one of the roles the plant kingdom plays is transforming light into life. Do you get what I am saying? Is there anybody out there that is still capable of hearing us? To genetically engineer plants and animals is no different than doing the same to humans. We all breathe the same air. All life forms are perfect, fulfilling their task within the tapestry of life. To manipulate them is to spit in the face of the Great Spirit and the eternal wisdom of creation. It is to say to her that you mistrust the way she designed the rising of the sun and shining of the moon. In nature, nothing is independent, everything is interdependent and connected, we are all one community, and to manipulate one is to do so to us all!

"What's happening in your human world? Have you stopped trusting in a wisdom that created your own perfect bodies, the most complex organism on earth, that you wish to now manipulate other bodies of life as far as possible away from their original source? Have you stopped trusting in the wisdom that has nurtured and sustained life from the time before time began?

"The next thing you'll suddenly do is breed GMO crows that are silent; well, that would surely spell the age of doom. Everything and everyone is born of the same divine source and is part of a never-ending spectrum of love bowing in reverence at the altar of creation."

Nobi is howling his words into the night while I am moved to tears. I didn't realise he was King of the Crows, though, really, I should have known. He stares at me with his eyes of love reflecting in the endless night, then he looks at the space where all things are heard and calls the night back to his attention.

"I am Nobi, King of the Crows, voice to the voiceless ones, and I want to talk with the ones who say GMO seeds are to the benefit of humanity, I want you to come here, look into my eyes and explain to me how this deadly technology is meant to restore the balance of life on earth.

"I, Nobi, brother to the butterflies and the bees will do whatever I can, to save my kin—the gentle small winged ones, for they are my relations in creation.

"I, Nobi, messenger of the winged ones; want to talk to all the idiots who propagate a fossil fuel economy which is responsible for killing the support systems of life on earth, while the marvels of nature are ready to give you all the power possible in a way that harms none in the process.

"I, Nobi, a good friend to all, want to remind you that we all share the water that we drink. Why is it so hard to find clean water, is it because they want you to buy it? Now you have even turned water into a commodity to be bought and sold on supermarket shelves. It is amazing how quick you are to conform every time one more of your birthrights are robbed by the corporations and turned into a commodity. What's next? Do you intend to turn the air that we all breathe into another item that you all must purchase and after a short outcry accept it as an inevitable reality?

"I, Nobi, King of the Crows, want to understand what it is you are spraying into the sky? What are all these white lines up there? They smell awful and I suspect someone is playing a really dirty game with the air we all breathe!

"Do you get what I am saying? Is anyone out there really listening? For if you are, I want to know what you intend to do, all of you! Do you intend to do something now or will you just watch it as a movie that is none of your concern?"

I know he isn't talking to me anymore. I don't matter, nor does he. What matters is this: will the night's echoes vibrate in the ears of the many and open their hearts to the call of the wild?

He suddenly turns back to me and with a soft voice whispers in my ear, "We have a visitor!"

At once an eerie silence permeates the sphere around us. It feels like the whole universe has pressed the pause button. The stillness in the air has an unnerving quality to it and for a moment I feel unsettled. The river, too, seems to be responding to something invisible taking place as she gathers more and more energy although her sound is hushed for a moment, like a silent assassin waiting to strike.

The silence is perfect, as though nothing in creation dare disturb it. A gentle peachy white glow appears over me; I wonder if this is some pre-death hallucination. Is the river preparing me for the moment I am swept away? The softest of breezes caresses my face with the same tenderness as a mother or a lover strokes their beloved in a time of illness. It reminds me of Nulla.

Suddenly my body twitches. A circle of crows descends from the sky in perfect silence and surrounds me. The world must have really turned upside down if crows have started practicing the ways of silence! I count them, twelve with Nobi amongst them. They are all glowing with same peachy white glow that first appeared in the sky above.

I tremble — the night of the high fever in the tribal village. What's happening? I feel my forehead to check if I am on fire again, however it feels cool. Nobi smiles, reassuring me all is well, while gesturing to me with a nod to relax.

What are they doing here, just a short moment before the river comes and takes me away? Are they going to try and force me out of my crumbling resolve? Lift me somehow with them into the sky's safety, a sanctuary offered to them alone?

I hear my breath slowing down to tune itself in with the prevailing silence. In . . . out, in . . . out, it meanders quietly and with my awareness on my breath I gradually feel calmed. An unfamiliar feeling overwhelms me, as though the universe itself is holding me in her warm embrace. Gentle delicate tears flow lovingly down my face. They feel so warm and reassuring. I am the peace I have always been seeking.

In an instant it dawns on me that I am a seeker no more. I am a finder forever. Seeking creates an unwanted schism within us. Finding affirms the reality of what is. I feel like hugging every particle of life in the vicinity around me, kissing the air that is offering me life from one moment to next.

All of a sudden, a wild piercing sound commands the whole universe to attention. It feels like the call of the earth coming from deep in the belly of the greatest of mothers.

And here she is, in front of me suspended above the river — the biggest, most awesome *eagle mother* to have ever graced creation. Her wings are ablaze with a myriad of lights, while her eyes tell the story of each songline ever sung and yet to be walked. The twelve crows and I are nothing any longer, just tiny particles within the eternal dance of creation as she rises again and again, from one dreamtime to another.

She appeared to me many years ago when I was a young man, fevering in a tribal village struggling for its survival. The village, unfortunately, had since been lost to the forces of greed, although the truth that she spoke to me that night is forever alive within the movements of life. How much of it have I personally embodied into my being, how total has my journey into trust been? The answer is evident in where I am at this very moment.

The eagle calls again, with a sound that is piercing something much deeper than my ears.

"I speak to all who share the sacred breath that we are,"

she calls all living beings to attention. "I speak for the river, I speak for the one and I speak within the one.

"I am the one.

"The time has come to make choices, for the choices you make now will reverberate in the waves of tomorrow. We are all moving towards an end and a beginning. Humankind is yearning for a new way. Still, the time for the promise of tomorrow is today. As the only species that is capable of destruction, it is your responsibility to be caretakers of life; make sure that the whole rainbow of creation is smiling again. Humans are the only particle in creation that takes and takes, while the rest of creation gives and gives.

"Humans are the only creatures that hate, hold negativity and self-destruct while the rest of creation is in a state of *being*. The time has come for a revolution in values and a realignment of the intent for your walk on earth.

"You carry within you the same DNA as a tree does. Have you ever watched a tree, its presence and purpose of being? What does it do? It nurtures, shelters, sustains, transforms and embraces the life around it."

The world surrounding me is aflame with presence: the presence of the river reflecting flow, the presence of the eagle mirroring the light of truth, and the presence of the night as the womb that eternally gives birth to the promise of a new dawn.

The eagle's voice gradually melts into the shadows of the night, as though it is spoken from the far reaches of a galaxy yet to be touched. At the same time, I feel it is my own voice emerging in remembrance of the silence that has brought it forth into manifestation.

Each and every one of us affects reality with every thought and action. We are powerful and ultimate creators and we can chart life on earth into a new direction. We have handed over our power to unreliable gods that have sown fear in our minds and sorrow in our hearts — gods that have separated us, rather than uniting us; gods that have called us to fear one another, rather than to embrace the diversity of our oneness.

Wouldn't now be the right time to chuck these gods away and replace them with the song of love and the abundance of sharing?

We cannot anymore afford to have anything distract us from our goal and vision. Every battle in life is won by the mind before it is even waged. Isn't this the right time to make our minds up about how we envision life on earth to be? Sure our vision must be to restore balance within and without — to be true caretakers of life, sharing this beautiful earth with all our relations.

The age of dominance is over, for we are seeing its folly and we are strong and trusting to step beyond into the land of the brave. We must tear the existing paradigm into pieces by our sheer will and determination and replace it with the kingdom of love and abundance.

The moment is ripe to discard this ruthless system we call *economy*. A system based on lies, illusion, greed and exploitation. We need to shift from a fossil fuel addiction to a renewable energy system, from a throw-away economy to a reuse-recycle society. From a growth-based economy, to a way of life that serves our basic human needs.

Once we run the show in a balanced way again, society will matter again and economy would be relegated to be the minor servant it is meant to be, rather than the driving force behind every human intent and action.

We must rely on new sources of media and create a real global free press, so we cannot be brainwashed anymore by media controlled by the gods of separation. In this age of globalisation, let us globalise dissent, globalise a revolution in values, and globalise love and care for each other.

Our resistance has to be real, not political theatre for the media. Gone are the days when getting painted in fairy floss is going to make a difference. It's all hands on deck time, when we walk the talk and dream the dream awake.

The time has come for us to truly sever our cooperation with evil, while at the same time creating a new future today. We must do everything to ensure the survival of laughter. Radical change will happen through the will of the people despite their governments, and isn't it true that each and every one of us wants change?

Yet this change must always start with the self and then embrace the whole.

The sound of the river is deafening, her waters slamming into her banks with tremendous speed and force, spray washing up the platform we are sitting on. She is letting us know that she has a voice. She roars her own sermon of truth and any moment now she will break beyond all her boundaries.

The eagle's voice emerges again from what seems like a space below the river, a space untouched, yet so familiar. Wait a minute; who is speaking here, is it her or me?

"There is no space of separation within the spirit of love." She commands the night again with the awesome presence of her voice.

"Walking with this knowing in your hearts will banish all fear forever. It is time for the warrior and lover within you all to join hands; they complement the great circle of life. Action within the world is born from the depths of silence." She keeps on talking with a voice that grows louder, yet feels so far away. Who is really doing the talking here? Am I just hallucinating, while the voice I am listening to is my own heart of hearts?

We are all divine. The whole human race is a bunch of amazing folk, all seeking the one thing—LOVE. We are powerful beyond our current belief. We are beautiful, extraordinary and we are choosing the power of love to replace the hunger for power. Within all of us exists a place where magic reigns supreme—a place where separation ceases to exist and unity is the song of life.

In the eyes of each and every one of us shines a light that

emanates from the same source. We are literally all brothers and sisters, mothers and fathers, sons and daughters to each other. Every human being is a celebration of a unique gift to the world and each and every one of us wants to shine. Some of us have been deceived, tricked and may have fallen between the cracks, yet we are all evolving, reaching out our hands towards the light that leads us towards the love that we are.

The problem is that, at times, we search for answers in faraway places while the biggest treasure house lies within us. It sits in our hearts, and that radiance, which shines in our heart, is brighter than any galaxy ever conceived in the Milky Way and beyond.

❋ ❋ ❋ ❋ ❋ ❋ ❋

I stare at the river; there is no one but Nobi by my side. The moonlight above reflects her madness, tinges of flying silver particles in a frenzied dance. Transfixed by her presence I see Nulla's face staring at me from the chaos created by the river's dance.

"Nulla!" I scream into the night, and all I can hear are the echoes of my voice.

"Nulla, where are you, why are you not here?" I keep on yelling, while the river answers my call with more and more of her gathering intensity and fury.

Where am I? What is going on here? Is the river Nulla? Is Nulla the river? Did I make it all up? I couldn't have — I've lived half my life with this woman. But, hey. . . wait a minute . . . aren't we all making everything up with every moment that passes?

Amidst the river's psychosis, I become aware of a crucial voice of calm and equilibrium. She is beckoning, whispering to me that we are all co-creating reality all the time; that this moment is made up by me as much as the moment makes itself up.

The river is thrashing wild, throwing an almighty tantrum so we all are at last forced to make up our minds. I have but a brief moment left to decide whether to embrace what Nobi has said, what the river is telling, and what I know beyond all doubt to be true—or do I stay sitting here and get washed away in the poetry of destruction?

We all have but a brief moment left to make up our mind, before this beautiful dream on earth is swallowed by the nightmare of economics, fear, separation and greed.

I look at Nobi, I never made him up, and he is as real as anything that I have ever known.

Delicate tears flow down my face, washing me with a promise of renewal. They are salty and they taste like the ocean.

About the Author

American by birth, Australian by fate, Jaman would probably prefer to consider himself a world citizen - acting locally wherever his feet are touching Mama earth, and always thinking globally.

Jaman has been involved as an active campaigner with many green issues such as old-growth forest protection and reforestation. As well, he has been active in campaigns for human rights and social justice. He also spends time spreading knowledge and initiating actions within the field of organics, permaculture and earth repair.

Jaman has spent significant time with two Australian aboriginal elders and credits them with much of the insight he has gained into our relationship with the earth and with one another.

He also studies Indian classical music with one of India's greatest legends Pundit Shiv Kumar Sharma.

In the past years he has called both Australia and India home as well as spending time in Slovakia.

Although he has written previously in the field of sustainability and permaculture, *I Crow River* is his first novel.

The next evolutionary step

Many of you may be wondering what could be done? What is it that you and I can do to effect the change that within our heart of hearts we all desire to see!

There are so many things we can do, there are so many ways we can make our voices heard and each and every one of us can effect change! We can plant a tree, nurture a garden, go on a march, sign a petition and join a singing circle. We can set up an NGO, create a community or volunteer and support the less fortunate. The list goes on and on.

Find your own way to get inspired and connect with people and organisations that are acting NOW.

We are in the process of developing a website which would act as a resource centre to inspire and connect.

You can find us on http://www.caferevolution.org and our blog jahcrow.blogspot.com

My elder Gaboo Ted Thomas would look every evening into the setting sun and sing - 'the best is yet to come', and yes! I truly believe so. We have the power, the will and the intention to make sure it does come.

For the earth and all beings, we act in love and courage.